# REPO MADNESS

# BY W. BRUCE CAMERON

*The Midnight Plan of the Repo Man*

*The Dog Master*

*The Dogs of Christmas*

*A Dog's Purpose*

*A Dog's Journey*

*Emory's Gift*

*8 Simple Rules for Dating My Teenage Daughter*

*How to Remodel a Man*

*8 Simple Rules for Marrying My Daughter*

## FOR YOUNGER READERS

*Ellie's Story: A Dog's Purpose Novel*

*Bailey's Story: A Dog's Purpose Novel*

# REPO MADNESS

# W. BRUCE CAMERON

REPO MADNESS

Copyright © 2016 by W. Bruce Cameron

A Forge Book
Published by Tom Doherty Associates, LLC
175 Fifth Avenue
New York, NY 10010

www.tor-forge.com

Forge® is a registered trademark of Tom Doherty Associates, LLC.

The Library of Congress Cataloging-in-Publication Data is available upon request.

ISBN 978-0-7653-7750-0 (hardcover)
ISBN 978-1-4668-5591-5 (e-book)

Our books may be purchased in bulk for promotional, educational, or business use. Please contact your local bookseller or the Macmillan Corporate and Premium Sales Department at 1-800-221-7945, extension 5442, or by e-mail at MacmillanSpecialMarkets@macmillan.com.

First Edition: August 2016

Printed in the United States of America

0  9  8  7  6  5  4  3  2  1

For Amy and Julie,
who have always been
so supportive of their baby brother

# REPO MADNESS

# Prologue

Gary Bruner drove his panel van down to the Ironton Ferry docks the Friday after Thanksgiving under the assumption that he would be free from harassment there—harassment of the police kind. That's how he resentfully defined the two incidents when he'd been pulled over and had his pot confiscated, even though he'd escaped arrest both times: police harassment. All he was doing was smoking marijuana, which he did nearly every day of his life, and then he gets harassed for it.

Gary Bruner was sometimes known by his nickname, "Burner." He'd forgotten who gave him that name or, to be truthful, why.

The panel van had belonged to a painter in its former life, and splatters of latex—egg white and orange parrot and hazy lilac—still riotously decorated the windowless interior. Gary thought it looked festive, and sometimes pictured himself cutting out pieces of the vehicle with a torch and framing them and selling them as art for thousands of dollars. But that would mean locating a torch and deciding which pieces and all that, which felt like a lot of work to Gary. Besides, then his van would have all these holes in it.

What made the van really special were the four theater seats to which he'd helped himself when the Star movie house closed several years ago. They were folding chairs, burgundy velvet where not worn down to shiny black leather, and he'd bolted them to the wooden floor of the van after using liberal amounts of duct tape to repair the puncture wounds in the cushions.

Two people were sitting in the seats now: a woman named Sharon, who looked to be maybe twenty-two years old, and Gary's friend Mick, who at twenty-four was a year younger than Gary and who had his arm casually draped around Sharon's shoulder back there, as if they were watching a movie and not bouncing down the highway on ten-year-old shocks. When Gary's brakes squealed them to a halt, he saw Sharon glancing at the arm and caught a flicker of irritation in her eyes. It suggested to Gary that Mick's play for Sharon was far from a done deal.

Sharon looked pretty good to Gary. She had short cropped red hair and nice light-blue eyes. She wore big looped earrings, which Gary thought was pretty sexy. She had on tight jeans and calf-high boots, which Gary thought was pretty sexy. Her eyes briefly met his in the rearview mirror.

Gary left the engine on and turned to the two in the back. "Let's see what you got," he suggested to his friend. Mick nodded and pulled out a ziplock bag and pinched out a handful of his new buy, finding his rolling papers and deftly packing a joint's worth of dope into what twisted out to be a very slender white stick. Sharon moved back a row to give him room to operate, which Gary found pretty sexy.

The van was the only vehicle in the parking lot. The restaurant, called the Landing, had once been a bait shop but now was one of the most popular dining spots on the lake. They served lobster rolls in there, Gary had heard. From worms to lobster—there was probably a philosophical comment about that he could make to impress Sharon, but Gary couldn't think of what it might be.

Because of the holidays, the Landing was closed, and the Ironton Ferry had ceased operations for the winter, though it hadn't yet been pulled out of the channel. There was no reason for anyone to drive down the ferry road from M-66, which was why there would be no police harassment tonight. Even still, Gary had backed the van into the parking spot so they could see up the driveway to the highway and also enjoy a view of the lake, which on this night was still and cold looking.

They didn't talk much as they passed the joint around. Gary tried to meet Sharon's eyes, but she mostly sat staring out the driver-side window, holding in the smoke and contemplating the dark water.

Gary tried to see things from Sharon's point of view. He and Mick looked pretty similar—both had unkempt beards and long hair. Neither had showered in a few days. Both were skinny. Mick had bought the dope, which maybe gave him some points, but Gary owned the panel van. Professionally speaking, both men were seeking opportunities at the moment, or at least were willing to entertain any opportunities that came seeking *them,* so Gary scored that one a toss-up.

"I'm going to roll another," Mick said, his voice strained as he talked past his held breath.

"I'm not feeling much," Sharon admitted.

Gary blew out a deep lungful. "I don't think it's dope," he stated flatly.

"What do you mean?" Mick looked offended.

"It's, like, the weakest pot ever. Where did you get it?" Gary asked. "The high school again?"

"No, it's good. You need to just let it work on you," Mick insisted.

The air was so polluted that Gary cracked his window, turning up the heat to compensate. The moon outside was glinting off the black water of the channel. "It doesn't even *smell* like dope," Gary complained. Sharon nodded at this, and Gary felt a gush of affection for her. "Are you from around here?" he asked her.

Sharon nodded. "Mancelona."

Mick, trying to demonstrate how potent his marijuana was, took in a huge lungful and barked it back out.

"And you and Mick, how long have you . . . ," Gary asked delicately over Mick's hacking and choking.

"Oh, we're just friends."

Mick stared at her through his red, watery eyes. This seemed to be new information to him.

"I have a boyfriend," Sharon continued in what Gary felt was unnecessary elaboration.

"You do?" Mick demanded.

Lights lit up the trees: a car had turned off the highway and was descending the curved approach to the ferry landing. A *fast* car. Gary watched out the passenger-side window as it careened down the hill toward them. "Whoa!" he blurted.

"What is it?" Sharon asked.

The car, a four-door of some kind, flashed past the parking lot as if rushing for the ferry. Except there was no ferry, just the gate that raised and lowered like a drawbridge. The gate was sagging outward toward the lake, Gary saw, less a barrier than a steep ramp, and in the seconds before the car hit it, he drew a mental trajectory and saw where in the channel the car would land.

Sharon screamed when the car hit the barrier, and was still screaming when the vehicle went into the water in a huge spray. The three dope smokers scrambled out of the van into the cold night air.

"What the . . . ," Mick said. They stood and watched numbly as the car heaved and surged in the lake, white foam dancing in its headlights, which lit the water up green as they dipped beneath the surface.

And then a man swam into the light, flapping his arms on the water. "Lisa Marie!" he was yelling. "Lisa!"

"Boat!" Mick shouted, pointing. A small aluminum rowboat lay upside down in the grass lawn of the cottage next door, pulled up twenty yards from shore. The three of them ran to it. Gary and Mick flipped it and saw there were oars inside. Gary fumbled to get the paddles into the locks.

"Hurry!" Sharon cried. She was sobbing, and Gary and Mick pushed the small craft down the slick grass and into the shallow water. When Gary stepped into the lake, it was shockingly cold.

The guy in the channel was still yelling something, his voice anguished and audibly growing weaker. Gary sat and heaved on the oars, and Mick fell heavily, nearly capsizing them. "Jesus, Burner!" Mick snapped at him.

It took them no time at all to get to the man, who was floundering in the water. He was still shouting, screaming, *"Lisa!"* over and over. The car was now totally submerged, and the lights were pointing down into the depths, seemingly aimed at infinity. "Dude! Give me your hand!" Mick shouted, leaning out of the boat. Gary stopped rowing and went to help, and together they seized the guy's jacket.

"Careful!" Gary warned as they started to haul the man up. The boat was close to tipping—the dude was *heavy*. He was staring with glassy eyes up at the two of them and seemed incapable of helping himself aboard. There was a gash on his forehead, pouring blood down his face—in the ethereal light from the head lamps, it was black as ink.

They put everything they had into it and managed to get the man into the boat without winding up in the drink themselves. He was shivering violently.

"Call 911!" Mick yelled at Sharon. She turned and raced away. Mick looked to Gary with a stricken expression. "You think there is someone else in the car? Was that why he was yelling? Dude, was there someone else in the car with you?"

The guy didn't answer and looked as if he *couldn't*—his eyes were rolling up into his head.

Gary stared somberly at the sinking car, still visible but now a huge blurry shadow underwater, the taillights making the foam look like bubbling blood. If there was someone else in there, he didn't see how that person would survive.

Gary looked down at the nearly catatonic crash victim. "Hey," he said suddenly to Mick. "You know who this guy *is*?"

And then the car lights winked out, and they were swallowed by the night.

# 1

## Nothing Like You in the Literature

I flipped the light under the little sign that said JOHNSTON and then took my seat, pensively glancing at my watch. I was close to fifteen minutes late.

The small anteroom had a coffee table layered with magazines for every possible sort of person who might be seeking psychotherapy: fishermen, people who cared about fashionable clothing, people who wanted their houses to look like someone else's house, women who were pregnant or wanting to be pregnant or had recently been pregnant. I picked up one whose cover had a snowmobile straddled by a woman in a bikini. The girl and the machine were both impressively muscular. Maybe where she lived, that's how everyone dressed for snowmobiling.

I've never actually owned a snowmobile, but I've stolen a few.

The door popped open, and I blinked in surprise at the guy standing there—fit, wiry, fifties; short, sparse hair receding from a freckled forehead; green eyes. My regular psychiatrist was a trim and frankly attractive woman who I felt was really helping me because she laughed at my jokes. "Mr. McCann?" he asked.

I stood and tossed aside my magazine. "Where's Sheryl?" I asked.

He bent and arranged the snowmobile magazine so that its edges lined up with the magazine for people who dress their dogs in sweaters. I'm not an edges-lined-up kind of guy and didn't feel bad about my apparent negligence.

"You call your doctor by her first name?" he asked mildly. "Why are you late, Mr. McCann?"

"I had to repo a Mazda from a guy who got fired from his job for threatening his boss with a baseball bat."

"Oh?" He raised his eyebrows in interest.

I shrugged. "The guy still had the bat."

"Come on in. Dr. Johnston was in a skiing mishap. She's all right, but she won't be able to work for a few months, so I am helping out. My name is Dr. Schaumburg. Robert Schaumburg."

I followed him into Sheryl's office. There was a couch, of course, but I always sat in a chair across from her, and I settled into my habitual place uneasily. After eighteen months of dealing with one psychiatrist, I was feeling awkward starting up with another.

"I've been reviewing her notes, to which I am allowed access under the terms of your probation." He settled into a soft chair, tapping a thick green folder. My file, I gathered.

"Okay, so should we wait for her to recover, probably?" I suggested helpfully.

Dr. Schaumburg regarded me blandly. "We have no idea how long that might be, unfortunately," he responded finally. "Shall I call you Ruddick? Ruddy?"

"Ruddy. No one calls me Ruddick except those phone calls at election time."

"Ruddy, then. Are you still taking your meds, Ruddy?"

My discomfort increased. "Well, yeah, of course. Why do you ask?"

"People on your mix of medications usually exhibit small changes in facial muscle tone and general body movements. I'm pretty good at spotting those, and you don't seem to have any."

"Guess I'm just lucky that way."

"Under the terms of your probation, you are required to be on your medication. I'm sure Dr. Johnston advised you of this."

I used my facial muscle tone to give myself a frown. "Did you talk to her? Because this whole probation thing is BS."

Dr. Schaumburg settled back slightly. "Tell me about that."

I shrugged. "Not a lot to tell. A bomb went off. A couple of people got killed. I wasn't to blame for any of it, but I was in the middle of everything and the D.A. felt like I had to be charged with *something,* even though I did nothing wrong."

"Because you're an ex-con."

"Because I went to prison, yeah. So we worked out this sham arrangement where I would get probation for obstruction of justice, because instead of taking matters into my own hands, I should have called the cops and let innocent people get killed while we all waited for them to respond, I guess. Sheryl agrees it's ridiculous. I didn't *obstruct.* I *solved.* Things could have been a lot worse, let me tell you."

Schaumburg reflected on this. He looked at his notes. "You were in prison for . . ."

I blew out some air. "Murder."

"Because you were drunk and crashed your car and a woman died."

"I was not drunk," I corrected. "I tested well below the limit. And many people accidentally took that turn down to the ferry before they reengineered it."

He regarded me blandly. "But you *were* drinking."

"Yes." I bit off anything else I might add.

"You don't seem to have any remorse."

I wanted to stand up. That's what guys my size do when we're getting pissed off: We stand up. A lot of times that ends the conversation. But something told me that was not a good idea here, so I jammed my hands into my pockets. "No remorse? I think about that accident every day of my life. Didn't I plead guilty? Didn't I stand up in front of a judge and say I deserved to go to prison? Don't you think I would give anything to have it all back, to have her back? That I would have traded places with her if I could?"

"Lisa Maria Walker."

"Yes. That was her name."

"Your girlfriend."

"No." I looked away. "We had just met."

Schaumburg nodded as if I had just confirmed something. "Before that, you were something of a local hero," he observed. "Football star, NFL career all but assured. And now you are a repo man and a bouncer in a bar."

"You say that like it's a step down or something."

"You're getting agitated."

"Well, who wouldn't? It was the worst thing that's ever happened to me."

"I would expect someone on your dosage to be more calm. A deadening of response is typical."

Okay, now I wanted to stand up and also punch him in the face. He was needling me, picking at a deep wound to test me. "I *am* calm. Bob."

A tiny smile played on his lips, but it wasn't amusement. "All right, then. Has Dr. Johnston ever discussed with you something called dissociative personality disorder?"

"Mostly we discuss sports."

"Let's talk about the voices in your head."

I sighed. We sat there, silently regarding each other for a full minute before I nodded wearily. "One voice, actually."

"Under what sort of circumstances do you hear the voice? Is there something that triggers it?"

"I don't hear it anymore," I replied dully.

"The meds are working, then." He was giving me a look full of irony, and I didn't reply. "But you also told Dr. Johnston that there were times when the voice would take over your body."

"No, not 'take over.' Look, I had a voice in my head that said his name was Alan Lottner. That's all."

Schaumburg pulled out a pen and clicked it, positioning it to write something. I waited patiently. "Alan Lottner," he repeated. "Who was once a real person? Now deceased."

"He died, yes."

"And it turns out you are engaged to his daughter?" His green eyes flicked up to meet mine, glinting slyly.

Jesus, had Sheryl written down every single one of my personal secrets for this schmuck to read? "Yes, but that was just a coincidence."

"A coincidence."

"Meaning, I didn't know Katie when Alan showed up. Okay, I had met her, but I didn't know who she was. In relation to him, I mean."

"You met a woman you were attracted to and then started hearing her father in your head," he summarized.

I was developing a real dislike for this guy.

"It's not typical for someone who harbors the delusion of a voice in his head to tie it to a real person," he informed me. "Historical figures, maybe, but I've never heard of it being the father of a fiancé. Does she know?"

"Who, Katie? That I had her father talking in my head for a while? No, I guess none of the bridal magazines in your lobby suggested I should bring it up. He's gone now, anyway. Alan, I mean."

"Which makes you sad."

"What? No! Where do you get that? Did Sheryl say that?"

"Your reaction is interesting. Your . . . vehemence. Why do you deny it with such force? Would there be shame if you missed the voice?"

"Shame? No, of course not."

"Then what is the matter with admitting you might, at times, regret you no longer hear the voice?"

"What is the *matter*?" I repeated incredulously. "If I went around saying I used to hear a voice and I want him back? People would think I was crazy."

"Well . . ." Schaumburg gave a lazy shrug. "People. Perhaps. But in here, I think it is important to probe these areas."

"Okay, sure. Let's *probe*."

"What do you want to tell me about how you feel about the voice? Today, I mean."

"I want to tell you that the voice is gone," I replied firmly.

He looked amused. "All right, then."

I glanced longingly at the door. The clock said I had to endure just a few more minutes of this.

"Tell me about when Alan would control your body," Schaumburg prodded after neither of us had spoken for an awkward while.

"That only happened a couple of times. I would be asleep, and he would sort of take my body out for a spin. He never did anything bad with it. Like, he would fold the laundry, stuff like that."

Another long silence. I regretted bringing up the laundry—it made me sound pretty crazy somehow, even though doing my shirts was Alan's idea.

"I'm not able to find anything like your case in the literature," Schaumburg told me. "Schizoaffective disorder, which is how Dr. Johnston has classified your condition, is entirely separate from dissociative personality disorder, though people commonly make the mistake of believing schizophrenia means having a so-called split personality. In other words, patients never describe their alter ego as a voice; they just morph from one personality to another, spontaneously and, sometimes, conveniently."

"I see we're out of time and I'm sorry I was late," I replied sincerely. "It took longer to get that bat out of his hands than it should have."

"Did you hit him with it?"

"What? *No.* That's not how it's done. You think I would last long in this profession if I went around braining people with a baseball bat?"

"What if Alan were running your body: Would *he* hit some-one with a bat?"

"Alan?" I laughed. "No. A badminton racquet, maybe. Or he'd write them an angry note." I stopped chuckling at Schaum-burg's expression.

"You really miss him, don't you?"

I wasn't buying the sympathy. This guy was playing me, and I needed to pay more attention before I talked myself into trouble. "He's gone," I responded unequivocally.

"There have been cases where people miss the voices; they crave their delusions. You've perhaps seen the movie *A Beautiful Mind*? It's even hypothesized that some patients could so yearn for the return of their imaginary companions that they re-create the voice. Bring them back, in other words."

"Sounds like something we should talk about next time," I noted amiably, standing up.

"Why don't you sit down? I have some time before my next appointment."

It didn't sound like a suggestion. I sat, flexing and unflexing my fists on my knees.

"What is your pharmacist going to tell me when I call him to find out the last time you filled your prescription?" Schaumburg asked.

"Tom? That I was just in there last week," I replied with all the truthfulness my soul could muster. I had, in fact, been in there just four days ago, getting some medication for Katie.

"All right, Ruddy. I'm your doctor and interested in what is best for you. But if I call your pharmacist and find that, as I sus-pect, you have not been getting your medications, I'm going to report your lack of cooperation to the court. And you do know what that means, don't you?"

I licked my lips. "It means I would go back to jail," I finally rasped. I believed this bastard would do it, too—put me behind bars just for not taking some stupid pills.

"I'm glad we understand each other," Schaumburg said.

I thought about giving him the stare I had successfully used to close down bar fights and get people to hand over their unpaid-for cars, but I knew it wouldn't work here. Schaumburg had all the power. In the end, I just stared at him helplessly.

I did not know what I was going to do.

# 2

## Why Would Anyone Do That?

I jabbed at my cell phone. I used to hate the damn things—my fingers are too big for the tiny buttons on the screen, coverage is lousy when I'm in the backwoods, and they have a tendency to break when I get pissed off and stomp on them. I swore I would never replace the one I threw out of the truck window a while back. Then I got a girlfriend, who outvoted me.

I get outvoted on a lot of things.

I phoned the pharmacy, and Tom answered. I pictured him on the other end of the phone call: He looks so much like a pharmacist, I'm sure he knew as a kid that's what he would wind up doing. He was probably born wearing a white coat and a mustache. I told him what I wanted him to do for me, and he became pretty uncomfortable.

"See, Ruddy, the thing is, your doctors are sort of the head of your health care team. I pretty much can't refuse to talk to them, and if they ask about your medications, I can't say you're getting them refilled when you haven't actually ever done it," he told me apologetically.

"Could you stall for a few days, so I could get in there and pick them up?"

"I think we already got a call. From a Dr. Schaumburg? He

asked me to phone him back. Said it was pretty important we speak today."

I was parked in the clinic lot in Traverse City, where a light snow had fallen and frozen on my truck windshield, adding to the film of ice already there. My heater was on full blast, blowing air that carried only a hint of warmth. Two small circles of clear glass had formed right above the defroster vents, and I leaned down and peered through these at cars creeping by on the snow-packed streets. Only five in the evening, and the night was already settling in—this far north the sun can hardly be bothered to make an appearance in January. I could not possibly make it to Kalkaska before Tom closed.

"Could you maybe wait until tomorrow to call him back?" I asked hopefully.

"Ruddy . . ."

"I need a little help here, Tom. Dr. Johnston never even asked about my medications, but this new guy is a hard-ass."

Tom was silent in a way that suggested to me that he was turning something over in his mind. "New guy," he mused.

"Right. I guess Sheryl was in a skiing accident." I unconsciously rubbed my knee.

"The thing is, there's a protocol for him to follow. Dr. Schaumburg, I mean. I'm not supposed to discuss your medications with him until I get something from Dr. Johnston's office."

I seized it. "Right! This guy could be an imposter, pretending to be my doctor to extract information from you!"

"But why would anyone do that?"

"Look, Tom, I think the important thing here is that you make this Schaumburg prove he is who he says he is. Meanwhile, I'll come in and pick up my medications tomorrow."

Tom was silent again.

"What is it?" I probed as pleasantly as I could.

"Ruddy, you never picked up the prescription. I couldn't fill it now."

"Look. This Schaumburg guy says he wants to send me back to jail. For not taking medication! That's not America, that's like . . ." I tried to think of a country where it was illegal not to take pharmaceuticals. Jamaica? "It's just un-American," I finally finished.

"I can't lie to a doctor," he whined.

"I'm not asking you to lie. Not exactly." Though I wished he would. I bit my lip. "You just tell Dr. Schaumburg you can't discuss my case without the authorization, and I'll think of something."

Tom agreed that he could at least do that much. I hung up, feeling a sweat break out on my forehead despite the frigid temperature in the truck cab. "Okay, I bought myself a day," I said aloud.

I sort of got into the habit of talking to myself back when I had Alan in my head. A lot of people talk to themselves. It doesn't mean I need to be on antipsychotic medication. Schaumburg could kiss my ass. "There's nothing wrong with me!" I yelled. A woman walking past at that moment heard me through the windshield and frowned in my direction, reflecting disbelief at my statement.

"I'm pretty sure people who talk to themselves sometimes yell," I muttered to myself.

My wipers rasped across the ice, which showed no sign of breaking up. I called my boss, Milt Kramer, to see if any of the customers I was hunting for had decided to drop off their vehicles. No, but he had a new assignment for me.

"Mark Stevens. Seventy days past due, eleven hundred dollars. I'll text you the vehicle description. Mail comes back no forwarding, no phone. Bank says collect or pull it in."

"Stevens? The handyman guy?"

"He put contractor/builder/architect on his application."

"I know him. He's probably living with his friend Kenny; shouldn't be too hard to find."

Milt grunted. "Bank says he's pretty much been past due from day one."

"That's Mark."

"You, uh, had your doctor appointment?"

"Yeah, but it was a new guy, a Nazi."

"Oh. You tell him about Repo Madness?"

"No, because there's no such thing. You made it up. I tell the doctor about your diagnosis, he's going to want to put *you* on medication."

"I did not make it up. I'm telling you, enough time stealing vehicles, and the madness sets in. I saw a guy bigger than you just break down and sob right on the street. He had to leave the business, wound up teaching high school, poor bastard."

"Did this crybaby hear voices?"

"He wasn't a *crybaby,* for God's sake. He had Repo Madness, is what I'm telling you. Now, you still got your nerve, I give you that, but with voices in your head, telling you to join a commune, become a nudist, get a cat . . ."

"I don't have the voice anymore, and he never said to do any of that."

"Then why are you going to a psychiatrist?" Milt rejoined slyly.

"All right. Next time I see the doctor, I'll tell him I've got Repo Madness and I'm afraid it's going to make me cry."

Milt snorted. After my dad died, Milt sort of became a father figure to me, and banter like this was how we expressed affection for each other. "Hey, uh, Ruddy," he said in a change-the-subject tone. "I'm meeting my nephew for drinks after work, but not at the Black Bear, a different place." His voice sounded guarded.

The Black Bear was my sister's bar, where I worked as a bouncer. Milt's nephew Kermit had just married my sister, so whatever was going on sounded as if it was some sort of family stuff. I don't mind drama as long as I don't have to hear about it. "That's up to you, Milt. I won't tell Becky."

"Well, on Mark Stevens, get the money or the car. Copy?"

"I'm not saying 'copy,' Milt. We talked about this."

I disconnected and thought briefly about Mark and Kenny. The first time I ever met them, they both stuck guns in my face, but I sort of liked them anyway. I would be sorry to repo Mark's truck.

The Black Bear on my mind, I called in to see if any bar fights needed to be broken up. My friend Jimmy answered—my sister, Becky, had hired him to greet customers and serve food, and it was working out really well. Jimmy was handsome, almost ridiculously so, and had the perfect personality for food service—the first time he'd ever had a job for which he'd displayed any actual talent. He laughed when I asked him if my services as a bouncer were required—my sister had remodeled the place and turned it from a dingy saloon into a family restaurant where "happy hour" actually meant "happy" and not "a bunch of unemployed guys getting drunk and then punching each other." I was starting to feel pretty useless as a bouncer—not too many parents want you to put their toddlers in a hammerlock. The only altercations I had broken up recently had been between the Wolfingers, a couple who had been passionately arguing since the day they got married.

"I'm going to head over to the Smeltania festival," I told Jimmy.

"What's that?"

"You know, Boyne City? They put the ice shanties out on the lake today. Smeltania."

"Smelt? You mean the little fish?"

"Right. Hence, Smeltania."

"I thought they called it Shantytown."

"That is what most people call it," I admitted. "But the whole thing started because of the smelt runs. They elect a temporary mayor, have a post office out on the ice—it's a big deal."

"Sure," Jimmy said absently.

"So you're patronizing me now?"

"Huh?"

"My fiancée swing by?"

"Haven't seen Katie, no," Jimmy replied.

For Katie not to show up at the Bear was not terribly unusual, but we'd had a few disagreements over things lately, and I couldn't help but read some bad news into her absence. It was on my mind to ask Jimmy for some advice—he'd had a lot more experience with women than pretty much any single man in Kalkaska—but I wasn't sure how to phrase the question. That was the thing about women: I'd been studying them my whole adult life and knew less about them than when I'd started.

"Hey, so, after you've been to the Shantytown festival, are you coming to the Bear?" he asked.

"Maybe, yeah. Why?"

"I'm sort of in trouble, Ruddy."

I groaned a little. "What did you do, Jimmy?"

"Can we talk about it in person?"

I told him sure, but I hung up with a sense of foreboding. When we were kids, I had always been something of a big brother to my friend, and had helped him out of a lot of messes. But he was an adult now, and his problems were usually a lot more complex than when he would get a girl to do his homework and then turn it in, in her handwriting.

Finally my heater had grown some balls and was turning the frozen layer on my windshield dark with meltwater. When I flipped on the wipers, the ice fragmented into islands that broke and slid away. I turned on my headlights and chugged out of the parking lot and into the night.

Despite the cold, the Smeltania festival would be well attended, with Christmas lights, lots of vendors in heated tents, live music from shivering musicians, and plenty of alcoholic beverages. I wasn't going there to party, though. I had a different purpose in mind.

I was going to see if I could contact Alan Lottner.

The snow let up by the time I arrived at Boyne City, a pretty town of about four thousand people that grew up around the logging and fishing industry because the Boyne River flows into Lake Charlevoix right there. Once the logs and the fish were pretty much gone, the town fell on rough times, but it had recently reinvented itself around upscale condos, yacht slips, and fancy restaurants. I wandered the festively decorated streets, stopping for a burrito at the Red Mesa Grille, idly walking through the parking lots to see if any of my current clients had driven their cars over to be stolen. Strings of lights lit up the snow, guiding the people, who wore bulky coats and wandered around greeting each other heartily, happy in hypothermia.

A guy stood on a flatbed trailer and explained the history of Smeltania to a small gathering of people. The story was about as dramatic and exciting as a bunch of flimsy shelters on naked ice could possibly be. When the smelt went away, so did the "town's" name, but the shanties remained because for some people, nothing is more entertaining than sitting for hours at a time on a bucket and watching a hole cut in a frozen lake. Now some smelt had returned, and a huge banner gamely welcomed everyone to Smeltania, but the locals still called it Shantytown.

After the speech, a children's choir sang an original song that had been written by someone who had clearly never before composed music. I clapped my mittened hands when they were finished.

Vendors were selling handmade jewelry and Native American artifacts from China, and T-shirts with slogans on them. The woman I had come to see was Madame Revard, and her tent had a thick curtain of beads hung over the entrance.

"Come in," a woman's voice invited. Madame Revard, I presumed. I pushed the beads aside and entered. There was room inside to park two pickup trucks, which had sort of become a unit of measurement for me—occupational skill or Repo Madness, take your pick. A kerosene heater cranked out heat and a faint petroleum odor, and a bunch of candles provided glowing illumination. The whole thing looked like a huge fire hazard.

Madame Revard resembled pretty much everyone else in northern Michigan, a short woman with skin pale from lack of sun. She wore a pendant that hung on her forehead, as if she'd been trying to put on a necklace and it had gotten stuck. Her earrings matched the pendant, and she had a thick ring or two on every finger. Over time, I've noticed a corollary between the size and number of gaudy rings a woman wore and the likelihood I'd be repossessing her car. I decided to keep this piece of information to myself.

"Welcome," she murmured. "Did you come for a specific reason, or are you just curious?"

"You're a medium, the kind who helps people contact the dead?"

"I speak to those who have departed, and if they choose, they communicate back. Would you like to try?"

"Try. Sure."

"I ask for my fee in advance so that it is out of the way and not a distraction," she said smoothly. "Fifty dollars, and we will get started."

I gave her two twenties and a ten. I mean, why the hell not?

# 3

## Not from a Him

Madame Revard didn't say anything for a few moments. She had an array of small polished stones in front of her, and she picked a few of these up, holding them in her hands for a moment before setting them down again. It was the first time I'd seen a medium do that. One of them was a Petoskey stone, a spotted rock, unique to the area, cherished by collectors and by locals who liked to find rocks and sell them to people from out of town.

"A man is here," Madame Revard murmured. She glanced up at me, then looked away.

I sat silently, my arms crossed. It was not a good sign that she had scanned my face for a reaction, but I wasn't ready to give up on her yet.

"He is a very big man," she continued. "Your father?"

Well, I'm a very big man, so chances are my dad had been too.

"He says he used to play football with you in the yard," she elaborated.

That could be a guess, but something told me there was more to it than that. I didn't know where Madame Revard was from, but it probably was around here—not that many Hollywood celebrities had flown in for the Smeltania festival. When my dad died, it got a mention in the local press because I was still considered big news—the hometown jock who had thrown it all away when Lisa Marie Walker drowned. Almost the exact same story ran when my mom passed away.

Madame Revard closed her eyes. Her lids were painted a metallic-silver color, like a hubcap, contrasting strongly with her deep-red lips and the black points brushed into her skin at the outside corners of her eyes. I wondered if she got her makeup advice from dead people.

"He has something he wants to tell you. He's sorry for how judgmental he was? Something happened, and he was very stern with you. He says he was too harsh." She opened her eyes and gazed at me levelly.

I swallowed. Maybe this lady was a charlatan, maybe not, but her words still got to me. What kid doesn't want to hear his father say something like that? Lisa Marie had been under a blanket in the backseat of my car, sleeping off too much alcohol. To Dad, her utter helplessness made what I did that much worse. He never came to visit me in Jackson, though my mom showed up a few times. The day he died, a guard and a minister came to my cell to tell me. My petition for compassionate leave was denied. I closed my eyes briefly to suppress a flood of regret.

"Is there anyone else there? Another man, maybe?" I asked in a hoarse whisper.

The woman paused for a moment. Then she reached out and picked up a smooth stone. "Let me see," she murmured. "Someone you were close to?"

As if anyone would visit a medium to contact perfect strangers. I gave her a small nod when she met my eyes.

"You lived with him," she stated.

Alan had lived with me, actually.

"Yes, someone is coming forward now. He says he has been watching you, and that he is learning lessons from you he wished he had learned while he was alive. That you're his role model in life now, his guide, and he is glad you are teaching him."

Well, that was a lot of crap. If Alan had something to say, it would almost certainly be to complain about me being engaged to his daughter.

Madame Revard saw something in my expression. She set down the stone. "He has left," she murmured.

"The guy who was here last year was better at this," I said.

Her face hardened. "What do you mean?"

"The medium. He came up with some stuff that no one could know but my mother. Not just feelings, but actual facts from the past. It's why I keep trying—I've never been able to reach Alan, but sometimes I'm impressed. Persuaded there's maybe something to this."

"They can sense when you're skeptical. When you're not receptive. And they stay away."

"I'm very receptive."

"No, you're hostile." Her eyes flashed at me angrily.

I stood up. "I'm not hostile; I'm just built to look like it."

"Thank you for the session. Go in peace," she said dismissively.

I stepped outside the tent, and the cold air rushed up to freeze my face. "Well, Alan, struck out again," I said softly.

I sometimes talk to Alan as if he were still there. That doesn't mean I need antipsychotic medication.

The locals had been drinking long enough to set up a broom ball game on the ice rink. I stood and watched it for a minute: about a dozen people whacking each other with brooms that had the bristles wrapped in duct tape. They were supposed to be playing a sort of hockey, without skates and using a soccer ball as a puck, but mostly they were knocking each other over, falling to the ice and laughing uproariously.

As far as I know, only our species does this sort of thing.

I sensed someone standing near me, and turned. A young woman was looking up at me with an oddly intense expression. From the lights strung overhead, I could see she had pretty blue eyes and blond hair worn short, her bangs peeping out from her hat, which matched her scarf. Her bulky coat hid whatever curves she might have, but she was on the thin side. "Hi," she said. Her freckled cheeks were red from the cold.

"Hi," I responded with more interest than was appropriate for a man who was affianced. In my defense, she was really focused on me, her stare intent, and it made me feel attractive. I had been at the festival for a couple hours and had just about decided to leave, but if pretty women were going to chat me up, maybe I'd stick around awhile.

"I saw you come out of the medium's," she said. She glanced over at Madame Revard's tent.

"Yeah. She said Abraham Lincoln is proud of me."

Admittedly, not the most witty remark, but she was still staring at me and reacted not at all to this.

"I saw you last year, too. There were two mediums here, and you talked to both of them."

"You saw me last year?" I replied, puzzled. Why would anyone notice or even care?

"I'm kind of a medium too," she continued, as if answering my question.

"Oh?"

"You're Ruddy McCann. That football guy."

"Well, okay, but that's sort of known."

She shook her head. "No, I'm not channeling anyone for that. I mean, I recognized you."

"Okay." I slipped off my mitten and held out my hand. "Nice to meet you . . ." I put a questioning look on my face and left a blank at the end of my sentence for her to fill in.

"Amy Jo," she said with some reluctance. She kept her glove on as she shook my hand.

"So, every year you come to experience the thrill of Smeltania?"

She wasn't interested in light banter. "I have a message for you. From, you know, beyond?"

This was the strangest conversation I'd ever had with a

medium, and believe me, those people can get pretty strange. I regarded the young woman warily. None of this felt right, exactly, but she was clearly intent on telling me something. Could Alan be reaching out to me through her? It seemed pretty implausible, but if I wasn't at least a little open to the idea, why had I driven all the way to Boyne City?

"Okay, what does he say?" I finally asked. I thought about my wallet, which had a lone twenty and a few ones stuck inside. If Amy Jo were going to quote a price, it would be now.

But she was shaking her head. "Not him."

"Sorry?"

"Not from a him. It's from a girl."

"A girl," I repeated slowly.

"Yeah, um . . . it's important."

"Okay." I was completely baffled.

Amy Jo worked her lips a few times, looking as if she regretted ever approaching me. Then she leaned in closer, sharing a confidence. "It's from Lisa Walker," she said in a near whisper.

I went very still. The woman gazing at me so intently did not have the look of a prankster, nor a con artist, but I could not think of any reason why anyone would bring up that particular name to me. "That's enough," I said coldly, interrupting Amy Jo as she was getting ready to say more. "Who are you?"

"I told you," she replied. Her face held the anguish of a liar caught in an obvious fib.

"You're not a medium."

"Listen to me!"

"This isn't funny."

"She says she wasn't in the car!" Amy Jo blurted.

I stared at her, my anger rising. "What kind of person . . . ," I started to ask, but I stopped when she shook her head wildly, tears in her eyes.

Why would she be *crying*?

"No, it's true. Please. I know you think you killed her. I know about the accident. But you have to believe me. She wasn't in the car."

I realized my heart was pounding. Did she realize what she was saying? For a moment I allowed myself to contemplate it, and I nearly staggered with the implications.

"I have to go," she said, taking a step back.

"Wait. No!" I seized her by the shoulders, and her eyes widened in alarm. "Listen to me. You have to tell me everything. What do you think you *know*?"

"Lisa wasn't in the car when it sank. Okay? Please let go of me!"

I realized just how tightly I had been gripping her. I let go. "Not in the car? My car? How do you know?"

She backed a step away from me. "I said."

"You're not a medium! What is this?"

"Ruddy?" a woman called.

I turned, and there was my fiancée, Katie, her hands in her pockets, a stunned expression on her face. From her perspective, the conversation I'd been having must have seemed shockingly intimate.

I turned back, but Amy Jo was fleeing, tufts of packed snow flying from her boots. She was headed for the parking lot.

"Ruddy? Who was that?" Katie demanded, bewildered.

I turned away from the shock in her eyes and tracked Amy Jo as she slid behind the wheel of an old RAV. Her brake lights fired, but she had to back up to get out of her spot, and I caught a clear glimpse of her license plate. As a repo man, I'd developed a knack for memorizing plate numbers.

"Ruddy?"

I turned back to my fiancée. Her blue eyes were pained. A lock of her curly reddish-brown hair had come loose from her wool hat, and she brushed it away impatiently. "How . . . how did you find me?" I asked her, which had to be the worst question for me to ask. Could I sound more like a cheating man?

"You told Jimmy you were coming here. You told me you were on a repo. Who was that woman?"

"She said she was a medium."

"That's not what I mean, Ruddy!" Katie exclaimed. "You were holding her, having a fight!"

"No. No, no, no," I protested. "It wasn't like that. I just met her."

"You did not just meet her," Katie remonstrated, shaking her head. "You are lying to me."

"I swear, it's true."

"So you just met her? You were *holding* her."

"Yeah, but not . . . It wasn't like a hug."

"I could see it wasn't a hug! Ruddy, what's going on here? Can you imagine how it felt to see the two of you together?"

"Okay. Okay. I see how this could look. But you have to trust me."

"Trust you?" she repeated. "You said you would be working a repo. You lied to me, but you say to trust you?"

"I know."

Her shoulders slumped in defeat, and that alarmed me more than anything else she could have done. "I've been trying so hard to make things work lately, and now this—," she began mournfully.

"But there is no 'this'!" I interrupted. "I was just reacting to what she told me. That's all. I swear that's all you were seeing."

"What? What did she tell you?" Katie pleaded. "I want to believe you, but you're not telling me anything."

I took a deep breath. "She said Lisa Marie Walker wasn't in the car the night I crashed into the lake. When it sank, she wasn't in the car."

Katie blinked, caught off guard. "What?"

"That's what she said."

"How . . . ?"

"She told me she was a medium, but I don't believe her. I mean, she didn't act like any medium I've ever spoken to."

Katie frowned at me, confused. "You've spoken to mediums?" she asked after a pause.

I sighed. "Yeah, it's why I came here tonight." I gestured at Madame Revard's tent down the street, and Katie looked over at it without comprehension.

"To talk to a medium," she said.

"Yeah."

"Why would you do that?"

I was not going to tell her why. I could just imagine her reaction if I told her I was trying to reach her dead father. "The medium, Madame Revard, told me my father was sorry he was so stern with me, so judgmental. I think she means after what I did to Lisa Marie Walker. He was very . . . He felt I had really let him down, let the family down. The town, even. The only thing he approved of after the crash was when I pleaded guilty."

"Oh, Ruddy." Katie's expression softened. "I didn't know you were so . . . You never talk about that."

"I didn't want to tell you what I was doing tonight, so I said I was on a repo." That much was certainly true.

"But can't you see? That's the kind of thing I've been talking about. I wish you would tell me. I wish you would let me in, to trust me. You used to trust me!"

"Okay. You're right. Anyway, then this woman, her name is Amy Jo, came up out of the blue and said she saw me go into the medium's tent and that she had a message from beyond for me. From Lisa Marie. That Lisa Marie says she wasn't in my car."

Katie processed this. Of all the people in the world, only she knew the full story. How I'd met Lisa at a party. She'd been drinking and wanted to go for a ride. I was the college football jock, and she was a high school senior. After she drowned, everyone assumed I'd taken her out for sex, but actually, that never came up. I had just met her and was flattered by her attentions.

Soon after we got into the car, she felt ill and crawled under a blanket in the backseat. I stopped for beer in Charlevoix because that had been the original destination, but she never moved when I parked the car, and didn't answer when I asked her if she wanted anything. Driving back home, I made a fatal wrong turn, mistaking the steep drive down to the ferry launch for a bend in the highway. I didn't even see the ramp, and hit it going probably fifty miles an hour. That's what the sheriff estimated, anyway.

I got out of the car with the help of some people who had been sitting in a van, smoking marijuana. Lisa Marie didn't. Her body washed up right here in Boyne City five days later, blood full of alcohol, lungs full of water.

I wasn't lying to Schaumburg. There were many days when I would gladly change places with her.

Could she have gotten out at the 7-Eleven? I tried to remember if I had seen her when I got back in the car, if she had said anything, made a noise. It certainly felt as if she were still there.

And if she wasn't in the car, why did two searchers find her body floating in the cold gray waters of Lake Charlevoix?

"You've never seen her before? This Amy Jo?" Katie asked.

"I swear it."

"Why would she say that? About Lisa Marie Walker?"

"I don't know, but she seemed to believe it."

"Is there . . . Is it possible?"

"I don't know. But if it is, Katie, it means that my whole life went off course, that I lost everything I had, all for a lie."

We stared at each other. Light snow was falling, landing in the fur hood around her face and sticking there. Under any other circumstances, I would have been unable to resist pulling her to me and kissing her, but I just stood there. "What is it? Why did you come looking for me?" I asked finally.

"Oh." Her face fell. "Ruddy, I am so sorry. I have news."

She stood there and tried to control her emotions, and I stood there, waiting for whatever bad thing she was going to tell me, my heart thudding. "It's about Milt," she was able to say before she came into my arms, pressing her face to my shoulder. The rest of her words were muffled by my coat, but I still heard her.

"He's dead, Ruddy. Milt killed himself."

# 4

## Aloha Means Everything

Tom actually came out from behind the counter at the pharmacy, something I'd never seen him do. If someone had asked me, I would have speculated that after closing hours he slept in a box in the back. But he wanted to tell me how sorry he was about Milt, and he shook my hand with grim formality.

Tom's mustache is as bristly as a whisk broom and actually makes a scraping sound when he rubs it. It's a sandy color, like his hair—blond but with a lot of what could almost be dirt in it. "So, do they know what happened?" he asked me.

I shook my head. We sat down in chairs in the small waiting area. "It looks like he closed his garage door, started his engine, and then just sat there and drank vodka until the fumes got to him." Thinking of him dying like that always gave me a stabbing sensation in my gut, and this time was no different.

"Did anybody . . ." He struggled with how to put his question and then gave up. "This is such a shock."

"No one had a clue this might be brewing, as far as I know. I can't think of any reason for him to do this, though I guess there's no such thing as a good reason. But business has been good, we're getting more skip tracing work, he was healthy. . . ." I trailed off as a shadow passed through Tom's eyes. "What is it?"

"Nothing."

It wasn't nothing. I could tell. If Milt was sick, Tom might know—but of course he couldn't tell me. "How's his wife? How's Trisha?" he inquired after a moment.

I shrugged. "I haven't spoken to her, but I guess not well. It's just awful."

We both sat there quietly for a moment.

"What does this mean for you, then?" he asked finally.

"Besides losing my friend, you mean? I don't know. Milt *was* the business; it was always just him in that office. I've got some repo assignments I guess I'll follow up on and maybe get paid, maybe not. Either way, I feel like I owe it to him, that I'd be dishonoring him somehow if I just gave up. But yeah, I might be out of a job."

"I'm so sorry, Ruddy."

"Yeah, well, unemployed beats being in jail," I responded somewhat pointedly.

Tom's mouth became an unhappy line. "Look, Ruddy, your prescription is way more than six months old. I can't legally fill it."

"But if Schaumburg calls and you tell him I haven't been taking my meds, he says he'll violate me, and I'll have to do the rest of my probation behind bars."

Tom spread his hands. "I don't know what I can do."

"Well," I reasoned, "when Schaumburg calls you can say, 'Yes, Ruddy was just in here recently to pick up his meds.' That's not a lie, it *is* why I'm here."

"What if he asks if you've been taking your medications?"

"You tell him the truth. You don't know. Hell, Tom, how would you know if *anybody* was taking their medications, really?"

"You're asking me to lie to a doctor. I could lose my license."

"He wants to put me in jail! Just for not taking some antipsychotic medication! Is that fair?"

"Why haven't you been taking them?" Tom asked curiously.

I hesitated. I didn't want to tell him I was trying not to suppress Alan's chances of coming back, because that would sound like I did *need* the meds. "I don't like their effect," I finally replied evasively.

"Ruddy . . . I'm sorry," Tom said mournfully. "If Schaumburg asks, I'm going to have to tell him the truth. That's just how it is."

We held Milt's memorial service at the funeral parlor owned by Katie's mother, Marget. Katie begged off attending, saying she had to work, but I knew the real reason for her absence was that she did not want to risk having Marget try to talk to her. I didn't press the issue. Katie knew how much Milt meant to me, and I knew what Marget had done to Katie.

I saw her, though, Marget, standing silently in the back of the room. Her white-blond hair, thin and straight, could not have been more different from Katie's curly reddish-brown locks, though they shared the same electric-blue eyes. Marget stared at me in a way I knew meant she was going to try to engage me in conversation, which I dreaded.

I met Kermit's brother, Walt, for the first time. Walt looked a little like Milt, with pale skin and a lean body. Kermit was short and squat, the kind of guy coaches always thought would be tough to tackle but weren't. Where Kermit's darker skin color came from, I did not know. Both men both spoke about their uncle, praising him for his generosity and kindness, and I thought about how good a friend Milt had been to me, splitting the repo fee from the bank fifty-fifty, though it was his truck and his lot and his reputation that we operated on. His wife, Trisha, sat in the front row and sort of sagged against a man I later learned was her brother.

When friends were invited to talk, I stood and told everyone that Milt was the only person who would give me a job when I got out of prison. That he cared about me and if we had a slow period, he would advance me some pay so I didn't starve. Milt would have been disappointed at the way his big tough repo man's voice cracked, the way tears wet my cheeks, and how I had trouble finishing what I started out to say. Milt's kindness and fatherly concern for me had propped me up when I was in danger of going into a dark spiral of my own.

And the money helped, too. Being a bouncer didn't pay well or often—Becky gave me some of the proceeds when she was in the black, but it wasn't as if I had a regular salary. I didn't mention the part about bar bouncer not being a lucrative profession, though I guess a few people might have inferred that from the way I dressed. Nor did I speculate what I was going to do now, since I apparently was no longer a repo man. What I did say is that everyone was welcome to head over to Kalkaska for a wake in Milt's honor at the Black Bear.

Kermit came up to me to thank me for my words. As always with Kermit, there was an awkwardness between us, even under these circumstances. I told him how sorry I was, stumbled a little through the words *untimely, premature accident,* not sure what you're supposed to say to the nephew of a man who likely took his own life.

"Well, not premature," Kermit murmured sadly. "Uncle Milt had cancer. It had recently metabolized to his liver."

"I had no idea," I replied, shocked.

"He wanted it kept a secret."

I looked involuntarily at the casket, oddly hurt Milt hadn't confided in me about his illness. Kermit followed my gaze. "Is that why it's closed?" I asked him.

I instantly regretted asking such a unfeeling question. Kermit shook his head. "No. Actually, he was impounded. The lid is down because he's not in there."

"Impounded?" I responded, baffled.

"Yeah. We thought the sheriff wasn't going to be investigatory, so we scheduled this as soon as possible. By the time we found out the law wanted to look into things, the onens were routed."

He saw me go blank at the unfamiliar word. "It's a Jewish thing, it means family of the dead. Uncle Milt's relatives. They're all here. But they don't know that my uncle . . . isn't."

"That's got to be really hard, Kermit," I said inadequately.

I wanted to say more, but Kermit was looking over my shoulder. "I think she wants to talk to you," he said, withdrawing politely as I turned and saw Marget coming at me. I froze in place, steeling myself. "Hello, Marget," I said in a tone softened to suit the circumstances.

"Hello, Ruddy. How is my daughter?"

"Katie's doing well. She started a new job as a receptionist in a real estate office. Same one that Alan worked in. And she took the test, the one to get her license to sell property. We haven't yet heard if she passed."

Marget's eyes fluttered a little. Marget was still married to Alan when he died. "I didn't know that," she replied quietly. "Well. How are the wedding plans going?"

"Fine," I said. They weren't fine, actually, but Katie wouldn't want me talking about that with anyone, especially her mother.

"Have you sent invitations?"

"Not yet."

She nodded. Her eyes wanted to ask me if she would be receiving one, but I knew she dreaded the answer.

"Well, I should get to the Black Bear," I said formally. "Free drinks, I imagine we'll be busy. Thank you for the way you took care of Milt."

"Ruddy. Can you talk to her? She won't return my phone calls."

"She doesn't want to speak to you."

"She's my daughter," Marget said in quiet anguish.

"Marget. You murdered her father."

She blinked at my words. She was the type of person who could look at you with warm sympathy, but I always knew there was something much tougher in there, and I could see it in her icy expression now. "There was an investigation. There were no charges. The D.A. said there was no evidence," she hissed.

"That doesn't change what happened."

My soon-to-be mother-in-law glared at me. "I would think that you of all people would understand."

"No. It's not the same. What I did was an *accident,* Marget."

"It is the same. I had nothing to do with what happened to Alan. *They* did it."

I regarded her outraged expression, waiting for the guilt to seep into it, but it didn't happen. Apparently, she had herself convinced of the truth of her words.

"I guess Katie doesn't see it that way, Marget. And I have to be honest: Neither do I."

"Well, here's the way *I* see it," she spat in icy fury. "My daughter needs me. When Alan died—"

"When Alan was murdered," I interrupted rudely.

She gave me a look of utter contempt. "When that happened, I was there for her, and I've always been there for her. Then you come along with your lies, an ex-con *loser* who steals cars from people, and you think you can take her away from me? You think I am going to let you do that? You know nothing about her. You're no good for her. You're no good for anybody."


I came up with several pointed, devastating things to say to Katie's mother once I was back in my truck. The conversation haunted me on the drive back because it peeled back the covers from my own insecurities. I really wasn't good enough for a woman like Katie, probably, but who would be? And lately, it seemed, I really did know nothing about her—I was having more and more trouble understanding some of the things she was saying. Clearly, I was doing a few things wrong, but I wasn't sure *what.*

I followed a caravan of cars to Kalkaska and hustled into the warmth of the Black Bear, where Jimmy had been standing guard over a mostly empty business. The mourners crammed up to the bar and things flipped pretty quickly into a party. Becky caught my eye and held up two fingers—the Bear would cover two drinks for everyone. I stood behind the bar and made mental note of everyone's tab.

I'd like to think Milt would have wanted this: a big gathering, people laughing and talking. In reality, though, I had trouble picturing him anywhere but behind his desk. He hadn't been in the Black Bear since my sister put in booths and a new kitchen and soft lights. All kinds of people came to the Bear now, not just guys who wanted to argue about snowmobiles or chain saws. Maybe that's why Milt stayed away—the place had lost its charm.

"Hey, Kermit, that was nice, what you said at your uncle's service," I told my brother-in-law. He regarded me warily, maybe looking for an insult. "No, I mean it," I insisted.

"Thanks."

"You think Milt would be glad the funeral ended in a party?" I gestured around the room at all the people.

Kermit gave it some thought, frowning. "I think he would be embracive, yeah."

"Embracive." I nodded. "Okay, sure."

"He may not have been the most conversable convivialist, but he would have enjoyed the festivities."

"I don't know, Kermit. Sometimes it's like your words come out of a sausage factory."

He blinked. "Sorry?"

"When I repo a car, I say, 'I'm here to repo your car.' I don't say, 'My . . . My inhabitance on your property is with the cause to, uh, reappropriate the collateral on your defaulted financial instrument.'"

He was back to eyeing me like I was the schoolyard bully getting ready to beat him up for winning the spelling bee, when I had really been trying to just have a little fun with him. Why did it seem that we were always at odds with each other? I might not have been friendly toward him when he started dating my sister, but that's because I didn't think he was good enough for her. And while I still held that view, it had more to do with my love for her than with my opinion of him. That was okay, wasn't it?

This was the sort of thing I used to be able to talk to Alan about.

I switched gears. "Hey, do you know any mediums? Like, local people? I'm thinking it is a lot like those psychics you used to be in business with."

"Media?" he pondered, his frown deepening. "No, a medium and a psychic are two different things. Media talk to dead people."

Was the plural of *medium* really *media* in this context? How the hell should I know?

"I *know* what a medium does, Kermit," I replied a bit peevishly.

He told me he didn't know any media. That's what he said; I'm not endorsing his use of the term.

I glanced at the clock—it was getting late—and lowered my head to my phone. Katie often had to put in evening hours at the real estate office, but she should have arrived by now. Thanks to autocorrect, I wrote: *Are you com get over? Coming!*

At that point the Wolfingers, Claude and Wilma, blew into the place like human typhoons. "We won a trip to Hawaii!" Wilma screamed, in a tone and volume of voice normally reserved for people who are being actively murdered.

Claude and Wilma were both sixty-two years old and it seems as if they'd been married a lot longer than that. When Wilma shrieked out her megaphone-level announcement, a baby in the corner started crying. Most people, though, shouted something like, "Yay!" even though we were thinking, *Oh no!*

You don't just *win a trip to Hawaii*. Not if you live in Kalkaska.

Claude raised what seemed to be a postcard over his head, waving it around like a winning lotto ticket. Everyone congratulated him despite the lack of plausibility. Claude's hands always look like he's been down at the jail, being fingerprinted—he's a mechanic at the local garage. White hairs sprout out of his nose and his spotted arms, and his head is mostly bald. His wife, Wilma, is part Native American, with beautiful dark skin, nearly black eyes, and a temper that flashes lightning quick. She has fifty pounds on her husband and is an inch taller than his five-foot-eight—we always say he's fighting out of his weight class.

"Ruddy!" Claude bellowed when he saw me. "We're going to Hawaii! All expenses paid!"

"That's great, Claude," I said as sincerely as I could.

"Drinks are on me!" he cried overenthusiastically. Everyone yelled, "Yay!" again.

"Actually, the first two are on the house," I corrected him.

"Even better!" he enthused. "This is the best day of our lives!"

I decided not to explain that the free drinks were due to Milt's passing. I turned and tracked Jimmy eyeing me and remembered he was in some sort of trouble. We nodded at each other, but things were too busy to chat.

Whether Milt would have enjoyed the conversable conviviality or not, the free drinks and the single round I let Claude put on his tab propelled the bar into a full-out celebration.

"In Hawaii, they don't have consonants, just vowels," Claude lectured a bleary-eyed group of revelers. "And aloha means everything: hello, good-bye, love, peace, eat, drink, lawn mower, doesn't matter: You just say aloha."

A lot of people frowned as they considered this, but no one challenged him.

"Honey, let me dance the hula for you," Wilma cooed at her husband. They were being amazingly noncombative with each other—I guess winning a trip to Hawaii can really smooth out the rough spots in a relationship.

Wilma put Claude in a chair in the center of the room and spooled up "Hotel California" on the jukebox, which I guess was as close as we could come to Hawaiian music. Everyone was laughing and cheering, but we all fell silent when Wilma started to move in a smooth, flowing, and frankly erotic fashion, her hips swaying, her hands carving the air like elegant birds. What the hell? No one had ever seen her do such a thing, or suspected she was capable of it. She was graceful and beautiful, and we were all entranced.

The dance ended with Wilma climbing on the chair and crashing with her husband to the ground. Then they made out on the floor until Claude needed to breathe. "Last call!" I shouted.

I checked my phone. No response from my fiancée.

By the time we'd broomed everyone out the door, it was just Jimmy and me. I locked the place and poured us a couple of short beers, and we sat underneath the bear—a taxidermied black bear that stood in the corner, its lips in a snarl, arms raised, looking fierce and ready to attack. I had nicknamed the bear Bob and thought he was kind of cute. He was the reason my father gave the bar its name. Legend had it Dad had shot the thing, but Becky claimed she was with him when he bought it at a garage sale.

As I get older, I learn more and more that memory is a tricky thing and that Becky's is wrong.

"Okay, so?" I prodded.

Jimmy swept his black hair out of his eyes and looked at his hands as if he were holding cards in them. "Yeah. I have a problem. With Alice."

"Alice. Alice Blanchard?"

"Yeah."

"Is she asking for child support? Because if she is, you know you need to pay it."

"No, she still won't take any money for Vicki."

Jimmy had recently found out he had a daughter, Vicki, now ten years old, by a woman he hadn't known was pregnant when they'd stopped dating. Alice Blanchard was married to a big shot banker in Traverse City now and had a nice life and was altogether hostile to Jimmy, but she allowed my friend to see his biological daughter.

"So she won't take money. . . . Wait, is Alice threatening to cut off your visitation? Because that's not right either."

Jimmy shook his head. "No, that's not it."

I was impatient with the guessing game. "I know she hates you, Jimmy. What's she doing now?"

Jimmy looked pained. "It's like this, Ruddy. I sort of started having sex with her again."

I stared at him. "I did not see that one coming," I confessed.

"We didn't mean to. We just couldn't help it."

"Sure, that makes sense."

"So I need your help."

"You need my help? How can I help? With what?"

"Alice thinks her husband suspects something."

"Wow, Jimmy." I shook my head. "This is a big mess."

"Tell me about it," he responded moodily. "And it gets worse. He told her one time that if she ever cheated on him, he would kill her."

"Right, well, a lot of people say things like that."

"No, Alice says he means it." Jimmy gave me a soulful look. "She's really, really scared."

# 5

## Why Would You Believe Something Like That?

My dog, Jake, stirred in his bed when I walked in the front door, giving me a mournful look with his basset eyes. His mottled body—brown and black and white—was coiled and ready for inaction, his flabby stomach as pink as a baby's butt.

"You know, for a lot of dogs, when their master comes home, that's a really big deal. They jump around, bark, lick. Or, you know, move a single muscle."

He sighed with disgust at the behavior of those other dogs. I went over to him and knelt to stroke his soft ears. "Hey, Jake. You get a lot done today?" He leaned into my massage. "Did Katie take you out?"

He shot me a coldly disapproving look at the word *out*.

"Okay, you and me, outside, leg up, in five minutes. Prepare yourself mentally."

I walked down the short hall and stood in the bedroom doorway. Katie was sitting up in bed, reading *Radiant Angel* by Nelson DeMille. She wore a gray flannel nightgown that looked like it had been issued by the Russian army. I was learning to read the signals: White clingy T-shirt meant she could be coaxed into feeling amorous. Lacy black meant I'd better be ready to perform. This one suggested I'd have better luck invading Poland.

I gazed at her, feeling the distance between us. Some random

seed of discontent had taken root in our relationship and flow-
ered despite any nurturing by either of us. "It was a nice funeral,"
I said by way of a greeting.

She set her book down and gave me a sad smile. "He was a
good man. Are you okay?"

I shrugged. "Doesn't seem real yet."

"I know. And then when it does sink in, you sometimes wish
you could go back to being in denial." I wondered if she was
thinking of her father. "So, did you see my mother?" She glanced
away, as if she didn't want to hear the answer.

"Yes."

"Did she speak to you?"

"Yes. She said the usual things. 'I'm no good for you, I'm a
loser' . . . like that."

She pressed her hands to her head in an odd headache gesture.
"My whole life . . . ," she started to say, and then she was crying.

I crossed over to her, concerned. "Honey? Katie? What is it?"
I put my arms around her.

She didn't reply for a moment. Her tears flowed silently, and
she reached for a tissue to wipe her eyes. Jake's collar rattled as
he came into the room, sensing something. He leaped onto the
bed, probing Katie's face with a wet nose and then a pink tongue.
She hugged him to her. "Oh, Jake," she said mournfully.

"Is it Milt?" I asked.

She shook her head, then shrugged. "Oh, a little, I guess. It's
more that I couldn't go to the funeral because of my mom. Which
is just one more way she's running my life, you know? And when
I went to work, answering the phones at Dad's old office, I
thought I was finally making my own decisions, but the only reason Dad worked there in the first place was because she got him
the job. Even now that I've taken the real estate exam, it still all
flows from her, you know?" She caught my noncomprehension
and laughed sadly. "I guess this doesn't make any sense."

"You're saying you feel controlled by your mother."

"I'm saying I don't know who I am anymore."

Something told me I was heading into a conversation I might not like, but that didn't stop me. "What does that mean?"

"I mean, I have these roles, like I'm your fiancée, my mother's daughter, and if I passed the test, I guess I'm a real estate agent, but who am I? Who is Katie Lottner?"

Jake and I glanced at each other. She appeared to be in real pain, a pain neither dog nor man seemed able to understand.

"I thought about going to the bar as usual," she continued. "And there's laughing and drinking, and then Wilma Wolfinger throws a beer in Claude's face. Like nothing happened, like Milt never died. And I realized, this is how every day goes now."

"Actually Wilma did sort of a Hawaiian lap dance for Claude."

She gave me a wan smile. "This topic is a little too emotional for you, isn't it?"

"No, no," I protested, though inside I was practically screaming, *Yes, yes.* I just couldn't escape the feeling there was something worse going on here than I perceived. "I just want to make sure . . . Are you still pissed off about that Amy Jo woman, at the Shantytown festival?"

"No. I told you I accepted your explanation."

I wondered if I should probe the difference between *accepted your explanation* and *I believe you.* I decided to leave it alone. I regarded my fiancée. Even with her face scrubbed of makeup and her hair pulled back in a scrunchie, she was still breathtakingly beautiful.

"It's just that we spend practically every night at the bar." She sighed.

"Because I work there. I'm a bouncer. It's not like they'd hire me to do that at the church."

"You work there. You get *paid* to work there?"

Was that what this was all about? I remembered reading somewhere that married couples mostly fought about money and sex.

I couldn't imagine what there was about sex to fight about, but money made sense. "Becky doesn't pay me in winter. The Bear really doesn't make a profit until the snow melts."

"That's not my point. It's not that you're not making any money; it's that you go there even though there's no reason. I just would like to spend an evening somewhere *else* for a change."

"Okay. We'll do that. It's a good idea. Let's go someplace nice." I mentally reviewed my financial status, which was broke and out of a job. Well, maybe not *that* good of an idea.

"No, I'm sorry. That's not what I even meant to tell you. Forget I said that." She gave me a serious look, and I felt my blood chill. There would be bad news now. "I think I found a place. In East Jordan. Like we talked about. Closer to work."

"No," I protested. "We said we would discuss it."

"No," she responded in disconsolate tones. "Please don't say that. We've discussed it a lot. The commute, our relationship, how things have been lately."

"You say 'our relationship' like it's this thing we keep in a closet somewhere. It's not a thing; it's us," I argued. I could feel the heat rising in my face, though I knew I needed to be calm and reasonable.

"It's really late, can we not fight about this now? I won't know about the place until tomorrow. I just really need to chill out and go to sleep; I don't want to go through this all again."

Well, I did. I wanted to go over this ridiculous idea that we were going to put a pause in our lives. We were betrothed; you don't suspend that for some sort of engagement vacation. But instead I came up with the most difficult word for me to utter in the moment. "Sure."

Katie sighed in relief and picked up her book in a way that suggested the conversation was over. I thought about asking her if she wanted to fight about sex, but instead went to drag my dog out into the cold. He really had to lift his leg, but his expression indicated he resented me anyway.

Katie slipped out before I awoke, and, of course, Jake didn't stir. I had a vague notion of my front door easing closed while it was still dark, and then what seemed like just seconds later my house was filled with daylight.

The morning was so nice, it hurt. We don't see much of the sun in late January, but on this day the air was full of dancing sparkles as the trees shook off their snow under a dazzling blue sky. I shielded my eyes as I stumbled to the repo truck, which barely started despite the dual batteries. The sun was doing nothing to cut the cold, which had driven temperatures below zero.

"Why on earth would the Wolfingers want to go to Hawaii?" I asked myself.

I drove to Boyne City for the second time in twenty-four hours. My route took me through the little town of East Jordan, where Katie worked, then through acres and acres of hardwood, the trees casting dark shadows in the brilliant sun, until finally I arrived at the shore of Lake Charlevoix and turned right. My heater had apparently decided to give up—even after an hour in the truck, I could still see my breath.

When I arrived in Boyne City, the shanties clustered out on the frozen lake looked like big animals huddled against the cold. I pictured the men sitting inside them, not moving, holding fishing rods, icicles hanging from their faces. Well, okay, the shanties probably had to be heated.

I kept driving north, and eventually the woods thickened up, blocking my view of the ice, until I turned off the road and into a neatly plowed driveway near a mailbox that read STRICKLAND.

Barry Strickland had been the sheriff until recently, when he resigned amid the scandal of an extramarital affair with a councilman's wife. It didn't seem to bother the townspeople all that much when the story came out, but Strickland immediately apologized and quit the office. He explained that he'd brought dishonor to the position. That was the sort of man I knew him to be—he had the strength and integrity of a steel beam.

The councilman's wife went back to her husband, and Strickland, long a widower, went to his cottage on the shore and now, ironically, did a little work for Milt, helping us find people who had disappeared with debts owed to banks and credit unions. He still had a lot of friends in law enforcement after thirty-five years working as a cop all over the state, and was dogged and patient as an investigator.

Patience wasn't exactly part of my own investigative technique.

Business had expanded, all due to ex-sheriff Strickland, and now anybody skipping out on their debts north of Grand Rapids had Milt's recovery service looking for them.

"Ruddy. Come in," Strickland greeted me after I knocked on his door. "Coffee's fresh. Sorry I didn't make it to the Bear after the funeral."

I told him it was okay as I stomped the ice off my boots and accepted a mug from him gratefully. We sat in chairs near the fire. Hard to believe he wasn't still sheriff; he sure looked the part—his eyes were blue and clear, his hair a metal gray.

"Been a beautiful day, but clouds are rolling in," he remarked. "Going to bring some precipitation." In the other room, the Weather Channel was running, sound off.

This was what happened when you lost everything due to a mistake: You wound up alone and miserable. I knew very well what Strickland must be going through. I'd had something very similar occur in my life.

Except now, of course, I had a shot at a second chance.

I handed over a slip of paper with Amy Jo's plate number on it. If her name even *was* Amy Jo. He accepted it with interest, but when I explained why I needed the girl's address, what she had told me, his expression grew flat.

"Oh, Ruddy," he said mournfully. "Why would you believe something like that?"

I'd given that a lot of thought. "I'm not sure I *do* believe it. But I've racked my brain and you know what? It's possible. I didn't check under the blanket when I got back in the car that night. I didn't even look at her, and if I talked to her, she didn't answer. I can't say for sure she wasn't in the backseat, but I can't say for sure she was, either."

"What difference could it make? No one is going to reopen the case. She died, and you pleaded guilty and did your time."

I shook my head. "I'm not thinking that far ahead. I just want to *know*."

Strickland regarded the paper with distaste. I knew just how much he hated this sort of thing. This had nothing to do with our skip tracing business; it was just Ruddy McCann chasing ghosts.

"Please, Sheriff. This girl was not a medium, I'll tell you that. I've been to about half a dozen, and none of them acted like her. I think what she said is because she knows something. Because she *saw* something."

Strickland grunted. "I've asked you not to call me Sheriff."

"Oh. Sorry. Barry." It sounded odd on my tongue, like calling your father by his first name.

In the end he agreed to get a friend of his to run the plate because, I think, he was too damned bored not to. He walked me to the door, and we both peered at the sky, which was filling with the expected clouds. He told me how sorry he was about Milt. We left it with that sentiment, though I thought I caught something in his expression that must have been mirrored in my own.

Looked like we both might need new jobs.


While I'd been talking to Barry, I'd gotten a phone call and a voice mail. I didn't recognize the number, but I knew the voice. "Ruddy, it's Dr. Schaumburg. Please call me back. You know why."

I did not call him back.

When the precipitation hit, it came down as something between sleet and rain, if there is such a thing. I stopped in East Jordan for lunch at Darlene's, a restaurant that serves amazing cinnamon rolls I'd reluctantly given up eating. I only had one.

I was only thirty yards from Katie's office, but something told me not to drop in. I sent her a photo of my cinnamon roll instead, hoping she'd take the hint and join me. Instead she sent me back a smiley face emoticon, which could mean something, or nothing at all.

The roads were impossibly slick as I drove away, and I kept my speed low and my gear in four-wheel drive, regretting that I'd taken the time to stop at Darlene's. I should have just gotten a cinnamon roll to go and also another one.

In Mancelona, a tiny town about fifteen miles from Kalkaska, I saw a guy named Tigg Bloom putting gasoline in a Chevy Suburban. I knew Tigg because a year ago I'd sat on his front porch and drunk beer with him until he admitted his brother's Kia was parked behind the pole barn at the far end of the field. I agreed not to mention where I got my information, and Tigg agreed to drink the rest of the beer.

Now it was Tigg's turn: He was more than ninety days past due on the Suburban, and had vanished. I tried the beer trick on the brother, but he was still upset about the Kia and tried to sic his Labrador on me. I threw a stick for the dog, who ran to get it and brought it back to me. Strickland had worked the file and reported that Tigg's relatives all said he'd escaped northern Michigan and was in Florida somewhere. When I chatted with Tigg, I'd ask him if he knew he was related to a bunch of liars.

By the time I'd cautiously U-turned on the icy road, Tigg was in his Suburban, headed back toward the way I'd come. I hung back, following at a safe distance.

A few miles down M-66 toward East Jordan, the road bends steeply downward into the Jordan River Valley, a hilly area scooped out by glaciers eons ago. At the crest of the hill, the vehicle in front of Tigg turned left, and I saw the Suburban's antilock brakes working to hold Tigg on the road as he stopped.

My vehicle didn't have antilock brakes. Instead it had a rust hole on the passenger side that I kept covered in cardboard. In a real emergency, I could always lift the cardboard and stick my foot out, but in this case I was moving slowly enough that by pumping the brake pedal and downshifting, I coasted to a stop on the ice-rinked highway without rear-ending my customer.

Tigg had been watching my approach with considerable concern, and I saw the relief in his eyes when I was able to halt. Then he sat upright.

"Damn," I breathed. He'd recognized me.

Tigg put his foot into it and rocketed away, and I gave chase. If I lost him now, I might never see him again—a lot of these guys will do a better job of hiding their vehicles once they've seen the repo man.

I racked a full fifty-five miles per hour onto the speedometer before my brain took over. You don't do a high-speed chase in the middle of an ice storm. I was moving much too fast for these conditions, especially considering I was now barreling down one of the steepest hills in the whole state. I lifted my foot off the gas, watching in frustration as the Suburban pulled away. He was really flying.

I touched my brake, and immediately my truck's heavy back end tried to slide up toward its front end. I turned into the skid, then looked up and gasped: Tigg had realized his mistake and was trying to stop, his vehicle jerking and sliding, fishtailing crazily down the hill. A school bus in the opposite lane was rumbling up the hill, honking frantically.

I lost track of Tigg and focused on getting my own rig under control. My brakes were *worthless*. When I touched them even lightly, my tow truck started to drift, and I was swaying back and forth over the center line. "Damn it!" I yelled. I was losing it.

Farther down, I saw the Suburban way over in the bus's lane, and then it flew back to the right side and hit the snowbank in a spray of snow and then it was in the trees, crashing into them so violently I could *hear* it.

The school bus was trying to get out of my way, but I had lost control, and I was weaving and sliding and desperately turning the steering wheel against the skid. *I was going to hit the bus.*

I could not let that happen. My front end swung to the right, and I took my foot off the brake and mashed down on the accelerator. All four wheels bit and I surged ahead, flying past the bus and off the road—*"Jesus!"*—and then the snowbank grabbed me and the truck flipped upside down and I rolled over and over until I slammed into the trees.

Yet with all that happening, I had time for a single thought before impact. That voice yelling, *"Jesus!"*

That wasn't my voice.

That was Alan.

# 6

## I Know You're There

I've been hit in the head often enough to know I don't like it.

When I awoke in the hospital, it was to the nauseating head pain that comes from a concussion. In football they happen despite the fact that you've got a helmet on your head, and when you're crashing your repo truck into the trees, you don't even get the helmet.

Becky was sitting in a chair, an Andrew Gross novel—*One Mile Under*—open in her lap. When my mom died, she left the family home to me, along with boxes and boxes of suspense thrillers and mysteries. I dug into them, and now our whole family is hooked on the genre.

"Did we win the game?" I asked her.

Becky looked up from her book and frowned at me. "Do you seriously believe you got hurt in a football game, or are you just being a jerk?"

"Are those my only two choices?"

She came over and smiled down at me. "They found nothing broken. They were worried you might have brain damage, but I told them there would be no real way to tell."

"Funny."

"They thought it might be a good idea for you to spend a couple of days here so they can monitor you."

"Not doing that," I replied.

"I know. I told the doctors you would be stubborn and unco-operative and grumpy." She patted my shoulder affectionately. I gazed up at her, somehow missing her even though she was right there. "What is it?" she asked quizzically.

"I don't know. Things are different between us now."

"Bad different?"

"No, not bad, exactly. I mean, I don't get to see you as much as I used to. Seems like you've sort of turned the Bear over to Jimmy. I guess I regret that. But you're . . . softer now, or some-thing. You seem happy. We never fight."

"I do miss the fights," she teased gently.

"It was just that when I woke up and saw you there, it re-minded me of other times, like when we were kids on Christmas morning and you would sit in that chair in my room and wait for me to wake up."

"You are on pain medication," she observed.

"So?"

"Perhaps they've got you feeling sentimental?"

"I actually feel pretty good except for the headache."

"I miss you, too, Ruddy. You should come over and see what I'm doing to the house. I ripped out the wall between the kitchen and the living room, and I'm putting in engineered flooring."

"I'd like to see it."

"As long as you don't try to help." She smiled.

From somewhere in our family DNA, Becky got the ability to remodel houses, build garages, and stuff like that. I got the abil-ity to watch her do it.

"Maybe marriage agrees with me." She gave me a level look. "Marriage to Kermit, I mean."

"I do remember who you married."

"Just suggesting that you maybe give him a break every once in a while. He really looks up to you."

I almost said, *He's so short, he* has *to look up to me,* but decided to let it pass. "Has Katie been in?"

The most momentary of shadows passed across Becky's eyes, and I felt my pulse rate kick up a notch. Something was going on, and Becky was picking up on it over the all-female telepathy network. "She said she would get off work early," Becky finally replied.

"You know she's looking at moving out. Just for the winter, I mean," I added hurriedly. "Because of the drive and everything."

"I know."

"Is there something you're not telling me? About Katie, I mean."

"No, Ruddy." Her eyes were open and honest.

But there was something I wasn't telling her, wasn't there?

"What is it?" she asked after a moment, reacting to something in my expression.

I shook my head. "Nothing."

There's a reason why hospitals are so boring—if they were fun, people would always want to go there. Becky was a good sister, but I could tell she was antsy, so after a few minutes of desultory conversation, I suggested she leave, grinning at the relief on her face.

After she left, I lay in the bed and looked at the ceiling for a long moment, debating what to do—though there really wasn't any choice.

"I know you're there, Alan. I can feel it."

"*When the truck rolled, I thought we were going to die,*" he replied.

"Okay, but you're already dead."

"*Nice. Thank you for that.*"

"Why are you here, Alan? Why did you come back?"

"*Back? What do you mean? I've been gone?*"

"Yeah. You've been away for about eighteen months now."

"*A year and a half? How is that possible?*"

"Well, how is any of it possible?"

We were quiet for a moment while we both considered what a good point I'd just made. "I missed you, Alan," I admitted. Becky was right: The drugs were making me emotional. "Having you gone has felt really weird, like being in the middle of a phone call and then realizing you lost the signal and for some time you've been talking to dead air."

*"Do you think they would let you take a shower?"*

I raised my arm and sniffed. "I'm fine."

*"You did not just do that."*

"So that's it? I tell you I've missed you for eighteen months, and your response is to want to bathe?"

*"You're right. Sorry, I just wasn't prepared for an onslaught of repo odor. Please continue."*

"Please continue," I muttered back sourly. I filled him in on everything that had happened since he'd gone radio silent.

*"Wait, you and my daughter are engaged?"* he interrupted, sputtering.

"Yes, Alan. Engaged to be married."

*"That's not . . . That is not a good—"*

"Deal with it," I said curtly. Then I told him what had happened with the girl named Amy Jo. "She's no medium, I promise you, but she was emphatic that Lisa Marie Walker wasn't in the car when it sank. So Sheriff Strickland, make that ex-Sheriff Strickland, is tracking her down for me so I can talk to her."

*"How are you going to support my daughter as a repo man?"* he demanded when I had finished.

"Are you even paying attention? If Lisa Marie wasn't in the car, it changes everything. My whole life would be different."

Alan sighed. *"I don't see how it's possible. Didn't her body float up onshore in Boyne City a few days after the accident? How do you explain* that?"

"I don't know," I said testily. "I don't have all the answers yet." I brooded in silence for a moment. "And we've got another problem. Or at least, I do." I explained to him about Dr. Schaumburg's insistence that I take medications to silence the "voice."

"*That's absurd. What difference would it make to take pills? I'm a real person!*" he declared indignantly.

I was quiet.

"*What is it?*"

"There's something not right. It didn't seem to bother you at all when I told you about the eighteen months. You've been gone, vanished, for all that time, and you just accepted it. As if you already knew. And all the questions you're asking me, they're the same questions I've been asking myself. There's nothing uniquely . . . Alan . . . about you. It's as if—well, Dr. Schaumburg said he was concerned I might want you back so much that I would sort of invent you in my mind."

"*The man sounds like a quack,*" he sniffed.

"I did just have a head injury," I mused. "Maybe that's what did it."

"*What was I supposed to say when you told me I've been gone eighteen months? What could I say? There's nothing I can do about it. To me it feels like I was taking a nap—I have no sense of time passing at all. And I'm asking* logical *questions.*"

"You're getting a little shrill in there, Alan." I was grinning, though—getting this cranked up was exactly like Alan Lottner.

Except, of course, I *knew* that this was how Alan would react. If he were a mental figment, he would have the personality I remembered.

He asked about the rest of the people in my life. He shared my opinion that Strickland was too good a lawman to have resigned, but agreed it was just like the man to have held himself to such high standards. For some reason, Alan was very approving of Becky and Kermit getting married. I told him about the Wolfingers believing they were headed to Hawaii and that Jimmy had "sort of" started sleeping with Alice Blanchard again. That one shocked him.

"*She hates him though,*" Alan protested in disbelief.

"I know. But that's just . . . Jimmy."

Alan was thoughtful for a moment. "*So, how much do you get for a repo?*" he finally asked.

"Alan, for God's sake."

"*Five hundred?*"

"Yes. Well, for skips. I get two fifty for a regular repo. And lately we've been getting these people who forget that they have to turn in their cars at the end of the lease. I get fifty bucks for that. Same deal as always, Milt splits the fee with me fifty-fifty. Oh. Yeah. Milt." I told Alan about Milt sitting in his garage, his motor running. "I wanted to believe it was an accident, but Kermit said Milt had cancer and that it had gotten into his liver, poor bastard. They're investigating it as a suicide. It looks like he drank a quart of vodka, engine going, until the fumes got to him."

Telling Alan about Milt punched a hole through the wall of denial protecting me from the reality of his death, and I went quiet while Alan processed his shock. Eventually Alan said all the right things about being sorry for my loss, but soon got right where I knew he would go. "*So with Milt gone, do you even have a job now?*"

Exactly the question I'd been asking myself. Again, nothing to suggest Alan was anything but my imaginary friend. "Trisha gets the business, I guess. I can't see her running it, though. I don't know what is going to happen. Maybe she'll put *me* in charge, who knows." I shuddered. "Just saying that gives me chills. Sit at a desk all day? I'll take my chances with Repo Madness."

"*What are you going to do if the business closes?*" Alan wanted to know.

I didn't have any sort of answer to that one.


Katie poked her head in around four o'clock. "Hey, Ruddy. How are you feeling?" She came over and kissed me, a quick one that hit mostly cheek. I felt a rising anxiety, even as Alan was making happy noises inside me.

*"I like her hair like that,"* he remarked.

I patted the bed next to me, and Katie went over and sat in a chair under the wall-mounted television. "Everyone says you're okay," she advised.

"Just hit my head. Nothing vital."

For her job, Katie wore what she called "grown-up clothes." She had come straight from work and was still dressed in a wool skirt and cashmere sweater that clung to her in a way I very much appreciated. She stuck a finger in her hair and started twirling it like a forkful of spaghetti.

*"She does that when she's upset about something,"* Alan advised me. I gritted my teeth. I knew what it meant.

"You look beautiful," I said, meaning it. I smiled at her and she glanced away and it felt like rolling over in the repo truck, my insides churning. I took a breath to steady myself. "Why don't you tell me what you came here to say," I suggested.

"I signed the lease. On the rental house in East Jordan. It's really cute."

Alan made a startled noise.

"Cute," I repeated, my voice tight.

Sadness crept into her eyes. "I told you we need time to think, Ruddy. It's not . . . I feel like we're not putting any thought into things."

"What sort of things?" I meant my tone to be as soft as hers, but a harshness found its way into my voice, unasked and unwanted.

"When I get my real estate license and start selling properties, it will mean more money, probably, but it would be a lot less regular. I mean, you can go awhile without selling a house or anything. So I'd need, you know."

*"A man with a better job,"* Alan suggested.

My anger flared. "Need what?" I nearly spat.

"To reduce expenses. And especially spend less time commuting in the winter."

"Oh."

"See what I mean, though? Why are we so scratchy with each other? You were getting mad, I can tell."

I didn't bother to deny it. "When are you moving?" I asked faintly.

She sighed unhappily. "Well . . . please don't be angry. I already spent the night there."

"*What?*"

"I was going to tell you. I left you a voice mail. I got trapped by the ice storm and decided it was safer just to stay there. I didn't know you were in an accident until I got Becky's message."

I was fixated on the idea that she had gone from suggesting she get a place closer to work to actually sleeping there. "Wait. You don't just move out without warning. Without talking about it. That's not right."

Her look turned forlorn. "Oh, Ruddy. I *have* been talking about it. You just haven't been listening. I told you I needed more space, that it seemed like when I moved in with you, I adopted all of your life and you didn't adapt to any of mine. I told you I didn't like going to the Bear every single night of the week. I told you I needed time to think. That I don't know who I am as an independent person, but only as extensions of other people. What did you think that meant?"

I opened my mouth, but nothing good wanted to come out of it. Sure, we'd talked, but I felt she had never explained how *significant* those conversations were. "Don't you love me?" I hated how that one came out plaintive, even begging.

"Yes, but I don't love my life, you know? I feel like we're stuck in a rut." She gazed at me, her blue eyes level because she was finally getting it out, what the real problem was. And I understood: Ruddy McCann, repo man, *lived* in a rut, and he had pulled her in with him.

"What about Jake?" I asked.

*"Don't try to make her feel guilty about a dog,"* Alan chastised.

"Oh. He stayed with Kermit and Becky last night, and he's with Kermit right now. This isn't . . . We're not ending the relationship. It's just a break; we're taking a break. The place in East Jordan is literally half a block from my job. It's nice. I walked to work this morning."

"Is there somebody . . . ?"

"No, Ruddy. I haven't met anybody else," she assured me firmly.

"Then don't do this," I grated.

Katie stood up. "I'm really sorry, but I need to go. I'm going to be late."

"You can't *go*. We need to talk about this!" I insisted.

*"Let her leave, Ruddy. She's feeling trapped, and this isn't helping,"* Alan advised.

Katie was shrugging on her coat. "We *will* talk more about it, Ruddy. Just not right now. I need time, I told you. That's all this is about. Honest. Please."

I sat up in the hospital bed, feeling ridiculous in the lightweight gown I was wearing. "I'll go with you."

"What? No, Ruddy, you can't." She checked her watch. "I'm meeting my new landlord. I'm sorry. But we will talk, I promise."

"Dammit, Katie!"

*"Oh, that's great. Yell at her,"* Alan jeered.

With a look that held far more sadness and regret than I thought was appropriate for a "break" where we were "not breaking up," Katie grabbed her purse and rushed out the door, checking her watch again in the hallway.

"Don't say anything right now, Alan," I warned him.

And, to his credit, he didn't.

———

They kept me another night just to prove that they could, but Jimmy was there in the morning to pick me up. I was stiff, aching everywhere, and groaned aloud as I settled into his car.

Alan was asleep.

When he was gone those eighteen months, I felt his absence as a lack, as a hollow sensation. In a lot of ways it was what I went through when I lost my dad—this odd, phantom-limb feeling that something was both there and not. Alan's return was like an increase in air pressure, a weight inside my mind—and of course you couldn't get the guy to shut up. But this was something different than when he'd vanished, this sleep—the feeling that he was there, but in a way that didn't register with the senses except as a dormant object. He'd slept before, the first time he'd come to visit, so this, too, was something my subconscious might easily be inventing for its own amusement. I wanted my friend back, so he was back. Then I wanted him to take a break, like Katie wanted us to take a break, so he went to sleep.

I texted Katie to say I'd been released.

*Good,* she responded. *We'll talk soon.*

About what, our living apart? I didn't want to talk about that.

Jimmy was pensive as he drove us back to Kalkaska. I watched him wrestling with something, giving him time. That's what you did with Jimmy—there was no sense in trying to pull his thoughts out of the oven before they were fully baked. "I never have done this before, you know," he finally remarked.

"Driven a car?"

He blinked at me. "No. Ruddy, you taught me to drive."

"I was kidding, Jimmy. Done what?"

"Slept with a married woman. I mean, yeah, I've slept with them, but never as more than just, you know."

"I actually don't know."

"I mean, just as a one-time thing. One night. Not . . ."

"You've never had an extended extramarital affair," I translated.

"Extended extramarital," Jimmy repeated dubiously.

"Why is it extended? I thought she said her husband would literally kill her if he found out. That's hardly encouraging for long-term prospects."

"Yeah, about that."

"What about that?"

"Alice says he knows. Her husband, I mean. He knows about us."

# 7

## The Deal with Uncle Milt

Jimmy's face looked apologetic as he laid it all out for me. Alice's husband was a guy named William Blanchard. According to Jimmy, he was possessive and jealous and had suddenly become very suspicious, at one point grabbing Alice's cell phone out of her hand and scrolling through it, looking for proof she was calling and texting another man.

"Did he find any? Proof, I mean," I asked.

Jimmy shook his head. "She erases everything."

"Well, hell, Jimmy. He's not really going to commit murder. He's a banker. Bankers cheat people; they don't kill people."

"Alice says he's got a dark side to him."

"Well, can I just say that maybe you shouldn't be fooling around with a married woman? Especially when her husband's got a dark side? Aren't there enough single women in the world for you?"

Jimmy looked reflective, and I wondered if he was seriously considering that maybe there *weren't*. He surprised me, though, with his next statement.

"We're kind of in love, Ruddy."

"Jesus, Jimmy."

"It didn't happen on purpose."

I thought about it. I had to agree: Falling in love didn't ever happen deliberately. That he had made the journey from lover to hated ex to father to lover again was no stranger than anything else that had ever happened. "So how do you feel about Vicki?" I asked.

"My daughter? She means everything to me," Jimmy replied, sounding surprised I would even ask the question.

"Could that be it, then?"

"What do you mean?"

"I mean, all of a sudden you have this adorable little girl in your life, your own daughter you never knew you had, and you love her and want to do right by her, and so maybe it seems like you should love the mother, too. That you and Alice and Vicki are a family unit—and her husband's a jerk, even a little abusive. You probably feel this is the best way to protect your daughter. It's pretty rational." I nodded at my impeccable logic. Part of me wished Alan were awake to witness my deft analysis.

Jimmy brooded over the truth of my observation for a minute. "You know, Ruddy, you can be a real asshole sometimes."

I stared at him, shocked. His ridiculously chiseled jaw pulsed, and he glanced at me, his eyes hot, before turning back to the road. "I'm not a kid. I don't need you trying to explain that what I'm feeling could be because of Vicki. I've been with enough women to know that this is different. I came to you because I have a problem. Alice is afraid of her husband's temper. She's worried he might hurt her or Vicki. You know how to handle stuff like that. That's why I want your help. I don't need you to try to talk me out of Alice."

I wasn't sure that Jimmy had ever been this angry at me before. "Sorry, Jimmy," I finally apologized. "I didn't understand the situation."

Jimmy nodded, still staring moodily out at the road in front of us. After a moment I turned my gaze in the same direction.

All right, I believed him: He was in love with a woman who was married to a potentially violent man. They thought they were covering their tracks, but William Blanchard suspected something was going on, and they were afraid of his reaction if he got any actual proof.

That didn't mean I knew what to do about it though.


My pickup was where I left it—at Milt's repo lot. Someone had taken the time to scrape the snow off my windows, and I saw why—there was a small piece of notepaper wedged under the wiper. *Please see me in the office. Kermit.*

I felt Alan stirring, and I let the note hang loose in my hand as I stared at the gray skies and concentrated on the sensation. It was exactly as I remembered it from the last time I'd had Alan as my brain guest, the odd feeling of a light bulb coming on and growing brighter. But if it were all my imagination, why would it be any different now than before?

*"What are we looking at?"* he wanted to know.

"*I* am looking at the sky," I responded. "You don't have eyes, so you are looking at nothing."

*"Good old Ruddy McCann,"* he observed after a moment. *"Always cheerful and friendly."*

"I'm just missing Milt. God, it's so tragic. I have to believe he was on some sort of medication that got him depressed—otherwise, he was so full of life."

*"So you believe it was deliberate? Suicide?"*

"Are you saying you don't?"

*"No, just the opposite. You said the cancer had spread to his liver."*

"Yeah. Probably pretty painful."

*"Not just that. You have liver cancer, you're not going to sit and drink a bottle of vodka unless you know it's your last night."*

"I didn't even think of that," I admitted. I continued to contemplate the sky. "I only wish he'd said something to me about it," I said softly. "Instead we just talked about Repo Madness."

*"Not exactly a victimless crime,"* Alan agreed. *"Leaves behind a lot of guilt, a lot of questions."*

I decided I'd had enough sympathy from the voice in my head. "Have a nice sleep?" I asked him.

*"It's not like you think. I don't get tired, and I don't get rest, but I do feel myself slipping into unconsciousness, and it's exactly what it's like when I used to doze off for a nap after an open house weekend."*

"And what about when I sleep?" I challenged.

*"What do you mean?"*

"You know exactly what I mean. When I sleep, if you wake up, what do you do?"

Alan was silent.

"Alan? What do you do, or I guess, absolutely *not* do, when I'm sleeping?"

He sighed.

"Dr. Schaumburg says I have a choice between having a voice in my head or dissociative personality disorder, which is where I fall asleep and you get up to do the laundry. I can't have both. So *you* can't have both. We clear? This time you must not, not ever, try to do something with my body while I'm sleeping."

*"I don't understand your problem."*

"I asked if we are clear."

*"Fine."*

I kicked at a chunk of ice, sending it skittering across the lot. "Let's go see Kermit," I suggested.

*"I can't believe you still wear those ugly rubber boots. Where do you even buy such things?"*

"From the repo menswear catalogue."

Kermit was in Milt's office. The effect was jarring—here was short, squat, dark-complexioned Kermit sitting behind the desk where the pale, white-haired Milt had always sat. I felt a flash of annoyance at the sacrilege. The body was still in the morgue;

what did Kermit think he was doing? Going through the drawers, reading Milt's files?

I brandished the note. "What the hell is this, Kermit?"

He blinked at me. "Uh . . ."

"You don't *summon* me, okay? This was like being told I need to go to the principal's office."

"Sorry. I mistook my intentions," he apologized.

"I don't work for you."

"I should have done it differently."

I turned to sit in the big overstuffed chair in the corner, but it was occupied. "Jake?" I demanded.

My dog regarded me mournfully. *Please don't make me get up,* his eyes pleaded.

"What are you doing here?" I asked him.

"He likes it here," Kermit responded defensively. "Katie asked me to look after him, and I thought it would be easier to just do it here."

*"That makes sense. Jake has someone to watch him all day,"* Alan observed in his maddeningly rational voice.

"He doesn't need someone to watch him all day," I snapped. Then I caught myself and glanced at Kermit, who didn't seem to think my statement was odd.

"I know, but I don't mind it," Kermit replied. "Kinda nice to have company. I'll be here every day now—my aunt Trisha put me in charge. That's why, after he was diagnosed, Uncle Milt wanted me to move here, so I could absorb the operation. My brother, Walt, was pretty pissed off, but all he would have done was sell the business."

*"So that makes Kermit your boss?"* Alan speculated, laughing.

"Oh. So in other words, I actually do work for you," I concluded. If the alternative was being unemployed, I thought I could probably adapt. I tried to shove Jake over so I could sit with him, but he saw my efforts as unwelcome. Eventually I sat on the arm of the chair, my hand unconsciously reaching down to stroke Jake's velvety basset ears.

"Uh, well, you could still contract with Kramer Recovery if you want. I don't know—maybe you're sick of repossessing cars."

"How would anyone ever grow sick of *that*?"

Alan snorted.

"So, Kermit, do you suppose that because of the cancer, maybe with medications, that's why your uncle . . . ?" I trailed off.

Kermit was shaking his head. "No way. This was an accident. My uncle would never commit self-suicide. He just had too much to drink."

"*Do* not *tell him about how a man with liver cancer wouldn't drink vodka unless he intended to kill himself,*" Alan instructed sternly.

I gritted my teeth. Of course I wouldn't tell him. "Sorry, Kermit."

Jake sighed. All this talking was disturbing his nap.

"Well, okay then, we'll resumption everything," Kermit continued. "But about your fee, there's a little problem."

I held up a hand. "Stop right there, Kermit. I can't take any less than what I'm already getting." Kermit looked really uncomfortable, and I bit back my anger. Who else was he going to get to steal cars for him? Why would he try to negotiate this? I was his brother-in-law: He knew I didn't take any money from Becky during the winter, not even when I tended bar and there was cash in the tip jar. "Seems like you've got something to say to me," I observed coldly.

Kermit squirmed. "Well, what was your deal with my uncle?"

"Half," I replied curtly. "Fifty bucks for these morons who don't understand about turning in their cars at the end of the lease. Two fifty for a standard repo. Five hundred for a skip."

"Yeah, but, Ruddy—"

"Yeah, 'but, Ruddy' what?" I interrupted testily.

"We transact two hundred just for opening file."

I stared at him, not sure what he was saying to me. "Opening file?" I repeated stupidly.

"Two hundred on assignation, plus two hundred for lease early term, a grand for a repo, two grand for a skip, plus expenses."

*"In other words, you haven't been getting half; you've been getting a fourth,"* Alan explained helpfully.

"I can do the goddamn math," I snapped at him.

Kermit nodded resignedly.

"So Uncle Milt has been *lying* to me?" I stood up, and Jake raised his head, concerned at the emotion in my voice.

"That's why effectuated immediately, your fee needs to be half," Kermit said rapidly. "I never knew the numbers, but even Becky says you were supposed to be getting half."

*"It's still not very much money,"* Alan observed.

I stared down at Kermit. He looked afraid, as if I were about to start ripping apart the furniture. I realized then that I felt bad that he would fear me. There was a time, before he married my sister, when I wanted him to be frightened—in fact, I wanted him to run away, leave my sister and me alone. But he stuck it out because he loved Becky. "I would never have known about this if you hadn't told me," I pointed out. "You could have made a lot more money."

Kermit raised his hands, palms up. "Wouldn't have been right though. You thought you were getting half. You should get half."

"You're an honorable man, Kermit. If Milt were here, I'd have a few words I'd want to say to him, but you're making it right. I appreciate your honesty." I held out my hand. "Boss."

He shook it. We grinned at each other. "Well, since there's been no dissolution," he said after a moment, handing over a repo folder. "Here's one from a new client. Bank in Traverse City says their regular agency said to go . . . now what is it when you petition the court?"

"Writ of replevin," I responded automatically.

"Right. Replevin. So they're giving us a shot. Be good business for us, Ruddy; their bank finances a lot of the local car dealers. Customer's name is Tony Zoppi. You know him?"

*"The Zoppi family? They're practically mafia; everyone knows about them,"* Alan whispered worriedly.

Why was he whispering?

"Never heard of the guy. Also, there are no keys," I pointed out, shaking the empty key packet.

"Yeah. The bank had complete neglection on getting key numbers."

"All right. But I don't have a tow truck, remember?"

"Yeah, it was totaled. What a mess. You okay? It's almost hard to believe you walked away from that one."

"I didn't walk; I was taken in an ambulance," I answered dryly. "Yeah, I'm down to one symptom." *A voice in my head.*

*"Symptom. So clever,"* Alan observed caustically.

"My point is," I continued, "without a tow truck, and without keys, how am I supposed to bring in Zoppi?"

"I don't know, but I'd love to land that account. We're getting plenty of Strickland skip business, but repos are pretty slow."

Jake and I exchanged a look. There seemed to be a veiled suggestion that perhaps I wasn't pulling my weight in the operation compared to Barry Strickland. Of course, all Jake was doing was *napping*.

"Oh, if you get it, call me and I'll rendezvous you at the bank," my new boss advised.

"The bank? You don't want me to bring it here?"

"No, they want it at the bank. You're supposed to ask for William Blanchard; he's the bank president. He specifically mentioned you by name, so your reputation predates you."

"William Blanchard," I repeated.

"Yeah." Kermit nodded.

I gave Jake a final pat on the head before I left.

William Blanchard. The man who was married to Alice Blanchard, who was having an affair with my best friend, Jimmy.

I decided to drive my pickup north to Traverse City and see if Zoppi was at his place of business, which was a furniture-refinishing place south of town. His family owned it and, according to Alan, half a dozen businesses that were supported by some huge crime ring involving drugs and murder and who knew what else.

"Like *The Godfather*," I mused.

"*What?*" Alan responded.

"That's the plot from Puzo's novel. I just read it; it was in my mom's collection. The Corleone family takes their proceeds from their illicit ventures and buys legitimate operations."

"*The book? You mean you never saw* The Godfather *movies?*" he demanded incredulously.

"Of course I've seen the movies, Alan," I retorted. "I'm a *guy.*"

"*Then what's your point?*"

"My point is that everything you're babbling about is in the book. Which I just read. Pretty coincidental, don't you think? And there isn't some huge crime family up here, Alan; everybody's too cold for that."

He was silent. "Alan?"

"*I don't* babble," he sniffed.

"Well, hey, the good news is that I still have a job and just doubled my money." I said it a bit aggressively, waiting for Alan to advise me it wasn't enough to make me a serious prospect for his daughter, but he was silent. I heard the boop of a siren and looked in my rearview mirror. A sheriff's department car was following me, its lights flashing. Sighing, I checked the speedometer and pulled over. They had me going five over the limit.

The man who got out of the passenger side was the man who'd replaced Barry Strickland—Grant Porterfield, the new sheriff. He was a little beady-eyed guy, short and fat where Barry was lean and solid.

The deputy driving was Dwight Timms, whose family had owned a bait shop for many years and was known for smelling like their products. Dwight didn't like me much—he and Katie had been all but engaged when I met her, and he was unhappy she picked a repo man over a heavily jowled, jarhead, sallow-skinned, dull-eyed moron with a mean streak and a badge to back it up.

I guess I didn't like Dwight much either.

"Sheriff," I greeted evenly, ignoring his deputy.

"Why don't you step out of the vehicle so's we can talk?" Porterfield suggested. Timms walked up on the other side of my pickup, covering me like I was a public menace.

I agreeably opened my door and stepped out, crunching snow under my stylish rubber boots. I rubbed my hands together but kept them out in the open. Cops like to be able to see your hands.

*"How fast were you going?"* Alan asked.

"Heard about your accident the other day," Porterfield noted. Timms was peering in through my windows, looking for smuggled AK-47s.

"Black ice." I shrugged.

"I heard you were chasing Tigg Bloom at the time. Repo man."

"Chasing? No, not true. I was behind him, sure, but I was just driving down the hill and lost it on the ice."

"That's not what Tigg says."

"How is good old Tigg?"

"His leg's broke, but he'll live. He's thinking of filing a criminal complaint against you."

"So his statement is that he saw me, thought I was somehow going to tow away his truck with him driving it in front of me, decided to drive off at high speed, went flying down a steep hill coated with ice, lost control, nearly wiped out a school bus full of kids, crashed into the woods, and I'm the criminal?"

Porterfield gave me a look I supposed he thought was hard

and scary, but I'd been glared at by Barry Strickland, who was a professional at it. "Well, either way, that's your last one," he said, leaning over to spit in the snow.

Timms came over to stand next to his boss, giving me a smirk. His hand was resting on the butt of his weapon. The guy was really starting to piss me off.

*"Last one what?"* Alan wondered.

"I'm not sure I understand, sir," I replied.

"No more repos in my jurisdiction. You want to pick up a car, you file a writ of replevin with the court, get it signed by a judge, and I'll send my deputies out to pick it up. We'll call you when it is in impound."

I stared at the two lawmen. They were both wearing identical challenging grins, loving telling me that I would not be able to make a living anymore.

What Timms wanted more than anything, I knew, was for me to lose my temper and take a swing at him. They'd pull their handguns, get cuffs on me, and book me for being disorderly, and my probation would be revoked. I'd wind up doing a couple years of jail time, just for the satisfaction of breaking his nose.

Might be worth it.

"Understood," I finally replied woodenly.

*"They can't actually do that,"* Alan intoned in an I-was-a-Realtor-so-I'm-an-expert-in-the-law voice. *"If it is legal, they can't stop you from making a living."*

"May I go, Sheriff?" I asked.

He spat in the snow again. He seemed disappointed somehow. "Drive carefully, Mr. McCann. Watch out for black ice."

I slid into my pickup and watched in my rearview mirror as the two lawmen settled in, said something to each other that made them both laugh, and then pulled a U-turn and sped off.

"Well, that's just great," I said.

*"I don't know what to do next. I guess get a lawyer and sue the sheriff's department,"* Alan speculated.

"I don't have the money to sue anybody."

*"But you just had the sheriff tell you that you can't do repossessions anymore. What are you going to do?"*

"Me?" I started my pickup and put it in gear. "I'm going to go repo a car."

# 8

## A Job Up Your Alley

I sat in my pickup and regarded Zoppi's Jeep Grand Cherokee—a pretty blue machine with sprays of frozen Michigan mud splashed out from all four wheel wells. The parking lot of the furniture-refinishing place was small and rutted and contained only a Dumpster, some snow-covered lawn chairs, and a decades-old Honda motorcycle on lifeless tires leaning against the back wall of the shop. I'd driven past the front of the place and looked in through the display windows, and it appeared the same person who had designed the parking lot had also decorated the showroom—furniture was haphazardly arrayed on the cement floor, some of it as dirty as the motorcycle.

Alan, of course, was in full priss. *"I am telling you, you don't want to mess with these people, Ruddy."*

"I'm going to make him an offer he can't refuse." I had no keys and no tow truck. How was I going to get my hands on the Jeep?

The sun was pretty close to setting. I figured Zoppi would be leaving his place of business soon, probably to go put a horse head in somebody's bed, if Alan was to be believed.

I parked well down the road, behind an abandoned cherry stand—in the summer you can stop at any one of a hundred family-owned stands lining the highways and buy a lug of sweet cherries fresh off the tree. In the winter there is nothing except maybe free ice. I grabbed a pair of pliers out of my toolbox, then hiked back to the parking lot and tried the door to the Jeep. Unlocked, but no keys under the rug or behind the visor.

*"Someone could come out any second!"* Alan hissed.

I popped the hood and went to look at the engine, cringing in anticipation of a car alarm, but there was none. I pulled the pair of pliers out of my pocket and disconnected the positive wire off the battery, letting it droop. I shut the hood, slapping the grease off my hands and onto my pants.

*"So now you have smears of oil all over your clothes,"* Alan stated disgustedly.

"Makes me almost as bad as the mafia, doesn't it?"

The furniture shop was in a cluster of faded retail buildings huddled together on this stretch of road, as if people had started to develop a town and then lost their nerve. To sit indoors and keep my eye on the Cherokee, I had a choice between pet grooming or a tiny café. I picked the café and settled down with a cup of coffee at the front window, logging into their free Wi-Fi.

Becky had started offering free Wi-Fi at the Black Bear, too. People start giving away everything for free, how is a bill collector supposed to make a living?

Alan made distressed peeping noises as I surfed the Web on my smartphone. *"I hate this. I just start to read something, and you change it,"* he complained.

I ignored him and was soon frowning at Wikipedia. "'A human body cools twenty-five times faster in cold water than in air,'" I read aloud.

*"So? What are we doing?"*

I glanced around the café. There were no customers, and the woman behind the counter had gone into the back room. "I'm thinking about what Amy Jo said. Lisa Marie wasn't in the car when it sank. What if that means she got thrown out? Maybe the back window was open. We hit the water going, what, fifty? That could propel a person pretty far. Maybe Lisa swam to the opposite shore that night. I was pretty out of it. And those stoners didn't know to look for anyone else. If she got tossed twenty yards or so, woke up when she hit the water, and headed for the opposite side, it could explain how she survived."

*"Twenty yards?"* Alan repeated skeptically.

"The point is, Alan," I responded agitatedly, "maybe what Amy Jo meant was that Lisa Marie started off in the backseat, but she wasn't in the car *when it sank*. The water that night was forty-eight degrees, which means by this chart I'm looking at, she could have gone more than thirty minutes without drowning. You could swim that channel in a third of that."

The woman came out from the kitchen. "You need something, hon?" she asked. She'd obviously heard me talking.

"No, I was just . . ." I gestured with my phone. She nodded in understanding and went back through the swinging doors. Cell phones have made it possible for all sorts of lunatics to operate in society.

*"So then what?"* Alan pressed.

I was frozen, though, staring at the screen. This habitual position reminded me that I hadn't texted with Katie in hours. I thumbed the message app and double-checked. Nothing from her.

*"Is that what I think it is? A conversation with my daughter?"* Alan asked excitedly.

"Yeah, I was just looking to see if she had sent me a text message. She usually checks in regularly." Maybe not when we were on a break, though. I scrolled back through the past to show him what I meant.

*"Well, that's revealing,"* he said dryly.

"What is?"

*"I'm looking at what she is saying. 'How are you feeling?' she asks. 'I miss you. What time will you be home?' she says. 'Thinking of you today. Can't wait for the weekend.'"*

"Yeah?" I had a feeling I was about to receive the benefit of another lecture from my fiancée's father.

"*Then look at you. 'Fine,' you say. 'Seven thirty,' you say. 'I have to work the bar Saturday.' See a pattern?*"

"You mean the pattern where she asks a question and I answer it?" I snapped, irritated because I understood exactly what he was getting at.

"*Don't you think she deserves more than just information?*"

"It's the information age," I retorted. "That's what texting is for." He was silent.

"Fine." I sighed. I thought about it for a moment, and then typed this: *It really meant a lot to me that you came to see me in the hospital. I was glad to see you. I don't understand why you need a break. I think it is crazy that you're moving out.*

"*Maybe just end it at* hospital," Alan suggested.

"But it *is* crazy that we're living apart. What the hell does a break mean when it is in the middle of a relationship? That's like saying, 'My legs are tired. I think I'll break one.' "

"*Just erase everything after 'glad to see you,' *" he insisted.

I did what he said and sent it. "Okay."

"*Okay. So tell me about Lisa Marie,*" he suggested.

"Right. So she gets thrown out of the car. If she spent much time in the water, she would have collapsed. She needed help. When I got to the hospital, I was unconscious, and I guess they warmed me up gradually."

"*So it's late at night, and she's gotten to the opposite shore. Many people there?*"

"In November? No, it's mostly summer places, but there could have been a few locals. She could have made her way to a house. Or," I speculated with growing enthusiasm, "what if a car came along and picked her up?"

"*Why would a car come if the ferry had shut down operations?*"

"Dammit, Alan, this isn't helping!"

"*Ruddy. You're forgetting that she died. She was found in the water. Five days later.*"

"I am not forgetting that," I snapped. "What I am saying is that if she was thrown from the car and made it to shore, someone would have helped her or they would have found her body right there. And whoever helped her . . ."

"*Whoever helped her changed their mind and dumped her back in the lake to drown,*" Alan concluded.

"Shut up, Alan."

"*Ruddy . . .*"

"Just shut up!" I glanced over, and the waitress was standing behind the counter, regarding me with round eyes. My phone was on the table, nowhere near my ear. I smiled weakly, left a tip, and went outside, my hands in my pockets. Alan wisely didn't say anything.

Zoppi, when he emerged though the back door, looked more like a bellhop than a criminal warlord. He was thin and pale, with jet-black hair that was more perfectly combed than a toupee. "Looks like he forgot his machine gun," I told Alan as I strolled over, acting nonchalant. Zoppi got into his car, reacting angrily when he turned the key and nothing happened.

"*So now what?*" Alan wanted to know.

Zoppi opened his door, and I was right there. "Hey! Car won't start?" I called cheerfully.

He was surprised but not suspicious to see me. "Yeah."

"Why don't I take a look? Pop the hood," I offered.

Shrugging and not at all grateful, Zoppi slid back into the car and tugged on the lever. The hood bucked up an inch, and I raised it. "Try it now," I called after pretending to do something to the engine.

Zoppi swore. "Nothing!" he shouted. "Goddammit!"

"Hey, okay, let's switch places," I suggested.

I slid in behind the wheel as Zoppi went around to the front. "Well, the goddamn battery's disconnected!" he shouted at me.

"Really?"

Zoppi moved the cable, and the second it touched the battery terminal, the interior lights came on and bells started to ping. I turned the key, and the engine caught. "Great!" I enthused. "Shut the hood!"

Zoppi reached up and slammed the hood down, and I had it in reverse and was backing away from him before he could even register what was happening. I kept going until I was twenty yards down the road, then pulled a snow-aided U-Turn and headed north to Traverse City.

*"What if the battery cable falls off and the car stops?"* Alan asked worriedly.

I was watching my rearview mirror but saw no signs of pursuit. Maybe Zoppi was trying to start the motorcycle. "It won't stop. Once the engine is running, it keeps going, even if there's *no* battery."

*"I think you made a big mistake, Ruddy. Now Zoppi knows what you look like."*

"Good. Maybe next time he sees me, it will remind him to make his car payments." I grinned at myself in the mirror, my soul full of the happiness that only making off with a good repo can give somebody.

*"I wish just once that you would listen to me."*

"That's funny, because I wish just once that you would stop talking."

Alan didn't have a retort for that one.

Half an hour later I pulled into the bank parking lot, went in, and asked to speak to Mr. William Blanchard.


William Blanchard was portly, with a neat, graying mustache and very short hair sparsely covering his head. He actually looked like a pretty friendly guy, and his handshake was warm and soft—hard to picture him hurting anyone; he looked like somebody's favorite uncle. He wore a sharp navy suit with a white shirt and a muted tie—a banker outfit, in other words. He blinked his light-brown eyes in surprise when I told him I had Zoppi's Cherokee in the back.

"That fast?" His face lit up in a boyish grin. "I just called it in to your boss yesterday."

"It was right there at his place of business."

Blanchard leaned back, his chair springs groaning in alarm as his considerable heft tested their strength. He seemed eager for details, so I walked him through my little ruse, and he laughed so hard, his face turned red. "Well, you are certainly the right man for the job," he concluded.

I optimistically interpreted that to mean we had just landed the account for Kramer Recovery of Kalkaska. I wondered if Kermit would give me a bonus.

"Do me a favor. Shut the door a minute."

The bank had locked the outer doors and most of the employees had left, but I did what Blanchard had requested. When I sat back down, his demeanor had changed somehow—less avuncular, more crafty, maybe.

"*Something's going on*," Alan suggested superfluously.

"So, Ruddy, I asked around about you," Blanchard said, his eyes watching me unwaveringly. "I know you're an ex-con, and I heard some people were threatening your sister's business and you took care of them with, uh, extreme prejudice."

Since that wasn't my interpretation of events, I opened my mouth to object, but he held up a hand.

"No, that's okay. Don't need to discuss that. Not why I asked you to shut the door. Have another job for you, something up your alley. Interested?" A small smile played at his lips, as if he had a wonderful gift he couldn't wait to give me.

I waited. I had stopped liking our Mr. Blanchard so much.

"All right," he said decisively. "Here's the deal. Last summer I took a group of guys out on my boat for a weekend cruise. All businessmen, clients of the bank—important clients. Had drinks, had some, uh, female company, played poker, fished. All fun, right? And one of my guests, we'll call him John, wasn't so good at cards the first night. He's not from around here, but after he lost a couple grand at Texas Hold 'em, everyone warmed up to the guy. Liked him so much, in fact, that on the last night, just to give John a chance to get some of his money back, we all decided to raise the table stakes."

"Let me guess what happened next."

Blanchard nodded, giving a cold chuckle. "John's luck got better. A *lot* better. After a while I had to issue some markers to a few people, which was okay by me." He shrugged. "I am a lender, after all."

"And so now . . . ," I prompted.

Blanchard slapped his meaty hand on his desk, suddenly furious. "And now those sonofabitches got together and decided they were played. They said John hustled them. And get this: They voted—they *voted*—that they shouldn't have to pay their markers to me. I told them it wasn't my fault, that no one made them keep betting, and that I had to pay their debts to John, but *they don't care.*"

*"I don't think this guy had to pay John anything, except maybe a fee to fleece his friends,"* Alan observed.

"Jesus," Blanchard muttered, bringing himself under control. "So. All right. I've got forty-three thousand bucks outstanding between four guys. I need you to go collect it. By whatever means necessary, *capisci?*"

*"He's asking you to go beat up a bunch of local businessmen. Can you believe this guy?"*

"I may not be the right man for this particular job, Mr. Blanchard," I replied slowly.

"I'll cut you in for ten percent of whatever you can squeeze out of those assholes," Blanchard continued. "You get it all, I'll round it up to five thousand dollars."

I stared at him for a long moment. "I'm in," I said.

# 9

## The One-in-Five Drop

Blanchard had a bank teller drive me back to the cherry stand where I'd parked. The guy looked like a twelve-year-old in a suit, a nice kid who tried to talk about basketball over Alan's strident insults. According to the voice in my head, I had agreed to become a contract gorilla hired to extort money from innocent businessmen.

"For chrissakes, Alan, all I agreed to is to go talk to a few people who owe some money. That's what I *do*," I pointed out when we were alone in my vehicle.

"*Blanchard said he told them if they didn't pay the money he cheated them out of, he was going to 'send someone.' That's a pretty obvious threat.*"

"Probably he meant he was going to hire Tony Zoppi. Oh no, wait. Tony doesn't even have a car."

"*Not funny.*"

"Did you hear the part where I'm going to make five thousand dollars?"

"*If you collect every penny.*"

"Oh, I'll collect it, all right. Then, I don't know, take Katie on vacation. Maybe we'll go to Hawaii with the Wolfingers."

"*I obviously won't allow my daughter to date a hired thug,*" Alan said icily.

I didn't advise that I couldn't think of any way he could stop me, because I was moodily reflecting on what Katie might think of my new assignment. She might agree with her father's interpretation.

My phone beeped as I was pulling up in front of my house. I looked down and saw a smiley face emoticon, followed by one blowing me a kiss. "Yes!" I exulted.

*"What's that? Did my daughter draw that with her phone?"*

"Um . . ."

*"She's always been so amazingly gifted."*

"And I'm not arguing with that, but actually the phone can sort of do it for you. They're called emoticons."

*"Really? So you can do one back?"*

"Repo men don't send emoticons," I replied darkly.

*"Right, you just send facts. 'I'm fine.' 'I have to tend bar Saturday.' But when you send what I tell you to send, she draws a face blowing you a kiss, with a little heart."*

"I did not send what you told me to send," I said testily. "Those were my words; you just suggested I make the text shorter."

*"Let's send her something back. Can you do a flower?"*

Because the buttons were ridiculously tiny, I wound up sending her a heart, a flower, and a cheeseburger.

A slow night at the Black Bear. Buoyed by all the money I was going to make off Blanchard, I sent a couple of beers over to the Wolfingers' table. Claude was wearing a lei fashioned from what looked to be some flower-shaped earrings from Wilma's collection. Since Wilma's tastes ran hot pink and electric blue, the effect was less Hawaiian and more Lady Gaga. They were still in the happy phase of their drinking, and raised their mugs in good cheer. Claude gestured for me to join them, and I nodded that I would, in a minute.

Jimmy was behind the bar, fiddling with a new wine bottle

opener Kermit had bought. He stuck a needle in the cork, pushed a button, and then pulled the opener out of the cork to an audible hiss. "I don't get it," Jimmy muttered.

*"It looks like it injects carbon dioxide into the bottle and forces the cork out,"* Alan observed pedantically.

"Here's an idea: Use a corkscrew," I suggested.

*"He should stop pulling the needle out. Just keep pushing the button,"* Alan urged, as if this was the most important issue facing humanity.

"Here." I reached out, and Jimmy handed me the bottle. I shoved the needle in and put my thumb on the button, and the cork popped out with a champagne noise. "There, technology saves the world," I pronounced. "So, Jimmy," I said as I watched him pour a couple glasses of Chardonnay for some customers in the corner. "I met your buddy William Blanchard."

He glanced up sharply, his dark eyes widening in alarm. "Yeah?"

I shook my head. "You don't have to worry about this guy. He's definitely a jerk, but he doesn't hurt people."

*"No, he hires you to do it for him,"* Alan observed snidely.

"He's as harmless as Tony Zoppi," I said.

Jimmy frowned. "Who?"

"I still think, though, that being with a married woman is a really bad idea, Jimmy."

The look he gave me then caught me up short. Jimmy's always been cheerfully black-and-white, shaking off adversity and facing the world with open optimism. It's an untroubled approach to life that I sometimes envy—I'm usually grappling with a little more complexity. But now in his gaze I saw deep conflict, a swirl of doubt and what-ifs.

"I don't know what to do," he said, putting into words what his expression was already saying.

He headed over to the booth to give our customers their wine, and I pensively watched him go, his tread heavy and burdened. "That's the thing about relationships, isn't it? You want them, but then when you're in the middle of them, they can really mess with your mind," I said aloud.

"*Spoken like a true romantic,*" Alan scoffed.

Becky heard me talking—she was plating a shrimp quesadilla for the Wolfingers. Her look was wary—she knew all about Alan, but as far as she was aware, the voice in my head had gone away a long time ago.

"Just praising the female brain," I told her.

She stopped on her way to serve the food. "You've got four messages from a Dr. Schaumburg. Who's he?"

"Sheryl was in some sort of skiing accident, I don't know what. He's my new temporary hard-assed doctor from hell."

"Well"—she gave me a searching smile—"he wants you to call him. He was pretty emphatic."

"I will, first thing in the morning," I promised.

"Are you in trouble, Ruddy?"

"Nothing I can't handle."

She gave me a small sister-to-brother smile. "Oh," she said, remembering something, "and Kermit wants to talk to you. He said he'd come by, so stick around for a while?"

"Sure."

"*She looks good!*" Alan praised. "*I like her new hair color. That gray skirt fits her perfectly. Is that necklace new? Kermit give it to her?*"

"Yeah, she's looking very nice," I agreed shortly, irritated because he'd noticed things about my own sister that I hadn't.

Jimmy rejoined me. I watched him fool around with a rubber stopper and a pump that sucked the air out of the wine bottle, keeping the contents fresh, somehow. Until Kermit showed up, we never cared if there was any air in or out of our wine bottles—we just screwed the cap back on and let the stuff rot. Next Jimmy went to Kermit's computer system and tapped in the order, which was somehow superior to writing it on a piece of paper. The computer also held our work schedules, which I ignored. "Jimmy.

I have a question for you. About . . . You know Katie is moving out, right? She's renting a place in East Jordan by where she works."

"Yeah, Ruddy, Becky told me." He gave me a searching look. "You okay?"

"Yeah, no, I'm fine. It's just that she said she needs some time to think. What does that mean? Got any ideas?"

"*What do you mean, what does it mean? She needs time alone,*" Alan answered peevishly.

I blinked once, hard, to send a signal that I needed him to shut up.

"Well, look," Jimmy replied uncomfortably, "Katie, I mean, she never has talked to me about it or nothing."

"Right. I'm talking women in general, here. Which you seem to know more about."

"Okay. Um, did you apologize?" he asked.

"For what?"

"For what?" Jimmy repeated, looking a little amused. "For, you know, everything."

"I have no idea what you're saying to me."

"She didn't move out for no reason. You're not listening to her."

"I do too listen!" I snapped, agitated.

"Okay, sure," Jimmy agreed soothingly. "Except she probably has been hinting at stuff you missed."

"She did say something about not wanting to spend every night at the Bear," I admitted.

Jimmy brightened. "Right! So apologize for that. And, like, anything else you can think of. That usually works."

"*I'm not going to sit here and listen to the two of you talk about my adult daughter like she's some sort of child to be manipulated with parenting skills.*"

"Anyone who wants to leave can leave," I stated.

Jimmy nodded. "Sure," he agreed.

"So say I'm sorry? That's it?"

"Yeah, and, you know. Change, maybe?"

"Change," I repeated. "Change into what?"

*"How about someone who doesn't agree to beat people up for money?"*

"I don't know, but I think women like it when men try to change for them," Jimmy explained.

"Ruddy! Come over and help us celebrate!" Claude shouted.

"Okay. Apologize. Change. Got it." I thanked Jimmy for his advice and went over to tell Claude to stop yelling. I settled down into a chair, noting Claude's ebullience and Wilma's darker expression.

"Everything okay, Wilma?" I asked cautiously.

"I wanted pineapple," she told me.

"Huh?"

"She wanted pineapple on the quesadilla," Claude translated. "But I told her we're not eating any of that canned crap. Next time I sink my choppers into a slice of pineapple, it's going to be straight off the bush, served to me by a woman in a grass skirt, in a glass full of rum and maraschino cherries," Claude declared.

*"Which come out of bottles,"* Alan remarked superciliously. I squeezed my eyes shut again.

"I wanted the pineapple in *honor* of Hawaii," Wilma pouted.

"Let me show you our ticket to Paradise, Ruddy," Claude said, reaching into his pocket and pulling out a small plastic case.

"Do you want me to get you a couple slices from the bar?" I asked her.

"No," Claude flared. "We don't want any damn canned pineapple!"

"I can have some if I want," Wilma stormed back.

"Then you might as well not even bother packing your bags for Hawaii, because you're ruining it!" Claude bellowed.

Wilma picked up her beer glass and threw what remained into

her husband's face. Blinking, Claude wiped his cheeks with a napkin.

"Get you another beer, Wilma?" I asked.

"Thank you, Ruddy."

I fetched two fresh beers and put some pineapple slices and cherries on a small plate. Jimmy tapped the order into the computer. My phone buzzed, and I checked it—Katie couldn't, or maybe wouldn't, make it to the Bear tonight. "Okay," I replied. Then, at Alan's urging, I texted her that I understood but would miss her—though it felt like I didn't understand *anything*.

I returned to the Wolfinger table—as usual, the tempest had flared and passed as quickly as a single bolt of lightning. I sat back down, and Claude reached out with thick fingers and snared a pineapple ring, popping it into his mouth.

"Take a look, Ruddy," he said proudly.

*"I don't get how they can throw beer at each other and then pretend nothing's happened,"* Alan marveled.

The plastic case he handed me contained a postcard announcing that the lucky recipient, identified as "occupant," had won one of the following:

A sample pak of hair products!
Deluxe mixing bowls!
A brand-new set of steak knives!
A factory fresh Jeep Laredo!
A glamorous HAWAII VACATION for two!

A toll-free number invited "occupant" to "Call NOW to claim your prize!"

"Claude," I asked cautiously. "How do you know you won the Hawaii vacation?"

"Because I called them!" he replied triumphantly.

"I called them," Wilma corrected.

"We called them," Claude amended.

"It was me," Wilma insisted angrily. "Why are you trying to take the credit?"

"The postcard was addressed to me!" Claude barked back. "By law, you aren't even allowed to call!"

"Hey!" I said. They both looked at me, blinking. "What did the people say when you called?"

Claude started to answer, but I gave him a look indicating that he'd better let Wilma talk.

"They looked up the number on their computer. It was so suspenseful, Ruddy, I couldn't even stand up. And then they said we won the trip to Hawaii!"

"Aloha, oy vey!" Claude shouted.

"Okay, it's just aloha, and quit yelling or Becky's going to make you leave," I said. I sat back in my chair, still holding the plastic-encased postcard.

"We're going to swim with dolphins," Wilma told me.

"Dolphins! We're going to swim with *whales,*" Claude boasted. "With . . . with octopuses, and stingrays!"

"I've never had a real vacation before, Ruddy. Not one on an airplane, where you go places and see things," Wilma breathed, her eyes glowing. "Not in my whole life. Our honeymoon, we stayed with Claude's parents."

"It was our own place over the garage," Claude explained defensively. "It wasn't like we were in the same room with them."

I noticed Kermit had come into the Bear and was chatting with Becky. "You guys mind if I show this to Kermit for a minute?"

They glanced uneasily at each other. I could see that parting with their postcard was like sending a child to the first day of kindergarten, but they finally nodded. I went over and handed the plastic case to Kermit. "Hey, you ever seen anything like this?" I asked him.

He glanced at it. "Oh yeah. It's a one-in-five drop."

"Say what?"

"See, it's legit, sort of. You get the postcard and you call in, and they try to sell you something, and you're hoping that if you agree to buy, it will provide confluence for them to give you a better prize, and then they tell you what you won."

Alan snickered, and I knew it had to do with the word *confluence*. I clenched my fists to hide my irritation.

"All right, but the Wolfingers won the trip to Hawaii."

"Sure. Almost everyone wins that one."

"What? You're kidding."

"Yeah, I mean, like one out of a billion wins the car, and they do give out some steak knives and the other crap. Like I say, it's completely legal. But pretty much everyone gets the Hawaii vacation."

"How can that be?"

"See, it's a Hawaiian *vacation*. So if you get over there, sure, there's a hotel room with your name on it. Probably has a view of a Walmart. But you got to buy your airplane tickets, pay for your meals. Like that."

Alan groaned.

"How do you know stuff like this, Kermit?"

"It used to be how I conducted my fiscals before I came up here," he explained.

I moodily stared over at the Wolfingers, who were gaily laughing, happier than I'd ever seen them.

"*We can't let this happen,*" Alan murmured to me. "*You heard Wilma. She's never even been on an airplane. This is the biggest deal of their whole lives. It will crush them, Ruddy.*"

I was thinking the exact same thing, but I had no idea how I was going to prevent the catastrophe from unfolding.

"Hey, Ruddy, good job on Zoppi. Blanchard says we get all his business from now on," Kermit advised.

"That's really great!" I enthused. I meant it, but I also felt a tinge of sadness that I was discussing repo biz with Kermit and not Milt.

"Plus, I got something pretty important to show you," Kermit told me.

"Okay, in a minute," I replied distractedly. I started to return to the Wolfinger table but then turned back to Kermit. "Can you find out who is behind this? The people running the operation, I mean."

Kermit nodded. "Yeah, I can probably do that."

"Thanks, Kermit."

*"He's actually got a lot of good qualities,"* Alan mentioned helpfully.

"Then stop laughing at how he expresses himself," I growled back, my teeth clenched and my voice soft, so no one would see me talking to myself.

Alan went quietly contemplative.

I handed Claude the plastic case, which he accepted as if I were handing him back a newborn baby. "Wilma, when you talked to the prize people, did you buy anything from them?"

"No," she said happily. "That's how I knew they were legit."

"They even gave us a credit card!" Claude interjected. Wilma frowned at him. "Tell him, honey," he urged, probably hoping to evade another beer facial.

"We got a new credit card with a five-hundred-dollar limit!" she announced. "They said we could use it on the trip!"

"In fact," Claude rushed in. "We get all kindsa free stuff from the travel club!"

"I wanted to be the one to tell about the travel club," Wilma complained. I put my hand on her beer mug, just in case she felt compelled to fling.

*"Travel club,"* Alan said disgustedly.

"So you joined a club of some kind? How much did that cost?" I asked.

"No, it's not like that. You pay a couple hundred dollars, but you get discounts worth thousands," Claude explained.

I nodded, sitting back. "And let me guess . . . they let you put your membership on your new credit card?"

Wilma nodded, and she and Claude started laughing, so happy they couldn't contain it.

"Okay, well . . . aloha," I told them.

"Aloha!" they chorused together, clinking glasses.

I went back over to Kermit. "All right," I said, "what's so important that you need to show me?"

# 10

## This Is Not Necessarily What It Looks Like

Becky followed her husband and me out the back door of the Black Bear, both of them looking oddly conspiratorial, as if planning to hit me on the head and stuff my body into the Dumpster. "What is it?" I asked suspiciously.

"Just look," Becky suggested.

It was cold in the alley, the harsh glare from the naked overhead bulb lighting up the fog from our breaths. It hadn't been plowed in a while, so the snow on the dirt driveway was rutted and packed hard. The light also illuminated a gleaming tow truck with KRAMER RECOVERY painted on its side. I gaped at it.

*"New truck,"* Alan said dismissively.

I looked back at my sister and my brother-in-law. "Really?"

Kermit and Becky nodded at me, beaming, their arms across each other's shoulders like parents watching their child unwrap Christmas presents.

I approached the new truck reverentially. It was the sort of vehicle a repo man dreams about. A T bar pivoted off the back— I could sit in the cab, flip a switch, and send the T bar out and under a parallel-parked car, locking the rear wheels and pulling the unit out of the tightest spot imaginable. A front winch matched the one in the back, black coils of steel gleaming like a parade sergeant's boots. Inside the cab, the seats were not spilling stuffing, and there was no hole in the floor. The radio looked like it worked, even.

"Only thirty thousand miles," Kermit noted. "Got it out of Flint. A one-man operation, decided to pack it in."

"Probably came down with Repo Madness." I nodded.

Becky went back inside while Kermit and I played with all the levers and knobs. "I'm going to be invincible in this thing," I predicted. Sending that boom crabbing sideways was more fun than I'd had in a long time. I picked up the Dumpster with it, grinning.

*"Can we go now?"* Alan demanded in a bitchy voice. He would have spent all day looking at tennis sweaters, probably, but put something of real value in front of him, and he was as petulant as a bored child.

"And wait, there's something else." Kermit showed me a little black box under the dash, in front of where my left knee would be. A black wire with a single silver pin connector attached to the metal box, which had a dusky red switch on one side.

"Self-destruct device?" I guessed.

"It's a GPS transmitter, so that I can track wherever you are at all times. And that switch? You flip it, and it sends a signal to all my mobile devices—my home phone even rings. So if you get into trouble, like, a hostage syndrome, you just hit that switch, and I'll know you need help."

"Huh," I said. I gently tugged on the connector, and it pulled right out of the socket.

"Why'd you do that?" Kermit asked, wounded.

"I don't want you knowing where I am at all times, Kermit."

"But what if you need my help?"

"Well, in that unlikely event, I'll plug it back in, flip the switch, and you can come rescue me." Kermit didn't appear particularly happy with the plan. "It's how I work. Nothing against you."

"Okay."

"In fact, I think I sort of do need your help on something. You know this deal with Claude and Wilma? The drop?"

"*One-in-five drop,*" Alan corrected me.

"One-in-five drop," Kermit corrected me.

"Yes, yes," I agreed impatiently. "What do you think it would cost to pay for their tickets? For them to fly to Hawaii, I mean."

"From Traverse City? I don't know, more than a grand apiece, I guess."

"Ah. Well . . . okay. I'm going to see what I can scrape together."

Kermit regarded me with surprise. "You want to underwire their fare for them?"

I could buy the tickets and still retain some of Blanchard's fee—if I collected everything from his gambling buddies. But there was a big difference between five grand and the funds I would have left. I thought about how much better it would be to use that money to take Katie on vacation or buy her something or just have a few bucks in the bank. "Yes," I decided firmly. "I don't want them to know about it, but yes, I want to buy their tickets."

"You're . . . That's pretty cool," Kermit told me. Oddly, he reached his hand out, and I shook it.

"So, look into what it would take. You're good at stuff like that," I told him. "I'm not."

"There are travel aggregators," he replied.

"Sure," I agreed.

"So, can I ask you a question? Something *you're* good at?" he queried somewhat pensively.

"Fire away," I said, waiting for Alan to come up with a list of things I was good at, like forgetting to bathe, which was a false accusation anyway.

"It's about my uncle," Kermit continued.

I gazed back somberly. "Okay."

"The investigation about Milt? Well, there's some kind of delay with the autopsy. The coroner who would normally execute it is out of town, and the next person in line had a death in her family. So it hasn't happened yet."

"And all of your family thinks he was buried right away." I nodded.

"Sure, but that's not it. I mean, it's not like they are going to find out my prevarication. No, I got a call. The guy from the prosecutorial office says that considering Milt's cancer, and no signs it was foul play, they're willing to just call it an accident instead of deliberation."

"So if you agree to no autopsy, they'll put accidental death on the certificate, instead of suicide," I translated.

*"They're trying to save the family's feelings,"* Alan observed.

"They're trying to save money by talking you into cutting corners," I told Kermit. I thought of Sheriff Porterfield, warning me he was going to put me out of business. What was happening to this place, anyway? "You know what? I say screw them. Maybe Milt had a heart attack. You want an autopsy to find out what happened, they should do one."

"Well, there's more complexity to it than that."

I nodded for him to go on.

"See, if the coroner rules it was suicide, then one of Uncle Milt's policies won't pay anything, and the other two won't pay the double indemnity for an accident. It's a lot of money."

*"Then why do it?"* Alan wanted to know.

"But how could they know that for sure? Your uncle probably just wanted to listen to the radio and think and have a couple of nips, and he fell asleep. Carbon monoxide hits pretty quickly, I think. No one can prove it wasn't an accident just by doing an autopsy."

Kermit's vision cleared. "Yeah, you're right."

*"So what good will this do?"* Alan demanded. *"He should leave it alone."*

"Did the prosecutor mention anything about the insurance?" I asked shrewdly.

"Yeah, he was the one who said I should see what the policies promulgated about suicide," Kermit admitted. "And there's something else. They found a bottle of vodka with him, but Uncle Milt hated vodka. So what was it doing there? Could an autopsy find out what he'd been drinking?"

*"I highly doubt it,"* Alan observed.

"Maybe," I replied, just to disagree with the voice in my head. "You should tell the prosecutor that the coroner should look into it."

"Yeah. Thanks. Becky said you'd know what to do," Kermit told me.

"Becky said that?" I asked, pleased.

"Yeah."

"Well, let me know that they find out. Hey, where's my dog? I want him to see the new truck."

"He's at your house. I drove him over," Kermit replied.

"It's, like, three blocks. You couldn't walk him?"

Kermit jammed his hands into his pockets, looking apologetic. "He didn't want to."

That sounded like Jake. "Okay, mind if I take him for a little spin in the new toy?"

Kermit slapped the side of the truck. "Have fun."

*"You're really taking the dog for a ride? You think Jake will honestly care?"* Alan challenged as I drove down the narrow alley.

"He's going to be amazed out of his mind. Besides, I know he would like to see Katie."

*"You're going to drive over to see Katie? Without calling first?"*

"Sure."


Jake actually did seem excited by the new truck, sitting up and sniffing at the dashboard and the CD player. I cranked up the seat warmers to keep my ass thawed so I could roll down his window and let him ride nose to the wind, his eyes full of the joy of being a dog. I punched on the radio and listened to a political commentary channel, a nonstop flood of one man talking, like having Alan Lottner on a speaker. Eventually I shut it off.

I used my repo skills to track down my fiancée. She'd said her new place was close to work, so I started at her office and cruised up and down until I found a small house with her car in the driveway.

There was another car parked right behind it.

I pulled over and sat in the street, contemplating. Who would be visiting Katie after eight o'clock at night?

*"This isn't necessarily what it looks like,"* Alan told me in a soothing voice. Which meant he was drawing the same conclusion.

"You're right," I said, my voice strained. I cleared my throat. "Probably a girlfriend."

*"Right. We should just go."*

The front door opened, and a man emerged, silhouetted by the interior lights.

He was a big fleshy man: Dwight Timms, Katie's former boyfriend before she upgraded to me. He was not in uniform, but he wasn't dressed for a date, either. He wore jeans and a heavy, bulky coat, looking like a balloon in the Macy's Thanksgiving Day Parade. I wondered if he had his gun with him, and if he did, if he could get to it through all that insulation before I punched his nose to the back of his head.

I was breathing shallowly as I watched him walk down the carefully shoveled walkway to his car. My hands were clenching the steering wheel. I noted Katie didn't kiss him good-bye. They didn't hug. Yet my heart was hammering inside my chest.

Timms caught sight of my truck and froze. I could not see his face—it was enshrouded by the harsh shadow from the streetlight—and I doubted he could see mine, either. But he could certainly read KRAMER RECOVERY on the side of the truck. We stared at each other, like two faceless phantoms in the complete silence of the snowy night.

"*Don't do it,*" Alan urged me. "*It's what he wants, Ruddy. He's hoping you'll come after him. Then you'll be in jail and you won't see Katie for years and you'll say good-bye to everything. Please. Just sit. Okay? If Katie looks out and sees you fighting, you'll lose her forever.*"

The last time I checked, I thought Alan was more or less in *favor* of me losing Katie forever, but I didn't mention this. I un-flexed my hands on the steering wheel, letting my air out in a long slow sigh.

"Okay," I murmured, though my pulse was still racing.

After standing there for what seemed five minutes, whatever passed for a brain inside Timms's head began to spark up and advise him he was out in four-degree air. He gave a derisive toss of his head and got into his car and backed out, flipping on his brights as he drove past me. I stared stonily ahead, my pupils whittled down to slits, and waited long enough for my vision to clear before I opened my truck door.

"Come on, Jake."

The peephole darkened as Katie eclipsed it from the other side, and then she opened the door and, thank God, she had a wel-coming smile on her face, though most of her joy seemed reserved for the dog. "Jake!" she greeted.

She held the door for us. I stamped my feet and looked around the tiny little living room. A wood stove was cooking in the cor-ner. Jake quickly decided the couch would be the softest place and jumped up to lie down before we got any crazy ideas about going back outside.

"*It's even smaller than it looks from outside,*" Alan murmured, ever the real estate agent.

I was heartened to see that Katie wasn't dressed for a date. She had on sweat pants and an old shapeless sweater, and no makeup. "I didn't . . . How did you find my place?" she asked.

"It came furnished?" I responded. The couch was ratty, there was a card table by the small kitchen, and a single wooden chair offered the only place to sit that wouldn't mean sharing space with a dog. I resisted the temptation to poke my head down the hall to see what the bedroom looked like.

"Yes, well, and I got some stuff from the Rainbow Shoppe. Ruddy, what's going on? You seem . . ." She shrugged.

"I saw Deputy Dumbbell."

"Sorry?"

"Dwight Timms. The worm farmer turned sheriff's deputy."

Katie's eyes turned cool. "So?" she challenged softly.

"I don't know, Katie, you tell me. Is that what *on a break* means?"

"Oh God." She looked thoroughly disgusted.

*"You need to back off,"* Alan commanded sternly.

"I don't know what you think, but Dwight is my . . . This is his place. He's my landlord. I'm renting from him. He came over because the oven wasn't working; it wouldn't light."

"So what are the terms of this rental?" I asked.

*"What are you implying?"* Alan hissed furiously.

The anger flared in her eyes and then turned to something like sadness. She shook her head mournfully.

"That question is completely inappropriate," she told me. "Dwight lists the rental with our company, and we manage it. My boss is waiving the fee so I can afford it. Why are you doing this? I don't want to fight. I was actually glad to see you when I opened the door. I was thinking of driving to the Bear, but it got too late, so I texted you."

"I just wasn't prepared to see your old boyfriend walk out of your house."

Sometimes in a conversation there's a point where it can go either way, and that's where I sensed we were. Worse, I knew we were at the precipice because I had forced us there. Instead of listening to Alan, I was heeding the needs of something base and unpleasant inside me.

"Well, I sure was," she finally said.

I stared at her in noncomprehension. "What do you mean?"

"I mean *I* was ready to see him walk out of my house. There is nothing going on between me and *Dwight,* Ruddy. God, give me some credit. That was a long time ago. He wanted to talk and asked if I had any wine, and I told him I needed him to leave. A little Dwight goes a long way, if you want to know the truth."

*"Thank God for that,"* Alan breathed.

I thought about Deputy Dumbbell's girth wrapped up in that big parka. "Is there even such thing as 'a little Dwight'?" I asked her. What I should do, I realized, was cross the room, take her in my arms, kiss her, and accompany her into the bedroom.

*"Don't try it,"* Alan advised me. *"Give her time, Ruddy. She just wants to laugh with you; that's all she's ready for right now."*

I didn't know how he knew what I was thinking, but I could see his point. I glanced over at Jake, who was sprawled on the couch. "I think my dog plans to sleep right there tonight."

Jake rolled his eyes at me, insulted I would drag him into the conversation.

"Jake, you silly dog, you can't sleep here tonight. I have to work tomorrow," Katie said.

Okay, I might be a big dumb repo man, but even I got that her statement was for me, not my dog.

"Okay, Jake. Let's go home."

Jake squeezed his eyes shut, feigning deafness.

Inspired, I told Katie that Kermit was my new boss and that I'd just negotiated a new pay package with him, and asked her if I could take her out to dinner, someplace nice, to celebrate my good fortune. She brightened and said sure, and we set a date for the next night, ignoring Alan's indignation. *"You didn't negotiate; you just accepted his offer,"* he advised me.

Unlike what happened with Timms, she did kiss me good night, a light peck on the lips, though she reserved most of her love for Jake. In a way I was grateful—before I did anything more passionate, I needed to have Alan take a nap.

My fiancée and I were living separately, but we had a date, she'd kissed me, and she loved my dog. I had no idea what was going on, but it seemed like I had a shot.

I woke up with Schaumburg on my mind, but I really didn't feel like talking to him, so I went to the library instead, jumping on the computer and looking for stories about Lisa Marie Walker. Alan woke up around the time I had finished with my notes, which I put on old-fashioned paper.

*"What are we doing?"*

I looked around carefully. The only other people were all the way across the room behind their desk. As long as I spoke quietly, I could converse.

"I'm going to let the *we* pass, though I've been doing all the work while you snoozed. I'm reading about the accident. I never did that, really, and since I pleaded guilty, there wasn't much to learn at the trial."

*"So?"*

"The search for Lisa Marie started that night. The stoners who pulled me out of the water said I was screaming some girl's name. The police moved pretty quickly, and they had divers out before dawn. Meanwhile, her parents had called to report her missing, and it was easy to connect her to the party I'd gone to. They woke up my friends, and they said the last they'd seen, Lisa Marie and I were getting into a car together. By the time I came to in the hospital the next afternoon, they figured she was in the car with me but that she had gotten out and must have drowned."

*"So that's the message. She drowned, just not in the car. That lines up with what that girl Amy Jo said."*

"I don't think that's it at all. The clear implication was that I was not at fault. She said, 'I know you think you killed her.' See? So something *else* happened to Lisa Marie."

*"Like what?"*

"Well, I don't know, Alan," I replied irritably. "But I got the medical examiner's name. He's no longer the M.E., but he is still listed as a practicing physician. I'm going to go talk to him."

*"What good would that do?"*

"You know, if you read a few murder mysteries instead of *Good Housekeeping,* you'd realize that in today's world, forensics solves everything. Maybe the M.E. remembers something that nobody cared about because I had already pleaded to the crime."

*"Well, obviously I'm reading the same book as you. I don't have much of a choice, do I? I'd prefer biographies, but you've decided we need to reread the Lee Child one."*

"Pretty good, don't you think? I see myself as a lot like the Jack Reacher character."

*"Except that he folds his clothes and keeps his kitchen clean."*

"I don't know where you get that."

*"He's ex-military. Organized, neat, disciplined. Simply could not be less like you."*

"You know what, Alan? I would appreciate it if not every conversation we have ends up with you complaining about some aspect of Ruddy McCann. Think you could manage that? You're a guest in my house and my body. Show some respect."

I must have raised my voice, because when I looked over at the counter, all three women were standing behind it, staring at me soberly. I waved in an everybody-talks-to-themselves fashion and left the library.

I really didn't want to speak to Schaumburg, but I was just reaching for my phone to call him when it rang. Caller ID told me it was Barry Strickland. We chatted about the weather for a few moments before he got down to it.

"I ran that plate," he told me. "Belongs to an Amy Jo Stefonick, twenty-three years old. You got a pencil?"

# 11

## Ask Her How She Knows

I headed straight to Ms. Stefonick's address in Petoskey, a lake-front city of about six thousand souls, most of whom would be inside on a day like this—frigid but partly sunny, the golden beams of sunshine slanting down through breaks in the heavy dark clouds every once in a while like stairways to heaven. I was pretty pleased with this analogy when I mentioned it to Alan, but he just said, *"Oh please."*

"So sorry that I am trying to find something pleasant to talk about," I replied.

*"It's not even original. And I can't stand that you're using your cupholders to store trash."*

"It's not trash; those are my receipts. The cupholder is my filing system."

*"Stuffing wadded-up scraps of paper into a hole in your dashboard is not a* system," he sniffed.

"You going to tell me why you're even more irritating than usual today?"

*"You're supposed to be giving Katie time to think things through, and then you're taking her out to dinner tonight. How is that giving her time?"*

"Okay. Let's say you're real, that I'm not just imagining you to keep myself company."

*"You can't seriously be back to that."*

*"If you are real,"* I continued stubbornly, "then you are her father, so you're hardly the person I would go to for advice on dating her. And not her father *now*; in your mind she's still a little girl. I mean, you missed the teenage years, when she discovered boys and went to prom. You missed when she moved to Detroit for nearly a year. She's a full-grown woman now, Alan. You want her to wind up with Deputy Dumbbell?"

He was quiet. I fidgeted. I had a great follow-up speech on the topic of what it meant if he were just a delusion, but his silence was robbing me of any pleasure in the argument. "Alan?"

His voice was raw with pain. *"How do you think it feels to know that, Ruddy? To know that I couldn't be there for her, to protect her from her worst mistakes, to give her advice. How can you be so callous to me?"*

Ugh. I was pondering how to apologize when my phone rang. It was, unfortunately, Dr. Robert Schaumburg.

"Ruddy, this is Dr. Schaumburg," he said curtly. "Your druggist keeps asking for some authorization form but hasn't bothered to fax it to me to fill out and sign."

Yes! Good old Tom.

"I want you to know I am sending a letter to the court today," he continued, "informing them you are in violation of the terms of your probation and, in my opinion, are a danger to yourself and others and should be picked up immediately."

Oops.

"I told you this would happen, Ruddy, that if you ignored me, it would be at your peril."

"I was in the hospital."

He paused. "Say again?"

"You can call over there and verify, or call the sheriff's office. I was in an accident during the ice storm and had to go to the hospital for a while."

I could hear him turning it over in his mind. "Why didn't you have the attending physician call me?"

"Doc, I got hit in the head. I was all bruised up. I was on pain medication. Which," I continued with more enthusiasm as something occurred to me, "I figured you would not want me taking in combination with the meds Sheryl prescribed, so I haven't been taking them since the crash. In fact, the medications don't seem to be in my house, and I promise you that if they were in the glove box when I rolled the truck, I'll need a new prescription."

I had rarely felt so clever—I hadn't even really lied.

"So which is it?" he asked skeptically. "You lost them in the crash, or you stopped taking them because you were worried about adverse drug reactions?"

*"Why don't you try faking a seizure?"* Alan suggested into my silence.

"I guess the point I'm making," I said finally, "is that I'm ready to go back on the meds, but I'm out, so if you could call in a prescription—"

"No," he interrupted. "I want to see you today, Ruddy. In my office. No excuses."

"Oh man, I have such a full day," I responded, thinking of Amy Jo Stefonick, my collection job for Blanchard, and my date with Katie.

"I have a four thirty. It's that or I send this e-mail."

"Four thirty would be wonderful," I told him with no enthusiasm. I had no idea how I was going to make it on time.


Before long I was turning up Mitchell Street, the main drag in Petoskey. The plow had shoved a wall of snow onto the sidewalks, and now the local merchants were out with their shovels, pushing it back.

There were three mailboxes attached to the outside of the

small house at the address Strickland had given me. Box 1A had the name STEFONICK on it, so I opened the outer glass door to 1A and knocked on the inner wooden door. My cheeks were numbing, and thick clouds of what looked like tobacco smoke billowed out of my mouth.

I was in luck: Amy Jo herself opened the inner door. I recognized her short blond hair and freckles. Her blue eyes opened wide when she saw who it was.

"Oh God," she said through the storm door.

"Hi, Amy Jo."

"Oh God," she repeated with more force. "What are you doing here? How did you find me?"

"I just want—"

She shook her head wildly. "Please! Leave me alone!" She slammed the door.

*"You sure have a way with the ladies,"* Alan remarked.

"All right, well, that is something I might say, Alan, but you would come up with something much more pissy," I retorted as I rapped my knuckles on the wooden door. The brass door knocker rattled as I did so, and I gave it a quick go as well. "Amy Jo?"

*"I am so tired of you playing this same tune,"* Alan said, sounding genuinely angry.

"Fine. Why don't you leave, then? Take a vacation. Go to Hawaii and stay at the Walmart. Amy Jo?" I knocked harder.

*"She wants you to leave her alone."*

"I repo cars, Alan. I don't leave people alone."

Finally she opened the inside door again. Her eyes were red, and she had a hand to her mouth. "I can't talk to you."

I was holding the storm door open and could feel the heat fleeing the inside of her house. "Just for a few minutes," I replied.

Defeated, she let me in. The wooden floors creaked under my feet after I slipped off my snowy boots and padded after her into the small kitchen. "I was going to have some tea," she told me resignedly.

"I would love some!" I responded enthusiastically. I never liked the stuff, but maybe Alan would appreciate it. We sat at a small round table, and the mug of hot liquid felt pretty nice in my hands. Amy Jo put some sugar in her tea and stirred it, looking into her cup, her eyes dead.

*"Please don't add any sugar; it's better unadulterated,"* Alan requested.

"Amy Jo."

She glanced up at me warily.

"You're not a medium."

She pressed her lips together and shook her head no.

"So what . . . ?"

She glanced around her small kitchen. "The first time I saw you going into a medium's tent, it was at the Venetian Festival in Charlevoix," she said.

The Venetian Festival is sort of the polar opposite of Smeltania. It takes place in the warm end of July and is a huge art fair and street carnival. At night there are fireworks and a parade of yachts in the harbor, rich people standing on the bows of their enormous boats, holding cocktails in their hands and staring at all the tourists sitting on the grass in the park, who stare back. I had ducked in to see if the mediums, or maybe the media, could connect me with Alan. I'd had no luck.

"I guess I'm not understanding," I confessed.

"Then I saw you last year at Shantytown, and I thought maybe you were trying to, you know, reach her. Lisa Marie Walker." She took a sip of her tea, and I did likewise.

*"She was pretending to be a medium as a ruse to talk to you,"* Alan advised me, as if I couldn't have figured that part out.

"You don't like the tea?" she said, smiling at my reaction.

"It's very different," I replied carefully.

"It's green tea," she and Alan said together.

"Haven't you heard of green tea?" she asked.

"Yes, I just had no idea people actually drank it." It was pretty bad stuff. I reached for the sugar bowl and, over Alan's loud complaints, heaped in a couple tablespoons. Now it tasted like sweetened bad stuff, which was something of an improvement.

"*Don't drink any more,*" Alan begged. I took another sip.

"So you knew I was going to mediums. And you decided to pretend to me that you're one, too. So that you could tell me something. What do you want to tell me, Amy Jo?" I asked her.

She looked away, then down. I let her struggle with it. "I saw something," she finally whispered.

"Saw what?"

She raised her eyes to mine, and I noted something new in them: regret. "That night. I mean, I didn't know what it meant at first, not until I was older, and you had already gone to jail."

It was prison, but I didn't want to interrupt her with a correction. I sat in silence—sometimes, when I'm trying to get people to tell me where they've hidden their cars, I'll just sit and they'll eventually fill the void with more information.

"I was on my bike. I saw you, and I knew who you were. Everybody knew who you were."

"Where did you see me?"

"At the 7-Eleven. You parked your car. I saw you get out and go into the store. And I sat and watched. I kind of had a crush on you then." She blinked at me a little shyly.

"So then what happened?"

"Then the back door of your car opened, and this girl got out."

I turned absolutely still.

"She went over by another car and threw up. I mean, she was pretty drunk; she could barely walk."

"Did she get back into my car?"

Amy Jo shook her head. "No, that's what I'm saying. A man came up and helped her."

"*My God,*" Alan breathed.

"Helped her?" I probed.

"He put his arm around her while she was sick. And then he led her down the street, and they got into a car. Or at least I think they did. I was actually watching you, because you had gone to the counter with some beer and you were showing your ID."

I closed my eyes for a moment. I felt a little dizzy. "Why didn't you tell the police any of this?" I asked faintly.

"I'm sorry, but I didn't even know about the accident until later, and then it was when I was in high school, doing a research paper on the history of the area. The night you crashed was the day after my birthday—a really *important* birthday. See, I got that bike for my birthday, and I rode it all day and all the next day, and then someone stole it right out of our garage. The night you crashed into the water, that was the night someone took it. I woke up the next morning and went out, and it was gone. So I'd never forget that night, the last night on my new bicycle."

"You still could have said something. You still could have told the police," I replied, my voice rising.

Her freckled face turned deathly pale. I had more than a hundred pounds on her, and we were alone in her small flat.

"*Ruddy,*" Alan soothed cautiously.

"I am so sorry," she told me, gulping back upset tears. "I didn't think anyone would believe me. I thought they would think I was just making it up to be famous. I was in high school when I figured out what I really saw. When you're in high school, there's a lot you don't understand about the world."

I took a breath. "Okay. Right. You didn't know. I get it. It's okay. Just . . . this man who helped Lisa Marie, can you tell me anything about him?"

She shook her head, a tiny motion. "I wasn't really looking at him. I was looking at you."

"Okay, but you did see him, even if just a little," I responded, forcing my voice to be gentle. "What do you remember?"

She swallowed. "He wasn't as tall as you are. He was sort of, you know, slender. I saw his hair. It was brown, but in the center it was missing, you know?"

"A bald spot?"

"Yes!" Momentary pleasure showed in her eyes—she was happy to have gotten this detail out—but then it faded. "That's really honestly all I can remember."

*"Ask her how she knows it was Lisa Marie Walker,"* Alan suggested.

Well, that was stupid—who else could it be? "Do you remember anything else? Anything at all would be helpful," I prodded.

She shook her head. Some relief was showing in her expression—the secret she had bottled up inside her for so long was out in the open, finally, and I hadn't yelled at her. Not much, anyway.

*"If she is only guessing it was Lisa Marie, then her testimony won't be enough to reopen the case,"* Alan lectured me. *"You have to ask her how she knows."*

Okay. "How did you know who the girl was?"

"Oh. Well, I didn't. I mean, not that night. But I did see her face. When she got out, she sort of stared up at the streetlight for a moment. That's how this whole thing started—I was reading about the accident, and I connected when it must have happened, after my birthday, but I didn't think much of it until I scrolled down to her picture and realized, oh my God, that's *her*."

Amy Jo apologized to me again as I was putting my boots on. I told her it was okay, though there were so many ways it wasn't, and got her to agree that if it came to it, she would be willing to tell the prosecutor what she had just told me. It wasn't the prosecutor she had been afraid of; it had been me, Ruddy McCann, repo man.

*"I guess I didn't realize just how important this conversation was going to be. I mean, I thought, you know, a medium. I don't really believe in any of that stuff,"* Alan murmured apologetically and, in my opinion, ironically, as I got into the tow truck. The person who claimed to be dead and talking to me didn't believe that there were people who could talk to dead people?

*"How do you feel, Ruddy?"*

"Feel?" I started the truck and steered back south. Time to see if I could collect some of Blanchard's money. "I don't even know. What am I supposed to feel? My whole life was ruined because of a lie. A lie even I believed. Should I be happy? Angry? I just feel hollowed out. My God. All I did wrong was drive her to Charlevoix. So I bear some responsibility, but not the way I thought. Maybe I failed to protect her, but I never killed *anybody*."

*"Somebody did, though. Somebody killed Lisa Marie Walker and threw her into the water."*

"Yeah. The guy who 'helped' her."

*"We have to find who did that, Ruddy. She was murdered. We have to find the man who did it."*

# 12

## Back in Jail

Herbert Yancy seemed like the best person from Blanchard's list to start with, because he owed the most money—more than fifteen grand—and would therefore garner me the biggest fee. Collecting him would get me almost to where I could afford the Wolfingers' tickets. Yancy lived on a bluff overlooking Torch Lake—a beautiful, shockingly clear body of water right off Highway 31 between Traverse City and Charlevoix. Yancy's driveway was so long, it could have supported at least one cherry stand, maybe a rest area and a traveler's bureau. He had a separate garage with five doors, the one in the middle oversized so he could park his sailboat or maybe an armored car full of gold bullion. The house itself looked to have more bedrooms than the average hotel, and a grand wooden staircase built of redwood between the garage and the house descended through the trees down to the beach below. Or at least I assumed it was beach— this time of year the lake and the shore were both frozen solid and coated with white.

I got sidetracked on the way to the front door. A ladder was leaning up against the house, and I could hear someone up there, moving around on the back side—the lake side—of the roof. I put my hands on the rungs.

*"We shouldn't climb up there,"* Alan fretted, so naturally I

climbed up there. For all his nervousness, there wasn't really any reason to worry—the foot of snow provided surer footing up top than I would have had in the summer. At the peak of the roof I paused to take in the view: It's a nineteen-mile-long lake, and from up there I could see practically the whole thing, the stark black trees in the white snow along the shore, the evergreens, and one lone ice shanty, trying to kick-start the next Smeltania.

There was, indeed, a person on the roof. A guy was sitting, his back to me, down toward the lakeside lip of the roof, messing with some wires. In the winter, as the snow melts, water trickles to the gutters, where it hits the air and refreezes, the ice backing up like a miniature glacier, which wreaks havoc on the shingles. To prevent this, homeowners like Yancy had heating wires zigzagging along the edge of their roofs to keep the water liquid and moving along. Homeowners like me climb up on their roofs with a shovel. The guy had earbuds in, which was why he hadn't heard me come down his driveway. I picked up some snow, made a loose snowball, and tossed it in his direction. I didn't mean to hit him, but it caught him in the back of the head.

He overreacted, leaping to his feet and spinning around. I guessed maybe I understood how startling it would be for this to happen: You're fooling with wiring, listening to rich people music on your iPod, and some repo man pelts you with a snowball. Not exactly how you thought your day would go when you first woke up this morning.

"Yancy?" I asked as he yanked the buds out of his ears.

"Who the hell are you?"

"Are you Herbert Yancy?" I repeated in a cold voice.

"Yeah?"

"William Blanchard sent me to talk to you."

I expected some sort of reaction but not what I got. Yancy's face paled in fear, his mouth dropping open. "Oh God."

*"Do you have to sound so hostile?"* Alan demanded.

"Look," I managed to say—and then the guy turned and ran.

On the roof! Where the hell did he think he was going? "Wait!" I yelled at him. I gingerly gave pursuit. We were running along the spine of the house and the fall on the lake side was a hell of a lot scarier than the driveway side, but I didn't particularly want to trip in either direction. "Would you just wait a minute?" I shouted angrily.

Though it was a pretty big house, it didn't go on forever. He was running out of roof, and the truth of this seemed to occur to him. He skidded to a halt, throwing a wild look back at me.

*"What did Blanchard tell these guys you were going to do to them?"* Alan wondered. *"He's scared to death."*

"We need to talk, Herbert," I declared sternly.

Yancy took a few steps in my direction, but he wasn't looking at me—he was staring at the twenty-foot gap between the house and the roof of the detached garage, backing up to make the leap.

"You've got to be kidding me," I muttered.

*"Don't let him jump!"* Alan shrieked at me.

Okay, how was I supposed to stop him? "Wait! Don't!" I shouted.

Yancy took off running, his stride lengthening, and when he leaped, it was graceful and athletic and he nearly made it, hitting the gutters of the garage roof hard before falling back and crashing onto the wooden stairs, bouncing and tumbling down them and finally coming to a stop in a heap at the bottom, sprawling on the frozen beach.

He wasn't moving.

Just great.

It took me a few minutes to get down to where Yancy had come to rest. *"Why did you have to do that? I told you not to climb up here! He could be dead!"* Alan babbled shrilly—that's right, I don't care what he says: The man babbles.

Yancy was conscious, but not in the mood to talk. I could see by the way his leg was bent behind him that the bone had snapped, and his wheezing suggested he might have broken a rib or two as well. I pulled out my phone and called 911, giving them the address.

I checked my watch. I needed to wrap this up quickly so I could make it to see Schaumburg by four thirty, but I couldn't very well leave Yancy by himself.

"Why did you run away?" I asked him disgustedly. "I just wanted to talk to you. Did you think I was going to throw you off the roof, so you jumped off instead?"

His eyes were squeezed shut so that he could concentrate on his pain, and he didn't answer me.

*"I can't see how your sarcasm is helping anything here,"* Alan chided.

"Whereas your complaining is oh so helpful," I snapped back. I didn't care if Yancy heard me arguing with myself or not. I kept glancing at my watch, tracking the time as it ticked away.

Eventually the sound of sirens built in the distance. I went up the stairs to wave at the ambulance when it came down the long driveway, looking uneasily at my timepiece as the attendants pulled out a stretcher. To get to Schaumburg's on time, I needed to leave *now*.

Which I did, getting an odd look from the driver of the ambulance when I gave him a thumbs-up and slipped behind the wheel of my new tow truck. He clearly thought I should stick around to explain why Yancy had decided to descend the stairs from the roof of his house, but I figured once the patient stopped feeling sorry for himself, he could tell them just as easily as I could.

*"Won't you get in trouble for leaving?"* Alan asked worriedly.

"Nah," I told him. "I'm the Good Samaritan here. If I hadn't shown up to dial 911, Yancy could have frozen to death down there."

*"If you hadn't shown up, he wouldn't have fallen,"* Alan argued.

"We don't know that for certain."

*"You have got to be kidding me."*

I was just turning onto the highway to head back to Traverse City when a sheriff's car came up behind me, moving very fast, its emergency lights on and flashing in an irritatingly ostentatious fashion. I eased over and the car followed me, stopped a dozen yards back. As I watched, Grant Porterfield and Dwight Timms got out of the car. The two of them were getting to be pretty chummy—it was almost cute.

Timms drew his weapon and pointed it at me. "Keep both hands on the wheel!" he shouted.

*"Don't worry,"* Alan told me dryly. *"You're the Good Samaritan here."*


The county jail hadn't gotten any more attractive since the last time I was there. I used my one phone call to ring up Kermit, asking him to please contact Schaumburg and Katie, and oh, by the way, come bail me out.

"Tomorrow," Porterfield suggested softly. In theory he wasn't supposed to be listening to my side of the conversation, but it was too quiet in the jail for him not to. "Nobody's getting bail this late in the day."

I was alone in the jail—the crime rate in Michigan drops with the temperature, which was why the sheriff had nothing better to do than harass the local repo man. Timms shut the bars behind me and then stood, grinning, like I was a new pet he'd just put in a cage. Porterfield didn't smile, though, when he came down the narrow hall, carrying a chair that he put down on the stone floor, making a harsh scraping sound. Timms looked around for a place to sit and then, grunting, sort of leaned against the wall.

"Ruddick McCann," Porterfield said with a sigh. "Did I not

tell you no more repos in this area? Then you go and beat up poor Herbert Yancy. You know he is a good friend of mine?"

"I didn't beat up anybody."

"That's not what he says."

Alan groaned. I stared at the floor—if Yancy was telling people I put him in the hospital, I doubted anything I could say would make any difference. I'd go back to jail on a probation violation while the assault charges worked their way through the court system, and then I'd go back to prison.

"Look at me now."

I glanced up into Porterfield's small pitiless eyes. He had leaned forward, his face pressed against the bars. "I told you no more re-pos," he said in an almost gleeful voice. "You disobeyed me. People who disobey me wind up right where you are now. We clear?"

I looked away. Timms banged on the bars with his stick. "Hey! Answer the sheriff!"

"Jesus Christ, Dwight! You about broke my eardrums!" Porterfield barked, backing away from the bars.

Timms turned even more pale than usual.

"You have absolute shit for brains," Porterfield seethed. "Did you not see that my face was right there? That *hurt*."

"Sorry, sir," the deputy mumbled.

Porterfield stood up, grabbing the chair. "I imagine you'll be our guest for some time," he told me. "You think of anything we can do to make your stay more comfortable, you keep it to yourself."

Timms smirked at me, and the two of them left. I stretched out on the narrow bunk and stared at the ceiling. "Well, at least I have a good excuse to give Schaumburg," I muttered.

*"If Yancy says you threw him off the roof, it is going to be your word against his,"* Alan observed helpfully.

"I do know that."

I lay there, feeling the jail cell get smaller and smaller, snuffing out any sense of the outside world. *"What happens,"* Alan asked me finally, *"if Yancy does file assault charges? Would they still give you bail?"*

"I imagine it will be easier for them to just violate me back behind bars for the duration of my probation."

*"God."*

"Yeah."

*"Okay, but what if it doesn't go that way? All you did is show up to have a conversation. Maybe Yancy will tell them that."*

"In that case, I have to convince Robert Schaumburg that the reason I couldn't make his appointment was legitimate. I could still wind up in jail." Which meant, of course, that I could say good-bye to any chance of getting back with Katie. Or finding out anything more about Lisa Marie Walker.

Breakfast was one of those boxes of cornflakes I used to eat as a kid, where the inside is lined in wax paper and you pour the milk right in on top of it. I sniffed the small container of milk before I added it, using a plastic spoon to finish the cereal off in about three minutes. A small cup of orange juice sealed with foil made up the rest of the meal, all brought to me by a deputy I didn't recognize. Alan slept through the culinary delights.

He was still asleep when the same deputy brought me lunch, and hadn't yet awakened when, without warning, the man I'd come to think of as Deputy Mealtime unexpectedly opened the cell door, motioning with his fingers that I should follow him. I followed him out into the front room, where Kermit stood, reading public service posters. We shook hands formally, like men at a funeral. The deputy had me sign some papers and gave me my personal belongings, Kermit hovering nearby. We all were taciturn, almost surly—it seemed to fit the occasion.

Once I was fully processed by the sheriff's department and certified safe to return to civilization, I followed Kermit outside to the repo truck.

"So?" I asked him.

"The guy in the hospital said you startled him and he fell off the roof. He said it wasn't your fault; it was an accident," Kermit told me. "And my lawyer filed a formal plaintiff with the court about the sheriff telling you not to repo. It's illegal constraint of trade to tell you that you can't do your job. This is a lawful business."

I gave Kermit an appraising look. "Wow, Kermit, I'm impressed."

He shrugged, but I could see he was pleased with the compliment. He told me my sister had followed him down in her car so that I could have the repo truck, which he had redeemed from the county lot—he and Becky were going to have a nice lunch at the Weathervane, one of the local restaurants. "You know what, I should do that. Take Katie there, I mean," I remarked thoughtfully. Kermit had successfully maneuvered the obstacle course from engagement to marriage. Maybe I could learn a few tricks from him. "I need to make up for missing our date last night."

"She said she understood when I told her what happened."

"Thanks, Kermit."

"Hey, uh, I decided to inquest the autopsy. On Uncle Milt, I mean."

"I didn't think you meant on yourself."

"I just wanted to say thank you. For your advice. It helped," he replied sincerely.

I told him to think nothing of it. "We're family, right?"

Kermit didn't reply, but his return gaze was full of surprise.


We said our good-byes, and I drove the short distance to the medical office where the former medical examiner, Dennis Kane, still practiced medicine. I told the woman at the counter that I didn't have an appointment, but that I had been referred by Dr. Sheryl Johnston, and then I spent an hour filling out forms.

The woman seemed displeased with my medical insurance, which only pays a claim if I've been hit by a meteor. I wrote on the checklist that the reason I needed to see a doctor was that I had a pain in my head.

When Alan woke up, he immediately began asking me strident questions about where we were and how we got out of jail, even though I clearly couldn't answer him with people in the waiting room. I snagged a key from the front desk, went down the hall to the men's room, and quickly filled him in, leaning in and talking to the mirror. It seemed slightly more normal to do it that way.

"*Did you call Schaumburg?*" he demanded.

"No."

"*Why not?*"

"Because I want to talk to this Dr. Kane before I do anything else. He's the missing link, I just know it."

Alan naturally didn't think that was a good idea. I invited him to stay silent, and returned to the waiting room.

Dennis Kane himself opened the door to the examining room. He was a medium-sized fellow with a long nose and jowly cheeks, pale skin, his white hair mostly clinging to the sides of his head, a few long wisps in front combed back. His glare was icy behind his wire-framed glasses. "Mr. McCann," he greeted.

I got up, smiling in a friendly fashion, but he turned abruptly away from me and led me down to his office—a small cramped space with mahogany shelves and a couple of black leather chairs. He did not invite me to sit. He stood, his arms crossed. "Why are you here?" he asked curtly.

Haltingly, I explained what Amy Jo had told me. That Lisa Marie had gotten out of the car that night. That some man had "helped her." I found myself talking faster as I came to the end of the story, because Kane stood very still, his mouth turned down and his eyes cold, not looking at all cooperative. "I thought you could tell me if there was anything in the autopsy, something that didn't seem quite right to you at the time," I finished lamely.

"Why in God's name would you do this? Drag up this matter?" he asked harshly.

I blinked. "Because if what Amy Jo said is true, it means . . . It means—"

"It is not true," he interrupted. He took off his glasses and shined them with his tie for a moment, and when he put them back on, his gaze was nearly hateful.

"I don't know what you are saying," I responded honestly.

"We both know exactly what I am saying. Lisa Marie Walker died as a result of your negligence. She was in the car that night. It's despicable to suggest otherwise."

"Despicable?" I repeated, feeling my anger rise. I thought of my years in prison.

"Yes, Mr. McCann. Because there was something I did not put in the report, something I left out, to spare the family. Something that proves without a doubt that you killed that poor innocent girl."

# 13

## Someone Knows Something

I stared at Kane. There was an odd reflection on his glasses from the overhead light, so that I couldn't precisely see his eyes, but the rest of him was rigid and hostile. As for me, I was shocked silent—even Alan had stopped talking. I cleared my throat. "What are you talking about?" I asked faintly.

"You know goddamn well what I am talking about." He shook his head, and the reflection flashed across his glasses. "I don't know what you think you were going to accomplish here today, but you made an appointment under false pretenses, and I want you to leave."

"Dr. Kane . . . I honestly *don't* know what you are talking about."

I've seen the look he gave me then—like I was the lowest life form on the planet. Usually I get it from people who are disgusted I am there to reinforce their obligation to pay back their loans, and I can often cheer myself up by driving away in their cars. Since that wasn't an option here, I felt myself growing frustrated and angry.

"Just leave." He made to move past me but stopped when I took a step, putting myself between him and the door. He peered up at me, a flicker of concern in his glassed-in eyes.

"We're not finished here. You said I know something. Tell me what you think I know, Dr. Kane."

His lips twisted into a disdainful sneer. "I never told the family the truth. I wanted to spare them the *pain,* Mr. McCann. But apparently your lack of humanity knows no bounds."

"Tell *me* the truth."

"You had intercourse with her that night. I recovered semen. Can you imagine? Bad enough that their little girl drowned in your car—first you got her drunk, and you . . . you . . ." He shook his head, unwilling to speak it.

*"Is this true, Ruddy?"* Alan whispered, shocked.

My heart was pounding. "Did you keep the semen?"

"What? Of course not! I would have had to put it into my report, then." He glared at me. "Satisfied? Now, are we done here?"

"Yeah. We're done." I pointed a finger at his face—a single finger, when what I wanted to do was feel his teeth on my knuckles. "Just one more thing, Dr. Kane. You think that proves she was in the car? It doesn't. It proves the opposite. The exact goddamn opposite."

Alan's questions followed me as I stormed out to the repo truck. *"What are you saying, Ruddy?"*

I got in and slammed the driver's side door. "Goddammit!" I shouted at the top of my lungs.

*"What? Tell me!"*

"If that pompous ass had just put that in his report, you know what a difference it would have made?"

*"No, what? How?"*

"It means, I would have known something was wrong. Because I might have forgotten a few things about that night, but I promise you, I never had sex with Lisa Marie. You don't forget something like *that*. I never so much as kissed her! I never would have pleaded guilty if I had known she had somebody's semen inside her. Maybe we would have hired a private investigator to look into what really happened that night. Or the guy's DNA might be on file with the cops. Maybe we would have found Amy Jo and gotten her story. Maybe somebody else saw something that night! My whole life would be different!" I started the truck and drove out of the parking lot, forcing myself not to let my anger express itself in a stomp on the accelerator. Alan's silence was somehow pensive as he experienced me controlling myself. "What?" I snapped at him. "What's your problem now?"

"*You keep saying that,*" he replied quietly.

"Saying what?"

"*That your whole life would be different.*"

"Well, it would!"

"*I don't disagree. But isn't that sort of beside the point now? You can't go back.*"

"Are you saying I should just let this whole thing drop?" I demanded, furious.

"*No! Of course not. I think something much worse happened to Lisa Marie than what anyone knows. There was semen inside her. She got out of the car before you drove into the lake, but she drowned anyway. We owe it to her to try to find out who did that to her. But it won't change anything. You can't get the years back. You'll still be who you are.*"

"You are wrong, Alan. It will change everything. You have no idea what it is like for me now. I used to go to the Dairy Queen or the bowling alley or the movies, and everyone was glad I was there. Men shook my hand, little boys looked at me like I was a superhero. Now people are embarrassed when they see me. The kids stare at me like I'm a suspect being interrogated behind a one-way mirror. All because of a *fiction.*"

Alan was silent. The old repo truck always shuddered its way down the highway, so much road noise that I couldn't have heard the radio even if it had worked. This one was quiet, the only sound a faint buzz from the knobby tires finding their grip on the pavement. I listened to the buzz for a while. "You don't understand," I finally muttered.

More miles buzzed by. *"Kane gave us something we haven't had up until now,"* Alan mused.

"How's that?"

*"Motive. Before, it didn't make any sense. Lisa Marie wasn't in the car. But she shows up in the water anyway. A man 'helped' her, but she still died. Why? It was a complete puzzle. Until you find out that she had semen inside her."*

"So she could have known the guy," I suggested, nodding.

*"Or he's a predator who came across a drunk teenage girl and saw an opportunity."*

"Jesus."

*"We need to find out everything we can about Lisa Marie Walker,"* Alan said decisively.

My phone rang. I picked it up and looked at the screen.

Time to talk to Dr. Schaumburg.


Schaumburg confessed that his conversation with Kermit left him slightly confused. "The man said you were reincarnated in jail."

"Well . . . reincarcerated, maybe." I gave a not-my-fault accounting of Herbert Yancy's swan dive off his roof. "So obviously, I couldn't make it to our appointment."

"It does seem as though every time we set up a time, something extraordinary happens to prevent you from making it."

"What, are you saying I wanted to roll the repo truck? To get arrested for some rich idiot falling off his own roof?"

"You didn't push him," Schaumburg observed neutrally.

"No, of course not. I was just there to collect an account for the bank." The ice I was skating on had grown thin under the truth, but it was still holding my weight.

"Could Alan have pushed him off?" Schaumburg asked quietly.

"What? Alan would have been afraid to even climb the ladder." I snorted.

"*I wasn't afraid,*" Alan tsk-tsked.

"Have you spoken to Alan lately?"

"Alan was just a voice, Dr. Schaumburg, something my brain made up." And that, too, was the truth. A version of it, anyway. Though from the continued noises Alan was making, I could tell he did not agree.

Schaumburg grunted. "All right, let's set a time for you to come in."

We agreed that we would love to reunite Tuesday morning.

I finally got a chance to repo a vehicle that was parallel parked on the street, right in downtown Traverse City. I pulled a Ford Edge from between an old Toyota and a new Audi and was out of there in five minutes. The whole experience improved my mood. Alan fell asleep while I was jockeying the Edge away from the curb. How anyone could fall asleep during such a glorious repo was beyond my comprehension.

Katie was having a busy day, but eventually was able to return my call for a quick five minutes. "They arrested you?" she responded incredulously when I told her why I couldn't make our date. "When the guy *ran* on a *roof,* and fell?"

"It was more like a jump, at least at first. The fall sort of came later."

"Was Dwight there?" she practically hissed.

I delighted in being able to tell her yes, of course, he was the one who put the cuffs on me. Too tight, by the way.

"So that's what this is all about?" she fumed. "Okay, I'll talk to him."

"What? No, don't do that," I urged.

"Why not? This is all some sort of juvenile power play. He calls you my bouncer friend. Like, 'Heard anything from your bar bouncer friend?' It sickens me."

"Do you tell him I'm actually your repo friend?"

She laughed. "I tell him you're my boyfriend."

"That's good." Actually, it was *great*. "Uh, I'd appreciate it if you let me handle Deputy Dumbbell. Otherwise, you know."

"It makes you feel less manly," she guessed.

"Of course not. I'm way too manly to feel less."

She laughed again. "Of course you are."

"If you need a demonstration," I said suggestively.

"In that case, I know just who to call," she agreed primly.

So she was not only not angry that I'd canceled our date because I'd spent the night in jail, she agreed that I should never have been arrested for something that wasn't my fault. Deputy Dumbbell's department had lost points, and she felt bad for me and agreed we should go out for dinner the next night instead. Plus, we both agreed I was manly. I scored it a solid win for Ruddy McCann.

I took the repo to Blanchard's bank. His lot had one of those wooden gates that rises when you put in your ID badge. I phoned the bank, and William Blanchard himself came out to card me in. He grinned and gave me a thumbs-up when he saw me dragging the Ford, turning his hand into a finger pistol that he fired and then raised to his lips to blow the smoke out of the barrel. "I get it: You're the gunslinger, I'm the gun," I muttered as I dropped the Ford next to Zoppi's Jeep. His ex-Jeep.

Blanchard invited me into his office and shut the door behind me. "I got a little something for you, boy," he told me, a sly expression on his face. He fished around in a drawer and tossed me a paper bag. I peeked inside and saw a thick wad of cash. "You like?"

"So Mr. Yancy paid?" I deduced.

"Yancy? Hell, boy, they *all* paid. There's five thousand dollars in that bag. You sure put the fear of God into the fellows on the boat. And by 'God,' I mean, of course, me."

Any affection I might have felt for him over the bag of money was waning in the face of his use of the word *boy*. I slipped the cash into my coat pocket. "For the record," I said, "Yancy fell."

"Yeah, well, some fall. You broke his leg and his collarbone."

"He fell," I repeated stonily.

Blanchard just grinned at me. Part of me wanted to take his bag of money and pitch it at his face, but it was a very *small* part.

Katie had texted me some emoticons while I was in with Blanchard: a heart, a glass of wine, and a piece of chocolate cake. When I returned to the repo truck, I sent her back a llama and a snowman. This is how people communicated before there was written language.

Alan woke up as I was pulling into the library parking lot. *"What happened with the repo?"* he wanted to know.

"There was a live grizzly bear in the backseat. I wrestled him into submission and dropped him off for Kermit to babysit along with my dog." Not so much as a chuckle out of Alan. A lot of imaginary people are grumpy when they first wake up. I shut off the engine. "Okay, Alan, we're headed into a library. That means if I look around and there are other people there, we have to be quiet. I can't talk to you if everyone can hear me. So you should be quiet, too."

*"Can I ask you something before we go in?"*

"Knock yourself out."

*"Did you ever take the antipsychotic medications? At first, I mean."*

"Nope."

*"Then how do you know you won't like the side effects?"*

"That's not why I don't take them."

I could feel him in there, mulling it over. I've always heard that humans only use 10 percent of their brains—was it really so crazy to suppose that the part of me that was Alan could tap into some of the other 90 percent for his own calculations? *"And you went to see psychics."*

"Mediums. Not psychics."

*"For me, though. Trying to get in contact with me. That's why you don't want to take the pills; you're afraid they will snuff me out, as if I'm some sort of psychosis and not a real person."*

"We done?"

*"Why? Why did you want me back?"*

"I honestly can't think of a single reason."

*"Ruddy."*

I blew out a breath. "I don't know. I don't think there is a reason, meaning, something I thought through, analyzed. It just *felt* wrong, somehow, when I couldn't talk to you. It helps to have you around, like when you stopped me from breaking Deputy Dumbbell down into his component parts, or when you told me I needed to give more thought to my texts with Katie. Or even talking to you about Lisa Marie Walker. You drive me crazy most of the time, but without you there, it gets too goddamn quiet." I fell silent, thinking of the irony of telling a voice in my head it was driving me crazy—if you hear a voice in your head, you've probably already been *driven.*

*"That's pretty much the nicest thing you've ever said to me."*

"Well, don't pick out your prom dress just yet, Alan. I'm only saying, when you're not around, I miss you. And when you are around, I want you to go away."

My Internet connection at home forces me to sip data through a straw, so if I want to get anything done, I use the free PCs in the library. I settled into a chair and demonstrated my technical expertise by logging into my e-mail.

*"What's Viagra?"* Alan wanted to know.

I, of course, couldn't answer him, because there were others at some of the computers to either side of the long table where I was sitting. The sheer unworkability of the arrangement—me silent, him babbling away—quickly became apparent when I used the search phrase "dead girl washes up onshore boyne city mi" because the first hit had nothing to do with Lisa Marie.

"*Wait,*" Alan commanded. "*This could be important.*"

Sighing impatiently, I read through the article. "*Slow down,*" he ordered.

A woman named Nina Otis fell off a car ferry and drowned. She didn't wash up in Boyne City—she was *from* Boyne City—but the distinction seemed lost on Alan.

"*So she's on the car ferry, the* Emerald Isle, *going from Charlevoix and Beaver Island,*" Alan mused, like he was Sherlock Holmes and this was a clue and he was waiting for Dr. Watson to catch up.

There was nothing to catch up to. Beaver Island is about fifty-six square miles of typical Michigan landscape—inland lakes, trails, beaches. It's a beautiful place—some of my favorite repossessions have been on Beaver Island. According to Nina's sister, Audrey, Nina was on her way for a surprise visit when she slipped unnoticed over the railing. It had nothing to do with Lisa Marie Walker.

About halfway through the trip, the captain of the *Emerald Isle* paged Nina. Her sister filed a missing person's report, but not much happened until five days later, when Nina was found washed up on the shores of Lake Michigan, just north of Charlevoix.

So, two women under entirely different circumstances drown, and their bodies are recovered in two entirely different places. The only thing they had in common was that it took five days for them to be found.

"*Hey, I wasn't finished!*" Alan protested when I changed back to the results page and pulled up stories on Lisa Marie.

It was depressing, reading the articles I'd skipped while it was all happening. The news accounts mostly got it wrong. I was identified as Lisa Marie's boyfriend. The stoners in the van were there for "late-night fishing." I was traveling at "excessive speed." That made it sound as if I had been going a hundred—I'd made a wrong turn that a lot of other folks had made. I was just the first one to go into the water.

Depressingly, there was nothing new at all to be learned from anything we read online. At Alan's insistence, I also searched for "missing women" in our area, and looked at other drownings.

Interestingly, at least to Alan, was the fact that a woman fell off the public docks in Charlevoix a few years ago, in November— the same time of year that I crashed into the lake. She, too, was found washed up in Boyne City after five days. The surface current must move corpses in that direction.

The article about Lisa Marie had a photograph, which I decided I needed in case I ran into anyone who might have seen something. I made the mistake of printing it out, because that got Alan all excited and he insisted on printing pictures of six other women who had vanished from the area who seemed to fit what he was calling the "victim profile," which was under the age of forty and female— hardly an exclusive group. Only three of the women—Nina Otis, who went over the rails of the *Emerald Isle* on the way to Beaver Island; the one who fell off the docks in Charlevoix; and another who vanished during the night from a sailboat anchored offshore in Boyne City—were pulled from the water. The other three were simply missing. I tried to signal my impatience with Alan's new hobby by clicking the mouse with extra force, but it was a fairly ineffective tool for expressing displeasure.

And I *really* disliked Alan's self-satisfied, approving "mmhmm" noises when I returned to the article about the woman who fell off the car ferry. There were a couple of things that were nagging me about the story.

Back in the repo truck, I fired up the engine and then sat in the parking lot, waiting for the heater to kick in.

*"I'm amazed no one has ever seen the connection!"* Alan enthused.

"And I'm amazed that after I told you to be quiet in the library, you talked the whole time," I replied.

*"Hey, don't just shove the printouts into the glove box; they'll get all creased."*

To shut him up, I pulled out an unused repo folder and placed everything inside. "We shouldn't be wasting our time on these other women," I groused. "I get that it's fun to play forensic detective, but we're trying to find out what happened to Lisa Marie Walker."

*"Then why did you go back to the story about Nina Otis?"*

I didn't want to tell him.

*"Ruddy? Why did you reread the story?"*

I didn't answer.

*"Ruddy?"*

You don't know the meaning of the word *pester* until you've had a voice in your head, insisting you talk to it. I put the truck in gear and pulled out of the parking lot. A light snow started to fall, batting at my windshield and lighting up in my headlights. "Well, I thought it was odd that the sister said Nina was going to Beaver Island for a surprise visit. How did she know that?"

*"What do you mean?"*

"The word *surprise* sort of implies you're not supposed to know about it. Yet when Nina Otis doesn't show up, the sister calls the police."

*"Nina's husband could have told her,"* Alan pointed out. *"As in, Hey, my wife is coming out for a surprise visit; don't tell her I told you."*

"Sure," I said dubiously.

*"What else? There's something else."*

I sighed again. "The captain of the *Emerald Isle* paged her. Why would he do that? I've been on that boat dozens of times, and the only page I've ever heard is when some parents are trying to track down their kids. The crew doesn't keep a roster; they take tickets like a movie theater, completely anonymously. So someone must have told the captain that Nina Otis was missing. Who did that?"

*"Oh my God, you're right. You think it was whoever pushed her off? Wait, that wouldn't make sense."*

"That wouldn't make sense," I agreed. "It wasn't someone who might have seen her go into the water, either. You don't page someone who just fell off the boat."

*"Someone knows something about the day Nina Otis died. The same way Amy Jo Stefonick knew something about Lisa Maria Walker."*

I didn't reply. I just watched the snow bend up into my headlights and then fly over the top of the truck.

*"Whoever it is, we have to find him, Ruddy. It could be our killer."*

# 14

## We Don't Know She Was Murdered

When I got home, I debated calling Katie, but Alan advised against it, so I did. I kept it silly and light. "You're more beautiful than a repo in the light of a midnight moon," I told her at one point.

"You're as romantic as a picture of a llama," she countered. We voted that hers was funnier.

Katie and I talked for an hour before we went to sleep in our separate houses, and we texted each other the moment I awoke. I felt pretty sure I was winning the battle to get her back. I emoticonned her a rocket and a piece of toast.

I took Jake with me on a quick repo assignment because it was just down the highway. He tried to ride with his nose out and his huge ears flapping in the wind, but after about five minutes the wind chill got to him and he pulled his head in with a disgusted look. I found the unit—a Mazda on blocks in the customer's front yard, hood yawning open, engine gone, seats gone, customer gone. I took pictures with my phone and sent them to the bank in Kansas that financed it. They would most likely just abandon the thing. Under Milt's regime, I would have received nothing for my efforts, but with Kermit in charge, I had a hundred bucks coming.

I still harbored a lot of affection for Milt, still missed him, but I didn't like the way he had treated me. If he ever decided to join the dead-guys-in-my-head club, we'd have a few words about that.

The last assignment Milt had given me before he died was a guy named Mark Stevens, whose file had now worked its way to the top of the stack. I had repossessed a lot of his family members over the years and didn't expect them to tell me much of anything on how to find their cousin, but his best buddy in life was a guy named Kenny MacDonell, so I figured if I found Kenny, I would be able to locate Mark.

I dropped Jake off at Kermit's office before I headed out of town and tried to ignore how eager my dog was to leave the repo truck. "You know you belong to me," I reminded him. He gave my hand an affectionate, reassuring lick. I think we both knew I was being condescended to by a basset hound. He curled up in his chair and sighed in contentment. Kermit was on the phone, so I didn't stick around.

It took me most of the day, asking around, to track down Kenny's mom, who lived by herself in a house trailer outside of Bellaire. Her driveway was plowed out and her walk shoveled, which Alan noted. *"Kenny probably lives here,"* he concluded shrewdly.

"Or maybe his mother drives a snowplow. You think of that, detective?" I knocked on the front door, little pieces of ice dropping from my mitten with the impact. The sky had completely bled out of blue and was a milky white, and the temperature was scraping the teens. While I waited, I had a fantasy that Kenny's mother would invite me in and give me a cup of coffee. I could taste the coffee, feel it warming my hands and my insides.

A woman opened the door as far as a chain would allow, her blue eye regarding me balefully through the crack. Even with that little of her face showing, I knew she was the woman who had gifted Kenny MacDonell to the world—same orange freckles and pale complexion, hair a dark red. I had met Kenny and his buddy Mark when the two of them barged in with shotguns and tried to hold up the Black Bear a few years back. I probably wouldn't mention that to his mom. "Mrs. MacDonell?" I asked.

"Who are you?"

"I'm a friend of Kenny's."

"He ain't here."

I hugged myself a little to indicate how much warmer our conversation would be at her table, with her coffee. "Do you know what time he'll be back?"

"Who says he lives here?" she responded with hostility.

*"She's not going to tell you anything,"* Alan predicted.

"Oh!" I gave her a surprised look, one of the chief psychological weapons we repo men deploy to extract information. "He moved? When was that?"

"I never said he lived here. I ain't seen Kenny in a long, long time." She made to shut the door.

"Oh my God! That's terrible!"

She hesitated, frowning suspiciously. The door was now open barely an inch.

"You must be worried sick! How long has he been missing?" I implored.

"I didn't say he was—"

"Have you called the police?" I interrupted anxiously. "I know how a mother feels when one of her children vanishes. Can I help you in any way, Mrs. MacDonell?"

"No, I'm sure he's fine."

"This is terrible weather to be homeless!" I squinted at the soulless sky.

"He's not homeless. He just hasn't been around in a while."

"He could be in trouble!"

She shut the door, slid off the chain, and opened it up wider, still blocking access with her body. "There's no trouble. He gave me two hunnert dollars a couple days ago."

I put a hand on my heart. "Oh, thank God. Thank God. So you know where he is, then."

"No. I don't know where—"

"I was so worried you were telling me something horrible had happened to my friend Kenny," I continued blithely. "He still doing construction at the East Jordan Iron Works?"

"No, he's remodeling a place on the lake south of Petoskey."

"That's good. He and Mark?"

"Yeah."

"Okay. One of those big places on the highway?"

"No, a small home off Townline Road."

Alan groaned, as if he had wanted her to keep it a secret or something. "Well, that is so good to hear. I know he's been down on his luck lately. Hey, if you see him, would you tell him his good friend Ruddy from the Black Bear stopped by?"

"What do you want with him, anyway?"

"Oh." I shrugged. "I just want to show his friend Mark my new truck."

*"I can't believe that worked,"* Alan muttered.

"The power of repo persuasion."

*"So when are we going to Beaver Island to talk to Nina Otis's sister?"*

"We're not. I can't see any reason why that will help us find out what happened to Lisa Marie."

*"But what about the possibility that all of the women we found on the computer were killed by the same man, a serial killer, like in all those books you make me read? We talked about this!"*

"No, *you* talked about it. I don't see the connection at all. Three of the women are just gone; they didn't even wash up on-shore."

*"People don't just vanish."*

"Alan, I make my living off of people who just vanish. It's what people do."

*"Where are we going?"*

"Home. I need to clean up. I have a date." I smiled at myself in the rearview mirror.

*"What? With Katie? When did this happen?"*

"You were asleep when I called her. Which is what I want you doing tonight, by the way. I don't need you chatting in my head while I'm trying to have a conversation with my girl-friend."

*"She's my daughter."*

"She's my fiancée," I retorted, hoping that was still true.

When I arrived home I put on a new shirt and a pair of pants that I'd sent to the cleaners. I shaved and made sure my hair was as under control as I could make it. I didn't have any warm coats beside the one that I wore to repo cars, but I put on a sports jacket underneath it.

*"How is it you can get your dirty socks on top of the hamper, but not in the hamper?"* Alan complained.

"It's just one of my many talents."

*"I can promise you Katie doesn't want to be with someone who can't even manage his own socks,"* he huffed.

"She wanted a guy. I'm a guy."

*"You're a slob."*

"Same thing." I put my socks in the hamper, though.

Kermit dropped off my dog as I was getting ready to leave— Jake took one look at me and rolled his eyes, going to his blanket on the floor, weary from a day of sitting in his chair. "Tough day at the office?" I asked him. I knew that the second I left the house, he would promote himself to the pillow on what I still considered to be Katie's side of the bed, feeling he deserved a little self-pampering after being at work all day.

I debated what to drive to pick up my date. The repo truck was much newer and nicer on the inside than my old pickup. It also had two winches and a giant mechanical arm capable of lifting a car, which she might consider overkill.

Regardless, I decided the nicer interior was the better choice.

Katie wore a new red coat I'd never seen before, very striking on her—but it made me uneasy, somehow, that she was buying beautiful clothing while we were on our break. She wore her work grown-up clothes under it, and I caught her eyebrows rising when I shrugged off my coat and she saw the jacket and the new shirt. What that expression meant, though, I had no idea.

I faltered when I saw that her finger was bare of the engagement ring I'd given her. Could she have forgotten it? The stone had come from my mother's small jewelry collection, a lucid, flashing diamond.

I knew that if we were permanently unengaged, she would give the ring back. If she didn't, maybe it meant what she'd been saying. We were on a break. Dating. Having fun.

The Weathervane is a beautiful hotel-restaurant built of gigantic rocks mined from the local hills and waters, including a ten-ton monster shaped like the state of Michigan. The place used to be a grist mill in the 1800s, and hugs the north side of the Pine River—a steel-lined stream, dredged deep, that cuts Charlevoix in two. A drawbridge over the Pine is the only connection between the two halves of town. From our table we could see the bridge and the river, jammed full of broken ice that rolled like the spiked back of a giant dragon. I had no idea why the river didn't freeze solid like all the other self-respecting water in the area.

My last-minute instructions from Jimmy the Wise One were to keep the conversation light and fun. Don't press her. When in doubt, apologize. Even if you're not in doubt, apologize. Apparently, women really like apologies.

Our waiter brought bread and butter. The butter was extremely cold, as tough to cut as the tension at the table. Here we were, engaged, on a break, on a date. What do you even talk about, under such circumstances? I asked Katie if she had ever seen the *Emerald Isle* coming or going to Beaver Island, which was far offshore, only visible on clear days.

"Just once. It barely fits in the canal!"

"The Pine is a river, actually. It was here before the white man showed up and lined it with steel plates. It's the only river in the United States to flow in two directions simultaneously."

*"Right. Correct her,"* Alan groused. *"Lecture her with useless facts. Make her feel like an idiot."*

"Sorry. I could be wrong," I told her. I gratefully held out my glass when the waiter brought the wine. "Sorry. Did you hear about the woman who fell off the *Emerald Isle* that one time a few years ago?"

"Yes! I was friends with a guy who knew her. Nita?"

"Nina Otis."

*"And now we're talking about murder. On a date,"* Alan scolded.

"We don't know that she was murdered," I said peevishly.

Katie gave me a puzzled look. "What do you mean? You think she was murdered?"

"No, sorry. It was just . . . I was reading about it somewhere one time, and I wondered why the captain paged her."

"He did that?"

"Yeah, it was in the paper. At some point, they called for Nina Otis over the ship's loudspeaker."

"Oh. Well, maybe by then she had fallen overboard."

"Sure." I waited for her to get it. Didn't take her long.

"Oh, but that doesn't make sense. How would they know who she was? And if she had fallen, they would have done more than just page her. Like, what was she supposed to do, say, *Oh, I fell off the boat, and the only reason I need to get back on is because I'm being* paged?"

We laughed together at that one, a simple, just-like-it-always-was type of laugh that reminded me how easily I could talk to her. I had to resist reaching for her hand. Her blue eyes had a lovely light in them.

I put that light out around the time we finished our salads.

"So ... how much longer do you think you'll need, to, you know? Think things through. About us."

"*Ruddy,*" Alan moaned.

Katie set her fork down stiffly, her posture straightening and her mouth settling into a line. I wanted to shout at her to wait, *Don't say what you're about to say!*

I got a stay of execution. "Couldn't we just enjoy dinner?" she asked softly.

"Yeah, right, sorry, of course. I'm sorry. Sorry."

By the time we'd finished the whitefish we'd both ordered, I'd managed to make her laugh by relating the story of how Mark Stevens and Kenny MacDonell came to rob the Black Bear with shotguns that were not loaded because they couldn't afford shells.

"And now these guys are your friends?" she asked, grinning.

"Well, yeah. At least until I repo Mark's truck," I told her.

Her bemused look could have been, *What am I doing out with a big dumb repo man?* Or it could have been, *This man has an open heart and a really nice tow truck.*

Now that I had a working radio, I listened to NPR while I drove, which was ten times more pleasant than listening to Alan Lottner. This made me something of a man of the world, and I chatted knowledgably about the euro, the inflation rate, the Federal Reserve, and other things that were apparently all connected together. At least seven times during dinner Alan said, *"Let her talk"* and as much as he irritated me, I did just that.

"A buyer this time a year is great, because you know if they're out looking at houses in this weather, they're serious. But if you get a seller who wants top dollar, you're going to work really hard and then get fired before the snow melts for not getting any offers," she told me.

"And why do you want to be in this business?" I replied.

Her laughter was rueful. "*So much better to be in the business of throwing people off their roofs,"* Alan remarked acerbically. I wanted to throw *him* off the roof.

I drove her home, putting on a new CD playing her favorite singer, Michelle Featherstone. We drove down M-66, and my mood darkened only briefly as we passed the turnoff down to the ferry landing. My eyes found the spot in the frozen lake where I figured my car went in. Despite Amy Jo's information and despite Alan's serial killer fantasies, seeing that place still made me slightly ill.

Katie reached a hand out and touched me, her face wistful and sympathetic. Instantly, I felt better.

I was in love with Katie Lottner. I couldn't really be losing her, could I?

"So things might not be what they seem," I said after a moment. "I found that woman from the festival. The one who said Lisa Marie Walker was not in the car when it sank? Her name is Amy Jo Stefonick. I spoke to her."

"And?"

I glanced over—Katie was regarding me intently.

"And what she had to say makes some sense. She says she saw me pull into the 7-Eleven that night. And while I was inside, she saw Lisa Marie open the back door of my car and get out."

*"Let's not tell her about the other part, the man who helped her. I don't want to scare her,"* Alan cautioned.

I bit off my irritation. Katie was watching me with round eyes. *"Then what could have happened?"*

*There, see, Alan?* The story made no sense without the rest of it. I told her about what else Amy Jo had seen, and she put a hand to her mouth. "This . . . My God, Ruddy, I don't know what to say," she commented when I was finished. "It changes everything."

"Yes, it does."

"Are you okay? This is huge." Her gaze searched my face.

"I'm okay. I'm still processing it. And trying to see if I can figure out, if she wasn't in the car, what really happened."

She squeezed my hand. "That's so *you*, Ruddy. Even though you didn't do anything wrong, you still feel responsible."

I pulled into the driveway and stopped, and we sat and looked at each other. She slid across the seat and kissed me, softly and gently, on the cheek and then quickly on the lips, and then she pulled back and gazed at me, passion and speculation in her eyes. This part of our relationship had always worked.

*"Ruddy! Stop!"* Alan yelled desperately.

I straightened abruptly. If I took things where I wanted them to go, it would be with her father right there, not just watching, but participating. There was no way I could subject him to something like that.

Why the hell wasn't he asleep?

"Is everything okay?" Katie asked me, a bit puzzled.

"Yeah, of course. I just . . . need to get home to the dog," I told her, loathing myself.

She smelled the lie and a coolness came into her eyes. At that moment I *hated* Alan Lottner.

"This was nice, Ruddy," she whispered after a moment. She slid away from me, and I controlled the impulse to go after her. "But . . ."

"No, please don't say *but*. There doesn't have to be any *but*, does there?" I pleaded.

She gave me an unreadable look. She seemed angry, somehow, or sad. "I just don't think you're the sort of man my father would have liked," she whispered. "It's like I can feel him disapproving or something. He always told me I could be anything I wanted to be, and now here I am." She gestured around the inside of the repo truck and shrugged.

"You *can* be whatever you want to be," I told her fiercely. "Look, you decided you wanted to sell real estate, so you studied and took the test and that's what you're going to do next. I'm proud of you."

"Thank you," she responded tersely.

"I mean it," I proclaimed desperately. I'd made her angry, somehow, and could feel the whole wonderful evening going down the drain.

"I know. I should go."

I walked her to her door but didn't try to kiss her again, and not just because of Alan. Something told me she wouldn't have accepted my affections at that moment. She slid inside her house, giving me a small wave, and I crunched down the snowy driveway to my truck. Alan was mercifully silent.

He and I didn't say a word to each other as I drove through town and turned onto M-66. I was focused on my driving and didn't even notice the sheriff's vehicle until it flipped its lights on behind me.

# 15

## You're Going to Be Mad

I was unsurprised to see Deputy Timms struggle out of the front seat of his patrol car, his belly pinning him under the steering wheel for a delicious moment. There was no sign of Sheriff Porterfield.

I rolled down my window. "Evening, Deputy. Where's your sheriff daddy tonight?"

Timms turned his flashlight up into my eyes, the beam so bright, I could feel heat. I clamped my eyelids down and waited patiently. Finally it dropped away. "License and registration, please."

I handed over the documents, and he yanked them out of my hand. Every single motion he made was an aggressive act—he marched his way back to his vehicle, stomping on chunks of ice with real force. The whole ritual of running my license was theater—he knew who I was, knew there were no outstanding warrants.

"*What a dick,*" Alan said.

I grinned. "He's the guy your daughter was going to marry before I came along," I reminded him. Alan didn't have anything to say to that.

Timms returned and handed me back my papers. "You know why I pulled you over?"

"Because you saw me out with my fiancée?" I responded. Even

in the desaturating light from his flashlight, I could see his face redden. This was apparently news to him.

"*Careful,*" Alan warned softly. Timms's grip on his flashlight was tightening, and I could picture him hitting me with it and then me taking it from him and hitting him back.

"You crossed the center line back there," Deputy Dumbell finally told me.

"That's bullshit."

"I'm citing you. These moving violations, they're expensive."

"Let me know if you have trouble spelling any words."

He sneered at me. "I guess you don't get it. My job is to make sure that every time you hit the road, you get a traffic ticket. One of these days, you and your Arab boss are going to get the message—no repos in Sheriff Porterfield's territory."

"Arab? Oh my God, you think Kramer is an *Arab* name?" I hooted.

He scowled. "I don't give a damn what kind of name it is. I'm just telling you what's what. I see you breaking the law, I give you a ticket and that's that."

"So wait, is it what's what, or that's that? They seem like two different things."

Alan laughed.

Timms handed me my traffic ticket. "Drive carefully and obey the speed limit," he mocked.

I waited until he was long out of sight before I scrupulously signaled and pulled onto the road, my speedometer a good five under the limit.

"*No idea what Katie ever saw in that guy,*" Alan groused.

"Yeah? Well, what about me?"

"*Sorry?*"

"Katie feels like you've been sending her messages that I'm not the man for her. Have you?"

"*I don't know what you're talking about.*"

"You don't? Haven't you been saying I'm not good enough for

your daughter? Well, take a look at the alternatives, Alan. How long will it be before her *landlord* figures out a way to get her back? You heard her: She's vulnerable. She needs to figure things out. And she's getting subconscious messages from you to dump Ruddy McCann and get back together with Deputy Dumbbell!"

*"You don't have to shout. I can hear you just fine."*

"Deflection!" I accused. "You're deflecting because you don't like the question. Let me ask you something, Alan. Have you noticed anything different about me and Kermit?"

*"What?"* he responded, truly puzzled by my shift in subject.

"Kermit Kramer. My sister's husband. Remember when I first met him? I despised the guy. And you kept saying that my sister loved him. And you were right. But I couldn't see it because you know what? Nobody was good enough for Becky. If it were up to me, she'd never get married. Just like nobody is good enough for your daughter. But she's going to wind up with somebody someday. And when I got to know Kermit, I realized, he's not that bad. That's what you've missed, these eighteen months. I looked for Kermit's qualities and then realized the most important one was that he loved Becky. The same way I love your daughter! So if you want to send her messages, tell her *that*."


I woke up early the next morning because my dog was snoring. I rolled over and gave him a gentle shove. "Jake. You're snoring."

He eyed me blearily, clearly not believing me.

My imaginary friend was asleep. "Okay, now you sleep, Alan. *Now,*" I chided him, thinking how much more convenient it would have been for him to wink out last night at Katie's. I would not even have minded if he'd snored.

I dressed and went into the kitchen. The folder with the printouts from the library was sitting on the table, though I didn't remember putting it there. I opened it and flipped idly through the pictures—Alan's lineup of supposed murder victims. I stopped dead when I came across a news clipping I'd not seen before—basically a recounting of the sad fate of Nina Otis, who had fallen off the car ferry and drowned. This one had a photograph of Nina on the boat itself, taken, the caption read, *most likely just a few moments before she fell unseen into the cold waters of Lake Michigan.*

The picture wasn't a very good one—Nina wasn't even the intended subject. Three young women were posing and smiling, and Nina, on the left, was both blurry and cut off by the frame. It looked as if she had been trying to get out of the way of the photographer when the picture was snapped.

I was troubled by two things. First, how could anyone identify the blurry woman when less than half her body was caught by the camera? And second, how the hell did the printout get into the folder? I knew I didn't put it there.

*Alan.*


As if sensing I needed to have a stern conversation with him, Alan slept through two repossessions that day, and was still asleep when I showed up at the Black Bear to see how my career as a bouncer was progressing. It was a lively night for early February—meaning, almost no one was there. Jimmy was at the bar, watching one of Becky's home improvement channels. It looked to me as if people were turning their garage into a rec room, which to me meant they would be parking their vehicles outside where they would be easier to repo.

I sat down with the Wolfingers, who were discussing the best time to take their Hawaii trip.

"Why wait until March?" Wilma pouted. "I want to go *now*."

"You don't go now," Claude said dismissively. "You wait until you're sick of winter."

"I *am* sick of winter!" Wilma responded.

"No, you're not!" Claude snapped, glaring at her. "You get

sick of winter in March, when it starts to sleet and the slush freezes at night."

I thought they both had good points.

Wilma shook her head, agitating her huge bejeweled earrings. "No. Stop trying to tell me how to think! I like March. The sun comes out. Sometimes."

"Jesus! I'm telling ya, you don't know what you're talking about! I've lived here my whole life, and March is the worst month!" Claude crashed his fist onto the table.

"I want to go *now*! You're not the only person who gets to vote!"

"Goddamn it, Wilma, do you see? You see? It's like you don't even have a brain. Everyone knows you don't go to Hawaii now; you go when I say!" Claude bellowed at her.

Wilma had perhaps a quarter of an inch of beer in her mug, which she tossed into Claude's face with the kind of accuracy that comes from years of practice. I wondered how many more times I was going to see that in my life.

"You can go now if you want, but I'm taking my trip in March," Claude told her as he wiped off his face.

"Fine."

"*Fine.*"

I stood up and reached for her empty mug. "You know what you should do? You should let Kermit help you with this."

They gaped at me, momentarily distracted. "Huh?"

"He's good at this. It's how he used to run his fiscals. Give me the card, Claude."

Claude handed over the plastic case with the one-in-five card in it. "Don't lose that," he fretted.

I went toward the back of the kitchen, where Becky and Kermit were working on installing a surveillance camera so that we could see that there was never anyone in the alley. I made a couple of photocopies of the card, telling Kermit I was ready to do the deal—buy the Wolfingers their tickets. I asked him to call the one-in-five phone room and make sure they would have their "vacation," their hotel room in the flophouse.

"When do they want to go?" he asked me.

"I'd say get them the hell out of here as fast as you can." I told him to let me know how much—I had the cash.

"You want us to split it with you?" Becky asked.

I shook my head, touched. "No, thanks. But I appreciate the offer."

The two of them glanced at each other, passing a married-couple message between them. "There's something else, Ruddy," Becky advised. They were both grinning as if they had another new repo truck waiting outside.

"Yes?"

"You're going to be an uncle!" Becky's eyes positively glowed.

"What? Wait, *what*? No kidding! That's amazing. I'm . . . amazed." And I *was* amazed. Just a few years ago Becky's options in the male department were limited to the drunken passes feebly launched at her at last call by swaying, slurring idiots who didn't see me glowering behind them. Now she was married and starting a family—everything had changed.

"We've been trying to be patrimonious for months," Kermit told me.

I had a vision then: Becky's children playing with *my* kids under Bob the Bear; me, not just Uncle Ruddy but Daddy, married to Katie, innocent of all crimes, a pillar in the community, with a responsible job. Well, I'd still repo cars, but more for the sport than for the money.

I gave Becky a hug and shook Kermit's hand and thought afterward I probably should have hugged him, too.

Becky told me they were keeping the news under wraps until she was further along, and I promised their secret was safe with me. I went back to the bar, floating on the good news. Jimmy hadn't moved. I put a fresh mug under the tap for Wilma. "Hey Jimmy," I hailed him cheerfully, "date with Katie went pretty well last night. I mean, really well. We didn't sleep together, but I think she wanted to."

"Okay," he said, still watching the TV.

"I mean, it seemed to go a little south at the very end, but almost because we didn't go to bed, if that makes sense."

"Sure."

"So, I thought maybe I should call her in a little while? Apologize a couple dozen times?"

He shook his head. "No. I wouldn't."

"Why not? I thought you always say women like it when you call them after a date."

"Not when you're on a break. Not when it didn't end good. You need to wait a few days."

I looked up at the screen to see what was so damn fascinating. Two men were putting up drywall. "Isn't there a book I can read or something? None of this makes any sense to me," I complained.

Jimmy just shrugged. "It's not supposed to make sense. It's relationships."

I grabbed a mug for Claude. "How's Alice?" I asked idly as I pulled on the tap.

Jimmy finally tore his eyes away from the riveting drywall demonstration. "Oh," he said.

That didn't sound good. "I'll be right back."

I gave the Wolfingers their refills. They were looking at Hawaii photos on Wilma's phone, compliments of Becky's free Wi-Fi.

The cell phone waylaid me on my way back to find out what had gone wrong with Alice and Jimmy. It was Katie's number on my caller ID, and I answered with real pleasure—maybe I shouldn't call her, but I certainly should answer if she called me!

Her voice was rushed. "Ruddy! I have to go to Grand Rapids. It's my aunt Kjersti. My mom's older sister. She's in the hospital."

"I'll drive you."

She paused. "That's really nice, Ruddy. I need my car, though.

I don't know how long I'll need to be there. They say she just collapsed."

"If you need me, I'll come down. Or I could drive you down now and tow your car behind us."

She laughed at this. "That's sweet. But I think I'll be okay. I'm going to go now, but I'll call you," she promised.

"Please do. And please drive carefully."

"I will."

"I'm going to miss you."

"Me, too. Ruddy? I need to get on the road."

"Text me when you get there."

"I'll send a soccer ball and a kangaroo," she vowed.

We hung up, laughing. I wondered if the cone of silence on Becky's pregnancy extended to Katie—I would have to ask.

"You know," I said to Jimmy when I returned to the bar, "my sister's in the back. You could put on the basketball game."

"No, it's okay. I want to see what's going to happen."

"What's going to happen is that they're going to finish putting up drywall," I predicted.

He gave me a blank look.

"So, what's going on? You and Alice. Something's bothering you, I can tell."

"I'm just . . . You're going to be mad."

"Oh?" I raised my eyebrows at him, truly surprised. I didn't really get angry at Jimmy, not with any heat.

"Yeah, it's about Alice. She's going to ask her husband for a divorce."

"Huh."

"You're not angry?"

"No," I replied. "Of course not, Jimmy. I've got no right to be angry. It's your life."

I wondered, though, how William Blanchard would react to *this*.

Alan woke up while I was at the Bear, but was uncharacteristically silent. I walked home, wondering why the sky was clear when it had been so cloudy all day. Jake was already back in the bedroom, his head on my pillow. His tail thumped when I stroked his ears.

I looked around my house—my very *clean* house. Either Jake had tidied up, or someone else had been at work.

I pulled out my tequila bottle and gave myself a generous pour. My Pavlovian response to the smell of the strong liquor was normally to go to my chair and pick up my Lee Child novel, but I resisted the urge. Instead I went to my small table, opened the folder, and pointedly pulled out the new Nina Otis article.

"*Look—,*" Alan began defensively.

"No, *you* look, Alan," I interrupted angrily. "What is the one thing you must never, never do? I don't care if my kitchen is dirty or my house is on fire—when I'm sleeping, you may not take control of my body. *Ever.*"

"*I just had an idea—*"

"I don't care!"

"*Please listen,*" he begged. "*I found out some things that are really important.*"

"How did you do this, anyway?"

"*I went to the Black Bear and used Becky's laptop. She leaves it there behind the bar most the time. Can I just tell you—*"

"That's breaking and entering," I thundered. "And using my sister's equipment? Do you know how furious I am at you?"

"*I didn't break. I used your key, and just listen. There's more to all this. You know the woman who fell off the docks in Charlevoix? The news accounts got it wrong. Nobody saw her fall. A witness said he saw her headed in the direction of the docks, and that she was carrying what looked like a bottle of whisky in a paper bag.*"

"So?"

"So don't you see? Lisa Marie gets out of your car, she's drunk, a man 'helps' her, and five days later they find her floating in the water. This woman is drinking heavily, she's got a bottle with her, she vanishes. And her body also doesn't show up for five days— pretty coincidental, don't you think? And what about the woman on the sailboat? Her husband said they were drinking a lot that night. He passed out belowdecks. Everyone thinks she went topside and fell off. But the water was calm, there was a full moon— wouldn't she yell? Wouldn't her husband hear the splash? They were anchored just twenty yards out—on a still night, wouldn't people onshore hear something? And her body washes up in Boyne City. Guess how many days after she disappeared."

"You're going to say five days."

"Yes! Well, four. Four days. But when her husband called it in, volunteers turned out in force—it was summertime, plenty of boaters to help out. They looked all over, starting, of course, right there in the lake at Boyne City. So where was she all that time?"

"She probably sank," I reasoned. "And then her gasses caused her to rise."

"Or, what if someone saw her on the boat? Somebody who has a thing for intoxicated women. Someone who could row out from shore, or something. He grabs her and, even if there's a struggle, her husband is zonked and doesn't hear it."

"Someone who likes to drown drunk girls," I summed up skeptically.

"Don't forget the autopsy on Lisa Marie. There's something else he likes."

"That doesn't explain Nina Otis," I pointed out after a few moments. "Even if she were drunk, there was no time to do anything on the boat except push her off."

"It's a two-hour trip," Alan advised.

"There's no place to do what you're suggesting. I've been on the boat."

"*Oh yeah? Every inch of it? Every compartment? And it's a car ferry—what if our helpful friend has a panel van?*"

I swallowed a slug of tequila.

"*God, that stuff is vile,*" he grumbled.

I ignored this. "Every single thing you say might be true, but they're all dead ends. Lisa Marie vanished, and the one witness has told us all she knows. A woman might or might not have fallen off the docks. Someone might have grabbed a drunk lady off a boat, but no one saw anything, or the cops would have been all over it. Maybe Nina Otis was pushed, but if someone saw that, they would have reported it."

"*They're not all dead ends,*" Alan insisted. "*You got the sister on Beaver Island. The surprise visit. Somebody paging Nina Otis—what if that was our man, luring her up to the bridge?*"

"She never responded to the page."

"*So she was ambushed on the way!*"

Jake had come out to see what all the yelling was about. He yawned pointedly at me—shouldn't we be sleeping? Wasn't that what night was for? And day, too, for that matter?

"Why is it so important to you to prove there's any connection? We're spending all this energy on something that might not have anything to do with Lisa Marie," I criticized.

"*But I think they* are *all connected. I think we're on to something. I think when the guy who took Lisa Marie read about your accident, it gave him an idea on how to dispose of bodies.*"

I was grimly silent, thinking that if Alan was right, my accident had provided the inspiration for several murders.

"*I think we should go to Beaver Island and speak to Nina's sister, ask her about the surprise visit.*"

"And what I think is that you're ignoring the point of this conversation, which is your unlawful appropriation of the body McCann."

"*I'm sorry, but the place was turning into a pigsty. I couldn't help it.*"

"That's ridiculous. You could, too, help it."

*"The cutlery was all in a jumble. There was no organization. Some of your water glasses were ends up and some ends down. It was driving me crazy."*

"There's a reason why *Alan* is an anagram for *anal*."

*"I just did what anyone would do."*

"No, you did what *you* would do. And you will never do it again."

*"Fine. Can we go?"*

"What could the sister possibly know?"

*"We can't answer that until we talk to her! Ruddy, it's the only next step we have. What else can we do?"*

Jake went to his blanket on the floor and collapsed with a groan. I pulled down the rest of my tequila. Alan waited anxiously, like a teenager who has asked to use the family car and is waiting for Dad to make up his mind. It wasn't so much that I thought Alan's idea made sense. It was just that if I didn't do this, I wouldn't be doing anything at all. "Okay," I decided. "I'll go."

# 16

## Then You Die

In the winter you can get to Beaver Island on a snowmobile if you don't mind the idea that you might hit open water and die. You can also drive your car across—the ice is thick enough except for where it isn't, and then you die. Or you can fly in a little two-engine airplane for a hundred bucks round trip. I picked the airplane.

Alan, as it turns out, equates *plane ride* with *plane crash*. As soon as he saw the tiny two-engine aircraft, he pretty much wanted to back out of the whole deal, but one of the consequences of being a voice in my head is you go where I go.

Around five hundred people live on the island in the summer, fewer in the winter. I was met by a guy in an ancient Jeep who I always call when I'm out on the island, looking for a repo. He was pretty surprised to hear from me because I've never once gone out there in the winter—you steal a car in the winter, the only way to get it to the mainland is to drive it on the ice, and then you die. His last name was also McCann, which was how I found out I had distant relatives who had once lived on the island. There was even a McCann House, which was both older and nicer than the McCann house in Kalkaska. He and I called each other by our last names. He was shorter and older and thinner than I, probably forty, and looked as if he had decided personal grooming wasn't worth the bother, his long reddish hair curling down and sort of blending into his ratty beard.

"Hey, McCann," he greeted me, holding out a gloved hand to shake. I got in the rattling old Jeep and told him I needed to see Audrey Strang—did he know her? He gave me a look—it wasn't as if anyone could have somehow escaped his attention on such a small island.

As was true of every trip on Beaver Island, it didn't take long to reach our destination: four neat little cabins in a row next to a main house, all of them well maintained log homes. A fancy sign proclaimed that we had arrived at AUDREY'S B&B. I told McCann I'd text him when I needed him to pick me up, waving at him as he backed down the driveway. There was far less snow out on the island than I'd expected—the little strip of land was too small to have lake effect. Still, snowmobile tracks in and out of the driveway told me that Audrey, who McCann said was a divorced lady, didn't use a car in the winter. A woman in a front window watched me trudge to the front door and I waved at her, too.

*"That's got to be Audrey Strang,"* Alan sang, positively giddy to be alive after the bumpy plane ride.

She opened the door as I was walking up the wooden steps and stomping the snow off my toes. "You don't have a reservation. Are you here for a cabin?" she asked, letting me in. She was an attractive woman, probably fifty, with short sandy hair and hazel eyes. Her home was nice and warm, and she wore a sweatshirt with a moose on it that matched her eyes. The sweatshirt, not the moose.

"No, ma'am. I'm here to . . ." Well, I should have rehearsed this part. I fumbled with the papers I had shoved in my pocket. "I am wondering if I could talk to you about your sister. Nina Otis."

She blinked, cocking her head. "All right," she said slowly.

*"Don't just show her the picture. Talk to her first, get her com-fortable,"* Alan instructed me, as if I didn't make a living talking to people about their relatives.

She invited me to take off my coat and told me she was just making some coffee, which sounded really good to me. While she ground some beans and put water in the coffee maker, she asked me if I was a cop. I said no, my interest was personal. "All right," she said again.

When she heard my last name, we walked through the tenuous relationship I had to the McCanns still on the island. We chatted a bit about her bed-and-breakfast business, and she revealed that she was going to leave in a week to go to Florida. It was the kind of drawn-out conversation that icebound people indulge in.

"I'm glad I came out when I did, then. I would have hated to miss you," I told her.

"*We could have called ahead,*" Alan observed, and not for the first time. I'm a repo man, so it sort of goes against my nature to phone people and tell them I'm coming.

I detailed for her what bothered me about the newspaper story—the "surprise" visit. She nodded warily. "Tell me again why you're asking?"

Here we go. I explained that I was looking into the drowning deaths of some local women, because I was blamed for one of those deaths, but now had reason to believe I wasn't involved. She asked me a lot of questions about that, and I answered truthfully, revealing everything except the fact that I had a dead Realtor in my head, who was making impatient noises over how long this was taking. Most of the information I've gotten from people has come from sitting and talking about something else until they felt comfortable enough to tell me where Uncle Bob was hiding his Chevrolet.

We had both finished two cups of coffee when I brought out the out-of-focus photograph. "Anyway," I said, smoothing out the piece of paper.

"Yes, of course," Audrey murmured. Her hazel eyes went milky for a moment as she remembered. "I'm actually the one who identified her in this shot."

"Really? It seems pretty blurred."

"Oh. I know. But that's her. I recognize the outfit."

*"It's just an outfit,"* Alan protested. *"Jean shorts and a red shirt?"*

I cleared my throat. "Is there something unusual about the clothing, then?"

"Oh no," Audrey said, shaking her head. "No, that's just the sort of thing she always wore."

"You think you would have recognized her without the clothing?"

"Maybe by the hair—that's how she wore it, long with a flip. Otherwise, no, it's a pretty bad picture."

"Ah. So . . . how did you know about the surprise visit? Not much of a surprise if she told you about it."

Audrey got up and poured a little more coffee for herself. I shook my head when she gestured with the pot in my direction. "I suppose it doesn't matter anymore," she said with a sigh, sitting back down.

"Sorry?"

"She was coming to see me, but it wasn't a surprise. She was coming to spend the afternoon in one of my cabins. With her . . . boyfriend."

"With her boyfriend."

"She was married to someone else at the time. So, you know."

"I see."

"Nina's husband was killed in a car wreck last summer, and the boyfriend's divorced now. I can't imagine anyone would mind me talking about it."

*"Find out the boyfriend's name!"* Alan practically squealed.

"Does the boyfriend live here?" I asked instead.

"Here, on Beaver Island? No. I forget what he did for a living, but he had some business here, or at least that's what he told people."

"So was he on the boat that day, the *Emerald Isle*?"

"Yes. He came straight here when it docked. He was pretty frantic, but of course he couldn't call the cops. I had to phone them and say she was coming for a visit. I don't know why I said it was a surprise. I guess because it was hush-hush. Their plan was to go back on the last boat. Her husband didn't know anything about it. Didn't suspect a thing." Audrey sighed, remembering.

"So he was the one who paged her. The boyfriend."

She brought herself back to the present, focusing on my face. "What do you mean?"

"She was paged. The loudspeaker called her name. He must have been looking for her," I elaborated.

"That sounds right."

"And what is his name?"

"David Leinberger. God, I haven't thought about him in several years."

"Tall guy, sandy hair? Maybe forty years old?" I guessed.

"Yes, you know him?"

"We've met, yes." I drummed my fingers on the blurry photograph. "Audrey . . . do you think there's a chance David might have had a reason to hurt Nina? Was she demanding he get a divorce, anything like that?"

"Oh!" Her eyes brightened in surprise. She considered it but then shook her head. "No, and there's something you need to hear, Ruddy. Nina had a problem with alcohol. At the time of the accident, her drinking was pretty much out of control. David, too, for that matter—I sometimes thought that was the main reason they were together. So I never doubted for a minute that Nina could have gotten drunk and fallen off the ferry. Her car had dents all up and down."

Alan drew in an audible breath. I bit my lip in irritation—how could he do that when he had no lungs?

"They don't serve booze on the *Emerald Isle,* though," I objected eventually.

Audrey shrugged and gave me a sad smile. "I imagine she had a few before boarding. She even drank at breakfast."

I refused an offer of pie until I found out it was raspberry. We had more coffee, ate pie, and talked about nothing of consequence. Alan moaned with pleasure at the pie. When we were finished, I texted McCann and advised I was ready to go back to the airport. I told Audrey how sincerely I appreciated her help, and she invited me to come out anytime. For just a minute, there was something flirty in her gaze, but we shook hands formally when McCann's Jeep showed up.

Alan fell asleep, waiting for the pilot to come fly us back to the mainland, but it was a quick nap and he was back as I steered the repo truck out of the Charlevoix Airport parking lot. "*Where are we headed?*"

"I have an appointment with Schaumburg, remember?"

"*Oh. Right,*" he said dismissively, as if having the psychiatrist threatening to send me back to jail was no big deal.

"Are you satisfied now?"

"*What do you mean?*"

"We know what happened to Nina. Her sister said she was an alcoholic. She got drunk, waiting for the ferry. She got on the *Emerald Isle,* and she and David Leinberger didn't find each other. She tries to dive out of a photo being taken by some tourists because she doesn't want anyone knowing she's making a little trip out to Beaver Island for hanky-panky. Probably she's trying to avoid being seen. Maybe she gets sick and leans over the railing to throw up, and that's it—she goes in. Meanwhile, Leinberger can't find her and eventually goes and has her paged."

"*I can't believe that's how you interpret it,*" Alan scoffed.

"Well, what the hell do *you* think, Alan?"

"*I think there's a man out there who preys on women who have had too much to drink. I think he grabbed Nina on the boat* and pulled her into his panel van. Maybe he held her captive on Beaver Island somewhere. Did you think of that?"

"No, and you didn't either," I retorted. "You just came up with it now."

"What difference does that make?"

"You know what? I could ask the same of this whole day. What's the difference? We're right back to zero on Nina Otis and have even less to show for figuring out what might have happened to Lisa Marie."

"We need to talk to David Leinberger."

I groaned.

"You said he was a friend of yours, right? Let's go ask him about Nina. Audrey said he's divorced, so what difference does it make?"

I was silent.

"Ruddy? He's a friend?"

"Not exactly."

"What do you mean?"

"He's a client."

"A client? You don't have clients. You . . . oh," Alan said as he got it.

"Right. I repossessed his car."


Dr. Schaumburg feigned surprise when he opened the door to his waiting room, where Alan had fallen asleep and I had nearly joined him, relaxing in an overstuffed chair. "Why, Mr. McCann, you actually came to your scheduled appointment," he marveled dryly.

He invited me in and asked me a bunch of questions that were really none of his business, so I sort of hunched my shoulders and answered curtly. I was fine. Yes, recovered from my injuries. Yes, positive that Yancy's dive down the stairs was not my fault. Glad to be here, sorry to have been so negligent. No, I had not heard from Alan Lottner. (This was true; I didn't ever hear him, not technically, not with my ears.)

"I have samples to get you started on your meds," he told me. He handed over some blister packs of little pills, along with a typed-up instruction sheet. He wanted me to call him if I had any one of what seemed like a pretty gruesome list of potential side effects. I put the pills in my pocket, nodding, thinking I would flush them down the toilet on my way out of the building.

"I want you back in ten days for a urine test," he said, fixing his eyes on me like a general giving me a direct order.

"Sure," I grunted.

"We both know what will happen if you fail the test."

"I won't fail. My urine is great at tests." Not so much as a smile flickered on his face. I stood. "We done?"

"No, we have some time. I want to hear more about Alan. Why do you suppose you've not heard from him?"

I was going to say, *Because of the medication I've been taking,* but I bit it off. "I have no idea what Alan's been up to," I finally responded evasively.

He mulled this over. I felt myself getting angry.

"What does his voice sound like?" Schaumburg probed.

"I don't know. Like a voice. Are you telling me you never have a voice in your head? Never say to yourself, you need to start going to the gym? That you should have asked out that one girl in high school, that you can't forget to mail your check to the tax people?"

"That's different than having a voice with a separate identity," Schaumburg informed me pedantically. "Having your own voice in your own head is pretty common. Having a voice that thinks independently, that urges you to do things you might not otherwise do—that's another matter entirely."

What really irritated me was how spot-on his observations were. If it weren't for Alan's pleadings, I would be focused on

Lisa Marie Walker and wouldn't have flown out to Beaver Island.

"You seem angry," he noted after a moment.

"Well, yeah, I guess it pisses me off that you're so smug about all this."

"Am I smug about this?" he answered, looking mildly surprised. "Tell me more about that."

"You act like I'm a danger to society, like I'm criminally insane."

"I never used any of those words," Schaumburg objected softly. "I just want you to see that what you've come to regard as normal is not actually all that common. Your own voice, as I said, sure, telling you not to eat that bagel." He patted his stomach. "But a voice belonging to someone else, that's actually very unusual."

"Is it?" I grated. "Let me tell you, I hear another voice all the time, and it's not Alan Lottner. Yeah, that's right; raise your eyebrows. It's my father's voice. I've heard it my whole life, always telling me to work harder, to throw another hundred passes, to study more. And you know what he says now? He says that I brought shame to the family. That I took a fantastic opportunity and flushed it down the toilet. That he never missed a game, never missed a practice, was there for me every mile and minute of every day, and then I drove into the lake and ruined everything!" My voice had risen to a hoarse shout, and I could feel my pulse in my temple. "Is that crazy? Do I need a pill for that, Doctor? Because I know a lot of guys who feel the same way about their dads, and nobody tells them they better get on medication or they'll be sent to *jail*."

After a minute I calmed down, wondering how much damage I had just done to myself.

"No, you may be right," Schaumburg shocked me by acknowledging. "You and your father were very close, weren't you?"

I nodded, rendered mute by my own emotions.

"Children often strive to please their mothers and fathers. And often our biggest achievers, our top performers, felt that in the end they never measured up to their parents' expectations. My own father was also a psychiatrist, at the University of Michigan. He never understood why I moved my practice up here, instead of making a fortune in the city. To him, just because my wife loves it here was not any sort of reason for such a sacrifice— he and my mother got divorced, because his career always came ahead of family. I don't hear his voice, but I do feel his disapproval every day that I deposit my meager little paycheck." A sad smile drifted onto his lips. I had heard quotes around "meager little paycheck" and knew those were his father's words.

"Is this so much different, then? I've got this voice—I *had* this voice," I interrupted myself in correction. "Always questioning what I was doing, wanting me to be more than just a repo man if I was going to date his daughter. So? A whole chorus of fathers, telling me I've got to do better."

"Yes, I am afraid it is different, Ruddy," Schaumburg replied. "You have a treatable disorder. But the medications will help you deal with it. We'll talk about that at our next visit."

After a second I realized what he was saying: My time was up. When I got to the door, he softly called my name. I turned.

"Don't forget," he said blandly. "Urine test. Ten days."

# 17

## Who Is Rachel Rodriguez?

I had a message on my phone: Kermit.

*"Hey, Ruddy. It's Kermit. Kramer. I conducted a few inquisitions into Claude and Wilma's one-in-five drop, the Hawaii scenario. So the room itself, the phones, is being run by a guy my brother familiarizes with, and it's our customer who is behind it all. William Blanchard, I mean. He provided the capitalization. Uh, Jake says hi."*

Alan woke up on the way to Gaylord, a town of close to four thousand people due east of East Jordan. I told him what Kermit had to say, that Blanchard had bankrolled the whole Hawaii vacation thing.

*"I still don't get how it makes money,"* Alan confessed.

"I don't either. Next time I see Blanchard, I'll ask him. Hey, Alan, I've got some good news."

*"You've decided to go to the gym and lose fifty pounds,"* he guessed.

"What? I don't need to lose *fifty pounds*."

*"Even five would help. You've got to start exercising."*

"It's winter. Every animal gains weight in winter."

*"No, animals starve in winter. Only humans gain weight in winter, but if they go to the gym, they gain less."*

"Why are we even talking about this?"

"*Our pants are tight. They're not only ugly, they're uncomfortable.*"

"They are *my* pants and you know what? Forget it. I'm not telling you anything."

"*No, tell me.*"

"I'm just some fat guy in bad pants. And Jimmy Growe is an idiot, and you laugh at the Wolfingers—you're the most intolerant person I've ever met, Alan," I stormed.

He was silent. I stared moodily at the empty road ahead of me.

"*Okay,*" he finally said quietly.

"Okay what?"

"*You may have a point. I never intended it, but I see how some of my remarks might cause offense.*"

A few more miles rolled by. "*What did you really want to tell me?*" he asked hesitantly.

"All right. It's a secret, but I guess I don't have to worry about you telling anyone, do I? Guess who's having a baby."

"*Oh my God, no,*" Alan moaned.

"What? Wait, you think it's Katie? And all you can think of to say is 'God no'?"

"*It's not her?*"

"Of course not."

Alan sighed in relief.

"It's my sister, thanks very much," I told him. "I'm going to be an uncle."

He congratulated me sincerely and told me I needed to buy a gift. "Like, now? I thought that's for the baby shower," I objected.

"*No, that's what you do if it is someone close to you; you get a gift right away.*"

"Like, a baseball mitt, maybe? Hockey mask?"

Alan laughed, knowing I was joking. Or hoping, anyway.

David Leinberger was easy to find—he ran a tax preparation

and accounting service out of a converted Victorian house, just two doors down from the bank that financed the Chevy Malibu I'd repossessed from him. I guess the people in the bank were too embarrassed to walk a few yards down the street and ask for their collateral, so I drove the forty miles from Kalkaska and hooked him up. David came out to ask what was going on when I had the front wheels lifted off the ground, and communicated a certain amount of displeasure with events. He was my height and spent a lot of time poking his finger in my face. Experience has taught me that fingers aren't too dangerous unless they're curled around a trigger, so I let him point and swear and threaten while I finished putting the safety chains on, and he was still yelling as I drove away.

This would be our first reunion.

*"What are you going to say? What if he recognizes you?"* Alan fretted.

"I don't know; let's just see what happens."

*"We should have a plan."*

"My plan is to see what happens. Stop talking now, Alan."

The other half of the house was a defunct hair salon, the windows cloudy with dust, but Leinberger's side was tidy, the snow shoveled. The sign above the door to the small accounting business invited me to come right in, so that's what I did. There was a tiny outer office with a desk and a phone, empty of people, but I could hear someone in the back, moving around, so I waited, wiping the wet off my feet and onto the welcome mat.

"Hi!" David greeted me, coming out smiling. He looked in better shape than last time I'd seen him—he'd lost weight, it appeared. As Alan seemed eager to point out, I'd sort of gone in the opposite direction. His clothes were pressed, and he wore a sports coat—Alan's kind of guy, basically. "What can I help you with today?"

"Mr. Leinberger?"

I held out my hand, but before he could reach for it, his gaze darkened. "I know who you are," he said after a moment. "Mc-Cann."

"Yeah. Hi."

"What do you want?"

"Just to talk. Do you have a minute?"

"Talk about what?"

"That's what I want to talk about."

Okay, even I had to admit that didn't make a lot of sense. His facial features were hardening. "You need an accounting service?"

"No. Well, actually, I probably do, but I can't afford one."

"Then I can't help you." He folded his arms.

I sighed. "I was just out on Beaver Island, talking to Audrey Strang. You remember her?"

He regarded me warily. "So?"

"So, something has come up concerning her sister, Nina. I was hoping you could help me shed some light on a few things."

"You've got to be kidding me."

"I think it was you who went to the bridge and asked the captain to page Nina, am I right? You were supposed to meet up with her on the *Emerald Isle,* but you couldn't find her anywhere. But did you see her at all that day? On the boat, or before?"

"Are you stupid or something?"

"I do get asked that from time to time. Look, Mr. Leinberger. David."

"Did you notice my car out there, when you came in?"

I didn't know where this was going, so I just shook my head.

"That's because it's not here. It's in the shop. It's *always* in the shop. It's an utter piece of crap. I'd like a decent vehicle, but I can't get one. Because of the repo on my credit. I was just at the Chevy dealer last week."

"All I do is what the bank tells me, David."

"No. *No.* You didn't even talk to me. Tax season was just getting started. I could have gotten caught up in just a few days. You didn't have to repo my car! You know what it did to my reputation in this town when that happened?"

"*You just stole his car? Without even talking to him?*" Alan demanded indignantly. I wondered just what he thought a repo man *did*.

"I went through hell that year. My marriage fell apart, I lost Nina, business went to shit . . . but I was getting it back together. I had been sober for twenty-one days when you showed up. I could have told you all of that—I was *trying* to tell you—but you just drove off without a word."

"Would it make a difference if I told you I was sorry?"

"What do *you* think?"

"I'm here because something happened to Nina on that boat. And I'm trying to find out what. All I'm asking is for your help. I would think you'd care."

His expression was utterly disgusted. "Time for you to leave, McCann."


"I thought that went well," I said to Alan once we were back in the wrecker.

"*He didn't tell us everything he knows.*"

"Gee, ya think?"

"*You can really be unpleasant to talk to sometimes.*"

"You're right. You should quit talking to me."

Alan took my advice for about five minutes. "*I couldn't tell if Leinberger saw something on the* Emerald Isle *or not.*"

"If he didn't, then we've wasted a lot of time."

"*I don't agree. He might not have seen anything, but this is still an important lead, the best one we've got at this point.*"

"Listen to yourself. Lead. Says detective Harry Bosch. Leinberger was on the boat and couldn't find Nina Otis, so he had her paged. She didn't show up. What more can he tell us?"

"*You're forgetting the panel van theory.*"

"I'm not forgetting it; I'm ignoring it."

*"It's the only thing that fits all the facts."*

"Not necessarily. Maybe it happened exactly as everyone believes—she fell off the *Emerald Isle*. Just like the woman who got drunk and slipped off the sailboat; or the one who got drunk and took the dive off the public docks in Charlevoix. Maybe what we're really learning is that it's not a good idea to be intoxicated around deep water."

*"Because if you are, and you're a woman, you're going to drown and wind up floating to shore five days later with semen in you,"* Alan finished for me.

I thought about this for a moment. We were literally at the turning point—the place where, taking the back way, I would turn left to get to Kalkaska. Instead I remained on M-32, pushing on.

*"Where now?"* Alan asked, sensing a change of plans.

"So, okay. Let's go to Charlevoix and ask around, see if we can find anyone who saw Nina that day, before the boat left for Beaver Island."

*"That would have been in the newspaper,"* Alan objected.

"Not necessarily. If you saw a woman having a couple of drinks before she got on the boat, would you call the cops or a reporter when you found out she'd fallen off?"

*"I would, yes."*

"That is right, Alan. And I'm sure they would have given you another merit badge for your Cub Scout uniform. But normal people would just shrug it off."

He went back to not talking to me.

Deputy Timms swung out after me as soon as I crossed the county line, as if he'd been sitting there, waiting for me. My ticket was for "following too close." I shoved it into the middle of the pile of citations in the glove box.

The downtown stretch of Charlevoix wraps around a round lake called, well, Round Lake. The Pine River, about which I spouted worthy facts to Katie, runs from Round Lake under the drawbridge to Lake Michigan. Lake Charlevoix is on the opposite side of Round Lake from Lake Michigan and is the same body of water that connects most of the places where I do my work: Charlevoix; Boyne City, where bodies float up; Ironton, where I drove into the channel; East Jordan, where Katie worked. In the summer, the *Emerald Isle* tied up at the docks on Round Lake, right at the place where the drunk woman had fallen into the drink and drowned. I had no idea where they parked the car ferry in the winter.

I parked out in front of the row of shops on the Round Lake side of the main drag, stopping in front of what used to be the Star movie theater and is now a couple of retail stores. I experienced my first kiss in that theater, with a girl named Susie. I'd heard recently that Susie had gone on to become a sister at the Carmelite Monastery of the Sacred Hearts, but I doubted our kiss had anything to do with that.

At the end of the row of shops, positioned so that it would have the best view of the car ferry, was a bar named, appropriately enough, the Ferry Bar. "Where do you think someone would go to get a drink or two before getting on the boat?" I asked Alan.

*"Maybe,"* Alan conceded. *"So what are you going to do? You can't just go in there and start asking people if they remember if Nina was there that day."*

"What I'm going to do is go in there and ask people if they remember if Nina was there that day." I grabbed the folder with the pictures of the missing women. The sky was cloudy, but the air was warm, so warm that the snow in the eaves was starting to turn gray with meltwater and drip in a rainlike patter to the ground.

The Ferry Bar was not as big as the Black Bear, but otherwise wasn't much different—just a small-town saloon, though the wall was decorated with pictures of boats and a bunch of nets and fishing crap. Not nearly as classy as a dead stuffed bear, in my opinion. I walked in and got the sort of assessing glances you see from regulars when someone they don't know shows up, though I imagined that in the summer, the place was jammed with tourists. That's why I like the Black Bear: Our summer crowd isn't really any different than our winter crowd. Nor is it hardly ever a "crowd."

The guy behind the bar was what Jimmy calls "cue bald"—a shaved skull gleaming in the overhead light. He was almost my height but very thin. I've spent more than a few hours of my life in bars, and slipped onto a stool with practiced ease, asking for a beer. "This your place?" I asked Cue Bald.

"Yeah. Wade Rogan." He extended a friendly hand.

"Ruddy McCann." I waited for a reaction and got it. He frowned a little, trying to place the name, so I nodded. "Yeah, from the Black Bear in Kalkaska," I told him. Not the guy who drove Lisa Marie Walker into the drink—more and more, that guy was fading away.

"Ah, the competition!" He grinned at me. He had narrow dark eyes but a friendly smile, the kind of happy look that keeps people coming back for a drink. Nowhere near as handsome as Jimmy Growe, but the same joyful personality type.

"You do siphon off a lot of our business," I agreed. "People driving thirty miles so they can watch your TV instead of ours."

"You and your wife own that place, right? Becky, Betsy?"

"No, Becky's my sister. I'm not married, but I'm engaged to Katie Lottner."

He gave me no reaction to that one. I couldn't believe he hadn't heard of her—it seemed to me that every man in a seven-county area would know who she was.

There were two other men at the bar who, if this were a movie, would be Guy at Bar #1 and Guy at Bar #2. They looked like they'd been sitting there so long, their pants were adhered to their stools. They didn't react to me or Katie's name at all—it seemed as if their reflexes were pretty well anesthetized.

"How long you had this place?" I asked Rogan.

"About ten years. I worked here a little before I bought it. I was a dentist down state, but I really always wanted to own a bar up north. My partners decided to buy me out of the practice, and the rest is history."

"That's funny, because I always wanted to quit the Black Bear and become a dentist."

Rogan laughed, and Alan made an impatient noise. I brought out my folder. "So, were you working the day that woman fell off the boat? Nina Otis?"

Rogan's expression shifted, looking not so much suspicious as wary. "Actually, no, I wasn't here that day."

I pulled out the photograph of Nina, the blurry one from the newspaper, and then another one that ran with her obituary. "You sure?"

"What have you got there?" Rogan asked, eyeing the other papers in the folder.

"I'm just looking into a few things."

"What sort of things?"

"Well. Missing persons. I work with Barry Strickland, the former sheriff. And we came across some unanswered questions on a few people."

"Can I see?"

I couldn't think of a reason to deny the request. I opened the folder and spread out the pictures like I was dealing cards. "A couple of these women were found floating in the lake a few days after they vanished. But these last three are more recent. They're still missing."

"Huh," Rogan said. I could see he was swept up in the mystery, because he had an excited look on his face. This was how I was going to solve this thing, I realized—I was going to get people to help me, ask people to ask people.

Rogan sifted through the pictures, stopping at one of them and regarding it carefully. It was a professional headshot, like maybe she was an actress or a model. She was quite pretty, actually. "Who is this?" he asked, holding the photo up.

"*Rachel Rodriguez*," Alan informed me when I hesitated.

I told Rogan. "So, have you seen her before? Has she been in here?"

"In the Ferry Bar? No, not that I know of."

"You know who you should ask is the mayor," Guy #1 piped up. I hadn't even realized he was conscious.

Rogan darted a look at him, as if angry at the interruption, then grinned. "That's right; anybody'd know, it'd be Mr. Mayor."

"The mayor? Of Charlevoix?"

Rogan laughed. "He wishes. Naw, of Shantytown. You know how they elect a mayor every year? It's pretty much a formality. Phil owns all the emergency equipment, keeps it in his shanty, so they can't really vote for anyone else, since the only real job he's got is to keep the emergency equipment handy for anyone who needs it."

"So how would he know if any of these women have been in here?" I asked, tapping the photo of Nina Otis because it was really only her I cared about.

"Because he spends most of his time planted right next to where you're sitting. Year-round. July, at Venetian festival, when the crowds are lined up to get in here, I won't let anyone sit on that stool. He's spent enough in here that I told him he's bought the thing. I'll bury it with him if he wants." Rogan laughed again.

"So he might show up here today?"

"Be surprised if he doesn't."

"Okay. Thanks. I'll ask him." I started to shuffle the pictures back into the folder, but Rogan reached out and picked up the photo of the woman who had fallen off the Charlevoix docks.

"Now her, I know, of course," he told me.

"*Of course?*" Alan repeated.

Rogan was nodding. He tried to look mournful, but on his happy face it just came across as something like embarrassment. "Yeah. She fell off the docks right behind here. I saw her."

# 18

## Looks Good on Paper

*"He saw her fall off the dock?"* Alan demanded with the stridency of a person watching a pet theory get shot to death.

"You saw her?" I repeated to Rogan.

"Yeah. I mean, she was in here."

"Oh, so you saw her *in here*."

"Yeah. I served her. She got a little lit, but not, you know, totally wasted. Got to be careful about that." Rogan gave me an insider's smile—purveyors of alcohol are always gauging the line between increasing sales and increasing liability. "She said she didn't drive here, though. So, you know."

"So you served her drinks, but you didn't actually see her fall off the docks."

"No, I saw that, too."

"Ah."

Alan groaned.

"See, I left early that night," Rogan explained. "Can't remember why. And as I was backing out of the garage—I've got a one-car stall underneath here that I park in during winter, and it was November—I saw her heading down to the docks. She had a brown bag, and I saw the neck of what I'm pretty sure was a bottle of Maker's Mark sticking out of it. You know, the red wax at the neck? She wasn't walking really well, like maybe after she left here, she took a few pulls on the Maker's."

*"So he didn't see her fall,"* Alan summarized excitedly.

"So you didn't actually see her fall into the water," I pressed.

"Oh no. No, and I told the cops about her going to the docks. I guess—maybe I should have tried to help her." The guy's facial muscles couldn't really do guilt, either.

"No one can blame you," I told him. "You didn't know what was going to happen. Sometimes things occur and you feel responsible, but you're not." Like me. Like how I had felt responsible all these years for something I now believed I did not do.

"Thanks, man," Rogan said sincerely.

I waited around for the mayor of Shantytown to show up, but there's really nothing to do in a bar in northern Michigan but drink, and after my second beer, I got bored with that. I gave Rogan a nice tip and told him to stop in the Black Bear sometime. I gave him my repo man business card and asked that he have the mayor call me. "Kramer Recovery," Rogan read out loud.

"Yeah, it's the company Strickland and I work for."

On the way back to Kalkaska, I got pulled over by Dwight Timms again.

"Have you got a crush on me or something, Dwight?" I asked mockingly.

He wanted to know if I'd been drinking, and when I told him I'd had two beers in two hours, he made me do a roadside sobriety test. Another deputy pulled up to watch the fun, but I touched my nose and leaned back and walked in a straight line like a circus performer, and he finally let me off with a warning. That's how he put it: "I'm letting you off with a warning." He didn't tell me what, exactly, he was warning me about. That the local deputies were stupid?

I went to see Kermit to get my dog and vent a little bit. "Timms hasn't let up, Kermit. He says he's going to pull me over every time he sees me," I complained. "Can't you get an injunction or something?"

Kermit thought it over. "I could put a camera in your unit."

"My . . . unit?"

"The tow truck."

Alan laughed.

"I'm not sure what good that would do," I said.

"You get him to say he's harassing you with deliberation, I think we can injunctify him."

"Injunctify," I repeated. "Well, let me think about it. Would the video camera have a shutoff, like the emergency Kermit transmitter?" I asked, thinking of my date with Katie.

"You mean, could you unplug it?"

I grinned at him. "Yeah, like that."

"I suppose."

Something occurred to me. "Hey, are you going to get back into financing, like your uncle?"

"Yes, I think probably so. I don't know a lot about buying paper, but I get calls sometimes."

"Buying paper?"

"You know. The car dealer writes a contract, and I repurchase it from him. Some of the people around here can't get financing because the credit logarithms score them so badly, but we know who they are, so we can figure on servicing the paper without too much trouble."

*"Real estate is the same way. The loan originator often sells the mortgage off for servicing,"* Alan lectured me.

I leaned down and stroked Jake's ears, putting my face very close to his. "Alan," I whispered to my dog, "shut the hell up." I straightened. "Well, there's a deal I want you to do. His name is David Leinberger. We repo'd him a few years ago, back when he was a drunk and his business was going south. Now he's sober, his client base is up, and he needs a break. I think he would be a good risk." I told Kermit to call the Chevy dealer in Gaylord.

He nodded, writing it down. "If you vouch for him, I'm sure it's a good deal," he said.

"Yep," I replied, hoping it was true.


*"Ruddy McCann, repo man with the heart of gold,"* Alan pronounced skeptically as I opened my front door for Jake. *"Or maybe the repo man willing to have his brother-in-law risk investing in car paper so the guy will talk to us about Nina Otis."*

"Okay, Alan? First, don't say *car paper*. It sounds stupid. Second, Leinberger doesn't talk to us, because there is no us. And third, I thought you said I was a war criminal for stealing his Malibu. Now I'm helping him get a replacement and I'm a bad guy for doing that, too?"

With Alan hovering in disapproving silence, I called Katie. She answered breathlessly. I couldn't imagine what she might be doing in Grand Rapids that would cause panting—making out with her aunt's doctor? Well, I didn't like *that* image insinuating itself into my mind. My grip tightened on the phone. "Hi!" I chirped, trying to sound lighthearted but coming out more like I was being strangled.

"Ruddy! Hang on a second."

I listened intently. I heard some bouncy, high-energy music get abruptly cut off.

"Okay. I'm back," she told me.

"What are you doing?"

She hesitated, like there was something she didn't want to tell me. I wondered if I wanted to hear it. "Okay, um, so don't laugh. It's Zumba. I'm at my aunt's house, taking a break from the hospital."

*"How is this your business?"* Alan wanted to know.

"What? Zumba?"

"It's, like, dancing."

"Oh." I thought about it. "You know, maybe I should do that, too."

Katie laughed.

"No, I mean it," I insisted. "Then if you wanted, some night we could go Zumba dancing."

"You're killing me here."

"You'd be surprised at how good I am at things like that."

"I'm going to wet my pants."

"What is it?"

"You just . . . Oh my God," she said, laughing so hysterically, I started chuckling in sympathetic response.

"What? Why are you laughing?" I demanded, though that's how we spent more than a minute, just laughing, her hysterical, me clueless.

"You have to Google it," she finally advised. Then we talked about her aunt, for whom there was still no diagnosis, and then her mood darkened. "Oh, and my mom is here," she stated, voice heavy.

*"That makes sense. Kjersti is Marget's sister,"* Alan informed me.

"How is that for you?" I asked carefully.

She puffed out a breath in a way I knew meant she had blown an errant thread of curly reddish-brown hair out of her eyes. "Not good. She keeps wanting to talk to me, and I don't want to talk to her. Does that make me a bad person?"

*"Of course not,"* Alan interjected.

Since I had been about to say the same thing, I changed my comment. "How do you feel about it?" I parried, having learned from Dr. Schaumburg.

"I don't know. She's still my mom, you know? Even after all that happened. I just wish she would stop trying to explain herself. That's what's bothering me. She says you've been poisoning me against her, telling her things that aren't true. She says she had nothing to do with what happened to my father."

Alan and I were both silent. I knew that Marget had every-thing to do with it, but if the law wasn't going to enforce any punishment, wouldn't I be better off letting it go? "What I told you, I believe it, but that doesn't mean you have to, too," I ven-tured.

We wound up talking for another few minutes, but then she said she was sweaty and getting cold and needed to finish her workout. When we disconnected, I used my phone to watch a Zumba video. If I tried to dance like that, I'd hurt myself and everyone else in the room.

*"I think you handled that pretty well, Ruddy,"* Alan told me.

During the time I'd been talking to Katie, my phone had made the annoying beeps that indicated someone wanted to interrupt my conversation with my fiancée. Still chuckling, I pulled up my voice mail.

*"Ruddy, it's William Blanchard . . . ,"* the message began.

The smile dropped off my face. I didn't have to be a bar bouncer to know he'd been drinking, and his voice had that ugly tone to it that said the alcohol had only added fuel to an inner rage. He breathed into the phone for a minute.

*"I got another job for you. You're gonna like this one. It's more up your alley."* He laughed mirthlessly. *"More like what got you sent to prison. Call me."*

He fumbled with the phone, and it disconnected. I stood there, listening to the silence.

What got me sent to prison was murder.


I was pretty busy over the next few days. What Kermit called "lease terminals" came in batches: people who neglect to turn in their cars at the end of their lease and need a visit from the repo man to remind them of their duty. They were pretty routine—most people were sheepish, though occasionally I would run into someone who thought that at the end of the lease, he owned the vehicle and needed to have the contract explained. I got paid two hundred bucks every time I dragged one in—I averaged four a day for five days. Ruddy McCann was solidly in the black.

I phoned my new buddy Rogan at the Ferry Bar, and he told me he'd given Phil, the mayor of Shantytown, my card and the message to call me. He had no idea why I hadn't heard back. Phil was busy being mayor, maybe.

During the same period, Deputy Dumbbell ticketed me for going fifty-eight in a fifty-five and for parking too far from the curb. I texted and talked to Katie and dodged a couple of calls from William Blanchard, but finally he got ahold of me and demanded I see him at the bank immediately, so I drove over. I grabbed my photocopy of the Wolfingers' one-in-five postcard off the pile of traffic tickets in the glove box and headed in to see him.

Blanchard didn't look so well; there was a sallow pallor to his skin, and a bleary red in his eyes. I thought maybe the heavy drinking had continued past the night of his message. He pointed to the chair in front of his desk, and I took my time easing into it. "The hell you been?" he wanted to know.

"Busy."

"Get my messages?"

I nodded.

"Then why haven't you called me back?"

"Busy."

He didn't like that, and I didn't care, and he could tell I didn't care. He lost some of his outrage, realizing it wasn't doing him any good. "I call you," he said much more evenly, "it means I have something for you. But that doesn't mean what I have will last. It usually is *timely*."

"Sorry." I fished in my pocket and pulled out the photocopy. "Hey, I was wondering if you could tell me something about this?"

He looked at it lying on his desk, but didn't touch it. "Makes you think I know anything about this?"

"Word has it that the phone number there connects to a room you're operating."

"The hell does it matter to you?"

"A couple of friends of mine won a trip to Hawaii."

Blanchard settled back into his chair, regarding me intently. "Okay, so?" he finally asked.

"So, how does it work? I mean, I can't figure out how it makes any money. They got a credit card out of it and joined some club they can cancel for a full refund."

I'd seen the look in his eyes from people before, people who assume they're so much smarter than I am that I'm probably not going to be able to grasp anything they're going to say. "What do you know about banking?" he finally asked.

I shrugged. "You open an account, deposit your checks, and the bank takes it all away with fees."

His smile was cold. "In other words, not a goddamn thing."

I was getting irritated and, apparently, Alan could sense it. *"Easy,"* he warned.

"Right, not a goddamn thing," I agreed flatly.

Blanchard nodded. "All right, since we're going to be partners on a new venture, I'll lay it out. The value of a bank isn't its deposits, because that money belongs to somebody else—a deposit is actually a liability, because when they ask for it, you gotta give it back. It's the loan that's an asset—I loan a million dollars, and as long as the borrower isn't in default, I got a million-dollar asset on the books. You understand most of this?"

I understood all of it. I just sat and waited.

"All right." He pulled a paper clip out of a little bin and started unfolding the metal, bending the thin wire. From where I sat I could see the mutilated corpses of dozens of paper clips lying in the trash can. "I don't have the money to make a bunch of million-dollar loans, so I had to get creative. This one-in-five drop goes to people with lousy credit, people who haven't been able to get a charge account in years, though the poor bastards keep trying.

They call the number on the postcard, find out they've won something, plus they get a credit card through my bank, with a five-hundred-dollar limit. It's their lucky goddamn day. They don't give a rat's ass about the interest rate or anything, and most of them use the card to purchase membership in a travel club for three hundred bucks, because they get all these coupons to save them money when they get to Hawaii. Two grand worth of coupons, face value, so instead of paying two hundred bucks for a helicopter ride, they only have to pay one seventy-five."

"*Let me guess who owns the travel club,*" Alan said.

"These people have bad credit for a reason," I objected. "Don't they default?"

Blanchard grinned at me. "Yeah, though they usually make a few minimum payments first. It's not a bad asset until they're ninety days past due, and then here's the genius part—you're a bank in good standing if your delinquency as a *percentage of total outstandings* is below threshold. Long as I keep growing the base, the bank looks damn good on paper, especially with the interest rates I'm getting. We're for sale, and my bonus is based on our sale price."

"*This cannot be legal!*" Alan stormed.

I slowly reached out and picked up the photocopy, putting it back into my pocket. "Pretty smart deal," I observed with fake admiration.

Blanchard gave me a satisfied smile.

"So, why did you want to see me?" I asked.

His smile winked out, and his eyes grew cold. "Got kicked out of my own goddamn house," he told me.

"Sorry?"

"Wife asked for a divorce and hands me a paper to vacate. The bitch! Get this letter from her attorney saying they're going to audit all my books, think I've been hiding money from her. And listen to this: I'm going to have to pay child support for the kid. She's not even mine! Only adopted the brat to make the bitch happy."

"That's pretty bad," I observed without sympathy. "You in a hotel?"

"No. Got a place on the south arm of Lake Charlevoix, moved in there. That's not what matters. I can*not* have an audit by some asshole accountant, not now, not with everything going on. This is a critical time for me."

"I know what it's like to have relationship problems. Maybe you can work it out."

"Maybe you can work it out," he mimicked, so angry, he didn't care that he was using such a smarmy tone with the guy who'd thrown Herbert Yancy off a roof. "She said there's no-body else, no other guy, but I know that's bullshit. She's got all kinds of new lingerie."

I blinked, and he nodded.

"Yeah, I have keys and still check things out when she's not home. Be an idiot not to."

"*Jesus,*" Alan breathed disgustedly.

"Well." I cleared my throat. "I know a good psychiatrist if you want, you know, counseling."

"I do not want *counseling,*" he spat. "I want you to take care of this for me."

"Take care of it."

"You heard me. I can't have an audit. This whole problem has got to go away. My wife, I mean. I want you to make her go away. Permanently."

# 19

## It Isn't Her

*"Blanchard is asking you to commit murder,"* Alan informed me tensely and altogether unnecessarily.

"Go away permanently," I repeated.

"Don't have to spell it out more than that, do I?" Blanchard asked silkily.

"No, you don't."

"You interested?"

*"Of course not,"* Alan said.

"Yeah," I replied. I had an idea. "If the money's right, hell yeah."

Alan made the sort of noise you'd hear if you backed your car over a chicken, but I kept my face professional killer cool.

"Oh, it's a *lot* of money. I'll tell you where and when. Can't be any screw-ups on this," Blanchard lectured me. "You do exactly what I say."

I decided an assassin would care more about money than step-by-step instructions. "How much?" I growled.

"Ten percent when I give you the go-ahead. Rest when you finish the job," he responded tersely.

Now we were both talking like television thugs. "Sounds good." I nodded. My mind had already left the conversation, though—I was thinking of how to turn this to my advantage.

*"Ten percent of what?"* Alan asked testily. *"You just agreed to a price that means nothing."*

"Except you didn't say ten percent of what," I pointed out smoothly.

"Fifty grand."

The whole thing was ridiculous—I wasn't going to kill anybody—but I couldn't help but reflect for a moment on how fifty thousand dollars would improve my life. Blanchard's face was sly: He could see me thinking about it. "That's five grand up front," he informed me, apparently believing I couldn't do the math.

"Five grand now, the rest after." I nodded again.

"No. Not *now*. See, this is why you have to do exactly what I tell you. I have to set it up so it doesn't look like I had anything to do with it. You don't make a move until I say. No money until then."

I've read a lot of books with contract hit men in them and never heard of an arrangement like this. He was supposed to give me the money when I agreed to the job, wasn't he? I decided not to argue, though. "I'm in," I declared.

We didn't shake hands when I stood up to leave. "This is our last meeting," he informed me. "Now on, you bring in a repo, you deal with my credit manager, Maureen. Ask for her."

Since he already knew about my repo job, I gave him my professional business card from the Black Bear, one of a dozen Becky had printed for me on her computer. That meant I only had eleven left.

"Of course I'm not going to kill Alice Blanchard," I informed Alan as I closed the door to the repo truck.

*"I can't imagine what you're thinking."*

"I'm thinking that my best friend, Jimmy, has fallen for a woman who is leaving her crook husband and that, if I play this right, William Blanchard won't be in a position to give them any more problems."

"*What does that even mean, 'play this right'? Play it how?*"

"I haven't figured that one out yet. Maybe I'll get Alice to join me on the roof."

"*Very funny.*"

Alan fell asleep soon after that, while my tires hummed on the drive to Gaylord. The melting trend had continued, so that every car was covered in muddy splash, and standing pools of water leached out from the snowbanks piled high on the side of the road. Whenever someone passed me going in the opposite direction, I had to turn on my wipers and hit the windshield washers.

In two days I would be peeing into a plastic cup for Dr. Schaumburg. Sighing in resignation, I opened my glove box and pressed my pills out of their blister packs and into my hand, swigging them down with a bottle of water.

Maybe, if the damn things worked like they were supposed to, Alan would never wake up.


This time there were two people waiting in David Leinberger's foyer, plus a young, painfully thin man at the desk who asked me to take my seat and offered to hang my coat and give me water or tea or coffee or a soda. I picked coffee and settled in with a magazine for professional tax preparers.

Oddly, there is no magazine for professional repo men.

Alan woke up and announced that we were in Leinberger's office, which, obviously, I already knew. I guessed the pills hadn't kicked in yet.

The couple ahead of me took about half an hour, shuffling out with glum, just-went-to-the-proctologist expressions on their faces. I guessed they wouldn't be getting a refund from the tax man this year. Then the skinny kid told me I could go on in to the back office.

David Leinberger didn't get up from his desk or offer to shake my hand, so I pretended I was so interested in the decorating, I didn't notice any slight. His office windows had beautiful wood trim, and the light fixtures were all antique, which made his desktop computer seem somehow out of place. I sat in a leather chair without being asked.

"Nice Chevy out front," I complimented. "New?"

"You probably think I owe you something. Like you did me a huge favor," he responded.

*"You did do him a favor,"* Alan said indignantly.

"No," I replied, shaking my head, "you don't owe me anything. I just did what I could to put something right. You said I should have listened to you before I hooked your Malibu. I decided you had a point."

Leinberger thought it over. "Okay," he said finally. "Thanks for that. So, what do you want from me? Something about Nina, right? Mind telling me why?"

I explained that I was looking into some deaths, some local women. That it was a missing persons case, but that I had developed a personal interest in the unexplained drownings. I mentioned Lisa Marie Walker and a few others, but Leinberger showed no reaction.

"So you think Nina's death is unexplained, somehow? I thought the autopsy showed water in her lungs and a lot of alcohol in her system."

*"So she was intoxicated when she drowned,"* Alan declared excitedly.

This was more than I knew, but I kept my face neutral. "There are just some things I'm trying to get a handle on," I responded. I brought out the photograph from the newspaper and slid it over to him. He picked it up, frowning.

"Her sister explained what was going on," I continued. "Between the two of you, I mean. I don't care about any of that; that's your business."

Leinberger looked unhappy. "Not the sort of thing I want getting around."

"I'm not telling anybody anything. I'm just trying to understand what happened that day."

"Yeah." He shook his head sadly. "Me too. She was so young. The thought of her drowning . . . God, I feel bad about that. If I'd only been with her, I'm sure it wouldn't have happened."

*"Tell him he shouldn't blame himself,"* Alan urged sympathetically.

"I'm sure it isn't your fault, David. Did you see her at all on the boat?"

"No. We were supposed to meet up top, toward the front. When she didn't show, I sort of looked around, then I went to the bridge and asked them to call her name."

"Which they did?"

"Yeah. She never responded."

"So something happened to her. Something after this picture was taken, but before you had her paged."

"Could be. But this picture isn't Nina."

I went very still. "Sorry?"

"The woman in the photo here. The one with the blurry face. It isn't her. It's not Nina."

In the silence that followed, the only sound was the whisper of noise from the second hand on the large clock on the wall. My mouth was open, and I was staring in shock. "It's not?" I finally managed to ask.

Leinberger shook his head.

*"Audrey said it was!"* Alan blurted.

"Her sister says it's her."

"Well, sure, but it's not. See how long her hair is? Nina got it cut short, like, a few days before. Audrey wouldn't know that, because Nina said she was going to spring the new look on her sister when they got together. Also, I saw these three girls that day. They were from Arizona State. You know, the women who

are always drinking margaritas and yelling 'woo-hoo'? That's
who they were. They were standing right where Nina and I were
supposed to meet. I remember them handing a camera to someone to have their picture taken. Believe me, Nina wasn't there."

*"Ask him if he remembers the woman who is in the picture,
then,"* Alan urged. I didn't see what that had to do with anything,
so I ignored him.

"What do you think happened that day?" I asked.

Leinberger shrugged uncomfortably. "She would have been
drinking. I think she fell off the boat. Only . . ."

"Only?"

"Well, her credit cards were maxed out. I had to give her the
cash for the ferry ticket. If she was drinking before she got on
the boat, then someone was buying her drinks."

*"The Ferry Bar,"* Alan declared. *"We've got to get the mayor
of Shantytown to call you back."*

"How about you? Did you maybe have a couple of drinks
before you got on the ferry?"

"Yeah, a few."

"Were you at the Ferry Bar?"

He shook his head. "No, I never go in there. There used to be
a place down the street, really quiet, private." He smiled ironically. "You're only as sick as your secrets. I ducked in there for
a couple. Nina didn't. Not there, I mean." He frowned at me.
"What are you saying? That she didn't fall? That maybe someone pushed her?"

"Well, the theory seems to be that she got drunk and fell over
the railing. But nobody saw her that day. And you're telling me
she maybe couldn't even afford to buy her own drinks, and that
you searched all over for her. Now we find out this picture is of
someone else. What I get from all this? We don't even know for
sure that Nina ever got on the boat."

The next day, I felt hungover, which was unfair, because I had had nothing to drink except orange juice before retiring. I swung my legs out of bed and felt like swinging them back in, and as I stood up, all I could think about was that perhaps my day might arrange itself to afford me some nap time. It was as if my medications had given me Jake's personality. Alan was snoozing as well.

I called Barry Strickland and told him I'd like to stop by and talk to him. Then I took my pills like a good little patient, washing them down with strong coffee, and heading in to take a shower. The coffee didn't so much wake me up as make me irritable. "Nice of you to join me," I muttered when I felt Alan stir.

*"Did we have breakfast?"*

"No. I had breakfast. You didn't wake up, so you missed it."

*"It's just . . . I'm hungry."*

"Well, you haven't had anything to eat in more than a decade, so yeah, I can see why you'd have a few cravings."

The ride to Strickland's took me through East Jordan, so I picked up the cinnamon roll at Darlene's that I felt the universe owed me since I'd passed it up the day I'd crashed the old repo truck.

*"Okay, that's the last thing you should be eating,"* Alan lectured me sternly.

"That's good, because it *is* the last thing I'll eat. Until lunch, anyway."

*"It's fat and sugar. Why not eat a vegetable, for once?"*

"I'll eat a salad tomorrow."

*"Tomorrow?"* he squawked.

"Look, this was a one-time treat because I was really hungry, for some reason." That reason being that one of the side effects of my new meds was food cravings—I'd looked it up. "I know I shouldn't be eating the things. I'm giving them up. That's the last one."

*"Well, good. I feel a lot better,"* Alan told me.

"That's my goal in life: to make you feel better, Alan."

Strickland opened his door for me. "Nice little storm rolling in tomorrow," he told me. We settled down into our habitual chairs in his living room.

"So I've got this thing that's a little . . . unusual," I told him. "And also, I need another favor."

That reminded him about Amy Jo, the supposed medium, and he asked me how that had panned out. I told Strickland what she told me, and he watched me without expression. "Somebody helped her. The victim. Prior to the accident. And she drove away with that person," he summarized.

"Right. So if Lisa Marie wasn't in the car, but she shows up five days later, floating in the drink, then whoever it was helped her die." Which meant I still felt that I had failed her.

"Anyone ever come forward who saw the same thing?"

"No." I shrugged. To an extent, my mood mirrored his skeptical expression. Spoken out loud, my words sounded desperate and delusional.

*"Tell him about Nina Otis,"* Alan urged.

"So what's this other thing?" Strickland asked. A certain wariness came into his steely eyes.

"Yeah. You know William Blanchard, president of that little bank in Traverse City?"

"Heard of him, yeah."

*"Why are we talking about that?"* Alan complained.

"He just hired me to murder his wife."

Strickland had a cup of coffee halfway to his mouth, and he halted it there for a long moment before completing the journey and taking a deep gulp. When he set the mug down, the gesture seemed to indicate he wouldn't be picking it back up for a while. "Explain what you just said."

I went through it all. When I was done, Strickland had some questions.

"Jimmy had no idea about the child?"

"No, sir. He just found out maybe two years ago."

"And now Alice Blanchard and Jimmy are sleeping together, and she asked Blanchard to move out, and that's why he wants her murdered."

*"Not exactly,"* Alan said, trying my patience, because that's precisely what I was going to say.

"Yeah, he's living in his summer place down the lake from here. But actually, I think Blanchard's problem is the idea that Alice's attorney wants to hire an accountant to look through his books. I think he's been hiding money from her, probably the IRS as well."

"Why you?"

I shrugged. "He's not real detailed. He's heard I was in prison for murder, and someone gave him bad information about what happened a few years ago, so he thinks that when I heard my sister was in danger, I went out and killed the two guys threatening her." Strickland had been intimately involved in that episode and didn't need it explained to him.

"Who else knows about this?" Strickland asked.

*"Just me,"* Alan advised. I knew he was trying to be funny, but it irritated me anyway.

"Nobody."

"You need to go to the state police with something like this."

"Sure, okay, except as far as they are concerned, I'm an ex-con serving out probation. I thought maybe you could help pave the way. Besides, they're always doing you favors; don't you want to do one in return? I'm picturing the newspaper stories— it would go a long way toward redeeming your reputation if you prevented a murder, don't you think?"

It took him a minute, but eventually he grunted and nodded. "I'll make a few calls," he said.

We finished our coffee and stood up, but Alan was stridently objecting. I sighed. "You got time for one more thing?" I asked Strickland.

I showed him the folder with the photographs, and to his credit he didn't roll his eyes or shoot me skeptical looks. I put Rachel Rodriguez and the other two local "just missing" women in one pile, and Nina Otis, Lisa Marie, the woman Rogan saw heading toward the docks, and the one who fell off the boat in Boyne City in the other, the "found in the lake" pile. I walked Strickland through the nagging elements in Nina Otis's case.

"You've been on the *Emerald Isle*," I told him. "It would take you, what, maybe five minutes to search everywhere on the boat? But Leinberger couldn't find her. If she fell off before he could look everywhere, she'd be in the Pine River and two hundred people would have seen it. And everyone stands at the railing, looking at the water—how do you miss an adult woman going overboard? The whole theory has always hinged on the fact that she was supposed to be on the *Emerald Isle*, and that her sister identified the girl in the photograph as Nina Otis. But if it wasn't her, isn't it more likely that she was never even on the boat? So yeah, her death still could have been an accident—but it didn't happen the way it says in the reports."

Strickland's gaze was unreadable. "I would agree," he finally said. "What are you proposing?"

"I'm wondering if the investigations turned up anything that didn't make it into the papers, something that maybe didn't fit the circumstances as precisely as the news stories implied," I said.

Strickland pulled out a pad of paper and wrote down each of the victims' names. I waited respectfully. "All right," he said. "I'll ask." He glanced up at me. "Meanwhile, you let me know the minute Blanchard contacts you, understood?"

"Got it."

I had a couple of repos I needed to follow up on, plus I wasn't that far away from where Kenny MacDonell's mother said he and Mark Stevens were remodeling a small home, but in the end I wound up just driving back to Kalkaska. Weighed down by my medication, there was no joy in repossessions that day.

"*Why don't we go to Charlevoix? Maybe the mayor of Shantytown has shown up. Maybe someone else in the Ferry Bar saw Nina and could tell us who was buying her drinks that day. Or maybe she was in one of the other bars. Ruddy? Why don't we do that?*"

"I think a better use of my time and body would be to take a nap," I told him.

Alan maintained a huffy silence all the way home. With a weary sigh, I opened the front door, glancing automatically at Jake's blanket. My dog was still at Kermit's, of course, and it just seemed like too much effort to go retrieve him.

I went into my small kitchen and poured myself a glass of water, and something hit me very hard on the back of the head.

# 20

## The Perfect Job for a Murderer

The shock of the blow sent me reeling, literally staggering into the wall, where my legs went weak and I slid to the floor. I looked up and had the vague impression of a person standing over me, raising his arms, holding something. He swung like a woodsman splitting a log, and I rolled away and felt the shock wave when he smashed his club on the floor, the blow so ferocious that the weapon bounced out of his hands.

Stupidly, I watched the man dart after it as it rolled away. It was a chair leg, the kind that has been turned and spindled. He was a stocky guy, not tall, gray haired. He stooped to pick up his club, and I got to my feet, feeling wobbly.

*"Ruddy!"* Alan shrieked at me, which wasn't at all helpful. I forced myself to cross my tiny kitchen and was still driving with my legs when my attacker raised his club, but I got inside the swing and punched him in the gut, the air and the fight leaving him in a gasp. He crumpled, holding his stomach.

I took a deep breath, fighting the queasy feeling. Now that I had time to process it, the blow to my head seemed to be bouncing around inside my cranium, ricocheting like a bullet. When I thought of it, I kicked the chair leg away, and it rolled into the living room and under the couch.

*"Zoppi,"* Alan murmured. *"I told you not to mess with them."*

The guy lying in my kitchen was at least sixty years old. His thin hair was neatly trimmed, and he wore a heavy woolen shirt and new Danner boots. He had a portly gut with what felt like twelve inches of give when I buried my fist in it, and was otherwise soft and out of shape. He looked like a retired accountant who had purchased some expensive outdoor gear for a weekend in the wilds of northern Michigan. "The local mafia must be in pretty sorry shape if they sent you," I told him. I rubbed the back of my head, finding no blood but a lot of tenderness that would need ice if I wanted to be able to move my neck the next day.

He got to his hands and knees. "Screw you," he said, panting twice between the words.

"You try to stand up, I'm going to make you lie down again," I advised.

He stared at the floor between his hands, visibly gritting his teeth. "After everything you have done to us, to find out what you're trying to pull now, you sonofabitch . . ."

I cocked my head at him and was rewarded with a stab of pain between my eyes. I made a mental note not to rotate my neck. "Now I what, exactly?"

"Leave us alone!" he roared. "For God's sake, show a shred of humanity and leave us the hell alone!"

He raised his eyes to look at me, wet, pain-filled eyes, and I recognized him. "Oh," I said.

Alan sensed something. *"Who is he?"*

Ignoring my threat to put him back down, my would-be assailant used his hands on his knees to straighten himself into a standing position. "What the hell are you doing?" he whispered. "What is wrong with you?"

"Look. Mr. Walker. I don't know what you've heard—"

"I've heard you've been telling people you didn't kill my daughter, you lying bastard!"

Then he came at me again, swinging his fist, but I've had a lot of drunks try the same move on me, and it was easy to step out of the way, catching his arm and twisting it a little. "Easy," I told him, squeezing him tightly. "I don't want to have to hurt you, sir."

The fury went out of him, and he sagged. "Goddammit," he muttered.

"Look, you want something? A Vernors, maybe?" I offered.

He gave me a fierce look.

"All right, then," I said. "I'm having one, though." I picked out a can of Vernors ginger ale and pressed it to the back of my head. The cold felt good, fleetingly, but an army of pain troopers had assembled at the base of my skull and was attacking the rest of my cortex in a flanking maneuver. I found some aspirin and gulped a couple, warily watching Mr. Walker, who was standing and staring sightlessly at the dusty shelves where my football trophies were all stacked. I'd pulled them out of the closet when I'd started dating Katie.

"I want you to leave us alone. Leave *her* alone," Mr. Walker said woodenly.

"I understand how you must feel. But a witness has come forward. Someone who saw your daughter that night. Who says Lisa Marie got out of my car at the 7-Eleven and drove off with someone else."

He turned to face me. "I wanted to kill you. I wanted to take a hunting rifle and remove you from our lives, but my wife wouldn't let me. I've got two other children. But they're grown now. So I'm warning you this one time. Stop it. Stop ruining our lives. Because if you don't, I'm going to shoot you in the goddamn face."

I stared at him. He looked like he meant it.

*"Ask him who told him,"* Alan blurted.

I frowned, not getting it.

*"Somebody called him! Find out who. Whoever did it was hoping this would happen, that you'd be warned off. Ask him who called."*

"Mr. Walker. How did you find out I was looking into the case?"

He sneered at me. "My daughter is not a case, McCann. My daughter was a living, loving, wonderful person who you let drown in the back of your car while you swam to safety."

"The person who called you did it for one reason, which was to get you to come here and get me to stop. He *wants* me to stop, which means I'm getting closer to him than I thought. Who was it? Who called?"

"For God's sake. You're serious," he said wonderingly.

"Just give me a name."

"I don't owe you a goddamn thing."

"Give me a name," I repeated patiently, "or I will call the police and tell them you came into my house and tried to kill me with a chair leg. You'll go to jail. You want that?"

"Screw you," he spat. I could tell, though, that my threat had landed on him, could see it in the self-disgust building on his face. I waited. After a moment he looked away. "I don't know. Someone called my firm and left a message. All it said was that it was a friend, and that you were spreading lies about my daughter, saying you didn't kill her, that someone else did it. That you're looking for the real killers." He said this last part with a sarcastic set of air quotes hanging in the air.

"Mr. Walker. I stood up in court and said that I was responsible for Lisa Marie's death—"

"Don't say her name!" he interrupted harshly.

I nodded. "All right. That I did it, that I should go to prison. But now a witness says I didn't do it, because your daughter was not in the car. I don't know if that's true, but I'm starting to believe it might be. And if it is, it means the person who put your daughter in that lake has never been punished for it. Don't you want me to try to find out who it is?"

"You," Walker responded after a long moment, "can rot in hell."

I lay on my couch, a bag of frozen peas pressed to my neck, until Kermit brought Jake home, and then I went to bed with my dog. Katie was at her aunt's bedside and couldn't really talk, so I let her go and tried not to pay attention to the throbbing in my skull. Getting up the next morning was the most difficult task I'd ever undertaken in my entire life, a grunting, wheezing repositioning of myself as an upright human. My neck felt as if a shark were trying to eat its way out of it, my stomach was heaving, and a muscle under my eye was fluttering like a butterfly trapped in its cocoon.

The only thing on my schedule that day was to pee in a cup. I wondered if I was up to it.

*"The pain goes from behind the ears all the way down the back,"* Alan complained.

"Do you think I don't know that, Alan?" I responded in irritation. I scrambled some eggs, and Jake came out of the bedroom and gave me a *What, no bacon?* expression.

I vaguely registered that the house looked neat and clean. It seemed unlikely that I'd been picking up after myself, but I couldn't exactly remember *not* doing so, and anyway, the alternative, which was that Alan had defied my orders and continued to be the midnight housekeeper, meant having a fight, and I just didn't have the energy for that at the moment.

I called Barry Strickland, wincing as I tilted my head to cradle the phone with my shoulder. He grabbed it on the first ring, and we exchanged pleasantries. "You get much snow over there?"

I turned and looked out the window. A soft, smooth layer of white stuff coated everything. "Yeah, looks like six or seven inches."

"Didn't get that much here."

"So I have a question for you. Just go with me for a minute."

"All right," he replied cautiously.

"You know this thing I'm looking into. How Lisa Marie got out of my car that night."

"Oh. I thought this was going to be about Blanchard. I talked to my contacts; they want to meet with you."

"Okay, sure. No, this is about Lisa Marie. What do you know about Dennis Kane?"

"The medical examiner? I know he was incompetent. A couple of convictions were reversed because he botched the autopsies. He's not even a forensic pathologist; he's a general practitioner. We've got a good one now. Kane's not been M.E. for, what, more than three years?"

"Do you know him personally?"

"I've spoken to him, sure. What's this about?"

"I was just thinking, if you were going to murder somebody, wouldn't that be the perfect job? They pull a body out of the water, and you're the one that put it there. You find exactly what you want to find, and you miss anything that might incriminate you."

*"Where is this coming from?"* Alan demanded.

When Strickland replied, I heard something in his voice, a caution, as if he were trying to figure out a way to let me down gently. "Ruddy. I know you like to read mysteries, but I have to tell you, life isn't like that. There's almost never any mystery to it. Usually a robbery goes bad, a husband loses his temper, two guys get in an argument. Murder is always simple and usually stupid. Smart people don't kill people."

"All right, but yesterday afternoon, when I got home, Lisa Marie's father was waiting for me in my living room. With a club."

"A club?"

"A chair leg, like what you can get at the hardware store. He hit me with it."

"Is he okay?"

I laughed mirthlessly. "He hit me in the head and you're worried about *him*?"

"No, I'm worried about you. If you put him in the hospital,

the judge is going to revoke your probation, even if it was justifiable."

"He's probably got a sore stomach this morning, but he walked out of here under his own power."

"All right."

"But you have to wonder why he was here. He said someone left a message at his company, saying I was running around denying I had done anything to his daughter. But I'm not. Very few people know anything about it. There's you. There's the medical examiner. And that's it. Whoever called Walker did so just to stir things up, maybe to get him to come here and put my head in telescopic sights."

*"It's not just Dr. Kane who knows. You told David Leinberger,"* Alan reminded me.

"I told this guy Leinberger that I was looking into a missing persons case," I added, "but I didn't explain who Lisa Marie Walker is to me."

*"If he is the murderer, he would know that,"* Alan argued. *"And what about Audrey Strang?"*

I put my hand on my phone. "Audrey Strang couldn't leave *semen,*" I hissed.

"What was that? I didn't catch it," Strickland said.

"Oh, I was just . . . talking to my dog."

Jake, sprawled on the couch, opened one eye but otherwise didn't move.

"I can find out if Kane has ever been suspected of anything," Strickland advised me, "but I know he's never been convicted of a crime."

"Can you get a copy of Lisa Marie's autopsy?"

*"Oh, and you told the bar owner, Wade Rogan,"* Alan interjected.

"I don't know, Ruddy," Strickland waffled.

"Can you try? Please?"

Strickland thought it over. "All right, I'll try," he told me.

We hung up. "Alan," I said, "you know how hard it is to carry on a conversation with you yammering away?"

"*So you've got Leinberger, Rogan, and then the mayor of Shantytown, and Rogan said he told him why you wanted to talk to him. Amy Jo Stefonick knows—maybe she told somebody else. Audrey Strang could have told somebody, too.*"

"Amy Jo said the guy that night had a bald spot. Leinberger doesn't have a bald spot. And Rogan's isn't a spot; it's his whole head."

"*You don't know Leinberger doesn't have a bald spot; you didn't look. And it was night; maybe Amy Jo is mistaken. And people do go more bald; maybe Rogan's spot got to the point where it got easier just to shave his skull.*"

"If I didn't already have a headache, you'd be giving me one."

"*And what do you expect Lisa Marie's autopsy to prove?*"

"You know what? I've pretty much had it with you. Anytime you get an idea—like how practically every woman who has ever vanished around here was killed by the same person who murdered Lisa Marie, even though there's not a shred of evidence, and three of the women didn't even drown; they're just gone—I'm supposed to take you seriously and fly to Beaver Island and traipse out to Shantytown to track down Phil somebody. But when I get a really good idea, like maybe the reason why the good doctor Kane didn't save the semen was that it was *his*, you piss and moan like I'm wasting your time."

"*Oh my God. Good doctor,*" Alan breathed. "*That's it!*"

"What?" I replied suspiciously. It didn't sound like Alan's reply had anything to do with my rant.

"*He wasn't a good doctor. You heard Strickland.*"

"Are you going to answer what I just said? I made some damn important points there."

"*He's been out of office for three years.*"

"And?"

"*Two of the three women who vanished did so in the past*"

*three years. But the ones who drowned were while Kane was medical examiner."*

I could hear the excitement in Alan's voice, and it irritated me. "Please get to your point so we can go back to mine," I said icily.

*"What if Lisa Marie was the first? The man who took her from the 7-Eleven couldn't have known you were going to drive into the lake; he was just being opportunistic. Then when he reads about your accident and how they're looking for Lisa Marie, it gives him an idea on how he might dispose of her body."*

"And it works," I added, catching on.

*"Yes! But only because the M.E. is incompetent and doesn't mention the semen. Let's say our killer thinks that maybe he figures he can get lucky twice. So, sure enough, he sees some guy buying Nina Otis drinks, and kidnaps her, and when he's done, he tosses her in the lake. Next he boats out to a party on a sailboat, slips aboard, and takes a drunk woman captive. He sees a woman getting intoxicated on the public docks and snatches her. Each time, he gets away with it because Kane is not a good doctor."*

"But now," I finished for him, "we have a new M.E. One who can't be counted on to miss things. So he has to come up with a new MO."

*"He's doing something else with the bodies."*

I thought it over. "You said two out of three."

*"Yes. Kane was still M.E. when Rachel Rodriguez vanished."*

"Not every body tossed into the water is going to wind up in Boyne City," I speculated.

I could practically feel Alan deciding not to remind me that Nina Otis didn't float to Boyne City. I was grateful to be spared the nitpicking. *"So Rachel Rodriguez could have sunk,"* he agreed. *"She could still be at the bottom of the lake."*

"Makes sense. Of course, maybe the reason the women who vanished in the last three years haven't been found is that *Kane*

knows he can't pull the same trick anymore. He's no longer M.E."

"*I suppose*," Alan said condescendingly.

"God, you're a joy to be with. Come on, Jake. I'll drop you at
Uncle Kermit's; Daddy's got to go urinate for the doctor."

Dr. Schaumburg asked me how I was feeling, and I told him I
felt bloated, hungry, I had a headache, a muscle twitch, irritable
bowels, and was in a bad mood. He told me that when I came
back in for another test in ten days, he would see about adjust-
ing my medication. I didn't tell him that some of the symptoms
might have had less to do with the pharmaceuticals and more to
do with having been brained with a chair leg.

I left the little cup in his capable hands and went out to try to
find future repo Mark Stevens and his soon-to-be-ex–pickup
truck. Through a process of elimination I found the place—most
of the houses were summer homes, unoccupied in the dead of
February. Fresh tracks in new snow up one driveway led to a
small place with sawhorses in the front yard and a stack of new
lumber off to one side. No one was home, and the vehicle that
left the tire prints was not around.

My headache receded a little when I met up with a guy who
decided he didn't want to pay for his Toyota because it stopped
running. When I explained what a repo would do to his credit,
he gave me a check, shaking his head over his plight but not
blaming me. I'd get a hundred dollars for making the collection,
part of the two-hundred-dollar fee that would be added to the
end of his car loan. He shook his head over that, too.

Alan was asleep when I ate a burger for lunch. I threw away
the bag and then, after a moment, opened the glove box, got out
my medication, and threw that away, too. I didn't know what I
would do in ten days when I had to take another urine test and,
at that moment, I didn't much care.

Alan woke up and ran me through a review of everything we knew about the "case," which was frustrating because once we took out our speculations, we really knew almost nothing.

Maybe it was just psychological, but I felt measurably better with the medication in the trash can and not in my bloodstream. I stopped in the Bear for a moment, and Kermit said the flights for the Wolfingers were all set. The tickets cost a little more than expected, because the people at the "Grand-Prize Center" insisted hotel reservations could only be made a week in advance, forcing an airline penalty that was probably further disincentive to collecting the Hawaiian vacation. I gave him thirty-two hundred bucks, thinking I had just wiped out my fiscals.

Darkness was settling in when I turned down my street in Kalkaska. I parked in the street and looked at my house. Footprints tracked up the sidewalk to the front door from the car pulled over by the tree Jake had decorated that morning. Katie's car. She was obviously back in town, and now she was in my house.

I got out of my truck and headed in to find out what was going on.

# 21

## Lisa Marie's Autopsy

My small table was set for two. A tall candle burned in the center of it, putting out a warm light. Something good was cooking, and as I slipped off my shoes, Jake came up to me, wagging. "Are the two of you having dinner?" I whispered to him.

The bathroom door opened, and Katie came down the hallway. "Oh! Hi, Ruddy."

She stopped about five feet away from me, smiling. She wore a pair of jeans I hadn't seen before, snugly fitting, and a silk blouse that matched her blue eyes. Her hair had been cut and was curled up softly on her neck.

"*She's beautiful,*" Alan said breathlessly, articulating my feelings exactly.

"Hi," I managed to say, instead of *Oh my God* or something. "How's your aunt?"

"It turned out to be mononucleosis," Katie said. "Can you believe it? She's, like, in her late fifties, but she never had it as a teenager, and when you get it this late in life, they have trouble diagnosing it. They thought it was Lyme disease, because of the fatigue, but then she turned yellow and her neck got all swollen."

Katie was not wearing her engagement ring. I swallowed back my disappointment. "So, she's fine?" I ventured.

"She's really sick, still, but yeah. She's going to fully recover."

"*That's good,*" Alan observed, probably just to remind me he was there.

"You look . . . amazing," I told her with feeling. "I like your haircut. It's cute."

She smiled at me. "I'm making that chicken you like," she said.

"Sounds great," I replied. I felt precarious, like one wrong word and I'd fall into a hole and be unable to get out. I so, so did not want to say a wrong word.

Katie went into the kitchen, dug in her purse, and came to me, holding a small envelope. I accepted it without comprehension—it was full of business cards. I pulled one out and saw her picture on it. "I got my license. I'm an official real estate agent!" She spun in a tight circle and then came into my arms.

"Congratulations! That's wonderful!" I told her.

She eased out of our embrace far too soon, heading back into the kitchen. "I really missed Jake, so I picked him up at Kermit's. He was so excited, he practically ran to my car!"

"He ran? I can barely get him to get out of his chair." I gave Jake an accusing stare, and he glanced away guiltily.

Katie poked her head into my refrigerator and pulled out a bottle of champagne. "And I was thinking, I have this big news, who can I tell? Who do I celebrate with? And it just seemed . . . I wanted to celebrate with you."

My mouth was a little dry. "Good decision. You want me to open that?"

"You are, after all, the professional barman."

I took the bottle from her, and now we were standing very close, smiling into each other's eyes.

"*Ruddy . . . ,*" Alan warned.

I glanced away, sensing her puzzlement as I did so, and focused on peeling the foil from the champagne. It was my fault—I'd actively tried to connect with Alan, I'd wanted him back, and now he was here, in my head, ruining my life. The cork popped out, and I blinked. Katie put a hand on my back as I poured, and I knew that when I filled the glasses, we would clink them and sip and then put them down and kiss long and deeply, that I would touch her through that silk blouse and that she would lead me down the hallway. The chicken would be overcooked.

But none of that was going to happen as long as Alan was here.

The bubbles boiled up in the thin flutes, giving me a reason to stay focused on my pouring. Alan made a distressed noise because he could feel my rising excitement, knew what I was thinking, knew he couldn't possibly live through what was going to happen next.

So I went into my head, wandering its corridors, turning the corners, and descending deeper into myself. I pictured Alan, not as a person but as a presence, finding him there in my consciousness. I mentally reached out to him and strongly, and firmly, pushed and pushed until he was forced into the darkest recesses of my mind, a closet with a door that I could close and lock. When I finished and resurfaced, Alan was gone.

I turned and grinned crookedly at my fiancée. We sipped champagne, we folded into each other's arms, and as we went down the hallway, all I could think was that if I could force Alan away, it meant he wasn't real.

I had a mental disorder. When I was talking to Alan, I was really only talking to myself.

The chicken cooked for an extra hour or so, but it was still pretty good. We opened a bottle of wine after the champagne, but neither one of us was really interested in drinking much more. It seemed more important to go back down the hallway to the bedroom for act two.

Later we lay sprawled, legs entangled, the candle from the table now on my dresser, tracing a bright-yellow circle on the ceiling. Katie's head was on my chest.

"I guess I was surprised to see you," I ventured, when what I really wanted to ask was, *Are you back for good?*

She sighed contentedly. "I figured a few things out."

"Oh? Care to share?"

She looked up at me. "We never dated."

"Sorry?"

"I think that's what's been bothering me the most. When I lost my home, I moved in here, like, same day. We barely knew each other at that point, and then from that moment on we were living together. Instead of being that wild, fun time of exploring and learning about each other, I was over here, trying to figure out how to fit all my stuff into your closet. You know? It kind of took the romance out of it."

"Well, but we did have a rather intense moment together," I offered mildly, thinking back to *how* she lost her home.

"Right. Not the most romantic of circumstances," she replied levelly.

"I get it," I told her.

"I couldn't understand why I wasn't happier when we got engaged, but now I know. You gave me a ring, but we were living as if we were already married. Did I want that, a life predecided because I had no other place to live? You move in with someone because you love them and want to be with them all the time, not because your house trailer was destroyed. You get engaged because you want to be married, not because you already are."

I searched for something to say. "I'm sorry for everything," I murmured. An apology worthy of Jimmy Growe.

"No, no, you did nothing wrong. In fact—God, Ruddy, that thing I said, about how my dad wouldn't have liked you, I was just being a bitch. I thought you were denying me sex to prove some kind of point, and it pissed me off. I said what I said to get back at you. I'm so sorry."

"I would never deny you sex to prove a point or for any other reason."

She chuckled. "Actually, I think my dad would have loved you."

"Maybe not *loved*," I responded cautiously.

She rolled and propped herself up on one elbow so she could look into my eyes, her gaze earnest. "I think I started questioning everything, not just how our relationship skipped dating and went straight to me picking up your socks from on top of the hamper every day—"

I groaned softly.

"—but us. *You.* I started having doubts about you. But then my mom helped me see the other side."

"Your mom," I repeated stupidly.

"Yeah, she was there, you know, at Aunt Kjersti's bedside. It was kind of hard not to talk to her."

"And your mom said you should give me another chance?" I tried to picture Marget arguing on my behalf, and couldn't make it work.

"Oh God, no." Katie laughed. "Just the opposite. She says you're a loser, and that you've told me all these lies about how my dad died, and I can do so much better, and how she always liked Dwight, he's got a real job, you know, not stealing cars but a decent career with a pension and benefits." As she spoke, Katie's voice took on the vaguely Minnesotan lilt of her mother's accent.

"Sounds like I'm growing on her."

Katie grinned at me. "I guess I've just never thought much of my mother's advice on matters of the heart. Or anything else. If she disapproves of you, that's the best endorsement a man can get."

"I'll try to continue to earn her distrust."

Katie's eyes searched my face. "But I do love you, Ruddy. There's so much stuff with my mom, and I hardly see any of my girl-friends, but I know, no matter what, I love you. Being away from you, missing you, taught me that. Now that I have my own place—I've never lived alone before; I had roommates, and having a trailer on my mom's property didn't count. But now that I have my own place, I feel like for once in my life I've got freedom of choice. So: I choose you."

"I choose you, too, Katie."

"So we'll figure it out."

"Yeah. We'll . . . date. Go to the movies. I'll ask you to prom." She laughed.

Katie slept in my bed that whole night. Jake spent a lot of it hunting around for a place to lie down—he liked having her back but didn't believe it meant she could reclaim her pillow.

I was awake for much of the time, watching Katie sleep in the glow of the moon. I could understand just how close I'd come to blowing it. She was right; we hardly knew each other when we moved in together, and because it was my house, she adapted to my ways, while all I did was grumble about the number of her items in the bathroom. I silently vowed to myself that from that moment on I would always put my goddamn socks in the hamper.

I didn't hear her get up, but the sound of the shower running dragged me into consciousness. I felt the sore spot on the back of my neck and gingerly rotated my head, wincing. When I stood up, Jake turned in circles and sprawled across the blankets, relieved to have the bed all to himself.

I went in to make coffee. Katie smelled it and came in for a cup, wearing only a towel, and I expressed my enthusiasm for this convenient outfit by reaching hungrily for her. She laughed. "Okay, now I have to get ready for work."

I volunteered to cook breakfast. This time, at Jake's insistence, I made bacon, too. Katie ate and I watched her and she smiled at me watching her. "Might be fun to do this again tonight," I finally ventured.

Her gaze was frank, and I steeled myself against what she had to say while she considered her words. "I have a six-month lease on the place in East Jordan," she finally said. "With the roads iced up, it's going to take me more than an hour this morning. When I walk, it's eight minutes."

"Okay, then."

A small smile crept onto her lips. "Maybe some nights you could sleep over there."

"I would really like that."

She went back to finish getting ready, and I stealthily set the plates on the floor for Jake to lick. It's just easier than scrubbing them at the sink, and the dishwasher would sterilize them anyway. When Katie emerged, wearing her work clothes, her face carefully made up, she was so pretty, I felt a pleasant hollow sensation in my chest. She came to me and kissed me good-bye. "I'm getting lipstick on you," she breathed.

"It's okay."

She motioned to Jake to say good-bye. Watching her lean over my dog, stroking his ears, I did something I wouldn't have expected: I reached out to Alan, and I invited him back in. I felt his presence inside me like an increase of internal air pressure, just the slightest change of my sense of being.

"Hey, Katie," I said as she turned to go. She stopped, her hand on the front doorknob, raising her eyebrows.

"I know that if your father were here, he would tell you how proud he is. How much it means to him that you're following in his footsteps in the real estate business. That he knows that part of what you're doing is an homage to him, honoring his memory. He's watching you, Katie, and I promise you he is so, so happy right now."

She tightly pressed her lips together, her eyes shining. Inside, I heard Alan weeping. I went to Alan's daughter and pulled her into a long, hard hug, an embrace all for him.


I didn't tell Alan what I had discovered—that he was a completely fictional presence in my head—because I didn't want to hurt his feelings. What would be the point? I was a repo man with a voice in his head. It didn't mean I needed to be on anti-psychotic medication.

I didn't tell Schaumburg, either. "Your urine test was positive," he advised me on the phone.

"Good. I was up all night, cramming."

He grunted, which is maybe what psychiatrists do instead of laughing. "Are you experiencing any side effects?"

"Yeah, I feel like crap."

"There's usually a period of adjustment. You'll probably feel better soon."

I didn't feel like advising him that the main adjustment was that I'd thrown the medication in the trash at the Burger King and actually was feeling better, thank you. We made an appointment for the next urine festival, me wondering what I was going to do about that. "How is Sheryl doing?" I asked hopefully.

"Dr. Johnston is recovering but is not expected to return to work until the fall."

"Ah."

"So you're stuck with me, Ruddy."

"I did get that that was what you were telling me."

"*I don't like him,*" Alan remarked when I rang off.

"Yeah, well, he wants to see you gone from my head forever. Not the greatest basis for a long-lasting friendship."

"*Not that. It's his manner. He's very dictatorial.*"

"He's got the power to send me to jail just by writing a letter. I think that might turn anyone into a dictator."

"*That's not exactly what I meant by dictatorial.*"

"If we're going to start parsing vocabulary words, I'm going to turn you over to Kermit."

After dropping Jake off at the office, I went out to the junk-yard where Tigg Bloom's Suburban wound up after he went tree smashing with it. He was refusing to accept his insurance company's offer, and the bank needed it off their books as a huge delinquency, so they wanted me to take it, and then the settle-ment conversation would be with them. No one noticed when I put dollies under the rear wheels and towed it away—people were dragging vehicles in and out of the place all the time.

With that taken care of, I stopped by the Ferry Bar. Phil, the mayor of Shantytown, had been in, but not recently, and no one could remember the last time he had been there.

*"Some friends. They can't even remember if it was yesterday or this week?"* Alan asked indignantly.

I knew from working at the Black Bear that friends in the bar are a different category from friends anywhere else. Being a sup-portive fiancé, I handed out Katie's business cards to everyone there. One guy said he already had a real estate agent, but I gave him a hard stare, and he took one.

"She's hot," Rogan the bald-headed bartender told me, leering.

"She's my fiancée," I corrected him.

"That's what I meant."

"Hey, Wade. Let me ask you something. Have you told any-one about what I talked to you about? You know, how I'm look-ing into the missing women, the ones who drowned, and Lisa Marie Walker?"

"Yeah, I told Phil that's why you wanted to talk to him."

"Huh. Does Phil have a bald spot?"

"A what?"

"You know. Like on the top of his head, is he missing some hair?"

"He's missing a *lot* of hair." Rogan rubbed his own skull and grinned. "Maybe it's the air in here."

"Okay. And hey, I'd appreciate if you didn't tell anyone else about my investigation." I felt embarrassed saying the word *in-vestigation* but didn't know what else to call it.

Rogan made a zipping-the-lip gesture and winked at me.

I slid in behind the wheel. "You know, I like the vibe of that place," I told Alan as I steered toward Boyne City.

*"Yeah, nice serial killer hangout."*

I cocked my head. "Are you making a joke? You? Alan Lottner?"

*"No, I'm just pointing out that our mayor seems to have vanished the moment he found out you wanted to talk to him about Nina Otis. And by* vanished, *I mean ran off."*

"Okay, because for a minute there I thought I detected some humorlike content in your statement. I was just saying, the Ferry Bar is a nice place. That's all. I like the guy who runs it."

*"Maybe you should take Katie there. Be an entirely different experience than a night at the Black Bear Bar."*

"Now you're pissing me off." I didn't tell him that yeah, that's actually what I had been thinking, that Katie might like the place.

*"And I'm glad you're buddies with Rogan. One of our suspects."*

"No, our suspect is the medical examiner Dennis Kane. I'm thinking I should go back there and ask him."

*"Ask him? As in, 'Hey, did you murder Lisa Marie Walker?'"*

"Why are you in such a pissy mood? Aren't you getting enough sleep? Maybe you should take a nap."

*"The inside of this truck is filthy."*

"Yeah, because it's winter, Alan. My boots get coated with snow and mud. You want me to go to the car wash? Spray the truck with frozen water?"

*"You could mop it out."*

"Repo men do not *mop.*"

*"We're going to Boyne City,"* he noticed. *"To visit Shantytown, talk to the mayor?"*

"No, we're going to meet Barry Strickland and the state police. I set up the appointment while you were sleeping, which is what I wish you were doing now."

Strickland had agreed to come out of his cave and meet at

Café Sante, a restaurant owned by the same people who run my favorite Mexican place, the Red Mesa. The café has a beautiful outdoor terrace and sits right on the shore of Lake Charlevoix, not too far from where Lisa Marie's body was pulled from the water. Today the lake was a sheet of ice, and the wind howling straight out of the north had driven the wind chill to negative ten, so I didn't imagine there would be many people sitting on the patio.

Strickland was already in a booth and waved me over. "I just got a call. They're both running late."

"Both?"

"Darrell Hughes is joining us."

Darrell Hughes was the prosecutor who insisted I had to be guilty of something even though I didn't commit any crimes, back when I, as Blanchard mischaracterized it, "solved Becky's problem with extreme prejudice." My probation with Sheryl, and now Dr. Schaumburg, was D.A. Darrell's brilliant idea. Strickland correctly read my expression. "He's not my favorite person either," he stated apologetically.

I ordered a cup of coffee. Through the window I could see the tiny ice shanties of Shantytown. The wind was blowing crystalized snow against the glass like a sandblaster, and the small buildings out there were barely visible. The idea of going there in search of the mayor, trooping around from shanty to shanty, some of them a hundred yards apart, was very unappealing. One of them had what looked to be a thirty-year-old Pontiac station wagon parked next to it.

"I can't believe people drive their cars on the ice," I told Strickland.

He shrugged. "It's thick enough. I'd probably drive. I don't have any interest in ice fishing, though."

"You know anyone who does? Someone who could introduce me around?"

"Not really. Why, you looking for a vehicle to repo out there? Most people drive clunkers to get to their shanties."

"Something like that," I replied evasively.

"Uh-huh. The other thing, then," Strickland concluded shrewdly. "Lisa Marie Walker."

I took a noncommittal sip of coffee.

He nodded, making up his mind about something. His normally hard demeanor changed somehow, and I gave him my full attention. "So . . . ," he began. "About that. I got my hands on the autopsy for her. Absolutely no surprises in the M.E.'s report. High blood-alcohol content. Some facial bruising, but she'd been in a car accident. No other injuries. Water in the lungs. Died of drowning."

I absorbed all this, disappointed. I didn't know what I had expected.

*"What's he not saying?"* Alan asked.

I glanced up at Strickland and saw him gazing back intently. If anything, his expression had become even more un-Strickland-like. Uncomfortable, maybe. "All completely normal," he told me. "And then I saw the photographs."

# 22

## This Is Huge

The expression on Strickland's face was one I'd never seen on him before: uncertainty. He seemed almost hesitant to continue.

"What about the photographs?" I prompted tensely.

"Ruddy, I want to clear the air with you on this. When you came to me with the story of this girl and what she claimed to have seen that night, I did not for a moment believe she was telling you the truth. I didn't know why she would lie, but her story seemed improbable. No, impossible. I really didn't think there was anything to it. So I dismissed it out of hand, though in all my years as a lawman I thought I had learned by now not to discount anything, to treat everything as evidence. I'm sorry for that."

I nodded at him, swallowing.

"I told you the medical examiner was incompetent," he continued.

"Yes, you said that."

He shook his head in disgust. "There's no way Lisa Marie Walker spent five days in the water. Even really cold water. I've seen bodies pulled from the lake, and they look pretty rough. She was *pristine*." Strickland sighed. "So I went back through and read the autopsy again, and saw some things that were missed. For one thing, she was floating."

*"But bodies float; that's how we find people who drown. The decomposition gasses make them float,"* Alan argued.

Strickland nodded as if he'd heard the voice in my head. "I know, you expect them to float. But there's an order to it. A corpse floats at first, then it sinks. Then, as it decomposes, it comes back to the surface. In the postmortem, the lack of decomposition is noted by Dr. Kane and explained away as due to the cold water temperature. But five days? Also, she was nude. And I've seen that, too. I can't explain why, but when I was a cop in Muskegon, there was a body that had been in the water for a couple of months, and the clothes had come off somehow. Washed away or something. Rotted, maybe. But five days?"

"You're saying she wasn't in the water very long."

He grunted. "My opinion, she probably went in the night before she was found."

"So she wasn't in the car when I drove into the lake."

"I do not believe she was."

I sat back, waiting to feel it: elation. Vindication. Or even a sense of time wasted, of a life ruined over a lie. And I felt . . . nothing.

*"My God, my God, this is huge,"* Alan breathed. At least *he* was feeling something. Maybe that's why I invented him, to process things I apparently could not.

"So now what? Can you get your hands on the other autopsy reports?" I pressed.

"The other . . . So you really believe that list you gave me is all murder victims?"

"Have you checked them out?"

"No. Tell you the truth, the list is still sitting on the kitchen counter." He held up a hand. "I only saw the autopsy photographs yesterday, Ruddy. Up until that point, I was just going along with you to help you work this out in your head, to get past what I thought was a sick joke. I didn't expect to find anything in the file. Those photographs hit me like a punch in the gut."

"But now you do believe me."

"I do believe that something happened to Lisa Marie Walker that wound up with her dead body being pulled from the lake."

"There's more." I told Strickland about the semen.

He looked thunderstruck. "Dr. Kane *withheld* that?"

"It's what he told me."

"That's a criminal offense."

"I imagine so."

Strickland incredulously shook his head. "I don't suppose he kept it."

"No, he said then he would have had to put it in his report, and that would have caused agony to the family."

"The man is an embarrassment. I don't need to tell you. . . ." Strickland stopped, fixing me with his steely eyes. "Would it have been your semen, Ruddy?"

"No, sir. I never so much as kissed her. In fact, once she climbed in the backseat, I never *saw* her."

"I don't think I can get into the other files, not without a reason," Strickland told me, addressing my question.

"Why did someone let you have the file on Lisa Marie?"

He looked sheepish. "I explained that you and I are working for Kramer, and I wanted to check into your past." He looked past me, over my shoulder. "Here they are," he told me.

State Police Captain Cutty Wells had an iron grip, a disciplined posture, and a no-nonsense gaze. She also wore lipstick and a uniform that completely failed to camouflage her feminine curves. Her curly hair was styled in a blunt, fashionable cut. Her nails were sculpted and painted pink. I found myself a little tongue-tied as we were introduced, sorting through my reactions to this tough woman with her military bearing and stylish tastes. She looked to be a few years younger than Strickland—fifty, maybe—but was clearly very fit.

*"She's a knockout,"* Alan gasped, sounding like a teenage boy
with an instant crush.

The D.A., Darrell Hughes, was the kind of smarmy jerk who
grew up rich, went to law school on Daddy's dime, knew what
kind of sweater to wear on a sailboat as opposed to a yacht, and
expected everyone to love him and laugh at his jokes. The kind
of guy who wears suits that cost more than my truck and who
has a Rolex on his wrist.

Well, I actually didn't know anything about his background
and his suit didn't really look all that expensive and his watch
was one of those cheap digital jobs, but I liked the angry feeling
I got when I pictured him living a life of privilege. He was blond,
with striking pale-brown eyes, a smooth complexion, handsome features. He looked so much like a district attorney that he
always ran unopposed, the opposition giving up the second they
saw one of his campaign posters.

"Mis-ter McCann," Hughes said to me, drawing out his words.

"Darrell," I greeted, shaking his hand.

He grinned at me. "Okay, then. First-name basis." They both
sat down at our booth. "So, you want to tell me how it is that
Blanchard called you, of all people, for this thing?"

Both Strickland and Cutty Wells gave Hughes a cold look.
He gave an oh-I-got-caught-I'm-so-bad non-apology grin and
shrugged. "I'll let these two ask the questions."

"Let's not mention any names," Cutty suggested, glancing
around the room. The place was virtually empty. Hughes shrugged
again.

*"She's not just beautiful, she's smart. She really has it together,"*
Alan murmured.

We talked for an hour about the individual who had made the
murder-for-hire proposition, speaking euphemistically about the
"candidate" who wanted to "contract my services." If the restaurant staff overheard anything, they probably assumed we were
planning the D.A.'s reelection campaign.

"All right," Cutty summarized. "He's got some sort of plan he's going to tell you about, and that's when he's going to pay you."

"*Not exactly,*" Alan disagreed for my benefit alone.

"Actually, I get the impression he *doesn't* have a plan—not one that's fully baked, anyway," I corrected. "I have the feeling he doesn't usually think too far ahead." I reflected briefly on the party boat where he had fleeced his friends without considering they might figure out it was a setup and refuse to pay, but elected not to mention it to the state police. "He knows he'll be the first person anyone will look at, so he is trying to come up with something bulletproof."

"Maybe he's got a plan for *you,*" Hughes suggested, his grin indicating he kind of hoped so. He made a gun out of his hand and pointed it at me.

"*This guy is a douchebag,*" Alan observed. I frowned over his use of a word I'd never before heard him utter. It was as if some of my personality were leeching through the blood-brain barrier into his.

"All right. We'll get ready to wire you up. He calls you, any-time day or night, I want you to ring me here." Cutty passed me a card with a phone number handwritten on it—her cell, I presumed. As I took it, a faint waft of her perfume gave my senses the barest touch, and I could almost feel Alan swooning.

"Need to get money from him. The crime is exchanging something of value for the . . . the service," D.A. Darrell lectured me in a professional D.A. voice.

"Get the money," I agreed affably.

Cutty glanced around the table. "All right, then. We wait for him to make the next move."

"Hey, Darrell, before we go, I have a favor to ask of you."

Darrell looked at me expectantly, anticipating how much he was going to enjoy turning me down.

"My probation. Since I'm involved in the 'recruitment' of the 'candidate'"—I gestured at Cutty meaningfully—"I'm thinking we could call an end to my visits with the psychiatrist. She's on temporary disability leave anyway, and this new guy is having trouble getting with the program."

Darrell had started shaking his head at the word *probation*. "Can't do that. The judge is the only person who can change the terms."

"Well, could you speak to the judge?"

"Not sure why I should do that."

"I'm not sure why I should take Blanchard's call."

Strickland and Cutty were glaring at me.

*"You said his name out loud,"* Alan chided.

Hughes gave the others a can-you-believe-this-guy? expression. "Are you trying to *bargain* with me, McCann?"

"I'm pointing out that I'm putting myself into a risky business, and I could use a favor in return," I responded.

Hughes clearly wasn't going to grant my request.

"For God's sake, look at the bigger picture here, Darrell," Cutty suggested pleasantly. Strickland made an affirmative noise, and Hughes looked blandly at his two companions for a moment.

"All right. I can't promise anything, but I'll send an e-mail," D.A. Darrell agreed.

The wind had lessened a little by the time I drove down the road where Mark Stevens and Kenny MacDonell were allegedly working. This time the pickup I was looking for was pulled up to the garage of the small house with all the construction materials lying around in the yard. Towing it out would be no challenge at all. I was a little disappointed—I had this fantastic new weapon in the fight to affect repos and was hardly getting a chance to use it.

As soon as I got out of the tow truck I heard it—a loud boom coming from the house. Not a gunshot—more like an impact, as if someone were taking a sledgehammer to the walls. Curious, I went up the front steps. *Boom.*

*"This isn't good,"* Alan fretted, so naturally, instead of knocking, I opened the front door and poked my head into the house.

"Mark? That you?" I yelled.

"Up here!" he yelled back.

I found some stairs and climbed up them. The interior of the house was warmer than the outside, but not by much. At the top of the stairs and down the hall, Kenny and Mark were setting a six-by-six fence post on the floor. Both of them were panting.

"Hey, guys."

They were a lot scruffier than the last time I'd seen them. Mark's rodent-brown hair and scraggy beard were oily, and the beard looked like a flock of crows had been at it. Kenny's pale Irish skin was red and chapped from the cold, his orange hair sticking up in unruly tufts and cowlicks.

"Ruddy!" Kenny greeted. They both slipped off their work gloves to shake my hand, but then Mark's expression changed as he connected my profession to his pickup truck.

"What are you guys doing?" I asked curiously. The fence post seemed out of place.

"We've been hired to remodel this dump," Mark explained.

"We also get to live here, which is sweet. We'd been living in Mark's brother's ice shanty out Boyne City way," Kenny enthused.

"Okay, but what's with the fence post?" I asked.

"Oh yeah." Kenny nodded. "See that air conditioner?"

The bedroom he pointed to was directly over the garage, I figured. In the window was a massive air conditioner, almost the size of a small car. It appeared to be a half-century old and, when I examined it more closely, actually had the word CHRYSLER etched into a metal plate on the front. The plastic cover had been removed, and the front coil was pretty dented up. "Looks like this Chrysler's been in a fender bender," I commented.

Kenny thought this was pretty funny, but Mark was still eyeing me suspiciously. "No, what it is," Kenny said, "the thing is stuck. So we're taking this fence post and ramming the sucker out."

"Why not just disassemble it?" I asked.

Kenny shrugged. "This way is more fun."

"Ah. Well, I'm glad to see you guys working. You get some money up front this time?"

Kenny nodded vigorously, ignoring Mark's warning glance. "Oh yeah. Thousand bucks each, then two fifty a week."

"That's going to work out, then," I replied, looking at Mark.

"Sure will," Kenny agreed blissfully.

"So you're four payments behind, Mark. That's eleven hundred dollars."

"I can pay something next week," he offered.

"Wait," Kenny interjected. "What are we talking about here?"

"How much do you have on you?" I pressed.

"Nothing." Mark glanced away.

"Kenny, how much have you got on you?"

"On me? Money? A few hundred," Kenny responded.

"I need eleven hundred bucks."

"Is this about the truck?" Kenny asked.

"He's a repo man. What do you think?" Mark demanded.

"Okay, but we need the truck," Kenny replied.

"Eleven hundred dollars," I said, my hand out.

Mark reached into his pocket and pulled out a crumpled wad of bills. He had just over eight hundred. I turned to Kenny.

"But no, that's not what this money is for!" Kenny protested. "This money is our starting money; it's, like, fun money. Next week's money, that's the bill-paying money,"

"I'm about two seventy short," I replied.

"It's not my truck! It's Mark's truck."

"You said we need the truck," Mark reminded him. "You want him to take it? How are we going to get the lumber and all the other crap we need if we don't have a truck?"

Kenny counted out the rest of it like he was saying good-bye to his children.

"There's going to be a collection fee added to the end of your contract now," I told Mark. "Two hundred dollars. You actually don't have to pay it, but it will show up on your credit if you don't."

"My credit," Mark snorted.

*"Ask him about Shantytown,"* Alan suggested.

"So you guys have been staying in Shantytown?"

"Yeah." Kenny nodded. "It was fun at first, fishing every day, but after a while I'm like, 'Wouldn't it be nice to like shower or something?'"

"You have running water here?"

"Not yet. Power is supposed to be on today, though, so we'll have heat and then we'll get water," Mark replied.

*"Shantytown,"* Alan insisted.

"You guys know the mayor of Shantytown?" I queried, biting back my irritation.

"Phil? Oh yeah." Mark nodded. "Everybody knows Phil. He's famous."

"What's his last name?" I asked.

The two men looked at each other and then shrugged. "Mayor?" Kenny guessed.

"His name's not Mayor," Mark sneered disgustedly.

"They call him Mr. Mayor. So, you know, that's as close to a last name as I know of," Kenny explained defensively.

"Would you guys be willing to meet me out there tomorrow morning, show me around, introduce me to the mayor?"

"Sure. We got nothing better to do now that you've got all our money," Mark pouted.

"But look at it this way: at least you can drive there," I responded. I looked at the fence post. "You guys want a hand with that thing?"

The three of us hoisted the big beam off the floor. It was

pressure-treated wood and weighed what felt like fifty pounds. We awkwardly gripped the thing and strode over to the air conditioner and hit it. *Boom.* The Chrysler rocked in its frame.

We grinned at one another. This actually *was* fun.

*"Hey, Ruddy?"* Alan said.

"Let's take a running start," I suggested.

We backed up.

*"Wait!"* Alan said urgently.

Mark yelled, "Go!" and the three of us ran across the room. We hit the air conditioner with such violence, the thing *exploded* out of the frame, landing a second later with a horrendous crash.

*"Isn't Mark's truck parked directly underneath the window?"* Alan asked into our triumphant whooping.

# 23

## Wrong About Everything

Mark and Kenny were high-fiving each other, but I had dropped out of the celebration. Alan had a good point.

"Awesome!" Kenny shouted. "Man, we hit that thing."

"Boom!" Mark enthused.

"Did you see? We *hit* that thing."

"Boom!" Mark repeated.

"Damn!"

"Boom!"

We all went to the rectangular hole in the wall, through which light snow was fluttering. Everyone went quiet when we saw what the air conditioner had done when it landed on the roof of Mark's pickup. The windshield was opaque with spider webs, and the monstrosity itself lay cradled in a huge dent in the top of the cab.

"*Boom,*" Alan observed with sincere irony.

"Huh," Kenny said, rubbing his chin.

"Uh, I changed my mind. You can repo the truck," Mark advised me.

As long as I was so close, I cruised over to the Ferry Bar. The same two guys were sitting on the same two stools, wearing the same clothes and drinking the same beers. I wondered if Rogan took them out back and hosed them off every once in a while or if he let them decompose in place.

"Hey, Wade," I said as I slid onto the seat next to the empty one reserved for the mayor. Without me having to ask, he pulled down the tab on the same brand of beer I'd had last time. I liked that. "You seen Phil?"

Rogan regarded me with friendly eyes. "You know what? I haven't seen him in quite a while. This keeps up, I'm going to have to let other people sit on his stool."

"*Maybe he's gone south for a vacation,*" Alan suggested.

I decided I didn't want that to be true, so I didn't mention it. "Let me ask you something," I said instead. "How did he act when you told him why I wanted to talk to him?"

"What do you mean?" Rogan asked, polishing a glass.

"Did he look . . ."

"*Furtive?*" Alan suggested, as if I guy like me would ever say a word like that aloud.

"Scared?" I asked. "Alarmed?"

"I don't get what you mean," the bartender responded.

"Well, what did you tell him?"

"I just said you were a private detective looking into some missing persons cases, and you had this whole list of women, and that one of them on your list was Nina Otis, who fell off the boat on the way to Beaver Island. That you wanted to talk to anyone who might have seen her that day, the day she fell. And I gave him your card."

"Did he say anything to *you* about Nina Otis?"

"No. I was a little busy, though. Why?"

"Just seems strange. You ask him about Nina Otis, and he vanishes."

Rogan's eyes crinkled as he thought about it. "Yeah, I guess that is pretty odd. You think he might have had something to do with it?"

"Honestly, no. I've been thinking—you know who would be the perfect person to get away with a murder?"

*"For God's sake,"* Alan said disgustedly.

"Who?"

"An M.E. Medical examiner. Any clues left on the body, why, they don't show up in the autopsy, do they? Hair and fiber, fingerprints . . . *semen* . . . You're the perfect guy to do it."

"Whoa," Rogan said, with admiration. "That's pretty smart."

*"He's no better a suspect than anyone else on the list,"* Alan muttered.

"But I do have to talk to Phil. What's his last name, anyway?"

Rogan frowned. "You know, I never heard it. He's just Phil."

"Do you know which shanty is his in Shantytown? I am supposed to meet some guys there tomorrow to show me around, but they've recently busted their windshield and might not show. I'm not relishing the idea of walking all the way out there—the things are scattered for what looks like four square miles."

Rogan laughed. "I don't know anything about Shantytown, Ruddy. Not my thing, sit in a box and look at a hole all day."

I told Rogan thanks, especially when he waved off my payment for the beer. "Most interesting conversation I've had all year," he told me. "Good luck with everything."

Alan was fuming, I could just tell. As soon as we were outside, he jumped on me. *"What are you doing, telling him everything?"*

"I didn't tell him anything," I corrected testily. "He revealed some information."

*"Like what?"*

"Like Phil hasn't been in."

*"We already knew that."*

"That as soon as Phil heard what I wanted, he took off and hasn't been seen since."

*"That's not what the man said."*

"You know what? I've been in this business a long time, trying to find people. And the best way to get information is to give information."

*"That makes no sense whatsoever."*

"Whereas having an actual argument with a voice in my head is so totally sensible. I don't know why more people don't do it. Think what a perfect world it would be if everyone went around *arguing* with a damn voice in their *heads*!"

Cruising down M-66, I mentioned to Alan that we would be close to Katie's work and maybe should stop in to say hi. He thought that was a bad idea, which helped me make up my mind to do it. She was busy on the computer but seemed genuinely pleased to see me, and when I asked her out to dinner, she told me her boss had brought in some fish he'd just caught and suggested I eat at her place, proving Alan completely wrong about everything. I mentioned I had an appointment the next morning in Boyne City, much closer to her little rental house than Kalkaska, and she said that was pretty convenient. I couldn't have agreed more.

*"Are you and my daughter back together?"* Alan asked me sourly as I drove home to pick up some clothes.

"I'm not really sure," I replied honestly. "We're apparently not officially un-engaged, but we're not talking about getting married, and she's not wearing her ring. We sleep in separate places, except when we don't, and she's invited me to dinner tonight."

*"Except when you don't,"* he repeated gravely.

Oh yeah, the dad thing.

*"When did that happen?"*

I sighed. "Remember the morning she was heading off to work from my place, first day as a licensed real estate agent?"

*"Ruddy . . . I can't promise you I will be asleep when I need to be. And you can't ask me . . . She's my daughter."*

I didn't think it was time to tell him about my newfound ability to push him away when I needed to. We would just get into a

huge argument, him insisting he was a real person and me pointing out that if I could force him to leave, it meant I was making
him up.

"Let's just handle that when I need to. I promise I won't make
you be part of anything," I vowed.

He was silent, though I could sense him worrying about it.
And after a while, I found something of my own to worry about.

Could I make him leave if I wasn't on the medication?


Becky wasn't at the Black Bear, so I parked the tow truck at the
repo lot and walked the few blocks to the house she and Kermit
shared. I knocked and entered, calling, "Hello?" over the unmis-
takable sound of a circular saw biting wood.

"In the garage!" Becky yelled back. I made my way to the
door just off the kitchen, noting that some of the cabinets had
been taken down from the wall.

Becky's garage had been turned into a workshop. She smiled
at me, raising her safety glasses. "Hi, Ruddy! What's in the box?"

"It's just a gift for the baby. A Michigan State blanket." I
waved the box at her. Alan made an approving noise because the
gift had been his idea. Becky opened the box and held up the
square of green-and-white cloth, grinning.

"Thanks!"

"So, what are you doing?" I asked.

"I'm building a pantry for the kitchen before I lay down the
new floor."

"No, I mean what are you *doing*? You're pregnant. You can't
be sawing wood. You need to be resting."

"Oh, stop. I'm fine."

"*Women can work pretty much right up until they're due, if
they're careful and healthy,*" Alan informed me. He had been
married to a woman who gave birth a single time, so that made
him some sort of expert.

"Won't the wood fumes be bad for little Ruddy Junior?" I asked.

"Wood fumes," Becky repeated, laughing along with Alan. "And what if it is a girl?"

"I don't know. . . . Ruddette?"

"You kill me."

"I just came by to see if it is okay if I leave Jake with you tonight."

"Oh?" She raised her eyebrows.

"Date. Katie." I was grinning.

*"You just came by to tell your sister you have a date with my daughter and are presuming you'll spend the night with her,"* Alan translated moodily.

"That's really good, Ruddy." She walked up to me and gazed into my eyes. "How are things with her?"

"She came back from downstate with a change of heart. She said she talked to her mother, who said such terrible things about me, Katie figured I must be a nice guy after all."

*"And you were going to tell me this when?"* Alan demanded angrily. *"Katie spoke to Marget?"*

"I knew she'd come around," Becky said encouragingly.

"I don't want to blow it with her."

"You won't. Just be the man she fell in love with the first time." I liked that one. "Thanks, Becky."

She looked around her workshop. "Well, I'd ask you to help, but I don't want to have to do everything all over again."

"Very funny." We were both grinning, though.


Alan jumped on me the moment I left my sister's house. "So sorry I didn't mention Katie talked to Marget," I apologized. "I've had a lot on my mind."

*"So she's forgiven her mother for what was done to me?"* Alan asked, anguished.

"I don't know that. But, Alan, would that really be so bad? Marget is her mom. She raised Katie. Don't people eventually have to forgive? Move on?"

*"Like you moved on from Lisa Marie Walker?"* Alan retorted.

I felt my face flash hot despite the cold air. "I get that you can't take a swing at me from in there, but if you're trying to get to me, that one didn't even make any sense. I did move on, got on with my life, and now I'm back in it because I'm looking for the truth. Because as much as I owe it to myself, I owe it to her; because I may not have driven her into the lake, but I did drive her to the 7-Eleven. Because I care that someone murdered her. Which you know damn well. Try going back to insulting my trousers; you had better luck with that."

*"Hey, I'm sorry,"* he said after a pause. *"You're right: I'm angry, but I shouldn't be upset with you. It just feels like Katie's choosing sides. Picking her, Marget, instead of me."*

"Your daughter isn't very easy to figure out, I'll grant you that. But the one thing I can tell you is that she'll make up her mind without help from anybody else."

Back at the repo lot, I told Kermit he and Becky would be taking care of my dog for the night. "But you'll be here for the Wolfingers' send-off party, though, right?" he asked me.

"Oh yeah, that's tomorrow night? I wouldn't miss it."

"Becky is launching a luau."

"I will be there for the countdown and takeoff."

I bent down to tell Jake he would be sleeping at my sister's place, but that I would be back and he needn't worry that I was abandoning him. It worked: He seemed pretty unworried.

*"I know what was going on with your sister,"* Alan advised as I walked home.

"Becky? Do tell."

*"You know there is no such thing as wood fumes, and that she's not going to hurt herself when she's not even showing yet. You're acting dumb and protective to let her know you care*

*about her and you're going to love her baby. Instead of just com-*
*ing out and telling her."*

"No such thing as wood fumes?" I demanded with exagger-
ated incredulity.

Alan sighed. *"Are you ever going to get a haircut?"* he replied
irrelevantly.

I ran a hand through my hair. "Just getting more handsome
every day," I proclaimed.

At home I changed into my one nice pair of pants and a
sweater I'd been wearing to social occasions since the late nine-
ties. When I sniffed it to make sure it was still fresh smelling,
Alan nearly had a seizure. I threw a few clothes into an overnight
bag and made sure I took my heaviest boots and gloves—it
would be cold out there tomorrow, on the ice of Shantytown.
If Kenny and Mark didn't show up, I'd be forced to knock on a
few doors.

The Black Bear showed up on caller ID just as I was heading
out to the truck. It was Jimmy. We exchanged how-ya-doin's as
I cranked up the engine. "Hey, could you do me a favor?" he
asked me.

"Shoot."

"I lost my cell phone. Would you call it for me? Maybe I can
hear it ring if it's around here."

Alan snickered.

"Jimmy . . . couldn't you just call it from the phone you're using now?"

"Uh, well, I thought that the sound of it in my ear might make
it so I can't hear my cell."

"Okay," I said. "But you could hold it away from your ear if
you wanted."

"Hey, yeah, that would work!" he agreed cheerfully.

"Say, Jimmy, you got a minute?"

"Pretty dead here," he grunted agreeably.

I told him where I was with Katie. "I think it sounds good," he told me when I was finished. "Like she's working things out in her life, and she sees you as part of that."

"You think I should talk about the wedding?"

"Only if she brings it up," Jimmy advised.

"Got it."

"*I cannot believe you're getting advice about dating my daughter from this moron,*" Alan sniffed.

We rang off. I set the cell phone in a cupholder and started down the road. "Alan," I said after a moment, "you may not ever, *ever,* call Jimmy a moron. You got that? He's like a brother to me. You do that again, and I will never speak to you."

"*I'm sorry.*"

"All your questions will go unanswered. I'll stop discussing Lisa Marie, Nina Otis, and everyone else with you. You'll be alone in the world." *Or maybe I'll just make you go away forever,* I thought to myself.

"*I get it. I said I was sorry. She's my daughter, Ruddy. I don't like you discussing strategy about her, like she's a hill the squad needs to take in a war.*"

"You'd rather have her with someone who doesn't care enough to try to figure her out? To give her what she wants? Because I know Deputy Dumbbell is awfully convenient. That's who her mother, Marget, with her overbearing influence, wants her to marry."

That shut him up, leaving me to ponder: Since when did Alan ever use a military analogy?

Strickland phoned me as I was pulling up in front of Katie's house. "Going to be sub-zero all week," he informed me.

"Great, I'm going to Shantytown tomorrow. Wait, do you know which hut belongs to the mayor?"

"Hell no. The mayor? He's not a mayor; the whole thing is idiotic. Just a bunch of guys sitting in small boxes, drinking themselves into a stupor everyday."

"It sounds pretty fun, the way you put it. Do you know the mayor's name?"

"Phil somebody."

"Okay, thanks. Good to know."

"Well, the reason I called."

"Yes?"

"I ran your list past a buddy, and we got a hit on one."

"A hit? They found her? Was she drowned?"

"Yeah, they found her. Rachel Rodriguez. But she's not drowned. She ran off and got married to someone her family didn't approve of. She lives in San Diego now."

"Lucky her."

"Yeah. It was in the high seventies there. Dry, though; they could use some rain."

"Any action on anybody else?"

"No, that one just came up right away. The case was old, you know, almost four years ago when she vanished."

I thanked him and hung up. "So we can cross that one off the list," I reasoned to Alan.

*"Right, but that doesn't mean I'm wrong about the others."*

"I'm not saying you are wrong, Alan. Aren't I going to Shantytown tomorrow to try to track down Phil, last name unknown by everybody, your prime suspect in the Nina Otis murder?"

*"So you agree it was murder."*

"I don't know that."

*"You said murder."*

"Jesus, Alan! I'm just trying to figure stuff out. You say Nina Otis was killed and maybe by the same person who did away with Lisa Marie Walker. We've got nothing on Lisa, but maybe the mayor can tell us who was buying Nina drinks before the ferry left, if she was in the Ferry Bar. It's the most tenuous lead I've ever heard, but it's the only one we've got so far."

*"Okay."*

I looked at Katie's tiny rental house. The light was on inside, glowing yellow through the curtains. Her driveway and walk had fresh snow from the other day on it, tracked with evidence of her arrivals and departures. I would grab the shovel from the back of the truck and scrape it away for her.

*"What are we waiting for?"* Alan asked.

Okay, this was it. I couldn't possibly have a date with Katie with her father there, yammering at me, so I went into my mind. I thought of Alan, searched for him. I wasn't on antipsychotics, but I could still feel him, like cotton stuffed into my head. I mentally went to that Alan presence, and, when I got there, I pushed.

# 24

## Why Would Anybody Lie About That?

When I woke up the next morning, the sun was bouncing off the snow, and there were neither clouds nor heat—a blindingly bright, painfully cold day. I could tell we were pushing the thermometer down into record-low territory and reflexively thought of calling Strickland for a weather report.

"I don't want to go out there," Katie moaned next to me.

"Then don't. Let's stay in bed and keep each other alive with our body heat." I demonstrated just how much I could raise our temperatures for a moment, and then she pushed me away with a laugh. "I have to go to *work*," she chided gently.

I went out and started Katie's car for her and scraped the ice off her windows, then ran back into the house so I didn't lose any extremities. When I walked her out and she saw her car, she turned and gave me a look that caused my internal organs to flutter.

As she drove away, she blew me a kiss, and then I got into my own vehicle and invited Alan back—just sort of reopened my mind. "Morning, Alan. You might want to turn up the heat in there today. It's not going to make it to zero."

He grunted.

"So, where did you go last night?" I asked, curious about how it felt from his end when I shut him out of my mind.

*"Go? What do you mean? I fell asleep. Isn't that what you wanted?"*

"Sure."

We drove to Boyne City and pulled up in front of the coffee shop where I told Mark and Kenny I'd meet them. When they arrived, I saw that they had dented the roof of their truck back up from the inside, maybe by using a chunk of the same battering ram we used in the assault on the air conditioner. It looked like an elk had tried to kick its way out of the cab.

Plus there was no windshield.

They were both wearing full woolen face masks, white chunks of ice clinging to the front where their mouths were. They slid into the booth across from me and pulled off their masks, looking shell-shocked as they gazed at me almost without recognition. Their lips were blue, their faces drained of color.

Kenny said something to me, but his mouth was so numb, I couldn't understand it. I told him to be careful with the coffee—it was hot, and I didn't want him burning himself.

"I sort of thought you boys might stop at the junkyard and get yourselves a new windshield," I drawled.

Mark was staring at his coffee as if his brain had disconnected from the rest of him. Kenny was shivering. "We're kind of short on funds, and we don't got any more credit there," Mark slurred.

"Yeah, but you can't drive around with no window on a day like today. You'll *die*."

"We tried driving in reverse but the other cars got mad at us," Kenny replied. "So then we took turns for five minutes each, one person driving, the other person ducked down under the dashboard to stay out of the wind."

I thought about it. "Here," I said. I pulled out my wallet and laid five twenties on the table.

Mark stirred, showing life for the first time. He mumbled something like, "Huh?" only not as articulate.

"That's what I get for collecting payments instead of pulling in a repo, that fee I told you about," I explained. "My contribution toward the windshield. You guys want breakfast?"

Kenny's eyes were shining like a kid's on Christmas morning. Mark raised his coffee to his lips and slurped. "Thanks, man," Mark said. "My cousin owns a body shop in Petoskey. With this we got enough to buy the glass and he'll carry us on the labor."

I nodded. I knew both Mark's cousin and the body shop—I'd affected a repossession on the former from the latter. "After we go out and talk to Phil what's-his-name, I'll tow your truck to Petoskey for you," I offered.

*"You're the nicest repo man in world,"* Alan noted sardonically. I wondered if it was his forced ejections from my brain that were making him so cranky.

We got so toasty warm in the café that stepping back outside caused us to gasp in shock. Eyes watering, we trooped in single file out toward the shanties. The wind had blown away loose snow, and some brave or stupid soul had driven a plow all around the area so that we were walking on white ice that felt like concrete underfoot.

There were several huts that were nice: prefabricated jobs on runners. More often, though, they were tiny little shelters built of weathered wood and plastic sheeting. Some had stovepipes. Many of them looked ready to fall over.

I was glad to have my guides. There were no people visible and, judging by the lack of smoke from the metal chimney pipes, there was virtually no one inside the things, this sub-zero day. Kenny and Mark led me straight to my destination.

Phil the mayor's place was larger than many, but not all, of the places, a solid but old-looking shelter that felt randomly positioned off to one side, not at all in the center of the "town."

Kenny pounded on the door, using a gloved hand, then surprised me when, after no one responded, he reached up and opened the door. I followed him inside, though.

The place was, I was sorry to note, unheated. A portable toilet at one end had a curtain for a modicum of privacy, and at the other end there was a bunk bed built at head height. In between these two places was a hole the size of a basketball hoop, a black circle in white ice. There was a trapdoor in the floor to cover this hole, but the trap was open.

"You pretty good friends with this guy?" I speculated.

Kenny shook his head. "Not really. He just lets people come in if they want. See, he's got the emergency equipment." Kenny opened some cupboards. I saw medical supplies, a flare gun, and other miscellaneous safety stuff.

I reached out and picked up a red metal can, a stout sixteen-ouncer with a cone top. "I haven't seen this in a while," I marveled. "Didn't know they still made it."

"*What's starter fluid?*" Alan asked, reading the label on the red can.

"This stuff is for the old clunkers people drive out here, the ones that have carburetors. It's ether, really volatile. You pour the ether down the throat of the carburetor, and it gives your engine an extra kick."

Mark and Kenny nodded, unimpressed. "Stove's not going," Mark observed.

"Yeah. And look, the fishin' hole's froze over. I think Phil hasn't been here for a couple of days," Kenny added.

"*He hasn't been at the Ferry Bar recently, either,*" Alan observed unnecessarily. But I knew what he was thinking: Had we identified our murderer?

"Let's go get some kerosene," Mark suggested.

We trudged fifty yards to a flimsy hut with canvas for a door. Inside was a guy who sold kerosene. Incredibly, and in complete violation of the law, he stored the stuff in clear, one-gallon glass jugs. He had two walls of his place lined with the containers, all on shelves. He told us he would let us take a couple back, and put it on the mayor's account.

"He's recycling jugs from an apple cider mill?" I asked, reading the label on the jug we were carrying as we headed back to Phil's place. Something else illegal—you weren't supposed to put petroleum products in old cider jugs.

"It's a sweet deal," Kenny told me. "See, he has this orchard, so in the fall he puts up the apple cider and makes people pay him a deposit for the jugs. Then, when they bring the jugs back in, he fills them with kerosene—he's got a huge tank next to his garage. He sells the stuff out here, and by the end of winter he's got all these empty jugs, ready to be refilled with cider again."

"Does he clean them first?" Alan and I asked at precisely the same moment.

Kenny frowned. "I don't really know."

"Kenny. Think about it. Of course he rinses them out," Mark chided.

"I don't know. The kerosene would sorta sterilize things, wouldn't it?"

We filled the stove at Phil's shanty and pushed the starter button and were rewarded with a blue flame and what felt like no heat whatsoever.

"Maybe he got up in the middle of the night to use the toilet and fell in the hole," I observed, only half joking.

Kenny nervously shut the trapdoor.

"Sorry about the wasted trip," Mark told me.

"Oh no. It wasn't wasted at all," I assured him.


After I dropped the boys and their truck off in Petoskey, Alan had an odd request: He wanted to go back to Boyne City. "Why?" I asked him. "I think it is pretty clear our man has flown the coop. I was thinking my next move would be to ask Strickland to check into good old Phil, find out his background. He's our man. He sat on his personal stool and bought Nina Otis drinks and then grabbed her somehow."

*"Just humor me,"* Alan suggested, as if talking to him wasn't humoring him. Pretending he *existed* was humoring him.

So in the name of humor, we drove back to Boyne City. Just as we hit the outskirts of town, Alan asked me to slow down. I accommodated him, looking blankly around. Here the trees were as thick as on Strickland's property—we were pretty close to his house, in fact. I wondered if I should stop by to make my request in person and find out how he felt about what a cold day it was.

*"There,"* Alan said.

I looked. I saw no there there, no there anywhere. "What?"

*"Did you see it?"*

"See what?"

*"Go back."*

Feeling a lot less humorous, I nonetheless swung the heavy truck into a ponderous U-turn and went back up the road. *"Stop right here,"* Alan told me. Across the street, on the lake side, there was a mailbox nearly buried in snow, a plowed gravel driveway disappearing into the trees.

"What is it?" I demanded.

*"The mailbox. See the name?"*

I did see. "Rogan." I thought about it. "You think this could be our dentist turned bar owner?"

*"I don't know why not."*

"Rogan's a pretty common name."

*"Okay, sure."*

I put on my light bar so that people would know I was on official business and got out and crossed the road, opening the mailbox over Alan's objections that I was committing a federal offense. The mail was all addressed to Wade Rogan.

"It's him, all right," I said.

*"Do you think the house is on the lake?"*

"Probably."

*"So why would Rogan tell us he didn't know anything about*

*Shantytown? If he lives on the lake, he's looking at it all winter long."*

I thought about it. "Let's see if he's home and ask him," I suggested.

*"What? No, I don't think that's a good idea."*

I drove down the driveway, which was shouldered with five feet of snow on both sides. Rogan lived in a two-story home with stained wood siding. A snowmobile was sitting uncovered but clean by the steps to his front porch—most people who leave their machines outside put heavy tarps on them when they're not in use. I knocked on the door, but no one answered.

His driveway curled to the right to a detached garage, but there were tire tracks in the snow right down to the ice. I followed them on foot. Alan was right: You could see all of beautiful downtown Shantytown from Rogan's place.

I decided to find out where the tracks led. It was hard but not impossible to see where to go once I was on the ice: Patches of packed snow bore the marks of several car trips, and anyway, they were headed in a straight line. I knew where we would wind up long before we got there: a newer model ice shanty, made of metal, a heavy padlock securing the door. "So not only does he spend all winter looking at this place . . . ," I mused.

*"He has a shanty of his own,"* Alan finished for me.

"He said ice fishing wasn't his thing."

*"Right."*

"Why would anybody lie about *that*?"

*"Obviously, to hide something,"* Alan speculated.

"Hide what? That he likes to ice fish?"

I started my truck and headed home, glancing at the mailbox as I drove past it. I didn't know what it meant that Alan read the name on the mailbox when I didn't even notice it. Obviously, though, my eyes must have glanced at it without registering what I was reading—otherwise, Alan wouldn't have seen it. So maybe it lodged into my subconscious, and my subconscious told Alan. Or maybe Alan *was* my subconscious.

*"So we've got the M.E. who either lied or didn't notice that Lisa Marie hadn't been in the water very long and who didn't report the semen or think it was strange she was naked. You've got the mayor of Shantytown who vanishes the minute he hears you want to talk to him about Nina Otis. And you've got Wade Rogan the bartender telling us he doesn't know anything about Shantytown when, in fact, he's a resident."*

"Rogan seems like the weakest suspect," I suggested. "It's a pretty big jump from not admitting you ice fish to being a serial killer."

*"There's something else,"* Alan advised.

"What's that?"

*"Remember when you showed Rogan the pictures of the missing women? When he saw Rachel Rodriguez's photograph? He asked you who it was. Rachel Rodriguez, who Strickland told us isn't dead. She's in San Diego. Maybe the reason Rogan didn't know who she was is because he didn't kill that one."*

"Geez." I rubbed my forehead. "Okay, but also Rachel Rodriguez was sort of the prettiest one. Maybe he was just reacting like any guy would, wanted to know who she was because he thought she was hot."

*"I wouldn't react like that."*

"Okay, any guy but you, Alan."

My cell phone rang. I reached down and answered it, enduring a sigh from Alan, who felt it was unsafe for me to talk and drive.

"Ruddy? Time to make good on our arrangement."

It was William Blanchard.

# 25

## Time to Kill Alice Blanchard

Blanchard was living in his vacation place on Lake Charlevoix, so I expected that he would want to meet nearby. My grip on the phone tightened, though, when he named the time and place.

"Eight a.m. Parking lot, Ironton Ferry landing," he said, still affecting a tough-guy terseness. "Tomorrow morning."

I was silent.

"Know the place?" he asked.

"Yeah. You're serious. That's where you want to meet."

"Nobody around. Ferry's obviously not running. Yeah. Got a problem?"

I couldn't hear any guile in his voice, no sly taunt. He obviously knew nothing about my history with the place. "No problem," I grunted.

"See you then."

"Right."

"And I'll have your money."

"Good."

He was quiet for what seemed like a minute. "Okay," he replied slowly. He hung up.

*"Something happened at the very end, there,"* Alan observed.

"I know. It's like he thought of something, but I don't know what." I called Cutty Wells, and she picked up on the first ring.

She wanted to meet at the state police station in Cadillac, Michigan, which was a forty-five-minute drive from Kalkaska but would put me an hour and a half away from the Ironton Ferry, so we decided we had to be there at five o'clock in the morning. When I say, "we decided," I mean that Cutty told me what time to be there, like a coach stating what time practice began. She didn't say please.

"*That's pretty early,*" Alan the detective noted.

"They better have donuts," I agreed.

The Black Bear was packed for Claude and Wilma's send-off. Becky roasted a pig and brought in fresh pineapples and served mai tais. Wilma tried to teach the women to do the hula, standing underneath Bob the Bear in what a less cultured person might say was a somewhat incongruent juxtaposition.

Katie wasn't there—the cold snap had layered a lot of black ice on the highway, and I didn't want her to risk it. I told her how much it meant to me that she was willing to make the trip, and I could tell how pleased she was to hear it.

"*I hope their hotel isn't some rat-infested hole,*" Alan murmured as he watched Claude improvise what he claimed was a "male hula." Claude slid his hips sideways and then did a cobra movement with his upper body, arms flailing as if they'd lost their inner bones. Laughing, a half dozen men tried to imitate the motion, spilling their beers on Becky's new wooden floors. If Schaumburg had been there to see what the men were doing, he would have been handing out antipsychotics like crazy.

"Yeah, but it's Hawaii, right? Even if the hotel has a view of a junkyard, they can still get to the beach," I replied. There was so much noise in the bar, no one noticed me talking to myself.

"*Hope so.*"

My eyes tracked two guys coming in out of the cold. One of them was bigger than I was and wore a plaid vest over a clashing plaid flannel shirt in a style I assumed Alan found distasteful. His brown hair matched one of the colors in one of the plaids, and even under the thick cloth I could see he had weight-lifter arms. The other guy was smaller and ferret-faced, with sharp features and jet-black hair. I knew him.

"*Tony Zoppi,*" Alan moaned.


Zoppi saw me wading through the people involved in the choreography, and smirked. I pushed a few revelers aside until I was standing in front of our new guests in front of the door.

"Nice party," Zoppi greeted, sneering a little.

I knew the big guy in the bad plaid too, I realized. His nickname was Buck, and he played high school football a few years after I did. He eyed me carefully, sizing me up in a way I'd seen before in this very bar.

"Let's go outside," I suggested. I reached up to the hook by the front door and snagged my coat, shrugging it on. Zoppi watched all this, an amused expression on his face.

"*Ruddy,*" Alan murmured. "*You sure this is a good idea?*"

I wondered if Alan wanted me to sprint to the repo truck and summon Kermit with the emergency Batphone. We walked down the street half a block so that we were standing directly under a streetlight.

"Did you think I wouldn't find out who took my Jeep?" Zoppi wanted to know.

I was watching Buck's hands, which were shoved into his pockets. I couldn't be sure he didn't have a weapon. "I assumed you would."

"Well, I want it back."

"So why tell me? Call the bank."

"You know who I am?"

"Yeah, you're the guy who skipped making his car payments and then helped me repo his vehicle."

Buck took his hands out of his pockets then, flexing them, and I relaxed. No weapon. He looked tense, ready to get into it, wanting to get it over with.

"Nobody pulls that kind of shit on me and gets away with it," Zoppi stated in an I'm-very-impressed-with-myself voice.

Under that streetlight, the odd orange glare bouncing off the snow, we could see each other very clearly. Good. Moving slowly, I took a single step forward, eyes on Buck, an expression on my face I'd learned to wear in the yard at Jackson State Prison.

After a moment Buck glanced away, and I knew he'd never done any time.

"You really want this, Buck?" I asked softly.

Buck seemed surprised. Probably he didn't realize I would know his name. Then I read the glance he threw at Zoppi perfectly: He was trapped now, and was going to have to go through with this even though he was afraid. We were big guys and would probably hurt each other, but he and I both knew I would hurt him more.

*"How do we know Zoppi doesn't have a gun?"* Alan worried. But I knew he didn't—he wouldn't have brought his big bad bodyguard otherwise.

I made a decision. "You want your Jeep? It's parked out in back of the bank in Traverse City."

Zoppi looked me up and down. "You think I'm stupid?" he asked.

"Well, you let me take your car when I didn't have keys or a tow truck; you think I think you're a genius?" Zoppi scowled and looked expectantly at Buck. "So that's where it is. At the bank," I told the bigger guy. "That's why you came here, to find that out." Buck blinked, absorbing it, and then nodded slightly. I looked at Zoppi. "So either we get some blood on the snow, or I go back to my party and you go pick up your Jeep. But I'm hitting you first, Zoppi."

Zoppi's face weakened, his mafioso fierceness collapsing like the facade it was. I stared at him, ignoring Buck. When neither of them said anything or tried to take a swing at me, I deliberately turned my back on the two men and returned to the Black Bear.

The mai tais did nothing to help me get out of bed in the morning when the alarm sang at four a.m. Only by gulping coffee from a thermos did I keep warm and awake enough to arrive on time at the state police post—a squat one-story brick building with patrol cars and three civilian vehicles in the parking lot—one of which I recognized as Strickland's.

Proving it is better to be a psychosis than a real person, Alan had gone back to sleep as soon as I bid good-bye to Jake, who looked at me as if I'd gone insane. I didn't even try to get him to go pee in the frigid darkness.

We all met in a back room with a large mirror on the wall. Strickland looked irritatingly alert, and D.A. Darrell looked irritatingly arrogant. Cutty Wells looked sleepy, but she'd put on her makeup, and her hair was perfect. Everyone was drinking coffee. I was introduced to two uniformed state policemen but forgot their names. One of them shoved a tray of donuts toward me, and I sighed in gratitude. As I took a bite, Alan woke up—right, I had to drive down here in the dark by myself, but he wakes up for the sprinkles.

"We got permission to enter the restaurant there. The . . ." Cutty turned to Donut Cop.

"Landing," Donut Cop and I said together.

"Right. The Landing. It's closed, but the owner's a great guy and gave me a key last night. We'll be inside, covering everything. Also have two unmarked SUVs that will take up position on M-66 after the target arrives. This is the camera," Cutty continued, passing over a Detroit Tigers baseball cap. "Full video and audio. Point of view, so keep looking at him the whole time."

"It's the Tigers. I'm more of a Cubs fan, myself," I objected.

Everyone stared at me. "Come on, guys; it's a joke," I explained. "Who in his right mind would be a Cubs fan?"

"*I love baseball,*" Alan informed me.

"I think what you're not getting here is the seriousness of the matter," D.A. Darrell lectured. I nodded and reached for another donut, taking a huge bite as he pontificated. "Conspiracy to commit murder. We need you to wrap this up perfectly."

"You want me to wear a baseball cap and look at him. Check," I said agreeably. It sounded like something I could probably handle.

"This is your backup. No camera, just audio," Donut Cop said, passing over a stick of gum. "Put it in your coat pocket. It's very sensitive, so try not to move around too much."

"What happens if I chew it?"

The two cops in uniform grinned, but everyone else wore stony expressions.

"It's what you get on tape that matters," Cutty told me. "As much of the plan as possible. Try to get him to say he wants you to murder his wife. Sometimes it works to say something like, *Any preference on how I do it?* because he might respond that he wants you to shoot her. But draw him out. Talk about it with him."

"*She really is attractive,*" Alan gushed.

"You'll be good at this, Ruddy," Strickland told me.

"And get the money. To convict," the D.A. told me, pointing at my face, "it's something of value for a contract to commit murder."

I could tell by the expression on Cutty's face that there was something about this that she didn't precisely agree with, but she didn't argue. Instead she gazed at me, her eyes intent. "Ruddy, two phrases. You get the money, the 'thing of value' "—I detected a faint sarcasm—"you say *bingo.* That tells us to move in. But if there's any danger, just say *not good.* My team will be on him in seconds."

"*Bingo* for money, *not good* for trouble," I repeated dutifully.

"Don't screw it up," D.A. Darrell warned.

"No, I'll get something of value," I agreed jovially. "About that. The money. It goes into evidence, right?"

"Right. To be presented at trial," Hughes said.

"And then when does it get released? After conviction, or what?"

"What do you mean?" Cutty asked.

"How long before it's no longer needed as evidence?" I elaborated.

Strickland was staring at me with a pained expression. "Ruddy . . . the government keeps the money. You don't get any of it."

I had been reaching for a third donut, but now I frowned. Everyone was nodding in happy confirmation.

"What did you think, that you would get the money?" D.A. Darrell chuckled in a derisive way that seemed to beg for someone's fist to split his lips.

"Uh, are you maybe forgetting that I spent a few years talking to a bunch of convicts every day?" I retorted. "Half of those guys got paid money to set up their buddies for a fall or to give information leading to a bust; it's what they do for a living when they aren't being criminals. So yeah, Darrell, I thought maybe as compensation for getting my ass out of bed to drive to Cadillac at five in the morning and then wearing the hat and carrying the gum, that when you were done showing the jury what five thousand dollars looks like, I might just get to hang on to some of it. Like a reward. You can't pretend you've never done something like that before. It's how this works. I've heard it a thousand times."

"You're helping with an investigation. Bringing a man to justice. That's your reward," D.A. Darrell retorted.

I sat back and regarded the officers. "Not good," I muttered.

"We *are* grateful for your—," Cutty started to say.

"Let me ask you guys a question," I interrupted. "What would have happened if I had gotten the five grand but waited to call you until after I had spent all the money? Would you not be interested in having me wear your hat? Tell me to forget the whole thing?"

Nobody wanted to answer that. I bitterly processed the unspoken answer to my question.

"Let it go, Ruddy," Strickland murmured.

*"Perhaps talking to the convicts gave you the wrong impression,"* Alan suggested gently.

"Hey, sport, I wrote the letter to the court," D.A. Darrell said in a what-more-do-you-want? tone of voice.

"Thanks," I replied listlessly.

The boys in uniform tested the hat camera and the gum backup, indicating they could receive both signals perfectly. "There's also a chip in the hat," Donut Cop advised, "as a backup to our receivers. The chip will be recording everything. You are good to go."


The sky was turning gray, everything on the ground white with snow or black with shadow as I cruised up M-66. Even with my big fat tires, when I came to the hill where I had rolled the last truck, I slowed, creeping along in low gear.

I didn't see the state police SUVs when I drove to the road down to the ferry landing. I assumed they would show up after Blanchard rolled in. I was early by twenty minutes, which gave Alan plenty of time to lecture me on why I should have known I wouldn't get to keep any of the money. "You turn in someone for not paying his taxes, you get a reward," I argued. "This is about murdering someone. Isn't that worse?"

*"Not the same thing,"* he responded.

"I met a ton of guys who set up stings and got to keep some

of the proceeds, but I guess I'm taking my time and risking my life for no reason."

*"Isn't the hat probably recording right now?"*

"Crap!" He was right, of course.

Well, a lot of people talk to themselves.

I glumly surveyed my surroundings. Even though I now believed something else had happened that night, sitting here stirred up all the old feelings of guilt and grief until I was almost sick with it. I believed I was innocent, Alan believed I was innocent, but my soul still blamed me for the death of Lisa Marie Walker.

Blanchard was ten minutes late. He came slowly down the road to the ferry in his Cadillac Escalade, then did something curious, driving all around the parking lot, peering at the woods, at the lake. I watched him impatiently. Finally he pulled up next to me and motioned for me to get in.

If he drove off, the government SUVs would follow, but he left the big machine in park. I climbed in. "Pretty damn cold out there," I griped.

He eyed me for a minute. "Yeah," he finally said.

"Nice car."

He didn't reply. Okay, enough friendly conversation—time to draw him out. "So what's the plan? Walk me through it," I suggested.

"Time for that," he grunted.

"Sorry?"

"Plenty of time for that," he elaborated. He was still gazing at me as if he wasn't sure who I was.

*"He suspects something,"* Alan fretted. *"Maybe the fact that he had to remind you he would be bringing the money is bugging him."*

I sat, the hat pointed like a rifle, not letting my irritation with Alan show on my face.

"You look tired," Blanchard said.

"Yeah, I was up late last night. Those friends of mine? The one who got your postcard? They're flying out of Traverse City this morning, headed to Hawaii. We had a big send-off."

Blanchard didn't say anything.

"So, you said you would call me when you figured out how to get away with killing your wife," I prodded.

Blanchard looked around the parking lot. "How is the repo business?"

"It's okay. How's the banking business?"

"*He's being evasive. He's not going to talk about the murder,*" Alan advised me starkly. "*He knows something's up.*"

"It's good." He looked at his watch the way people do when they've decided to leave. He was bailing.

"Actually, things could be better," I blurted. Blanchard glanced up at me, curious, and I nodded. "I got Sheriff Porterfield on my ass all the time. He says I'm not allowed to do any self-help repossessions, that they all have to go through his department. Kermit's lawyer got him warned off of shutting me down directly, so instead he has his lard-assed deputy giving me traffic tickets for all sorts of bogus reasons."

A glimmer of the old crafty Blanchard showed in his eyes. "That right?"

"My glove box over there is stuffed full of the things. It's really putting a crimp in my ability to hook repos, including for your bank."

"Well," he replied slowly. "I might be able to do something about that. Do a little business with the good sheriff from time to time."

My turn to say it: "That right?"

"Party I had on the boat? Let's just say Porterfield walked away from the table with a little money in his pocket."

"He was on the boat," I stated, talking strictly for the hat.

"Yeah."

"With the girls. The hookers."

He looked scornful. "Telling me you got a problem with that?"

"No. I'm just surprised that a lawman would take the risk of stepping out on his wife after what happened with Barry Strickland. Especially with prostitutes."

"Strickland was an idiot. He didn't have to resign."

"I agree." I knew Strickland could hear us right now, and wondered what his reaction to this conversation would be. And I was awfully glad to get this admission on tape—wait until this part of the conversation was played for the jury!

"Well. All right," Blanchard said. It was the way you ended a discussion, an all-right-nice-talking-to-you sort of thing. "I'll get back to you on that."

*"It's over."* Alan sighed, frustrated.

I needed to figure out a way to keep the conversation going. "So, Mr. Blanchard, let me ask you a question."

He regarded me warily.

"What kind of hotel are Wilma and Claude going to find when they get to the islands?"

"Hell should I know."

"Some sort of hovel?"

He shrugged.

"You know what? The money you brought today? Keep it," I told him.

He looked puzzled.

"Here's what I want instead," I told him. "Claude and Wilma Wolfinger. I want you to get them a nice room at a hotel right on the beach. They arrive tonight; I want them to be blown away by the accommodations. Okay? Have them met at the airport by one of those guys holding a sign with their name on it. They call me and tell me how wonderful their room is, we're a go. Otherwise, no deal."

*"Darrell Hughes is going to have a heart attack,"* Alan observed, but he sounded gleeful as he said it.

Blanchard was staring at me. "You're serious."

"That's what I want."

"Craziest thing I ever heard of."

I shrugged. I had a voice in my head. Crazy was just how I rolled.

"That's going to cost me more than five thousand dollars," Blanchard said, a calculating look in his eye.

"Well, there's this travel club you can join to get discounts," I told him.

He stared at me and then, unexpectedly, threw back his head and laughed. It went on and on, a gasping, rolling mirth. I sat and watched—there were literally tears in his eyes. I kept the hat focused on him even though I was starting to get a crick in my neck. "Oh God, that's hilarious," he sputtered. "Jesus. Oh God." He wiped his eyes. "Got to say, Ruddy, I was worried about you. Figured maybe you went to the cops. Ratted me out. But now"—he laughed again, shaking his head—"no cops would be in on anything like this."

I wasn't laughing back. "We got a deal?"

"Okay. Yeah, why the hell not? You slay me, McCann."

I had all their flight information in my e-mail on my phone, and I wrote it down for him. "This is too much," he said, shaking his head some more. "Killer with a heart of gold."

"I told you they were like parents to me," I reminded him.

"Yeah, well, I wouldn't do this for *my* parents. Okay." His face got serious. "I've got it all worked out. You do this right, you do exactly as I say, and they won't blame you, they won't blame me. But only if you follow my plan to the letter."

"Sounds good."

"It *is* good. It's perfect." Blanchard had a merry expression on his face, but there was hate in his eyes. "The person they'll arrest is the asshole my wife is seeing. I found out who he is: a guy named Jimmy Growe."

# 26

## Something of Value

"They'll blame Jimmy Growe," I repeated faintly.

"Yeah. You know him?"

"No. Well. I may have heard the name before."

Blanchard's smile was ugly. "So get this. He's the guy who knocked her up. When I met Alice, my wife, she had this little girl she was raising by herself, and all she told me was the guy's first name, Jimmy, and that he ran out on her and left her with nothing. She *hated* Jimmy. And now . . ." He pressed his lips together.

"You sure it's him?"

"Yeah, I'm sure. Dumbass left his cell phone there. I found it yesterday; it was in the couch cushions. It rang just as I was crossing the living room."

"How often do you do that? Go into your house?"

"Hell do you care?"

"You're right. I don't care."

"So here's the deal. When she goes to bed, Alice always leaves her cell phone on a charger I gave her. So last night, while she was sleeping, I went in and sent a couple of nasty text messages from Growe's phone to hers. Then I erased the messages off her phone, but not his. Threatening messages, like, *I'm going to kill you bitch*. Get it?"

I decided Blanchard would prefer if I were stupid. "No, I don't get it." This meant that I had to listen to both Blanchard and Alan explain to me that it laid down motive.

"*By erasing the messages from her phone, she won't suspect anything,*" Alan concluded. "*But the messages will be on* Jimmy's *phone.*" Then Blanchard said essentially the same thing.

"I'm going on a date tomorrow night. All night long, so I'll have an alibi." Blanchard winked cleverly.

"One of the girls from the boat?" I guessed, because otherwise I had trouble believing someone like Blanchard could be so confident about the "all night long" part.

"Want to focus, here, pal?" Blanchard suggested softly.

I supposed he thought he sounded threatening, so I did my best to look threatened.

"Want a date after all this is over, I'll introduce you. But right now I say jump, you say how high." He glowered.

"Yessir," I replied with an admirable lack of sarcasm.

"Here's a key to the back door of the house," he continued, tossing it to me. "Once you're in, leave the door unlocked. They'll assume she was negligent. You take this." He handed me Jimmy's phone. "Tonight send a text like, *I'm coming to kill you now, bitch.* This time do not erase the message from her phone; that's important. Then you wipe this phone down and drop it at the scene. They'll assume he lost it."

"Should I put it back in the couch cushions?" Still the dumb repo hit man.

"What? No," Blanchard replied, looking disgusted. "You think the cops would find it there?"

"Okay."

"Repeat back to me what I said," Blanchard ordered.

I walked through it pretty quickly. Then I remembered I needed him to be specific. "You want me to shoot her? Stab her? What?"

"Don't want you to leave any evidence, so yeah, a gun's best. Too much personal contact otherwise. And for God's sake, don't touch her! You can get your rocks off somewhere else. You do it there, you go back to prison."

"*He really is a despicable man,*" Alan said.

"And don't wake the kid. Just in, do it, drop the phone, out. Wear gloves and wipe the phone! Jesus, you handle this okay?"

"I can handle this okay."

"You're not exactly inspiring confidence," Blanchard muttered. He was sweating.

"Relax. This is pretty close to what I do, only instead of breaking into a garage to steal a car, I'm walking in a door to cap your wife."

*Cap* was a term I got from the mysteries I liked to read.

Blanchard looked at his watch. "Jesus. Gotta go." He glared at me. "Don't screw this up, McCann, or you'll be answering to me." He gestured for me to get out of his vehicle.

"And . . . ," I said without moving.

"And what?"

"And I'll be hearing tonight from Claude and Wilma that they love their hotel. Otherwise, I don't do anything. That's the contract."

"Yeah." He didn't seem to find it amusing anymore. "I'll take care of Mommy and Daddy for you."

After Blanchard left, I went back to my truck and just sat there, waiting for something to happen, someone to come. Nothing and no one did.

"*Maybe they want to make sure he doesn't come back,*" Alan suggested when I squirmed impatiently.

Neither *bingo* nor *not good* seemed appropriate. Hey," I called, waving my hand in front of the hat. "You guys asleep in there?"

The back door of the Landing opened, and Cutty gestured me in.

*"She doesn't look happy,"* Alan worried. He seemed pretty concerned with Cutty's mood.

I walked into the restaurant. A rack of computer monitors was stacked off to one side, my friend Donut Cop sitting in front of them. As I looked at him, what was in my vision popped up on all the screens, because my hat was still transmitting. I looked left and right, momentarily fascinated by the bizarre perspective.

"What the hell was that?" D.A. Darrell bellowed at me.

There was just something about Darrell Hughes that begged to be aggressively ignored. I glanced around the room. "I haven't been in here since they rebuilt it. Looks really nice," I observed.

"Ruddy," Strickland warned.

"Can you not follow even one goddamn instruction?" D.A. Darrell stormed.

"I thought I did pretty well," I replied mildly.

"You did well? You fucked it up, McCann!" the D.A. raged.

"You were supposed to get the money," Cutty reminded me curtly.

"Yeah, but I was also told to get something of value for the contract to commit murder. You heard him say to shoot her, right?" I nodded to the video equipment. "The camera picked him up. And the 'something of value' is the hotel room. You heard that, too—he says it will cost him more than five thousand dollars. We even said *contract*."

*"Plus you managed to sort of keep the down payment money,"* Alan concluded. *"It's actually pretty clever."*

"You've broken the law," the D.A. seethed.

"Maybe Ruddy has a point," Strickland mused. "He got something of value. And Blanchard was pretty explicit about what he wanted done. You hear him? Shoot her so you'll leave less evidence at the scene."

"Give me that," D.A. Darrell snarled, reaching for the camera hat. I caught his hand by the wrist in mid-grab and held it. My grip wasn't gentle.

"Don't do that," I said softly.

Everyone in the room went very tense on me. I kept my eyes on the D.A., who glanced away.

"I think everyone needs to calm down," Strickland observed dryly.

"Ruddy, would you mind returning our equipment?" Cutty asked.

I let go of the D.A. and handed Cutty the hat and the gum. Hughes rubbed his wrist.

"What do you think?" Strickland asked the D.A.

"What do I think? I can't take a fucking hotel room to the jury. It's stupid."

*"It does seem to me that before you came up with the idea, Blanchard was going to call the whole thing off,"* Alan said.

"It may be stupid, but you weren't in the Escalade. I was," I objected.

"We heard every word," D.A. Darrell countered.

I shook my head. "No, it was nuanced. Blanchard was going to pretend he didn't know what I was talking about. He suspected something. It was the idea of the hotel that convinced him I wasn't wearing a hat camera and spy chewing gum," I asserted, glad Alan had mentioned that.

Everyone looked at each other. Strickland cleared his throat. "We had one like this when I was a cop in Muskegon," he offered. "Guy hired a C.I. to kill a liquor store owner who wouldn't sell his building."

*"C.I.?"* Alan asked.

"Confidential informant," I replied without thinking.

Strickland nodded. "Right, one of our informants. So we fabricated some pictures of the intended victim. Back then we had to use fake blood, but the stuff you can do with digital nowadays, wouldn't take much to make a couple of convincing photographs." He turned to Cutty. "You take Alice into protective custody?"

Cutty nodded. "The second we got the threat on tape, my men moved in. She's packing some clothes right now."

"Think you could get some digital pictures of her lying on the floor?" Strickland asked.

Cutty gave him an admiring look. "I got a guy so good with Photoshop, he can make it look like Ruddy beheaded her if we want."

"Wait. Wait," the D.A. said. He seemed mostly upset that this wasn't his idea, because when everyone did what he asked—took a moment to wait, wait—he didn't say anything for a long time. "Okay," he finally nodded. "I see it. But I still need money to exchange hands."

"I like the bank as the location for that," Cutty suggested. "Obviously, he's got money there."

"Lot of people, though," Strickland noted.

"Yeah, but every employee is behind bulletproof glass. And this guy thinks he's going to stay bank president, be Traverse City's most eligible bachelor," Cutty pointed out. "He's not going to queer that deal by opening fire on my people. We put a couple of our guys in the lobby, messing with deposit slips. Ruddy shows Blanchard the pictures. Once the money is handed over, we'll walk right in."

"*We could get shot,*" Alan fretted.

"I'll do it," I said.

"This time of year, no one would notice Ruddy wearing a vest underneath his coat," Strickland chimed in. I had wondered when he was going to sneak the weather into the conversation.

"All right. We fake the pictures right now. Get the victim and her daughter into protective custody. Tonight we'll post some plainclothes at the house, make sure Blanchard isn't so stupid as to do a creepy-crawly to check on McCann's handiwork. Next morning, we go in, Ruddy makes the deal, gets the cash," D.A. Darrell concluded, as if it was all his inspiration.

"All for no reward," I agreed sunnily.

Both Strickland and Cutty turned a glare on the D.A., who managed to bite off any retort he had been planning to make. Group therapy.

"What about the guy? Jimmy Growe?" Cutty asked.

Strickland knew of my relationship with Jimmy, and glanced in my direction.

"In my opinion, you should just leave Jimmy out of it," I said. "Have Alice call him at the Black Bear and make up some reason she won't see him for a couple of days. A mother-daughter thing. Jimmy's not . . . He's not the best actor, and honestly, he's not particularly good with secrets, either."

"So you do know him," Cutty observed.

"He's my best friend."

"Is it true? Do you know, then? I mean, the affair. Is your friend sleeping with Alice Blanchard?" Strickland asked.

I sighed. "Yes, it's true."

Strickland nodded, his mouth set in a line. I wonder if he was thinking of his own extramarital fling, and the damage it had wrought in his own life.

"That his cell phone, as far as you can tell?" D.A. Darrell asked.

I didn't see why that mattered, but I pulled it out and looked at it. "Yeah."

Cutty held out her hand, and I gave it to her. "We'll get screenshots of the threatening messages."

*"It's a good thing she's on this. You can tell: There won't be any screw-ups with her in charge,"* Alan praised.

I yawned, tired though it wasn't yet noon. By my calculations, Claude and Wilma were probably just over Illinois. If there was a car waiting to meet them when they landed, the deal was on.

"We're all set," Cutty stated decisively.

"No," I responded. "We're not all set."

Everyone glared at me. I was accustomed to being unpopular, so I just gave them a mild look back.

"How are we not all set?" Cutty asked me in a controlled and gentle tone.

"You heard Blanchard say he can fix my tickets? Porterfield's been trying to harass me out of business. Now you've got the perpetrator of a murder-for-hire scheme on tape, saying he's in bed with the sheriff on shady dealings. The thing with the boat? It wasn't just prostitutes—Porterfield and Blanchard brought in a card shark to fleece their friends. I want Porterfield investigated, and I damn sure want these tickets taken care of. Every single one of them is bogus."

It was quiet in the room, and then, one by one, everyone turned to look at D.A. Darrell. His eyes widened. "You're fucking kidding me," he said.

"Everything on the tape is going to come out as evidence anyway," Strickland soothed. "Don't you want to get ahead of that? What would it look like if, after hearing the tape, you left Ruddy twisting in the wind on all those tickets?"

"Jesus, Darrell," Cutty interjected, her patience wearing out, "can we get past this petty crap and nail us a killer?"

Darrell Hughes looked at me, his expression flat. "All right," he finally agreed. "You got those tickets with you?"


I could tell Strickland wanted to talk to me, so I dawdled, pretending to be doing paperwork in my truck, as a big white van came in and the cops loaded all their equipment into it. Strickland walked down to the frozen lake and peered at it, drinking coffee out of a paper cup. Finally it was just the two of us there at the ferry landing. It was, I reflected, a lonely, forlorn place. The ferry captain, a woman named Toni, was off in Florida, I'd heard.

Alan was respectfully silent. He knew exactly where we were, and even if Lisa Marie Walker didn't go into the lake with me, this was still the place where my entire life got derailed.

Strickland came back up to the parking lot and slid into the repo truck next to me.

"Spring still feels a long way off," he commented.

"Yeah, but in six months it'll be winter again."

"Pretty ballsy move, asking for the hotel instead of the money."

"All's well that ends well," I said.

"Yeah, maybe. Still a lot of things that could go wrong between now and when you walk into his office at the bank."

"I guess so."

"I'd appreciate it if, in the future, you clued me in when you're thinking of going off book."

"All right."

He gazed at me, approval in those steely eyes. I understood he wasn't really complaining—he knew I'd made the right call. He just had to say something for the record so I didn't take him too far off the reservation with me. "Phil Struder. That's the Shantytown guy's name." He apparently couldn't bring himself to say *mayor*.

"Struder," I repeated.

"His family called in a missing persons report on him around the first of the month. Said he didn't come home from the bar. He lives with his daughter and her family; his wife's been dead a long time."

*"Missing, or run away?"* Alan wanted to know.

"Any theories on where he went?" I asked.

"No. Except that his car was ticketed and towed for sitting right there in the lot down near where the Beaver Island ferry parks in the summer."

"Huh," I said, processing it. "Right by the Ferry Bar."

"So, why the interest?"

I briefly explained what I had found out about Nina Otis. Strickland's expression was entirely impassive—I couldn't decide if he thought I was crazy, or thought I was really on to something.

"I sort of have had Phil . . . Struder . . . in mind as a suspect. Seems awfully convenient that he hears I want to talk to him and vanishes that day. But I'm not so sure, now that I hear he abandoned his car. I don't know how you get out of here without a car, this time of year."

Strickland rubbed his chin. "I haven't told anyone about what you've been looking into, but maybe Cutty and I will sit down for a cup of coffee after we've taken down Blanchard. Like you said, I'm building a few favors."

*"Ask him if he knows if she is seeing anyone,"* Alan suggested preposterously. My psychosis was acting completely crazy.

We went our separate ways. I decided to hit Darlene's for breakfast, but sternly told Alan I was not going to get a cinnamon roll, that it was time for me to quit. When I got there, I ordered eggs and bacon and a cinnamon roll.

*"I thought you were going to skip it this time."*

"I saw they were down to just one left, and I panicked," I explained.

*"You said you wanted to lose five pounds,"* he reminded me.

"That's why I wasn't going to have a cinnamon roll," I agreed logically. I had my phone out and pressed against my face so I wouldn't draw undue attention, talking to myself in Darlene's. "So what in the world were you thinking about Cutty Wells, Alan? I'm not going to ask her out on a date, for God's sake."

He was quiet, and I had a sudden insight. "Wait, do you think *you're* going to call her? Like, when I'm asleep?"

*"Do you know how lonely it can get being me? There was something about the way she looked at us. What would be the harm?"*

"The harm? Have you not only lost your body but your mind, too? She was looking at me, not us, and even if I'm asleep, it would still be Ruddy McCann chatting her up. What do you think, you're going to date her, fall in love, get married? What am I supposed to tell your daughter? *Don't worry, honey; I'm asleep?*"

"*I don't understand what's wrong with a little fantasy,*" he whined.

"I'll tell you what's wrong. You have a fantasy about a voice in your head, and the next thing you know, it's ruining your relationships. Now, I know for a fact you've been doing a little cleaning at night—"

"*A little?*" he interrupted incredulously. "*Do you ever wipe your counters? Sweep your floor? Bother to mate your socks?*"

"Again with the socks. Jesus," I snapped. "Look, you can get up and play housewife if it makes you feel better, but that's it. No computer dating. No taking Cutty Wells Zumba dancing. Got it?"

"*You've got someone. I've got no one,*" Alan mourned softly. "*Sometimes a man needs a woman, if only to cuddle with.*"

"That's what Jake is for."

Alan was moodily silent for most of the rest of breakfast. "*Can we talk about the mayor's disappearance?*" he finally suggested.

"Sure. He could still be our man, but I don't get the abandoned car."

"*Think of where it was found. Right there at the Ferry Bar.*"

"Yeah," I grunted. "But I'm not sure what to make of it."

"*I wonder if the mayor was in the bar the night he disappeared? Maybe someone came along and helped him the way someone helped Lisa Marie.*"

"I don't know," I replied, taking a last swig of coffee. "Let's go talk to Rogan and ask him."

# 27

## Here for the Money

Kermit texted me that Jake had done his morning business. Actually, what he said was that Jake had *defected in the yard,* but I got the idea. I'd been up for five hours at that point, but for my dog the workday was just getting started. Katie texted me she had gone into the office. My family thus secure and my stomach heavy and happy, I cruised past the Ferry Bar, but it wasn't awake yet, so I took a drive over to Gaylord and got into an argument with a man who said he didn't need to make car payments because his installments came out of his paycheck automatically. I concurred that had previously been the case, but in October he lost his job over a disagreement with his employers over whether he did any actual work. No job, no paycheck; no paycheck, no automatic deductions. This was too much math for my customer, who sought to prevail in the disagreement by virtue of his superior belligerence. When I seemed unfazed by his anger, he sought to intimidate me by threatening to call his lawyer, and while he was inside his house making good on his dire promise, I hooked up his vehicle and drove away. By the time I dumped the thing at the repo lot, I had run out of energy—too little sleep, too many carbohydrates.

I went home to nap but found it difficult to get sleep because my dog wasn't on the bed. Alan passed right out, so I lay there by myself and thought about how different my life would be if I had just looked in the backseat of my car and noticed that Lisa Marie had gotten out. Maybe I would have gone looking for her. Maybe that one little change would have been enough for me not to drive down that ramp to the ferry landing and off into the icy waters of the channel. But even if I had gone into the drink, I would have told everyone I was by myself. They might not have believed me, but they would have had to check out my story. The cops might have located a girl on a bicycle, a girl who saw a man help Lisa Marie Walker after she got out of my car. And we'd have the semen, proving it was not me who had sex with her, and maybe, if Alan's theory was correct, the killer's DNA would be in a database somewhere.

I gave up on my nap when Dr. Schaumburg rang my cell phone. He told me he had a letter from the court. "Your probation is being lifted," he told me sadly.

"First I've heard of it."

"Ruddy, I strongly urge you not to see this as an excuse to discontinue treatment. You have a controllable condition, but it requires close supervision. Your medication needs to be monitored consistently."

"Sounds like a plan," I observed agreeably. "Nice talking to you, Bob."

"Wait, please. Some side effects are unavoidable, but they can be reduced. It's imperative you stick with the regimen I prescribed. I'm your doctor, Ruddy. Whatever the circumstances that brought us together, my role is to help you get well."

"And you've done a fantastic job. Thanks," I told him sincerely. "I'm all better now." When I said good-bye, all I heard in return was dismayed silence, so I disconnected the call.

My call with Katie was a lot more fun. We decided to see each other the next night, and I promised I had some interesting things to tell her—namely, that by then we would have gone to the bank and arrested Blanchard for the crime of hiring a repo man to kill his wife.

I stopped by the Black Bear and chatted with Jimmy, who told me Alice Blanchard and their daughter, Vicki, had gone to visit Alice's sister. "I didn't even know she had a sister," he confessed.

"You still worried about her soon-to-be-ex-husband?"

Jimmy shrugged, running a hand through his black hair. "She says his lawyer sent a pretty nasty letter, which she gave to *her* lawyer."

I clapped him on the shoulder. "I think things are going to be okay," I told him.

"I still can't find my cell phone."

"Something tells me it'll turn up."

Just then my own cell phone chimed, and I put it on speakerphone when I saw who it was, gesturing to Becky to join Jimmy and me at the bar.

"Ruddy!"

"Hi there, Claude. You and Wilma make it okay?"

"It's seventy-seven degrees here! Can you believe that? In February!"

Becky leaned in. "Are you at your hotel?" she asked, glancing at me.

"Our hotel!" he gushed. Then there was a loud rustling and a loud squawk from Claude.

"Ruddy? It's Wilma. This place is amazing. You should see our hotel room!"

"I wanted to tell him, dammit!" I heard Claude complain in the background.

"Everyone is here," I told her, and they all chorused hellos.

Wilma responded with a giddy squeal. "Wait, hear this? Hear this?" she asked.

What we heard was Claude telling her to give him back the phone.

"That's the ocean, guys! Our room is right on the ocean!"

"Tell him we've got our own refrigerator!" Claude ordered.

"It is so wonderful, you wouldn't believe it," she continued. "We got upgraded when we landed; there was a man waiting for us at the airport."

"Two TVs!" Claude bellowed.

Becky was regarding me suspiciously. I gave her an innocent shrug.

"It's the happiest day of my life," Wilma told me.

"If you're not going to tell him anything, then let me talk," Claude insisted.

There was a noise that sounded like Wilma had taken the phone and hit him with it. Then he was back. We agreed that he should stop talking to us and go have some fun, and rang off.

*"You're not going to claim any credit for the hotel, are you?"* Alan asked.

I didn't want to answer him in front of people, but I figured he knew the answer.

I wasn't really sure why, but Claude and Wilma, with their goofy, maladroit lives, meant an awful lot to me.

So Blanchard had made good on his end of the bargain. And, I didn't care what D.A. Darrell thought; he had definitely delivered something of value.


At ten the next morning I met Cutty and her team in a parking lot in Acme, a small town on the outskirts of Traverse City. Alan was awake and nervous. The cops had the same panel van. I was introduced to two plainclothes officers who would pretend to be customers in the bank, both of them women, both of them looking like the sort of law professionals you simply don't want to mess with, stern and tough and strong. I assumed Alan found them sexy, too, but he didn't comment. I was given the hat and the gum and a file folder with several photographs of Alice Blanchard lying on her bedroom floor, dark blood pooled at her head. The photos were impressively realistic and gruesome. The Photoshop guy was almost too good—the head wound was pretty graphic.

"Where is she really?" I asked Cutty curiously.

She smiled at me warmly. Was Alan right? Did she think I was attractive? *Why did I care?* I chastised myself. "She and her daughter are someplace safe—don't worry," she assured me. "Okay, this is a little different circumstance than the last meet, because he's gotten what he needs from you. Now you're just a liability. Watch his hands," she lectured me. "You don't like what's going on, same drill as last time, say *not good*. We hear that, we'll be in that office in five seconds. You drop to the floor. We'll wait to send you in until all the civilians are out and then we'll block anyone else from entering—the only people in there will be mine. When he gives you the money, don't count it, but makes sure it's cash. That's when you say *bingo*."

"Right, don't settle for travel coupons or something," D.A. Darrell interjected. Strickland and Cutty both gave him a look. He held up his hands and gave a false smile. "All right. And say something for the mic, like, *I did what you wanted and shot her in the head, so I'm here for my money*."

"You really need it to be that explicit?" Cutty demanded, looking exasperated.

The D.A. put an I'm-the-expert expression on his face and nodded solemnly. "Got to wrap things up tight for the jury."

Strickland and Cutty plainly felt this wasn't true but elected not to say anything.

*"Just don't take any unnecessary risks,"* Alan urged, as if he were part of the briefing team.

He became particularly agitated when it was apparent I couldn't wear a bulletproof vest under my coat. The thing was just too tight.

"The coat sort of shrunk over the years," I explained lamely.

The laughter that followed cut a lot of the tension, except for

Alan's. *"We really need that vest,"* he protested as one of the cops put it back into the van.

"I really think the risk is pretty low. You shout *no good* and hit the floor, he's going to have no idea what the hell is going on. By the time he stands up to see what you're doing, my officers will have their weapons drawn and in his face," Cutty said. "But it's your choice. We can hold off until we find a coat that fits over the vest." She didn't want to wait, I could tell. The hunt was on, and her vivacious eyes were alive with it.

"Let's do it," I said.

The wooden arm at the bank parking lot was broken off, and Zoppi's Jeep was gone from where I'd parked it with the other repos in the back. It would be fun to take it from him again. The two women cops were already inside when I arrived, filling out deposit slips or something at two counters. To my right were the tellers and a manager, all behind bulletproof glass. Straight ahead was an empty conference room, and to the right, in a glassed-in office, was Blanchard, talking on the phone. His eyes bulged when he saw me.

*"He seems surprised we're here,"* Alan said.

I knocked on his open door. "Got a minute?" I asked as he ended his phone call.

"The hell are you doing here?" he demanded, looking afraid.

Unasked, I slid into a chair in front of his desk. "I did what you asked me to do last night, so I'm here for my money."

"I never said to come here. This is where I work."

"You never said not to," I countered, sounding like the tough hit man I was supposed to be. "I came here after the Yancy job, remember?"

"That was completely different, you idiot! Close the door. Jesus."

I was supposed to leave it open but didn't see how I could

refuse. I eased it shut, momentarily meeting the eyes of one of the two female cops in the lobby. "I printed up some pictures for you," I told Blanchard, not having to fake a chill demeanor after the *idiot* crack.

He was so jumpy, I expected him to all but faint when he saw the fake murder scenes. Instead his face changed completely. His eyes widened, like a little boy unwrapping a birthday gift. He picked up the photo, then the next one, a gloating smile on his face.

There was something so ugly and reptilian about the way he was receiving this information, I felt a cold anger building in me. This was his *wife*.

*"It's almost sexual for him,"* Alan observed.

"I had to kill the kid, too," I blurted, not even realizing I was going to say it until the words came out. Blanchard stared at me. "She saw me. Sorry."

"I said not to touch her!" he snarled at me, his face turning crimson. Finally some emotion. So he did care about the child, at least.

"I had no choice." I shrugged.

"Well, goddammit, you fucking moron. I don't have any insurance on the *kid*. Won't get a dime for her, and now I'll have to deal with all the funeral expenses," he fumed.

*"My God,"* Alan said.

Enough. "I did what you asked. I shot your wife. I want my fee."

"Your fee." He shook his head wonderingly. "Just how stupid are you? Come in here the morning after my wife is murdered, before anyone has even found her body. Everyone in the bank has seen you now. And what do you think, I'm just going to hand you a bag of cash now? Place of business?"

"You handed me a bag last time. And it's a bank: Are you saying you don't have any money here?"

"I'm saying, I don't have any money for *you* here. Not that kind of money."

I stared at him, unsure what I should do next. We were hardly at *bingo*. Almost unconsciously, I turned to look at the two police officers, but they were both studiously ignoring me. One of them was laboriously counting out a small stack of one-dollar bills; the other was punching buttons on a calculator. I glanced back at Blanchard, and he was nodding furiously.

"That's right; even some customers have seen you. Now, here's the deal. Story is that you came in to discuss a repo, all right? See the damage to my gate? Tony Zoppi stole his Jeep back, the moron. You go get the thing, let him know he's messing with the wrong guy. Got it?"

"What about my money?"

He seemed impatient with me, as if the job itself should have been its own reward. "Need to think about where we can meet."

"Why not where we were the other morning?"

His eyes narrowed. "You don't decide this. I'll think of something and call you later today, all right?"

*"He hasn't even thought that far ahead,"* Alan marveled. *"He doesn't have a plan."*

Well, that was just how Blanchard rolled.

"Okay," I agreed. "My cell phone's almost out of juice. If I don't answer, just leave a message."

"Not *leaving a message*," he replied in a mocking voice. "You don't answer, you are shit out of luck."

"All right. Then call me at the Black Bear." I handed over another one of my professional bar bouncer cards, and now I was down to ten. I stood up. I didn't know if I had messed this up or not, but I hadn't gotten to *bingo* and felt like I needed to say something to salvage the situation. "Don't forget to call me. You won't like what will happen if you forget to call me."

He gave me a cold smile. "Don't worry. You'll get your money. Going to do lots of business together, you and me."

*"Lots of business?"* Alan repeated incredulously. *"More murders? How does someone like this get into banking?"*

I left the building, one of the two women cops coinciden-
tally departing at the same time. The other one went to the
teller window.

I smiled at the woman cop, who gave me a completely noncommittal expression in return as I held the door for her. I guessed
she was waiting to find out from her bosses whether we were all
happy with Ruddy McCann.

I noticed the panel van parked across the street as I got into
my repo truck, and followed it when it pulled out into traffic.

We went back to the same parking lot in Acme. The van side
door slid open and Strickland, Cutty, and D.A. Hughes all got
out, stretching their limbs.

"I think we got enough," Cutty told me. "But he really wants
some cash to change hands." She jerked her thumb at D.A. Darrell.

"What was the whole thing with the cell phone?" The D.A.
asked me.

"My cell phone is running low on battery, and I don't have a
car charger," I explained.

"Great," he muttered.

"What is your problem?" I asked.

"My problem is that you keep making changes to the plan
without authorization."

"Look . . . ," I said, the blood flowing to my face.

"Let's all relax," Strickland suggested.

We all stood around, relaxing. "So, what do we do now?" I
finally asked.

"Now," Cutty replied, "we wait for Blanchard to call you."
She eyed me. "This isn't going to go down behind bulletproof
glass. He might think it's best not to pay you anything. We better
get you a vest."

# 28

## Not Good

Standing there in the parking lot, I learned what cops do when they have too much time on their hands and there's no Weather Channel—they make contingency plans, and then they make contingency plans for contingency plans. They endlessly speculated on whether they should put people in the Black Bear to guard me, just in case Blanchard showed up unannounced and pulled a gun. In that case, I told them, I would take the gun away from him. This impressed no one. *But an armed presence might make Blanchard suspicious. Do we even want the Bear to be open? But to close it would incite unruly apprehension in the town.* (That's exactly how D.A. Darrell phrased it. He and Kermit would love talking to each other.)

All of this, Alan reminded me impatiently, predicated on the possibility that Blanchard might decide to deliver the money to me at the Bear instead of phoning me at the number I'd given him. Why would he do that? Alan believed, and I agreed, that Blanchard would probably want to meet me in some isolated place so no one would see us together.

I tried to imagine where that might be and grew defeated by the possibilities—this whole part of the *country* was an isolated place.

Eventually it was decided that I should go to the Black Bear and that Cutty would put a single man inside and watch the front and back entrances from outside.

"*For a phone call,*" Alan maintained stubbornly.

I was glad to be back in my truck and away from the debate team. My cell phone warned me it was a good day to die, so I phoned Katie and told her briefly that I wouldn't be able to make our date, that it was business. Mindful of the wise words of Jimmy Growe, I apologized at least a dozen times, until finally she was laughing at me. "It's okay. Tomorrow night," she told me.

"Tomorrow," I promised.

"This will be fun. Ruddy . . ."

"Yes?"

"Thanks for doing this. I'm feeling a lot better about things. Like I finally know who I am."

"If you love someone, let her go," I quoted somebody. "And if she comes back to you, she probably forgot something."

She chuckled delightedly. "Exactly. I know this has been hard on you, but I'm figuring things out."

"We're dating," I replied firmly. "Also, my socks are either mated or in the hamper. No exceptions."

"Oh *my.*"

I told her about the Wolfingers loving their hotel room, but at some point in the conversation my phone's battery shut down the connection.

On the way to the Bear I stopped at my home, earning me a questioning look from Strickland and Cutty, who were following me in Strickland's SUV. I trotted over to their window.

"I just need to run inside for a minute; give me a sec?" I requested. I didn't bother to look at Darrell Hughes in his car directly behind Strickland, but I assumed he was appropriately offended with my deviation from the agreed-upon plan.

I went inside and plugged my phone into its charger. As soon as some life came back into it, I texted an apology to Katie, along with an emoticon of a bottle of wine, a heart, and a basset hound.

No one can accuse me of not being romantic. Then I called the Ferry Bar and asked to speak to Wade Rogan.

"Hey there, Ruddy," he greeted enthusiastically when I identified myself.

We compared notes on how the bar business was doing and chatted about how much longer before the ice left and the people returned. Then I got to it.

"Hey, I was out to Shantytown."

"Oh?" he responded. "Excellent! Did you talk to Phil?"

"No. He wasn't there."

"Really."

"You seen him?"

"I don't think so. Hang on." I heard him ask if anyone had seen the mayor of Shantytown, and pictured Guy at Bar numbers 1 and 2 coming out of their stupor.

*Ask him about his ice shanty, why he lied,* Alan suggested while we waited.

Rogan came back. "Nobody's heard anything from him. I hope he's okay."

"I'm just wondering why you didn't tell me you have your own shanty out there on the ice."

"Now, what?" he responded slowly.

"Out in Shantytown. You have your own place on the ice."

Rogan was silent long enough for me to want to ask him if he was still there. *He's thinking,* Alan advised me. *Trying to figure out what he should say to that.*

"What are you asking?" he said, a lot less friendly sounding.

"Just curious why you said ice fishing didn't interest you. You said you didn't know anything about Shantytown."

"Ice fishing doesn't interest me. That's where I keep my iceboat."

Now it was my turn to be silent.

"Hello?" he asked.

"Iceboat," I repeated, just to have something to say.

"Yeah, you ever do that? It's a blast. The wind catches your sails, and you can hit forty miles an hour, easy. Where they plowed all the snow and it's like an ice rink out there? Come out sometime; you'll love it."

"Yeah. I mean, no, I've never tried it."

"You busy Monday? I usually take Mondays off."

"I'll have to check my schedule," I said. I don't even have a schedule; it's just something people say. I tried to picture lying on a fragile frame, skimming on the ice at forty miles an hour, Alan screaming in my head like a frightened child.

"Cool. Anyway, my boat cost me twelve grand, so yeah, I keep it locked up."

"Makes sense," I replied.

*"Ask him about Rachel Rodriguez,"* Alan prodded.

I sighed. If I didn't ask, Alan would bug me about it until next summer. "Hey, Wade, another thing. Remember there were those pictures of those missing women I showed you?"

"Yeah?" He sounded wary again.

"Remember what you said about Rachel Rodriguez?"

"I don't even know what you're talking about."

"She was the one, you said, 'Who is that?' The rest of them, you obviously knew who they were. But when you got to Rachel, you didn't recognize her. Which maybe makes sense, because I was wrong. She isn't presumed dead. The rest of them are, but she's still alive. The cops tracked her down."

Rogan was breathing into the phone.

"Just think it's odd," I continued. "You knew all the dead ones but didn't recognize the living one. Why would that be?"

I waited for what I knew would be his logical explanation, mentally preparing myself for Alan's protests. After a long silence Rogan hung up on me. I pulled the phone away from my ear and stared at it in disbelief. "He just hangs up?" I demanded.

*"You panicked him. He didn't know what else to do. He wasn't expecting that question."*

"Yeah. Maybe." I thought about it. "On the other hand, maybe I just pissed him off. I did pretty much imply he killed the other women."

*"Right, about that. Why did you do that?"*

"Because you told me to!" I snapped.

*"No, I said to ask about Rachel. I didn't say to accuse him."*

"I didn't accuse him, and if you want me to not say anything, then you should not say anything," I retorted, my anger flaring.

I left my phone charging, the repo truck in front of my house, setting off to Becky's bar on foot. I heard Strickland start up his truck and follow me, and the white van was already parked half a block down the street from the Bear.

I went inside and decided the police officer must be the tall guy in the corner booth because, besides Jimmy, he was the only person in the place. I snagged a seat at the bar and asked Jimmy if I could have a burger.

*"A burger? After you had the cholesterol special for breakfast?"* Alan huffed.

"Hey, somebody just called for you," Jimmy told me.

I went very still. "Yeah?" I replied cautiously.

Jimmy sorted through a short stack of papers next to the phone. "Yeah, it was sort of weird. I got a call and nobody was there, just dead air, but I could hear him breathing, you know? Then he hangs up. Then maybe two minutes later the same number comes up on caller ID, and this time the guy wants to speak to you. So I say you're not here and he asks me to leave a message." Jimmy squinted at his handwriting. "So it says, tonight, ten p.m., south tip of Holy Island." He looked at me. "Got any idea what that means? What's Holy Island?"

"There's a little island in the south arm of Lake Charlevoix. Maybe a dozen homes on it. You get to it by this short bridge," I told him. "Can I have the message? And you can skip the burger; I've got to run."

———

Holy Island is maybe fifteen hundred feet long and a hundred feet wide. It has a one-track road running down the length of its spine from the bridge to the southern tip. I imagined its residents, mostly summer people, spent a lot of their time pulling into driveways to allow their neighbors to pass. In the winter it appeared only a single home at the north end was occupied, though a plow had run all the way down to the turnaround at the other end of the island. The houses were buried in snow, three feet of it stacked on the roofs. Dark trees rose out of the untracked white, fading from view as the sun set.

I'd gone around the turnaround and was parked about twenty feet back up the road from it, facing north and blocking further progress for anyone else coming onto the island. Strickland had dropped his vehicle into low four-wheel drive and churned into position behind the southernmost cottage, which was locked up tight for winter behind me. No one on the road would see it.

Officers wearing white hooded snow cover were hiding just off the road and would close in behind Blanchard when he approached. A communications station was set up in the house at the north end, which luckily belonged to an ex-cop who was more than happy to take his wife out to dinner on the state's dime while his home was used to trap a snake.

I was pretty impressed with the setup. They even used brooms to hide their tracks in the snow, and with their white hoods on, they simply vanished from sight.

There wasn't a lot for me to do but wait. My cell phone, naturally, was still at home in its cradle, so I couldn't call anyone—a mistake I would never make again. I had my magic hat on, the listening gum in my pocket. The unfamiliar bulletproof vest was like a heavy blanket—I was wearing a borrowed coat over it, which I had unzipped because it was so warm with all the layers. Alan was thankfully not trying to talk to me—he understood it wouldn't help the prosecution much if the star witness spent the moments before the arrest arguing with himself.

It was twelve minutes past ten o'clock. Night had settled, but the blanket of clouds above had diffuse light in it, reflected from East Jordan to the south, Charlevoix to the north, Boyne City to the east. The white on the ground glowed back up at the sky.

In the rearview mirror, I was able to make out, just barely, the dark figure of a person wading through the snow toward me. I rolled down my window, wondering if it was Cutty or Strickland.

It was Cutty. Alan made a barely audible sound that I knew meant he thought she looked great in her white outfit. And she did, actually. "The men outside Blanchard's house say he still hasn't moved," she advised.

"Okay."

"For now the listening devices are turned off. My men will pop them back on when I tell them to. We'll probably need to give it an hour before we make any decisions. You all right with that?"

"I'm fine."

Cutty stamped her feet. She had an impatient expression on her face, which was lit from my dash lights. She wanted to get the show going. "How's your dog?" she asked finally.

I was surprised. I hadn't realized she knew I even had a dog. "He's fine. He's staying with my sister, Becky, tonight."

"That's good. What kind is he?"

"Jake? Basset hound, mostly. Maybe something else. Sloth, probably."

"Basset." Cutty nodded. "Amazing animals. Nose as good as a bloodhound's."

"He uses it to sniff out places to nap."

She laughed. There was something intimate in her gaze, then, and she leaned more into the open window. Clearly, we were developing a more personal relationship. And there was no denying the attraction: Her forthright, honest character and commanding presence were very alluring to me. So this was why she'd turned off the listening devices. I struggled to think how I was going to introduce Katie into the conversation, which I needed to do fast, before things got out of hand.

"Could I ask you a personal question?" she queried in a low tone.

Here it comes. I took the cowardly way out and simply nodded.

"How well do you know Barry?"

I blinked. "Strickland?" I responded stupidly.

"I've known him for years. Always on a professional basis. I've dropped a few hints his way recently, but he's not very good at picking them up. How do you think he would respond to being asked out by a woman? Is he too old-fashioned for that?"

Alan made a nearly inaudible noise, communicating disappointment. I thought about her question, turning it over in my mind. "Honestly? I think he's feeling pretty low about himself, because of that thing, the affair. He's not picking up hints because he just doesn't see himself as worthy. So yeah, I think you're going to have to take the initiative."

*"Tell her she's extremely attractive and that any man would be lucky to be with her,"* Alan babbled. I ignored him.

Cutty was nodding. "I hadn't thought of that," she confessed. She gave me a level look. "Thanks. I appreciate a man's perspective."

"It must be hard. With what you do, I mean. A lot of men might be intimidated." *Except maybe imaginary ones in my head.*

"Oh, you have no idea." She shook her head, and the simple loop of gold in her earlobe caught a flash of dashboard light. "To most men in the department, I'm a bossy bitch. Or I must have slept with someone to get to the top. Civilians treat me just as badly, either going all alpha on me to prove they're more manly, or dismissing what I do as almost like an embarrassment."

"Barry's a good man, Cutty. Toughest guy I know, but completely fair."

"Thanks," she said softly.

We smiled at each other. "All right," she said. "Well, let's see if our banker friend shows up."

"I think he will. Hey, Cutty, could I use your cell phone? I left mine at home."

"No problem." She handed it over and then walked away so I could have some privacy.

"*Barry Strickland is too old for her,*" Alan opined irrelevantly and incorrectly.

"And you're too dead," I pointed out.

I phoned Katie. It rolled to voice mail, and I told her I was working late on a repo but thought it would be wrapped up by midnight, and that I didn't have my cell phone because I forgot it at home and was calling from a friend's. Then I told her I loved her and would talk to her in the morning about our plans for dinner. It felt normal and stress free, and I disconnected with the optimistic sense that we were destined to fix everything that might be wrong between us.

Twenty past ten. I phoned the Bear.

"Black Bear Bar and Grille, Jimmy Growe speaking."

"Hey, Jimmy."

"Hi, Ruddy."

His voice sounded funny to me. "What's wrong?" I probed, concerned.

"Oh, it's just that Alice hasn't called. I've left a couple message on her phone, but I haven't heard back."

"I'm sure she's okay, Jimmy. I'll bet you she phones you by tomorrow morning at the latest."

"It's just not like her. Oh, hey, you got a message."

I gripped the phone. "Same guy?"

"No, huh-uh. From Katie. She was really excited, said to tell you she scored her first appointment for a listing and was going to see the seller, so she can't meet you tonight."

"Okay. That's funny, our messages must have crossed each other. I called her to tell her I couldn't meet her either."

"She said your phone is rolling straight to voice mail."

"Yeah, I left it at home."

"I can't even *find* mine," Jimmy complained petulantly.

I told him I thought things would be fine in the morning, and rang off. Then I put the phone back to my ear in case the hidden snowmen were watching. "Hello, Alan? It's Ruddy McCann. Hey, did you hear the good news, Katie being called out to look at a listing?"

*"It's really tough at first. But she's so beautiful, anyone sees the ad with her picture, they'd call her right away."*

I frowned at this. I didn't want some creep listing his house with her just because he thought she was hot.

*"I half expected Jimmy to say that Blanchard called to say he couldn't make it. He's what, ten or fifteen minutes from here? Why hasn't he left his house yet?"* Alan pondered.

I thought about Blanchard's call to Jimmy. The message had been clear as to the time and place. Then I sat bolt upright. "Oh no," I moaned.

*"What is it?"*

I hastily punched in the number to the Black Bear.

"Black Bear Bar and Grille, Jimmy Growe speaking."

"Jimmy," I said urgently. "I need you to think. When the guy called earlier today and said to meet on Holy Island, is that how you answered the phone? 'Jimmy Growe speaking'?"

"That's how I always answer," he replied simply.

"Okay. Thanks, Jimmy." I hung up.

*"That's why he just breathed the first time, and then disconnected. When Jimmy answered, he realized you not only lied about knowing him, but that you work with him."*

"Not good!" I shouted out the open window. "Not good!"

# 29

## I Do My Best Work at Midnight

For a moment nothing happened—it had to be confusing, since Blanchard hadn't yet arrived. But then the snow convulsed into several cops who rushed the truck, their rifles drawn. I sat, my hands conscientiously in the surrender position, until Strickland and Cutty came running up.

"He knows," I told them. "Blanchard knows."

Cutty reacted first, holding a walkie-talkie to her mouth. "Hit the house. Arrest the suspect." She turned to the circle of snow-camouflaged officers. "Stand down." She looked at me. "How?"

I told her how Jimmy answered the telephone at the Bear. Cutty's shoulders slumped.

*"I think the D.A. is going to be pretty angry about this,"* Alan commented.

"It's all right, Ruddy. These things never go exactly as planned," Strickland assured me.

Everyone waited tensely, watching Cutty. "Captain Wells," her radio finally crackled.

"Go for Wells," she answered.

"Ma'am, we've searched the house. Suspect is not here."

"Repeat that."

"Suspect is not here."

"Not there?"

"No, ma'am. His car's in the garage, and there are no foot tracks in the woods, but he's not in the house. I got a man checking the backyard right now, lots of tracks back there."

"Is there a road in the back of that house?"

"No, ma'am, just woods for miles. If he's on foot, we'll have an easy trail to follow. But the snow's pretty deep—I can't see anyone wading through it very far."

Strickland and I exchanged puzzled glances. Cutty raised the radio to say something but then just stood there, looking exasperated.

"Captain?" the walkie-talkie called.

"Go."

"There's a shed in the back and snowmobile tracks heading out into the woods."

Several of us groaned. Cutty keyed her mic. "How the hell could you miss a snowmobile?" she demanded icily.

"Ma'am, sorry, but there are snowmobiles whizzing all over the place here. His was probably just one of those that went by in the woods."

"All right," Cutty said. "Wells to base, pack it in. Suspect has fled. He could be anywhere."

"The Black Bear," I blurted urgently. "Maybe he's gone after Jimmy!"

Cutty nodded at me. "I've got two officers in the place. I'll tell them to stay alert."

Within ninety seconds police vehicles were hurtling down the narrow lane toward us, their light bars strobing so that blue and red beams bounced off the snow, seeming to touch the clouds. Under any other circumstances, it would have been pretty.

"Wells! This is District Attorney Darrell Hughes," the walkie-talkie squealed. "What the hell is going on? How could you let Blanchard get away?"

"No names," Wells barked back. She rolled her eyes at us.

"I asked how in the hell you could let *the suspect* get away," D.A. Darrell repeated harshly.

"What's important at this moment is finding him," Cutty snapped back angrily. I didn't hear what else the D.A. had to say because Cutty turned away and got into a vehicle. The evacuation of the rest of the state police proceeded quickly, until it was just Strickland and myself. After all the activity, it felt oddly still and empty, the two of us just standing there on that lonely single-track road.

"I've got a thermos of coffee in my vehicle," he offered.

"Why not?"

I followed him to his SUV, which he had parked at the very tip of the island, pointing toward East Jordan. "It's actually sort of pretty," I noted, nodding at the ice and taking a sip of not-very-hot coffee from the paper cup Strickland had handed me.

"I like the way it is never quite dark, unless it is snowing," he responded, nodding. "Not out on the lake. Full moon tonight, too, even though we can't see it."

"What will happen with the case now?" I asked.

Strickland shrugged. "I can't imagine Blanchard will get very far on a snowmobile. He'll probably find a place to hole up, maybe break into someone's summer cabin, but eventually he's going to come out into the world, and we'll get him. Then it's up to the D.A. I think we've got enough to convict, myself. Screw the physical hand-over of money; that's just Hughes trying to be the big dog."

"Sorry about the way it went down. If I had remembered to charge my cell phone, none of this would have happened."

"That's okay. I don't know what I thought would come of it, anyway. For me, I mean." He was gazing at the lake but peering into himself. "Felt good to be involved in something important again." He looked at me. "That's why I'm interested in what you're doing, the thing with the missing women. Though I don't guess that this little party is going to earn me the favor I wanted, which is to see the files on those other ones. And you know, eventually I'll just be back to skip tracing for Kramer Recovery again." He sounded forlorn and empty.

"Well, we've got the current sheriff at the scene of a gambling party on a boat with hookers; seems to me there might be an opening in the department," I pointed out suggestively.

"No, we've got Blanchard *claiming* Porterfield was there. Not the same thing."

"Did you hear what Blanchard said? That you didn't need to resign? Most people feel that way, Barry." It still felt weird to call him by his first name.

Strickland just shook his head sadly. "I disgraced the office."

"But you were a good sheriff. The man we have now, *he's* the disgrace. I think the public is more than willing to forgive you. You just need to forgive yourself."

Dark humor glinted in his eyes. "So what should I run on, the success of this operation?" He looked at me more closely. "You still have the hat."

"Oh. Yeah, it's turned off, Cutty said."

"It still records locally—to the chip, I mean. If anyone cares to review it."

"Great." I mentally reviewed everything we had said.

"*Nothing you need to worry about,*" Alan assured me. "*Pretty innocuous talk.*"

"I guess I should take off the Kevlar," I said, fingering the bulletproof vest through the borrowed coat. I reached up to unzip it, and as I did my eyes caught the flicker of a light, bouncing a bit, far out on the ice.

"*What's that?*" Alan asked.

The light was getting closer, moving fast and straight toward us.

"Sheriff," I said slowly, "do you see what I see?"

———

The snowmobile was still more than a mile out. "No way to avoid him spotting my vehicle," Strickland declared tensely. "He'd see the lights when I backed up."

"You think it's Blanchard?"

"I think we have to assume it is." Strickland reflexively reached for his belt and then gave me a rueful look. "I don't have a radio." He pulled out his cell phone and punched his speed dial. I looked out on the ice—the snowmobile was closing fast.

"Cutty, it's Barry. I've got an inbound snowmobile. I think it might be the suspect, coming to make his payment. Yeah. No, he's two minutes away, maximum. Copy that." He hung up. "This isn't good. They're twenty minutes out. He'll be here in one. If I open my door, the dome light will come on and he is going to see me sitting here. He'll take off, and we'll be back to where we started."

"Why don't you just duck down and wait here, and I'll go pull him off the snowmobile and sit on him until the rest of the team gets here?" I suggested. "He doesn't know this isn't my personal vehicle."

"Open the glove box and hand me my weapon, would you please, Ruddy?" he responded calmly.

*"Oh God,"* Alan blurted in alarm.

The Glock in the glove box had a trigger lock jammed into it. Strickland pulled out a key as I handed it to him. "Turn on your headlights," I suggested suddenly.

"What?"

"Your lights. I'll walk down, leave my door open, you crawl out the door after me. He won't be able to see you with the headlights in his eyes. I'll meet him on the ice."

Strickland nodded and flipped on his beams. Instantly, the world changed, flaring white in front of us, the surrounding landscape seeming to plunge more deeply into darkness. Strickland hid below the dashboard, and I popped open my door and stepped out and walked down to the ice, waving my hand.

The snowmobiler was wearing a helmet and goggles, so I really couldn't tell if it was our man. He slowed down as he came closer, stopping about twenty yards away, so that I had to trudge that far out to meet him. He turned off his machine.

"Mr. Blanchard?" I called.

He sat there, just staring at me. I figured Strickland was stuck in the trees back on the island—if he attempted to follow me out here, Blanchard would spot him as soon as the sheriff was on the open ice.

Twenty yards was sort of a long shot for a pistol. I'd have to handle this myself. "That you, Mr. Blanchard?" I called.

He reached up and removed his helmet and goggles. I crunched snow under my boots as I cautiously approached. It was Blanchard, his face unreadable as his eyes bored into me.

"You bring my money?" I stopped two yards away.

He didn't say anything.

"Hey. I've been freezing my ass out here; you're late. Not the best way to treat your partner."

"Partner," he repeated.

"*How do we know he doesn't have a gun?*" Alan hissed at me.

"You said, remember? That we were going to do a lot of things together. But it starts with my money." I pursed my lips, watching his eyes. *Come on, Blanchard, pull out the cash so we can get to bingo and end this thing.*

He looked down at his lap. "All right."

I moved to the side of the snowmobile, holding out my hand, and that's when Blanchard raised his pistol.

"Not good," I had time to say, before he pulled the trigger.

Two shots went into my vest, staggering me, and then the third one went right into my face.

I fell like a tree, landing on my back on the hard ice. I registered more shots, coming from my left, close and loud. That was

Strickland, returning fire. I stared at the sky, my ears ringing, pain throbbing in my chest, face stinging as if from a slap, and waited to feel the life ebb out of me.

"*We're hit, we're hit,*" Alan babbled.

"Shut up, Alan," I muttered.

"Ruddy?" Strickland's face hovered over mine, the shadows from the headlights carving black canyons under his eyes. "You hurt?"

"He got me in the head."

Strickland's eyes widened in alarm. He reached out with a gloved hand and seized my jaw, moving my head back and forth. Ice crystals on the leather glove stung my cheeks. "I don't think so. Probably just missed—the shock wave can feel like a hit if it comes close enough. You were only a few feet away."

"Oh. Right," I agreed, feeling foolish. "I know he got me in the vest." I patted my chest, wincing.

"You need an ambulance?"

I shook my head and sat up. "No. Wow." I glanced over at Blanchard, who was still straddling the snowmobile, his lifeless body twisted, his mouth open in outrage. "Neither does he," I observed. The white glare from the SUV's headlights made Strickland's shots to the banker's center mass appear black as oil. One of them went too high—above the eyes—and some of Blanchard's skull was missing. It looked even worse than the Photoshopped pictures of his wife, made all the more grue-some by the way his corpse still sat in the saddle, as if ready to ride away like a headless horseman. I glanced away, a little sickened.

Strickland grunted. "I came running the second I saw him pull the pistol. I thought he'd see me, but he was looking at you and nothing else. Not the brightest move, to walk right up to him like that, my friend."

"Repo men are known for their lack of intelligence."

He grinned, bringing out his cell phone. He dialed. I looked around the cold, bleak landscape, thinking how close I had come to dying. It didn't seem real.

"Cutty, shots fired. Suspect is 10-55. Roll your forensics team," Strickland said. "Armed civilian on the scene." He looked at me. "No, our C.I. is unhurt."

I probed the bruises under the vest. "*Ow,*" Alan complained.


Even though they had the chip in the hat, the police still wanted to take my statement, so I sat in the panel van and went through it all a couple of times. There wasn't much for me to tell, since all I'd basically done was walk out on the ice and fall down—Barry Strickland's conversation would probably take a lot more time.

It was just past twelve when the cops let me go. Cutty shook my hand, a wry look on her face, probably processing how my screw-up had saved the court system the cost of a trial. "The D.A. wants me to hold you here," she murmured confidentially.

"Great."

She shrugged, giving me a small smile. "I don't actually work for him, you know. I'd suggest you get in your tow truck and go home. Put some ice on those bruises; it helps. I got hit in the vest two separate times a few years ago, so I know how much it hurts."

I took her advice and slipped behind the wheel, waving jauntily at the state police as I drove over the Holy Island bridge. No one tried to stop me.

I cruised up the snowy county road to M-66 and paused there, considering. I was exactly equidistant between Katie's place in East Jordan and the Ferry Bar in Charlevoix. I had two distinct sore spots on my chest, my ears still rang from the near hit to the head, and I was awfully damn exhausted. Katie opening her door for me would be the most welcome sight I could think of.

On the other hand . . .

"Let's go see what's happening at the Ferry Bar," I told Alan.

*"It's after twelve. They close early in the winter,"* Alan objected.

I turned right, toward Charlevoix. "That's good. I'm a repo man. I do my best work at midnight."

# 30

## We Have Less Time Than We Thought

Charlevoix was buttoned up tightly. In the summer the streets flow with people and gaily lit boats bob in Round Lake and the air feels warm and exciting. This time of year, February not yet half over, people withdraw into the safety of their warm homes, abandoning the town. I saw literally not a single person as I cruised up Bridge Street. I parked two blocks away from the Ferry Bar—standard repo procedure. I grabbed Alan's case file and headed out. My footfalls were muffled by the snow, so the night was utterly silent. When I got to Rogan's place, it was closed and dark.

*"Would you quit touching the sore spots on your chest?"* Alan requested peevishly.

"They hurt."

*"I know they hurt! Stop touching them!"*

I remembered Rogan telling me he had a garage. I went around to the back of the bi-level building, finding four ground-level garage doors. I located which one was logically his, but it was locked. All right. I went back up to the front and peered inside. The only lights were the indicators on the appliances, green and red and blue dots in the darkness.

My elbow knocked out the glass above the doorknob, and I reached through and unlocked the door.

*"Ruddy!"* Alan blurted, sounding stressed for some reason. "Oops."

*"That's breaking and entering."*

"I know. I'll go inside; you stay here and watch for the cops." A little psycho humor, there.

*"What are we really doing here?"* Alan responded testily.

"I don't know, Alan. We're looking around, seeing if we can find anything. You're the one who thinks Rogan might be our man."

After ten minutes in the bar, all I could say for sure was that it was a place that served alcohol. If Rogan had made a signed confession, he had neglected to leave it lying out. Sitting right next to his computer screen was the key card to access it, and pretty much without thinking I swiped it, and the system came alive.

*"You know what you're doing?"*

"This is the same system we've got at the Black Bear. Of course I do," I responded.

Well, I really didn't. I had it in my mind to see if Shantytown mayor Phil Struder had a house account, but instead, after a bit of messing around, found myself looking at calendars. "Damn," I said.

*"Wait."*

"What is it?"

*"Can you check the date Nina Otis vanished?"*

"Sure. Want to tell me why?" Using the printouts from the folder for reference, I tapped the year, found the month, and opened it.

*"This is a shift schedule, right? Let's see if Rogan was really off the night she disappeared."*

That wasn't as easily accomplished as I would have hoped, but after a couple of stabs at it, I got the correct week up. It was summer, so three people worked that night.

One of them was Wade Rogan.

"Huh. And he said he wasn't here that night. Our friend

Mr. Rogan seems to have a problematic relationship with the truth," I noted dryly.

"*Not just that. Wait. Focus for just a second, okay? Focus. Okay. See it?*"

"See what?" I said impatiently.

"*See how he took the next four nights off?*"

"Huh."

"*Ruddy. What if the guy buying Nina Otis drinks was the* bartender?"

"Which," I mused, "was something the mayor could hardly have failed to notice." I thought about it, and then, with Alan's printouts reminding me of the dates, went back to work on the schedule. Rogan didn't own the bar the night Lisa Marie Walker vanished, but the next four days after telling the cops he saw a drunk woman headed for the Charlevoix docks, he was off work, letting himself get pretty short-staffed for a drinking establishment in the tourist season. He wasn't working the night the woman fell off the sailboat virtually in front of his home, nor did he report to work for three days after that. We saw the same thing for the two other missing women from Alan's list—the nights they vanished, Rogan was here, but then he gave himself a quick little vacation after that.

"Let's look around," I suggested. I went down the hallway to the bathrooms. The hallway itself was closed off by a curtain. The men's room was first, on the left, and then the ladies' was at the very end. An ancient wooden phone booth, inoperative and all carved up with initials and obscene comments, was positioned between the men's and the women's, so that the end of the hall was hidden from view.

On the other side of the hall from the ladies' room was a door with a wide-angle peephole in it. It was locked, but when I hit it with my boot a couple of times, it opened inward. Alan sighed. I turned on the light.

It was a tiny office—Rogan's personal work space. A desk, phone, and a chair. Photographs of someplace tropical, maybe the Wolfingers' beach in Hawaii, on the wall. Shelves with cleaning supplies and cans of salsa, things like that.

"So, Alan," I said. "Suppose you're giving some lady free drinks all afternoon. She's going to take the ferry to Beaver Island, but you're making them strong and she's gulping them down, getting tipsy. Eventually it's time for her to leave. You know she's going to want to use the bathroom after all she's had to drink. You come back here." I gestured to the peephole in the door. "And you watch. And here she comes. You open the office door, you step out, you grab her, you close the office door. It could happen in literally seconds."

*"She would have to be really, really drunk,"* Alan objected. *"Otherwise she'd fight it, maybe scream."*

I thought about the cans of starter fluid out in the mayor's ice shanty. It wasn't just an explosive chemical; it had long had another use. "Ether," I speculated. "You have a cloth soaked in ether. By the time she reacts—remember, she's hammered—she's sucked in the fumes and her lights go out. Or hell, maybe I'm making this too complicated. Maybe you just say, 'Come here a minute,' and she walks right in."

Alan pondered it. *"Then what?"* he asked.

There was a single door to my left. I thought it might be a closet, but when I opened it, I saw that it led to a dark, steep stairway. I fumbled for a light switch, found it, and flipped it on. A single stark light bulb showed the way down to the inside of a garage. "Huh," I said.

*"What is that thing down there?"* Alan asked.

At the bottom of the stairs, which pitched so steeply they looked spectacularly treacherous, a small chair incongruously sat on a metal rail. It was, I realized, a stairway elevator.

"Picture you've got a drugged, unconscious woman, and you

need to get her to the trunk of your car," I murmured. "No way you're going to be able to get her down these steps. So you put in a lift."

*"He's been doing this for a while,"* Alan said breathlessly.

"You might have missed a few with your list," I agreed. Inside, though, I was finally feeling something—rage. This guy ruined my life, and he *took* Lisa Marie's. He murdered Nina Otis. He was like a spider, lurking here, waiting for his prey to stumble down the hall.

I debated going down the stairs, but I didn't know what else I would be able to learn. From where I stood, it was a completely empty garage. I turned to flip off the light, and my eye caught sight of a peculiarly high shelf to my right, about six inches wide and a foot long, set off to the side of the upper doorframe. It was so high, I couldn't see what was on it, but when I felt around up there, I touched a soft cloth. I pulled it down, unfolded it, and stared at a hypodermic needle and a small glass vial. I turned the little bottle over and read the label.

*"What's Flunitrazepam?"* Alan asked.

"Not something they covered in repo school," I muttered. I went back into the office, and used Rogan's PC to look up what I had found. "Rohypnol," I announced.

*"Okay, and what is Rohypnol?"* Alan asked peevishly.

"It's like a knockout drug."

*"So . . . ,"* Alan replied slowly, thinking it through.

"So that's it," I finished for him. "He waits in his office. The drunk woman comes down the hall. He opens the door, gets her inside, sticks her with a needle, and she's out for hours."

*"He did it, Ruddy. He killed Lisa Marie Walker."*

I put the drug back up on its shelf and turned off the stairway light. "I need to talk to Strickland," I said.

*"What's that?"*

I could hear it plainly: A vehicle was pulling up behind the building. Briefly, headlights caused a yellow strip of light to flare beneath the garage door.

"If we tripped an alarm, we're screwed," I muttered.

Just as I was shutting the door at the top of the stairs, the garage door gave a lurch and began grinding upward, raised by an electric motor. It wasn't the cops.

Wade Rogan was returning to work.

*"Run!"* Alan blurted, panicking. I didn't run, but I didn't dawdle, bumping into a table as I made my way through the darkened bar. There was no way Rogan was going to miss the destruction to his front door—cold air was flowing in through the shattered glass as I opened it and stepped outside. I thought that, with a little luck, he'd fail to notice the abuse to the office latch, because kicking it open hadn't really left much damage other than maybe a gouge in the strike plate.

How much time, though, before he realized he'd had a break-in? And then what would he do?

"My guess is that the first thing he'll want to do is make sure his drug stash is still there. Then he'll probably call the cops," I speculated. I was running down the street, my footfalls muffled by the fresh snow, my breath steaming out in front of me.

*"Will he? His bar was broken into, and nothing is missing. He knows you're suspicious of him."*

"You might be right." Panting, I slid into my tow truck. "But we've got some time. He's not going to want to leave the door with that hole in it."

*"Time for what?"*

"We know where he is, which means we know where he isn't. I want to go check out his house, see if I can find anything there."

*"You can't be serious."*

I drove north, right past the Ferry Bar. I stared inside: It was still dark. "He's in his office," I said. "Or maybe he's still in his car, listening to a story on NPR."

*"Or maybe he took one look and he's already on the road, ahead of us,"* Alan suggested tensely.

"I don't think so. We'd see his lights." Highway 31 has a lot of straight road before the turn to Boyne City.

*"You can't honestly be thinking of going to his house."*

"Yeah, I can honestly be thinking of that."

*"Why? Why not just go to Strickland with what we've got?"*

"What we've got? *I've* got? Well, what exactly do I have? And how about when I tell Strickland how I got it?"

*"I think if you break into a place and discover evidence, if you're not a cop, it can still be used at trial."*

"And I appreciate your expert legal opinion, but even if that's true, all I have is circumstantial crap. Maybe, though, I can find something in his house. Don't a lot of these assholes keep trophies? I read that somewhere."

*"We're going to have no time at all, Ruddy."*

I put my foot hard on the accelerator. "Nah, we're going to have plenty of time. Ten minutes, easy. Maybe an hour, even."

*"God. What if he catches us?"*

"If he catches *me*, then I'll make him lie down and I'll call the cops."

*"He could have a gun."*

"Well, I've been shot already tonight. Wasn't that bad."

*"You had on a vest."*

"Just relax, Alan."

There wasn't a soul on the road this late at night, this late in winter. The trees flashed by, coated on their north sides by snow that flared white in my headlights.

I passed Strickland's place and thought briefly about going back and seeing if he had gotten home yet and maybe wanted to help me go shoot somebody else. In the end, though, I kept driving.

———

Rogan's mailbox had a red reflector on it that brightened as I approached. I turned and headed down the long, narrow driveway—it reminded me of the trip down the middle of Holy Island: just as dark, just as isolated.

When I got to his house, I decided to flip the truck around and point it back up the driveway so I could take off quickly. *"Hey, Ruddy,"* Alan asked as I was cranking the wrecker around. *"Where's the folder?"*

"Sorry?"

*"The folder. Our files. Did you leave it sitting out in the open for Rogan to find?"*

"Huh. I guess we'll have less time than I thought."

*"We have to leave now!"*

"Ten minutes," I promised. I checked my watch.

*"What was that? Is someone here?"* Alan asked.

"What? Where?"

*"Next to the garage. See? There's a car."*

I backed my truck up and swung it so the headlights were beaming directly on the vehicle next to the garage. I sucked in a breath.

It was Katie's car.

# 31

## The Mayor of Shantytown

I punched my fist through the glass door on the side of the house, unlocked it, and found myself in the mud room, the place designed for people to dump boots and snowshoes and coats in the winter. This one looked like every other mud room I'd ever been in—lined with hooks and benches—except for the incongruous presence of a large, new-looking freezer, hip high and four feet long, shoved up against one wall. The thing was so large, it made the mud room unusable for its intended purpose. I stopped, staring at the gleaming appliance.

"*You don't think . . . ,*" Alan whispered in horror.

I did not want to look in that freezer. Yet that's what I did, gritting my teeth and lifting the top. The missing snowmobile canvas was in there, white condensation frozen in fractal patterns across its black surface.

I moved the canvas.

A man, perhaps seventy years old, his eyes open, his face white with frost, was folded into the tight space, his mouth frozen open, as if he died screaming.

I'd found the mayor of Shantytown.

"*He knew Rogan was the person buying Nina Otis drinks,*" Alan murmured in shock.

"And this is how he shut the guy up." I plunged into the dark house, feeling for light switches. "Katie!" I shouted. "Katie!"

I listened. Nothing.

Leaping up the stairs two at a time, I ran from one bedroom to another, tearing open closets, diving to the floor to look under beds. One room was an office, piled high with folders and other papers. I was panting, sick to my stomach. I turned and dashed back to the main floor. Rogan could turn up any minute.

Bathroom. Master bedroom. Small study.

Nothing. No sign of her.

*"We've got to hurry,"* Alan begged. *"You have to find her, Ruddy!"*

"I know! Stop. Let's think. Think." I stood, trying to get my breathing under control, listening for any sign of her.

*"Wait. Rogan's shanty."*

My blood chilled. With the temperature so low, Katie could die out in that shanty, especially if he had shot her full of Rohypnol. I turned to leave the house, then froze.

*"What is it? Why are we stopping?"*

"Listen."

The low hum of a pump bringing up water from a well filled the air.

*"What is it?"*

"He's got a pump house. We need to find it."

I thought about it. I hadn't seen any cellar stairs on the outside of the house. The stairs must be accessible from the inside. I went to the staircase, but all the doors nearby were closets. No.

"It's winter. It would have to be heated or the pump would freeze," I explained. "If she's there, it'll be warm. Where is the damn thing?"

*"In every house I've shown, the pump is usually in the basement under the kitchen. Or the crawl space,"* Alan informed me urgently. *"It's where most of the plumbing is."*

"Makes sense." I checked my watch.

*"It's been ten minutes!"* Alan squealed in horror.

I ran to the kitchen. "You want me to stop looking?" I demanded crossly. I searched, my eyes darting into the corners. "No stairs," I noted.

*"We have to hurry!"*

I flung open every door I came across. No stairs. Frantic, I ran back to the kitchen, wanting to scream in frustration.

*"Wait!"* Alan shouted.

"What?" I snapped back.

*"Doesn't the table look out of place to you?"*

He was right. Instead of being in the nook where it belonged, the table was pulled to the center of the room and was resting on a rectangular rug. I lifted the corner of the small carpet and saw the seam in the shiny laminate. Trapdoor.

"Good work, Alan."

I shoved the table away and yanked the rug aside, popping open the door. A ladder led down to a dark room, and I descended quickly, nearly falling in my haste. I found a light bulb and pulled a string and gasped.

There was a mattress on the floor underneath the small shiny pump, which looked like a squat torpedo with a motor on top. Katie lay on the mattress, her hands and feet bound with duct tape, which also covered her mouth. She was unconscious.

"Katie. Honey," I whispered. I shook her gently, and her head lolled. Her eyes flickered when I ripped the tape off her mouth, but they did not open.

*"I want to kill him,"* Alan raged. *"Let's get a, a knife, let's—"*

"Alan!" I barked. "Stop it. We can't risk that he has a gun. He shoots me, he'll be free to do whatever he wants to Katie." I looked at the steep ladder and measured the difficulty of getting an unconscious woman up it. "Okay. We need a phone." I scrambled up the ladder and looked around the kitchen. No phone. Master bedroom. No phone.

"*The office!*" Alan urged.

I raced upstairs. No phone.

"*Who doesn't have a phone?*" Alan demanded.

"Some people just use cells now," I said. "It doesn't matter."

"*We have to hurry.*"

"Okay. Wait. I have an idea."

I ran through the mud room and out the door into the cold. The wind had kicked up, and the snow was coming down harder. I ran to the repo truck, yanked open the door, got under the dash, and stuck the connector back into the GPS. Then I hit the red switch, the emergency "Call Kermit" switch.

"Now"—I panted as I ran back toward the house—"I've got to get her out of there and into the truck. It won't be easy." I pictured wading in the snow and hated how long it would take with a woman slung over my shoulders. Then I got inspired. I stumbled over to the woodpile. Like a lot of people up north, Rogan had a wood sled—basically just a metal toboggan with a U-shaped handle at one end. You load the sled with wood and drag it to your front door, saving yourself dozens of trips.

"*What are we doing?*"

Rogan had stacked a dozen logs on the thing. I impatiently flipped the sled over, dumping them into the snow.

"Once I get Katie on this, it will be a lot easier to get her into the truck." I pulled the sled after me to the mud room door and went back inside.

"*How long have we been here?*"

I looked at my watch. "Twenty-five minutes." I dropped down through the door in the floor and went to my fiancée.

It broke my heart to see her in her professional clothes. Her first call for a listing. She'd been so excited, Jimmy had said.

It was my fault. I'd personally handed Rogan her business card. He didn't need to ambush her on the way to the ladies' room. She'd driven right to him.

It wasn't easy, getting her balanced on my shoulders. Gripping her with my right hand, I grabbed for the rungs with my left, powering upward as quickly as I could. Despite the cold, sweat ran down my forehead and into my eyes. Each step made me gasp with effort.

"*Hurry,*" Alan urged.

There were fifteen rungs, altogether, and by the end of them, my thigh muscles were trembling and I was panting for air. I laid her gently on the floor, catching my breath.

"*We need to move, Ruddy!*" Alan hissed.

"Right. Okay." I used the rug as a toboggan and dragged Katie across the smooth floor until we got to the mud room. Then I put my hands under her arms and walked backward, pulling her, her heels sliding. Both of her shoes came off—she had worn impractical, business-looking footwear. Her boots were probably in her car.

I got her outside and, without too much difficulty, laid her out on the wood sled, wrapping her in a blanket. To keep her from getting frostbite, I went back into the mud room, found some fur-lined boots, and jammed them on her feet. "Okay," I said. "We did it."

Then my head snapped up. Someone was coming down the highway, his lights flickering in the trees.

"Just someone passing by," I said quietly to Alan.

The lights slowed and then, with a long lazy sweep, turned down Rogan's driveway.

We had run out of time.

Within fifteen seconds his headlights had found my truck. Rogan stopped dead in his driveway, idling there. What was he thinking? His vehicle was a Hummer, one of those gigantic military transports. In the dark it looked like a massive evil beast, the steel bars welded to the front of an open fanged mouth. I turned away from it, staying to the shadows, not looking back even when Rogan stepped on the gas and surged ahead. By the time he halted at his front door, I was already down at the lake, pulling the sled, headed out onto the ice.

Out toward Shantytown.

Rogan had tied a stout cord to the right and left sides of the sled's handle, and I soon figured out why—with that loop of rope around my waist, I didn't have to twist back to grip the handle. I couldn't afford to drag it walking backward—I needed to keep my eye on the one shanty out there that had a light on in a small window. All the rest of them were dark, like sleeping pachyderms.

We were making slow but good progress. I was reminded of hitting the tackle sled at football practice—then, as now, it was about getting my legs under me and driving forward.

*"He's probably found the mess we made of his kitchen by now,"* Alan worried.

"Oh, you can count on that. He's trying to figure out what to do next. He knows we're gone, but he doesn't know where—though the ice is the only place anyone would look, unless he thinks we're hiding in the woods."

*"Is that what he will do next? Come search for us?"*

"My opinion? No. He'll run. He's got to have thought about it, that one day this could happen, that he could be discovered. He's figured this out. He's not Blanchard; he's got a plan."

*"Good. Let him run."*

"That's how I feel."

I stopped to catch my breath. The shanty with the light on looked as if it were fading away from me. I was headed straight into the wind, and the snow swirling around was making visibility almost impossible. "Whoever it is in that shanty, they probably have a cell phone." I thought of something. "Oh Jesus."

*"What?"*

"I don't know how Kermit's going to react when he gets my signal. What if he comes straight down Rogan's driveway?"

"*Wouldn't he call the cops?*"

"He doesn't know what's going on."

"*We have to hurry,*" Alan said simply, for what seemed like the tenth time that night.

I put more into it, my eyes on that little square of yellow glowing at the top edge of the shanty. We were a hundred yards away, the length of a football field. A familiar distance.

Suddenly there was light behind me, brightening the swirling snow. I glanced back.

Rogan had driven his enormous vehicle out onto the ice.

He was coming for us.

I made a decision. If I kept going straight, Rogan and I would get to the illuminated shanty at the same time. I jinked left, where three huts were grouped in close proximity. I doubted Rogan could see me—the storm would be reflected right back in his eyes. I could see him, though, and hear the roar of his engine as he came streaking across the ice.

Of the three shanties, I picked the one in the middle, which had a door secured with a loop of string. I flung it open and carried Katie inside, setting her down gently and tucking the blanket tight around her. The interior was tiny, barely large enough for her to stretch out. "Okay. You'll be safe, I promise," I whispered to her. Then I got the wood sled and shoved it into the small hut as well, closing it back up.

"*What are you doing?*"

"I can't outrun him and drag her, Alan. Now I can move, draw him away." I started running again, heading straight out onto the ice, going for the shanties in the distance.

"*She'll freeze in there! She'll die!*"

"If Rogan catches us, we'll *all* die."

I looked over my shoulder. Rogan was bearing down on the shanty I'd been aiming for, the one with the lights on. I *felt* the impact as the heavy truck slammed into the flimsy hut, turning it into matchsticks. Horrified, I saw a man tumbling away from the wreckage, sprawling on the ice, a dark figure against the white.

Rogan hit the brakes and skidded a good twenty yards, drifting sideways. His Hummer rocked on its shocks when it halted, the snow pouring down in the headlights. He put the thing in neutral and revved the engine, his lights pointing back toward the hut he had just destroyed. I saw the motionless man lying in the snow.

I gauged how much distance I would have to cover to get to the poor guy and drag him to safety. Rogan would certainly see me as I emerged from the darkness. I charged forward anyway.

"*Oh my God,*" Alan breathed as Rogan put his foot on the accelerator. All four of his tires spun, snow flying off the tread, but he gained speed and was moving at least thirty when he ran over the body a second time, crushing it.

There was nothing more I could do. I turned back and fled blindly into the snowstorm. When the lights suddenly lit me from behind, I knew he could see me.

I was out in the open, the sheds so spread out that dashing from one to another would leave me hideously exposed. The nearest hut was twenty yards away. I had to get it between me and Rogan. I sprinted as fast as I could, heading for the shadows pooling behind it. This was one of the flimsy ones, canvas and wood. "Hey, is anyone here? Can anyone hear me?" I shouted as I ducked down behind it. The wind whipped my words away.

The light was growing more intense as the Hummer came straight at the shanty I was hiding behind. Rogan had seen my flight across the open ice.

"*We can't stay here!*" Alan screamed at me.

"Wait . . . wait . . . Now!" I replied. I ran straight to my left, and the Hummer hit the shanty and obliterated it. The tent material fell across his windshield, temporarily blinding Rogan, and I used the opportunity to double back, running in the direction from which he'd just come, and then heading to my right. I knew where we were; this was near where the mayor lived.

Rogan leaned out of his Hummer and removed the tarp blocking his view. Then he got back in, spun around, and crashed hard into another shanty. One of his headlights went out.

*"We're nowhere near that one. Why did he do that?"*

"He's having fun. It's Whac-a-Mole. He's just going to keep crashing into them until he's wiped them all out."

*"What about the one Katie's in?"*

"I know," I said grimly. "We can't let that happen. I'm going to have to keep him focused on me."

Rogan had all the advantages—his four-wheel drive could get him moving quickly, and with his high beams on, he could light up the lake. He spun his wheel, turning a 360, and the headlights raked the ice like spotlights. I dove down as they swept by me, but then they stopped and came back, probing, and I knew he had glimpsed me. I got up and ran, throwing myself behind the nearest shanty.

*"Did he see us?"*

"I don't know," I answered, gasping for air. I looked around, not sure if Rogan was facing his lights directly at me or not. "I was inside this one," I told Alan. "The guy who sells kerosene in glass jugs." I slammed my fist on the wall. "Hey!" I shouted. "If you're in there, get out! Get out!"

Rogan's engine roared. I gauged the headlights on the other side of the shanty as they got brighter, wondering if he knew where I was.

Yes, I realized. Yes, he did. He was coming straight at me.

# 32

## If I Don't Keep Moving I Will Die

I waited as long as I could before I bolted away from my hiding place. It was the only advantage I had—I was more maneuverable, able to dodge, when he was close.

I was hoping that the kerosene shanty would be built more solidly than the others and would cause his Hummer significant damage, but the building collapsed like a house of cards, the debris bouncing off Rogan's hood and roof. He slid sideways.

I ran back the way I had come.

"Hey, McCann! Which one is she in?" Rogan shouted, the wind playing tricks with his voice. "Huh? Where is she?"

I turned and looked at him. He was waving a hand out his open window, and in the hand he clutched a lethal-looking pistol. I couldn't see his face inside the dark interior of the vehicle.

"*Why does he have his wipers on?*" Alan asked.

I made it to a metal shanty and peered around the corner. He was, indeed, using his wipers.

"Kerosene," I said. "He just drove through fifty gallons of the stuff. It's probably soaked into the snow on his roof and hood, too."

Rogan surged forward, heading for the metal shanty. Surely, the more formidable structure would put a stop to this.

*Wait. Kerosene.*

"*What is it?*" Alan asked, sensing something.

Rogan was coming. I ran around to the back of the metal hut, putting it between him and me, but instead of staying put, this time I headed out onto the ice, keeping in the shadows.

He didn't slam into this one. Instead he pulled up next to it.

"*What's he doing?*"

Rogan stayed in his vehicle, firing several shots into the shanty's body, puncturing the metal sides. The percussions sounded much weaker than the one that had sent a bullet past my head. "Is she in there?" he called mockingly, his voice barely audible above the storm.

I turned and headed for the mayor's place, heedless of the fact that I might be visible now.

Rogan fired more shots—anyone in there would be dead, the thin sheet metal no match for bullets. Then he sat there for a moment, and I could make out what he was doing in the reflection of his headlights off the sides of the metal hut.

Reloading.

I charged up the steps to the mayor's shanty and ran to the cupboard. I pulled frantically at the doors, hurling them open. Out spilled emergency equipment—bandages, food, a flashlight. I flipped on the flashlight and played it desperately around the hut. "Where the hell is it?" I cried. "It was right here!"

"*What are you looking for?*"

Finally I spotted the flare gun. I lost more precious time searching for shells, but then I had one, which I slipped into my pocket.

"*He'll be able to see the flashlight through the window!*" Alan warned.

I turned off the flashlight and turned back toward the door.

The shanty exploded, and I was thrown against the wall. Splintered wood rained down on me. Disoriented, I dropped to the floor, which seemed to be moving sideways. When I could, I crawled back to the door. Rogan had slammed into the back end and ripped the shed in half. I fell out into the snow onto my butt, gasping, then rolled.

"*Run,*" Alan urged. I got to my feet. The mayor's hut had finally administered some punishment to the Hummer: The engine was making a rattling sound. Still, it ran, and Rogan steered it toward my fleeing shadow.

I stopped and popped open the flare gun, slipping in a shell. "Okay," I said, raising the weapon. I pointed it straight at the kerosene-soaked vehicle as it bore down on me, and pulled the trigger.

The flare shell sparked and shot out of the barrel, going straight and true into the Hummer's blunt grill, where it ignited, a blinding spot of burning light.

"Boom," I said.


There was no boom. Rogan stopped, the front end of his massive truck so bright from the flare, it turned the storm into a blinding curtain. I stood transfixed in the single headlight, barely thirty yards away, and saw the dark shadow of his arm out his window just moments before he pulled the trigger. For the second time that night, a bullet shrieked past me so closely, I felt the crack of the shock wave. I dove into the snow, which had accumulated a good two inches, rolled to my feet, and dashed back toward the wreckage of the mayor's shanty.

"Why the hell didn't that work?" I panted. Rogan floored it, ignoring me for the moment and racing across the ice and flying into another tarp-covered frame, flattening it.

"Where is she, Ruddy?" he taunted into the wind. As he skidded to a stop, I could see the flare still burning an impotent bright red in his grill, etching a dancing dot in my vision when I closed my eyes.

"He's in no hurry," I told Alan. "As long as he doesn't let me get too far away, he can keep herding me back toward the shanties, which he's destroying one at a time. I need a new plan. Nothing is working."

"*No, look. It* is *working!*" Alan shouted hopefully. I glanced over and saw what he meant: Even in the glare of the headlight, I could see blue and yellow flames flickering on Rogan's hood and roof, but they were tiny and useless. Little drips of flaming liquid were trailing off the Hummer as it lumbered forward. Then Rogan floored it again, speeding straight at me. I was too far away from the nearest shanty, caught in the open.

Dodge too soon, and he could follow my movements. Wait too late, and I'd be in pistol range. "*Ruddy!*" Alan warned. I elected to wait. Rogan's arm came out of the window. I tensed and then darted right, a quick five steps, then jinked back left, trying to get to the mayor's ruined shelter before Rogan could run me down.

Rogan had taken the feint and then, when he overcorrected, sent his Hummer into a slide. I'd always been good at faking out linebackers. He wrestled with his wheel, too busy to fire.

"*He's toying with us,*" Alan said urgently. "*It's a game.*"

This time, when the Hummer rocked to a stop, I saw something new: black clouds rising from his lower windshield, almost as if the glass were on fire. His wipers, I realized. They were burning, melting, and the rubber was smoking. His truck really was on fire, the fuel floating on the surface of melting snow and dripping onto the ice. It was just that the kerosene wasn't volatile enough to pose any danger.

Volatile.

I made it to the mayor's ruined shanty and jumped inside. The roof had collapsed halfway, but I ducked under it, feeling in the disorganized spill of supplies and tools.

"*What are we doing? We're sitting ducks in here,*" Alan gasped in terror.

I pulled the flashlight out of my pocket and flicked it on. I found a screwdriver, and then my hand closed on one cone-shaped can, then another. "Starting fluid!" I explained. "Pure ether! Highly explosive!"

In other words, boom.

I stuffed the items into my pockets and rolled out through the hatch in the floor, squeezing myself in the small crawl space and scrabbling back onto the open ice.

When I peeked around the corner, I saw Rogan see me: His head was out the window, trying to peer past the smoke. He turned off his headlights for a moment, so that the only illumination came from the now sputtering flare, which abruptly extinguished.

*"What's he doing? Why did he turn off the lights?"*

"It's starting to get foggy. Maybe he thought he'd be able to see me better with his fog lights," I replied, but Rogan just sat there for a minute, his fog lights off. Ghostly blue and yellow flames licked the air—it was unholy, a vehicle straight from hell.

His lone head lamp came back on. Maybe he thought that in the darkness I'd try to run for a new shanty, give him a clue where I'd hidden Katie, and that he'd catch me out in the open. I saw him grinning, still enjoying being the bull to my matador.

Would he charge, or come fast? "I need him to come fast. If he comes slowly, I won't be able to dodge him, and he'll be able to line up his shot. I need one more charge," I gritted out as I pulled out a can of starting fluid and punctured it with the screwdriver. The sharp tang of the ether filled the air.

*"Then run. Draw him out. Make him roll down his right window and fire out that one, across the inside of the truck."*

I did it, breaking from behind the shanty and dashing hard across the ice. Rogan was twenty yards away and easily spotted me. I ran to his right. He accelerated, lazily steering after me. I heard his rattling motor closing in, and watched my shadow on the ground get shorter and shorter, and then I threw myself farther to the right.

All I did in college was carry the ball, but in high school I was the best passer in northern Michigan. Both of his windows were open, and I aimed for the large black square and threw that can in a decent spiral, ether dribbling out as it sailed in a flat arc, a ten-yard toss as he braked. Boom.

The can went over the roof of the Hummer and vanished silently in the night. Rogan slid to a stop twenty yards away, broadside to me, staring at me through his open right window. I knelt and punctured the second can. Blue flames dribbled off his roof, smoke rose from his wipers, but I swear I could see his white teeth smiling. He raised his pistol and I raised my can. He fired and I threw.

He missed and I didn't. The can clipped the doorframe and then fell inside. I braced myself for a second shot, but it didn't come.

*"You did it!"* Alan cried.

Still no boom, but after a moment, yellow flames filled the Hummer's interior. I saw Rogan beating on them, slapping at himself, but he'd gotten some of the fluid on him, and the fire wasn't going out.

His dome light came on as Rogan tumbled out into the night. He staggered, his arms ablaze, and then fell into the snow.

I didn't bother to watch the rest. He would put out the flames on his clothing or he wouldn't. He would come after me with the pistol or he wouldn't. Either way, he was on foot now—his car was burning more and more brightly, filling the foggy night with a brilliant orange light. He was still dangerous, still had the gun, but if it was a footrace, I knew I could beat him.

I ran. I had to get to Katie and drag her to safety while Rogan was still distracted.

The cold air sawed harshly at my throat, and my legs felt ready to give out—I'd asked a lot of them that night already. I pictured Rogan snuffing out the flames, rolling in the snow, and then retrieving his pistol and pursuing.

I lined up the lights of the shore with where I knew the cluster of three shanties would be, though the wind was whipping snow around, nearly blinding me.

"*It's the one in the middle,*" Alan reminded me unnecessarily as the three dark shapes suddenly appeared in my vision, less than fifteen yards away.

I went to the shanty and opened the door.


Once inside, I turned on the flashlight. Katie hadn't moved. I knelt by her, checking that she was still breathing. I threw the wood sled out the door, picked her up, and followed it, laying her down.

"Ruddy?" she murmured. "Where are we?"

I took off my coat and laid it on the blanket over her chest, the frigid air moving quickly to attack the sweat under my flannel shirt. "It's okay, Katie. You're going to be all right." I slipped the rope around my waist and strained forward. Less than two hundred yards to my truck. When I turned off the flashlight, I could see the lights of Rogan's house, barely discernable in the storm.

We made it maybe halfway when the howling wind simply erased the shore. One moment I could see a few lights dancing around in front of me, then next all was swallowed in fog and snow. It was a whiteout, except that at night it was a screaming, menacing blackness.

I turned on the flashlight, and it lit up the cloud that enveloped me but did nothing for my vision. I leaned into the wind.

"*We need to go back to the shanty!*" Alan told me urgently. "*You can't see where you are going!*"

The wind was unstable, buffeting me from all directions, making it difficult to keep my bearings, to know where to go. I stopped and looked back toward where the shanties were. They had vanished.

"I can't see *anything*!" I bellowed.

*"If you keep moving, you could wind up lost out here on the ice,"* he warned.

"If I don't keep moving, I will *die,"* I snapped back.

I kept moving. When I turned off the flashlight, hoping to see some glimmer from shore, the darkness was alive, swirling and dancing in front of me like a devil, urging me on. I thought of the ghostly figure of Wade Rogan, his arms on fire, staggering forward and falling down. He'd looked like a monster.

I walked until my instincts told me we were at the shoreline, but we weren't. The ice was flat and hard under my feet. I played my flashlight around, hoping a break in the fog would let me catch sight of something: a tree, a shanty, anything. I turned and looked at Katie. She was shivering, her eyes open but dull. I knelt by her and patted the snow off her.

"I am so cold," she told me.

"All right," I said after a moment. I lay down next to her, wrapping my arms around her and pulling her tight against me.

*"What are we doing, Ruddy?"*

"She's freezing."

*"We can't lie here! We'll all die!"*

"That's going to happen anyway, Alan. We're lost."

*"Please get up, Ruddy. Please keep going."*

"Wouldn't you rather it be this way? Holding Katie?"

*"Don't give up! You've never given up!"*

"God, you sound just like my father right now."

*"Stop it! This is Katie's life. You can't lie down!"*

I thought about it. "Okay," I said. "You're right." I leaned over and kissed Katie on the cheek, shocked at how cold her skin was under my lips.

I stood up and put the rope around my waist. I left the flash-light on—we were stumbling around at random, hoping by sheer luck to find safety, so it didn't matter that the glare blinded me. Maybe someone would see *us,* though that didn't seem possible in this storm. I just knew it gave me comfort, to have light, to be able to turn back and see Katie on the sled.

"*Thank you, Ruddy. Thank you for trying to save my little girl.*"

"Alan. I have to tell you something," I panted.

"*Yes?*"

"I always thought you were real. Even though I know you can't be, I always thought of you as being a real person."

"*Thank you, Ruddy.*"

"I'm glad you're with me now. I would hate to be doing this alone."

"*I won't leave you,*" he promised.

I staggered ahead for a few minutes, then stopped. My legs were trembling and weak, and I felt ready to collapse. "I need a break," I said, my hands on my knees.

Then something slammed into me.

I fell back as if shot, registering that something coming fast had jumped up from the ground, hitting me hard in the stomach. I didn't even have time to move and it was on me, a wet tongue finding my face.

"Jake!" I shouted. "My God!" I wrapped my arms around him, joyously clutching his wriggling stout body. "What are you doing here?"

Kermit. He must have come to the repo rescue and, naturally, he brought my dog with him. My dog, with his silly ears and astounding nose.

I untied the rope from the wood sled and used it as a leash. When I gave Jake the loathed instructions to "go for a walk," he pulled steadily in the direction of the nearest nap: the repo truck.

We were heartbreakingly close to shore—I had been trudging along parallel to it, but would soon have been back out on the open ice. Jake led me to solid ground precisely where I had started my trek that night. The progress onshore was harder— the couple inches of new snow slowed the sled, but now I saw the flashing light bar of the truck pulsing ahead of me, ghostly in the swirling fog.

I didn't see Kermit until we were about ten feet away. He got out of the repo truck, gawping at me. I let go of Jake, who bounded over to him.

"It's Katie," I explained curtly.

"Did she fall through the ice?" he asked, coming to help.

"Where's your truck?" I replied.

Kermit pointed up the driveway, and we dragged Katie over. "We need to get her to a hospital. Keep your heat on high," I panted as I struggled to get her sitting upright in the passenger seat. Her head lolled like a drunk's. "She didn't fall into the water, but she's been drugged. I'll tell you all about it when we get to the emergency room."

"Okay."

I looked at him, put a hand on his shoulder. "Thanks for coming, Kermit."

He straightened. "Sure."

"I'll follow in my truck with the light bar on. Jake will come with me. Let me have your cell phone, okay?"

He handed over his phone and got into his truck. Jake followed on my heels, but when I opened the passenger door of the repo truck for him, he stood, his nose lifted, facing the direction of the ice shanties, sniffing. Could he smell Rogan, out there somewhere, still alive? His gaze was intent and focused, though there was nothing to see. Maybe Rogan was close, staggering to shore, or maybe he had crawled into one of the huts for shelter. I watched my dog for a moment and then snapped my fingers. "Hey," I said. "Forget it, Jake. It's Shantytown."

# 33

## You Don't Have Much Time

*"We need to let someone know what happened,"* Alan told me.

"Yeah, I know that, Alan."

*"We should call Cutty."*

Keeping one eye on the road, I held up Kermit's cell phone and thumbed 911. Alan made a small grunt of protest that we weren't calling his never-to-be girlfriend.

"911, what is your emergency?" a man asked crisply.

For a moment my brain went into the mental equivalent of a four-wheel drift, as I tried to separate what I should say from all that I could say. I cleared my throat. "There's a man who was run over out in Shantytown. Sort of in the middle of the ice shanties, but the southern edge. The guy who did it was driving a Hummer, and it caught on fire."

"On fire. Who is this, please?"

"The driver's name is Wade Rogan. He was driving around smashing into the shanties, destroying them, and there was a man in one. He deliberately ran over the guy a second time. I don't think the, uh, the victim, survived."

"What is your name, sir?"

"You need to send the ambulance and the police. Wade Rogan has a gun."

"I need to know who is calling, and your location."

"Did you get it? Wade Rogan. He is armed, and he'll shoot any cop he sees." I hung up.

*"Let's call Cutty."*

I ignored him and phoned Barry Strickland. I expected him to sound groggy—it was three thirty in the morning—but he answered on the first ring.

"Strickland."

"It's Ruddy."

"Hang on a minute."

There was a rustling sound. I could hear a report about a big snowstorm on the East Coast, and then the volume went down and he came back.

"Did I wake you up?" I inquired.

"Can't sleep," he grunted. "All my years of duty, that was only the second time I've ever killed a man."

"You saved my life, Barry."

Strickland grunted again. "I should have realized Blanchard might come for you. We knew he was on a snowmobile. I put you at risk."

"I'd say Blanchard did that."

Strickland thought about it. "Him, too."

*"Are we going to talk about Wade Rogan?"* Alan asked peevishly. I thought I knew why he was so cranky—it was his theory that all the disappearances were linked, but I was going to get the credit.

"There's going to be a lot of activity out on the ice of Shantytown tonight. It has to do with Lisa Marie Walker."

I could feel Strickland going still. "Yes?" he responded cautiously.

"I know who killed her. His name is Wade Rogan. He owns the Ferry Bar in Charlevoix. He feeds women alcohol and then drugs them with Rohypnol. I think Lisa Marie might have been his first—he saw her get out of my car, realized how drunk she was, and just sort of picked her up. When the news came out that she had supposedly drowned in my car, it gave him the idea to toss her in the lake after he'd . . . had her . . . for a few days."

*"And then he realized the M.E. was incompetent,"* Alan urged.

I had sort of forgotten this, but it still irritated me to be reminded. "It wasn't a perfect murder at all," I continued. "Her body was in good shape; his semen was in her. Rogan was a dentist at one time; he had to know the forensics were against him. Except the man in charge of the county lab was our good friend Dr. Kane, who suppressed evidence and chalked up the lack of decomposition to the temperature of the water."

"Please don't tell me you've spoken to this Rogan and told him your theory," Strickland interrupted.

*"It's not a theory,"* Alan protested.

"There's more, though. The woman who fell off the *Emerald Isle,* Nina Otis, was in his bar, drinking, the day she died. She never got on the boat. He kidnapped her and did the same thing he did to Lisa Marie. And the woman who supposedly got drunk and slipped off the boat in Boyne City? The thing was anchored in front of his house. He probably saw her staggering around on deck and couldn't resist rowing out to see if he could grab her."

The phone in my hand beeped, and I pulled it away from my ear to glance at it—the 911 operator was calling me back.

"All right, Ruddy," Strickland said kindly. "I understand how attractive this is—it's an explanation that gives us a bad guy, a very bad guy, responsible for participating in a fraud that ruined your life. But cases like this just don't string together this easily. It takes hard evidence and proof."

Alan and I were both silent for a moment. I pondered how to convince Strickland without talking for an hour, and hit on the solution. "He tried to do the same thing to Katie tonight," I said bluntly.

Now it was Strickland's turn to be quiet. "Say that again," he finally instructed sternly.

I told him about Rogan luring Katie to his home, drugging her, and holding her prisoner in his pump house. About my escape onto the ice. "Rogan drove his Humvee out after me and started crashing into the shanties. One of them had a man in it, and Rogan deliberately drove over him. He killed the guy right in front of me."

"Where is the perpetrator now?" Strickland asked tensely.

Rogan had gone from being the subject of a wild theory to perpetrator. I felt a cold satisfaction. "He's out on the ice still. I burned him alive." I gave the rest of it to him, the phone beeping at me frantically. "I've already called 911. That's what I meant by a lot of activity."

"So you didn't actually confirm he was dead. For all we know, he escaped," Strickland speculated.

"Have you looked out your front window? No one could survive out there. But I did tell 911 that he was armed and would shoot any cop he saw."

"I have to call Cutty. Ruddy . . . you're going to need to make a statement."

"Okay, but not tonight," I responded testily. "Katie's headed to the ER. Besides, it's the middle of the night." I told him I would meet him wherever he wanted in the morning, the late morning, but that I'd run out of steam.

"I can't promise you anything. You have to understand, you're reporting a homicide, accusing Rogan of being a serial killer, and telling me you burned him to death in Shantytown. There's going to be an all-points on you the second I hang up with Cutty."

*"He's got to let us see my daughter!"* Alan objected shrilly.

"All right. I'm headed home," I stated evenly.

"You're not going to the hospital?" Strickland asked skeptically.

*"Ruddy?"* Alan demanded.

"I am telling you that I am headed to my home in Kalkaska," I replied pointedly.

Strickland was silent a moment. "I will advise Cutty that when

I asked you where you were, you told me you were headed to your place in Kalkaska," he finally agreed dryly.

"Thank you, Barry."

"You're not going to have much time before they get there. If you're not snoozing in your bed, they'll widen the search pretty rapidly, and I can't imagine the hospital won't be the first place they check."

"Thank you, Barry," I repeated.

We hung up, and I turned off the phone even as it began ringing in my hand. "Okay, Alan," I said grimly. "Let's go take care of your daughter."


The hospital in Charlevoix lies at one end of a neighborhood with expensive houses commanding fantastic views of Lake Michigan, and is so clean and efficient, it's a little hard to take the place seriously. They took *me* seriously, though—I passed Kermit on the highway, roared up to the emergency room, my light bar flashing, and stormed into the place, ready to shove people out of the way to make room for Katie if I had to.

The waiting room was completely empty, so I was not forced to use my bar bouncing skills to clear it. I had a doctor and an attendant lined up at the doors with a gurney when Katie arrived, though, and I needed to swallow back my reaction when she got out of the vehicle under her own power, her eyes a little unfocused as they found me. She gave me a weak wave as she lay down and was wheeled past me and through some double doors.

*"They should let us go, too,"* Alan fretted. *"We're family."*

"I think the doctors know what they're doing and don't want me standing there," I replied.

Kermit came up to me as I said this and nodded at my wisdom. "They have procedural trammels," he noted. "Otherwise, you could present."

"I can't argue with that," I replied honestly, handing him his cell phone.

"She came awake in the car. I think she'll have a full resumption, I really do. Her conversation held coherency."

*"As opposed to* this *conversation,"* Alan observed snidely. I thought, though, that he was feeling what I was feeling—relief. Whether she recovered or resumed, I thought the fact that she was confabulating with Kermit was a very good sign.

"You want me to wait with you?" Kermit asked.

"No, that's okay. You can take Jake home. You should be with Becky."

He didn't move, something obviously on his mind. I waited. "So, I know this is not a good time . . . ," he began. "I wouldn't bring it up if it weren't important."

"No problem. What's up?"

"It's about my uncle Milt." Kermit fixed me with a pain-filled stare. "The autopsy came back. The police were out to see me. Detectives."

"What's wrong?"

"They said he had low levels of carbon dioxide in his blood. Not enough to kill him. He was way past drunk, though, so much booze in him, he was practically restive in a coma."

Alan murmured, *"Carbon* monoxide," and I ignored him.

"Is that what they say happened? Alcohol poisoning?"

Kermit gravely shook his head. "No. Someone made him get drunk and then, when he was unconscious, put a plastic bag over his head until he suffocated."

I was thunderstruck. Kermit nodded at my expression. "Yeah. It wasn't suicide."

I tried to process this. "Do the cops agree with the plastic bag theory?"

"They found the bag, once they bothered to look for it. It was wadded up in the corner. I guess somehow they can tell it was used to kill uncle Milt. It's been ruled a homicide."

"God." I tried to shake off the feeling of unreality. "Well, you were the last one to see him that night. Did he say anything about meeting someone else?"

"Me?" Kermit frowned blankly. "I didn't see him that night."

"He said he was meeting you for drinks but not at the Black Bear," I answered, straining to remember the conversation.

"Why would I give business to my wife's competitors?" he asked simply.

Now it was my turn to look blank.

*"Either Milt lied, or Kermit's lying,"* Alan the detective chimed in. I tried to keep the irritated expression off my face. Alan wasn't even around when this all happened.

"Could you and Barry look into this?" Kermit asked. "The cops are going to investigate, but I'd feel better with my guys on it."

His guys. In that moment, I felt it: Strickland, Kermit, and I *were* a sort of team, weren't we? Just not Alan. "Sure," I agreed. "Of course. Wow. How are you doing with all of it?"

He shrugged. "It's pretty unreal. I'm not sure how I'm doing," he said candidly.

"I'm sorry. I mean, I don't even know what to say about something like this."

"I feel better just knowing you and Barry are going to check into it."

*"I have a couple of ideas how we might start,"* Alan mused. I blinked once, really hard, a clear signal for him to shut his non-existent mouth.

"So, do you have any idea who would do this? Who might have a motive to murder your uncle?"

"Honestly?" Kermit gave me a searching look. "Well, me, I guess. I had the most to gain." He wore a sadly ironic smile.

"I know *you* wouldn't do it, Kermit," I said levelly. I clenched my fist, hoping Alan would take it as a signal I didn't want to hear any contrary theories from him. "Strickland and I will get to the bottom of it, I swear."

"Thanks. So, you sure you don't want me to stay with you, keep you company?" he asked.

"No, thanks," I said. *I don't need company; I have a voice in my head,* I didn't say.

"Okay. Well, let me know if you need anything."

*"He's a good guy. You should tell him,"* Alan advised me.

I agreed. "Hey, Kermit." He waited. I cleared my throat, suddenly feeling awkward. "You, uh, saved my life out there tonight. By bringing Jake. That was genius."

"That was actually contingent happenstance. Jake wanted to go for a car ride."

"Huh. In my experience, Jake never even wants to leave the bed."

"Maybe he instincted something was going on with you. Dogs are amazing that way."

"Maybe. Well, anyway, I'm just really grateful, Kermit. You saved Katie's life, too."

"Why were you out in Shantytown anyway?"

"Oh." With that question, I suddenly realized how much nobody knew but me. "I'll tell you later, Kermit."

"Sure."

*"That's it? He saves your life, and you just say you're grateful?"* Alan chided.

I gritted my teeth. *Okay, Alan.* "It's kind of not the first time you've done that, Kermit. Pulled my fat out of the fire, I mean."

My brother-in-law nodded as if this had never occurred to him. *"Your fat? What Western novel did you lift that expression out of?"* Alan scoffed.

"I'm just saying, I'm glad you're married to my sister. I'm glad you're in my family. My brother-in-law. It means a lot to me."

"Thanks, Ruddy."

I did something pretty unfamiliar then: I put my arms around Kermit and gave him a hug, slapping him on the back a couple of times, hard enough to give him the Heimlich. "Take care of yourself," I said, my voice a little hoarsened.

Kermit gave me a smile. "Yeah, you too, Ruddy."


I discovered something about hospitals—they can look completely deserted, but when you leave the lounge and head back to the examining rooms, people appear at your side to ask you if they can help you. I used my bar bouncer voice to say I needed to see Katie Lottner, and within two minutes I was speaking to her doctor—a striking African American woman, thin boned, with fine features and large dark eyes. Those eyes were warm and sympathetic as she led me over to some chairs and sat in the one next to me. I could feel Alan inside, bracing himself, but there was something so reassuring about this woman's demeanor, the tension left me like a chill in front of a warm fire.

"Your girlfriend has mild hypothermia, but no frostbite. The drugs in her system seem to be wearing off on their own."

"Actually, we're engaged," I corrected.

She smiled more broadly. "Congratulations."

"*Would you let her talk?*" Alan shouted at me.

I blinked my eyes once, hard, to get him to knock it off. The doctor watched me curiously. "Are you okay?"

"Yes, sorry," I apologized.

"There is no reason not to expect a full recovery. She's been alert, but we're letting her sleep."

"Can I speak to her?"

A cool expression came into her eyes. "May I ask exactly how she came to ingest Rohypnol?"

My jaw dropped when I realized I was a *suspect*. Alan was sputtering indignation. Once again I found myself searching for the most economical way to relate a potentially enormous amount of information. It was fatiguing. I considered my words and had an idea. "Doctor, how long have you lived here?"

She blinked at the change of subject. "Seven years, why?"

"You remember Barry Strickland, then."

"Yes, he was the best sheriff we've ever had. Where are we going with this, may I ask?"

"If I give you his number and he says it is okay, will you let me see my fiancée?"

She looked troubled. "He's not the sheriff anymore, Ruddy. He doesn't really have the authority. There's a protocol I must follow."

"You have procedural trammels," I translated a bit bitterly.

She frowned over this one.

"There's no way I can see her?"

"I'm afraid we have to wait for the deputy sheriff to give the okay."

"Oh. So you called the sheriff?"

"Yes, I'm required to," she informed me without apology.

"That's good. That's really good. I'm looking forward to getting this all cleared up. Say, I need to use the men's room. Can you tell me where it is?"

# 34

## I'm Supposed to Be Here

Deputy Dumbbell was pulling into the ER parking circle just as I was getting ready to drive away. His light bar was flashing, and he was so eager to arrest and probably shoot fugitive Ruddy McCann that he nearly slid into a pole. He flung his door open and charged up the sidewalk, his hands on his belt, either to be close to his gun or to hold his pants up. He never looked in my direction to see his suspect watching him.

*"We're going to be caught,"* Alan worried.

"No, we're not," I replied. At some point, it seemed, I had given up lecturing Alan on the use of the term *we*.

*"He's going to talk to the doctor, who is going to tell him you're in the restroom. When he sees you're not in there, he's going to come out here to radio someone, and he'll see us."*

"No, he's not," I said. I started my tow truck and drove quickly across the parking lot, easing up next to the deputy's patrol car, which was still flashing. I yanked the lever, and the T bar slid out, repo quiet, and within seconds I had the car's front wheels off the ground. Whistling, I dove out of the cab, set the safety chains, and jumped back in. I eased away, moving silently on the snowy street. The storm had let up, though it looked like we'd gotten another inch since I'd been out at Shantytown.

"*You are stealing a police vehicle,*" Alan marveled. "*This is insane.*"

"You think this is insane? I know this guy with a dead Realtor in his head." I went straight down the street, still within sight of the hospital, and lowered Timms's car back down next to a fire hydrant. Maybe he'd get a ticket.

"*What do you think you're doing?*" Alan demanded.

"Buying us a little time."

"*You're going back to jail over this.*"

"Really? What do you want to bet that when Deputy Dumbbell comes out and sees his car parked a hundred yards down the road, he's going to be too embarrassed to tell Grant Porterfield what happened?" I drove quickly but cautiously, heading away from downtown Charlevoix.

I spent the night at Katie's house—when you live in East Jordan, you don't think to lock your doors, so I opened the front door and walked right in. I thought I would lie sleeplessly for hours, but as soon as the faint but familiar smell of her perfume on the pillow hit me, I blinked out.

It was nearly noon when I jerked awake. Alan was still snoozing. Cursing over the lateness of the hour, I showered and made myself as presentable as I could, then drove up M-66 to the Charlevoix Area Hospital.

I breezed past reception with an it's-okay-I'm-supposed-to-be-here wave, which didn't fool the woman who called, "Sir?" after me. I paused, though, when I saw Barry Strickland leafing through a magazine in the waiting room. I decided to duck in to talk to him first.

"Ruddy." He stood and shook my hand in his iron grip. "Quite a night."

"For both of us," I agreed. I searched my mind for Alan—still asleep.

"They found the victim out on the ice. The Humvee was there, too, tires melted, burned all to hell."

"And?"

He shook his head. "No sign of Rogan."

"Damn."

"Cutty wants to investigate your theory before jumping to conclusions, but Hughes wants to call it a serial killer immediately and hold a press conference. The Feds will probably take over, so the only way for the D.A. to get any glory is to talk to the media right away. The two of them are in with Miss Lottner now."

"And you're out here?"

He shrugged. "Official business. I'm not an official."

"Well, you should be. Sheriff."

He regarded me steadily. "We'll see."

I liked that. "I'm going to go visit my fiancée."

He shook his head. "Not a good idea, Ruddy. The D.A. is pretty sure you've committed a crime or two. He also told me he received a call from your psychiatrist."

"Schaumburg," I supplied with a sinking feeling.

"Right. Hughes feels you didn't give him the whole story when you had him write the court on your behalf."

"I am so, so worried about the D.A.'s feelings."

He smiled at that one. "If it helps, Cutty thinks you're a hero."

"She said that?"

"Not in those words, no."

"Ah. Well, I'm going to go see Katie, and I really don't care what the D.A. or Cutty has to say about it."

He looked troubled. "Cutty's all right. She's a good officer."

"I'll go easy on her," I promised, which made us both smile. Cutty did not need anyone going easy on her for any reason. I paused before leaving. "Hey, is there something between you two? You and Cutty, I mean."

He gave a start, looking, what, embarrassed? Guilty? "No, of course not," he denied a bit strongly. "Why would you ask that?"

"I thought I sensed something. Like, a connection," I responded smoothly. Ruddy McCann, the meddler.

He rubbed his chin thoughtfully. "From both of us? Or just me?" he asked.

I'd gotten to *bingo*. "Well, I've seen the way she looks at you sometimes."

He looked floored at this, so I left the room, grinning.

I knocked once on Katie's door and pushed it open. The D.A. and Cutty jerked around, startled, but my focus was on my fiancée, who looked wan but clear-eyed.

"Ruddy," she greeted softly. I went to her bedside and gave her a we're-in-public kiss, and as I drew back, I felt her father waking up.

"You shouldn't be here," D.A. Darrell said angrily.

"Where have you been, Ruddy? My men have been looking for you," Cutty asked with controlled frustration.

"I spent the night at Katie's house. I was too tired to drive to Kalkaska," I replied honestly. "Then"—I turned to Katie to apologize—"I overslept. I'm sorry. I woke up and came straight here. Barry Strickland filled me in on what happened on the ice, and told me Rogan is still at large." There, now Alan was up to speed.

*"Rogan got away?"* he gasped.

"So, how are you feeling, honey?" I asked gently.

"I have maybe the worst headache of my life, but otherwise I'm really fine. I'd like to go home, but the doctors want to keep me a little longer."

"Plus, we have more questions. For both of you," D.A. Darrell added aggressively.

"You need to leave," I said to him—a sentence I'd spoken, with exactly the same inflection, to angry drunks countless times.

The D.A. scowled. "Maybe you didn't hear me."

"Maybe you're the one who needs the headache," I countered.

*"Ruddy,"* Alan warned.

"I love it when men fight over me," Katie observed lightly.

"We do need to speak to you," Cutty told me.

"And I'm happy to do that after I've had a few minutes alone with her," I responded, pointing to Katie.

"I got a call from Dr. Schaumburg. Your psychiatrist. He says you're delusional, that you're a danger to yourself and others." D.A. Darrell sneered.

"Yeah, well, that still doesn't mean I need medication," I replied.

D.A. The cut his eyes to Katie. "I'm not sure you're safe with him alone," he stated pointedly.

I clenched my fists, unable to believe this guy would stoop so low. Cutty was regarding him with a shocked expression.

"Well, that's the stupidest fucking thing I've ever heard," Katie spat, her eyes sparking angrily. I stared, surprised: I had never heard her use the *f* word before in her life.

"*Wow*," Alan said.

"Ruddy saved my life. I'm not saying another word to you, you moron," Katie continued. "Get out of my room."

Hughes opened his mouth to retort. "Sir!" Cutty barked, stepping in front of him. He blinked, startled. "We need to go. Now," she declared sternly. Cutty would have made an excellent bar bouncer.

He regarded her blankly, and then disgust curled his lip. "All right. We'll leave. But this isn't over." He glared at me.

"I'll call you when we're finished here," I promised Cutty, completely ignoring D.A. Darrell.

As they left, I closed the door and leaned against it. "So," I said.

"So. God, Ruddy. Come here." She held her arms out, and when I crossed the room, she buried her face in my neck. "I was so stupid. It was such a great house, I was thinking of how I would advertise it, how well it would show when the snow melted, and he seemed so nice. He offered me a drink, and even though it was really strong, I sipped it because I thought, you know, sales, get the customer comfortable."

"You are not stupid. That guy, he's had practice at this."

"I hardly drank any of it at all. Then the room started spinning, and I felt so drunk. He was laughing at me."

"It's okay."

She pulled back and looked at me, her eyes moist. "But then I remember you picking me up. I felt so safe in your arms. I knew everything was going to be all right. And then it was cold and then you were hugging me and then I was in the car with Kermit. Because you saved me. You, Ruddy."

"Well, Jake helped."

She laughed, shaking her head.

*"You did save her, Ruddy. You saved my little girl,"* Alan praised.

"What did the cops tell you?"

She shrugged. "Not much. They said they were just starting their investigation, but that that guy probably has done things like this before. Kidnapped women, I mean. They said I was lucky to get away. No," she corrected herself. "The D.A. said I was lucky to get away. The nice policewoman said you saved my life, and if it weren't for you, they wouldn't even know what was going on."

"I'll bet you the D.A. was happy with that."

"Oh, very," Katie agreed sarcastically.

"So, is there anything you need? Your Nelson DeMille novel? Chocolate? More apologies?"

"No, but there is something you could get from my house. Would you mind?"

"Not at all. What?"

"My engagement ring?"

"Really?"

Katie looked around, and her expression turned sly. "Come here," she said to me. She lifted the thin blanket covering her legs.

Now it was my turn to look around. "Are you serious? I thought you had a not-tonight-I-have-a-headache headache."

She laughed. "The bed's adjustable. How can we resist?"

"I'm just not sure that's part of the prescribed treatment." I could sense Alan's distress with the whole subject.

"Well, maybe this isn't the place for that," Katie concurred. "We could make out a little, though."

"Or a lot, even," I agreed.

We smiled into each other's eyes. My heart was responding with an accelerated pulse rate. She held out her arms, and I decided the time had come to push Alan away, but when I looked for him, he was already gone. Apparently, my unconscious had taken care of suppressing my subconscious.

I was a repo man with a voice in his head. I had a dog, a fiancée, a pregnant sister, friends, and legal problems. A life, in other words. I had a life, and this woman was at the center of it. I awkwardly climbed into the hospital bed with my Katie, and she laughed as she encircled me with her arms.

# Epilogue

Mick's first thought was that the guy standing on his front porch was a cop, because he had that look, that air of grim authority. He was big, too: a big unhappy cop, there to do some big unhappy cop thing to Mick. Mick swallowed.

"Mr. Clayton?" the big guy queried.

Mick nodded nervously—there was just something about the guy's presence that came off as menacing. Mick found himself feeling guilty, though he wasn't exactly sure what it was he might have done.

"I'm here about your Escalade."

This made no sense to Mick. "Now what?"

"You have a new Cadillac Escalade? In your garage, maybe?"

"Yeah, but . . ."

"You haven't been making your payments. You haven't made *any* payments. I need twelve hundred dollars from you, or I'm going to have to take it in."

"Take it in?" Mick blinked rapidly. "Wait, that's what this is? You're, like, a repo man?"

"Yes, I'm exactly, like, a repo man."

"Okay." Mick shook his head. "Something's not right. The payments are supposed to come out of my checking account automatically. I . . . Oh."

"Oh?" the big guy repeated.

"Crap! Like, right after I bought the car, my identity was stolen. Some guy took some of my outgoing bills from the mailbox and made checks on his printer for my checking account and cashed them. He got, like, five grand before the fraud people figured it out. So I had to get a new checking account." Mick slapped his forehead. "So of course the payments haven't been coming out automatically."

"Of course."

"And now I'm behind?"

"More than sixty days," the big guy affirmed. "So I need to either relieve you of the burden of ownership of the Escalade, or I need to relieve you of the burden of twelve hundred dollars."

"This is . . . Look, I'm getting married."

"Congratulations. Twelve hundred dollars."

"No, I mean, that's why everything's so disorganized in my life right now. Yes, yeah, I have the money. Is a check okay?"

The repo man looked around the entryway, clearly sizing up Mick's life style. Mick anxiously made the same assessment. His fiancée had recently repainted the entryway, and there was a picture of the two of them in Maui, Mick and Marissa, grinning because he had just proposed to her—if a guy could afford to take a woman to Maui, didn't that imply he made a nice living and was good for a couple of car payments? Marissa certainly seemed to believe so.

"Sure, I'll take a check, as long as you can promise it won't bounce. That would be very unpleasant, if it bounced."

"No, no, I get that. Don't worry. Come in. It's cold out."

The repo guy didn't have to duck to come through the doorway, but he completely blotted out the thin sun for a moment as he filled the frame. "When you didn't respond to their phone calls, I guess the bank saw that as an indication of your attitude toward your payments, and they sent me to help you with your attitude."

"The phone calls?" Mick asked as he searched for his check-book in a drawer in the kitchen, which Marissa was still in the process of redecorating. "Oh man, like, a robocall? I got a couple when I first bought the car, trying to sell me an extended war-ranty, so I just started hanging up on those," he apologized. He felt a real need to explain himself. As he handed over his check, he hesitated, his eyes widening. "Oh my God!" he blurted.

"Problem?"

"You're that guy. McCann. Robby?"

"Ruddy. We know each other?" He pulled the check from Mick's fingers, using the delicacy of a parent separating a toy from a child.

"Yeah. Well, not really. We met once. And I was deposed for your trial. On tape, I mean, but they never called us to testify."

The repo man drew himself up, somehow getting bigger, but his voice was soft. "I pleaded guilty," he said. "So there was no need for your testimony. And you are . . ."

Mick nodded vigorously. "Yeah."

"No, I mean, who are you?"

"Oh! Right. Uh, I was parked in a van that night with some friends. My buddy Gary and I were the ones who went out in the rowboat. That was some night."

"Yes. Yes, it was." McCann had a reflective look on his face as he nodded. "I am sorry I never thanked you. Between the whack on the head and the water, I guess I wouldn't have made it if you hadn't pulled me out of the lake."

"Sure. That's okay. Your dad did."

"My dad? My dad did what?"

"Your dad thanked us. He had us in for a couple of beers at that bar? Is it still there?"

"The Black Bear. Yeah. It's still there." McCann was regarding Mick strangely. "He did that?"

"Yeah."

"That surprises me. He never said anything about it."

Mick pondered what to say about the girl who died that night and came up with nothing he couldn't be sure wouldn't piss this big guy off. Instead he changed the subject. "It's funny. I'm going to see them. They're coming to the wedding."

"I'm not sure who you're talking about."

"Right. So Sharon and Gary got married. You have to . . . It's hard to explain what an impact that night had on us. I mean, we're just sitting there, smoking some weed I bought that was the worst damn marijuana in the world." Mick smiled at the memory. "And then your car comes, and it was as if it crashed into *us* somehow. Hearing you yell for that girl, watching your car sink, barely getting you into the boat, it really brought home to us how quickly things can change, you know? Life seemed different after that. The three of us were together all the time, talking about it, and Sharon kept asking what are we doing, we're just wasting our lives, when something could happen and then it would be over, just like that." Mick snapped his fingers. "She was kind of my date that night, but she and Gary sort of clicked. They decided to get married and move to Grand Rapids, where he started working for Steelcase, and she's into some kind of computer security. And I looked at that and thought that if Gary Burner—that was his nickname, from, you know." Mick pinched his thumb and forefinger together and brought the imaginary joint to his lips. "If Gary *Burner* is going to get sober and get married and get a job, then what am *I* doing, you know? So I got an engineering degree from Michigan—go Blue—and now I work in the energy sector, decommissioning old oil rigs, mostly right around here."

"Go Green," McCann replied. Michigan State.

"So I guess what I'm saying is, you don't have to think about thanking me, that in some weird way I kind of feel like I ought to thank you. I get that it was tragic, of course. I just . . . If you hadn't come along, I might still be parked in that van somewhere, getting high and bitching about my existence instead of going out and doing something." Mick impulsively stuck his hand out and, after a moment, McCann took it, shaking it gravely.

"I appreciate you telling me all this," McCann said. "No one ever mentioned it to me before. I'm happy something good came of the accident. You want, bring your friends to the Black Bear when they're back in town. I'll buy you all a beer. The place is a lot like you—it was sort of going nowhere, but my sister fixed it up, and now we get successful people, families. . . ." McCann shrugged in a way that indicated he wasn't necessarily sure he was describing an improvement. "Hardly ever get a fistfight anymore."

"Yeah, sounds good," Mick said, knowing that with the wedding, they would all be too busy to take McCann up on his offer.

McCann nodded as if he knew the same thing. "Well, hey, normally there's a collection fee that gets added to the end of your contract. Two hundred dollars."

"Oh."

"My company will waive it though. Consider it a wedding present."

"Wow. Thanks. That's great."

McCann turned to go. "No," he said over his shoulder. "Thank *you*."

# ACKNOWLEDGMENTS

As a former repo man myself, I have to say that to do the job properly, it helps to be more than a little crazy. Picture creeping up on a house at midnight, jumping into a car, and sitting there cranking a nearly dead battery while lights come on in the house and you see shadowy figures grabbing their shotguns and running for the door. What sane person would do something like that? Yet despite the fact that I repeatedly did stuff like that, I'm not an expert on mental disorders, so in order to produce a realistic-sounding conversation between Ruddy and a psychiatrist, I received invaluable aid from Dr. Ira Handler. Thank you, Doctor, for your guidance.

I've had thankfully little exposure to criminal court, so thank you, Rob Whims, for your legal advice and alarmingly creative ideas on how to murder people.

In this era of search engines, you'd think I could research everything just by sitting at my desk, but it turns out some things require more nuance than a question that generates 345,000 "results." Thank you, Cantor Gary Shapiro, for being my go-to on the subtle ins and outs of Judaism. And thank you, northern Michigan, for supplying me with such rich and interesting people and places—every time I go there for research it's a delight. And yes, Darlene's is there in East Jordan, the Landing is right there where Ruddy drove into the drink in Ironton, and the Red Mesa Grille is in Boyne City, as is Café Sante. No amount of Google will relate how good Darlene's cinnamon rolls are, nor how amazingly peaceful it is to sit at the Landing's lakeside tables for a fabulous perch meal on a summer evening, nor just how great the Mexican food is at the Red Mesa. Nor will Google help you find the Black Bear Bar and Grille in Kalkaska—I made that place up.

Thank you, Tucker, for being as lazy in reality as Jake is in fiction.

Thanks to Connection House for all of the social networking stuff, including web design, that you've done for, what, seven years? You've been invaluable. Is that what it's called, social networking? Whatever it is, thanks so much, with particular thanks to Susan Andrews, Andrew Gupton (they're related), and Charlie Salem. Charlie, you are unreal. And thank you, Mindy Wells Hoffbauer, for helping the more than 300,000 Facebook fans of *A Dog's Purpose* enjoy and celebrate their dogs. It's an ongoing conversation—if you're on Facebook and like dogs, books, *my* books, animal stories, or animal rescue, come to the *A Dog's Purpose* page and join us. Okay, maybe if you don't like dogs, you shouldn't bother.

Speaking of *A Dog's Purpose,* when this novel, *Repo Madness,* is published, the DreamWorks/Walden Media production of the film of *A Dog's Purpose* will either be in theaters or so close to it our contractions will be two minutes apart. This would not be happening were it not for Gavin Polone, who is honest, hardworking, determined, talented, and quite handsome with a mosquito net over his face. Gavin is the producer of *A Dog's Purpose* and has championed the book and the movie from day one. He is also involved in two other book-to-movie projects we have going at the moment—I'm honored to be working with him.

Another great producer is Vahan Paretchan of Lifeboat Productions, who is working to see that a series based on Ruddy McCann the repo man will be playing on small screens sometime in the near future. Hopefully by the time you're reading this, we will have already shot the pilot episode! Currently it's being called *Repo Madness,* but that could change—for all I know we'll call it *Ruddy's Flower Shop.*

I'm a producer myself, you know. I produced *Muffin Top: A Love Story,* which was co-produced, co-written, and directed by Cathryn Michon, who stars in the movie, which is based on her novel *The Grrl Genius Guide to Sex (with Other People).* In other words, Cathryn may have been slightly more important than I was to the whole thing, but hey, I drove her to the set every day—otherwise, there would be no movie! So maybe I should get all the credit.

Cathryn lowered her standards about five years ago and married me. I get credit for that, too.

Maybe by the time this book is released, our movie *Cook Off!* will be in theaters. I produced that one as well, and Cathryn's efforts on that project was just as intense—without her, there would be no *Cook Off!,* which was based on another one of her books: *The Grrl Genius Guide to Life.* (I drove her to the set on that one, too.) Oh, I'm actually *in* that movie, in a brief scene that I will modestly tell you is the best in the whole film, even though it's only a few seconds long.

Tom Rooker and Elliott Crowe were intimately involved in both of the above projects. And, I'll cheerfully admit, so were hundreds of others—Tom and Elliott get special attention because they, like Cathryn, are still working on both movies. Turns out, when you make a film, you're never really *done.* You just occasionally go into remission.

Cathryn also reads nearly every draft of all of my books, providing substantial notes and helping me craft novels I can be proud of. I used to stand right there and ask her what she thought of each page, but through selective use of negative reinforcement she has corrected my behavior.

If this is the first novel in my "repo" series you've read and you'd like to read more, check out *The Midnight Plan of the*

*Repo Man,* which introduced Ruddy, Alan, and the cabin-fevered folks at the Black Bear to the rest of the world. There is also a sweet little short story entitled "The Midnight Dog of the Repo Man" that is available in e-book format—it tells the story of how Jake and Ruddy came to live together.

And, if you liked *A Dog's Purpose,* please consider reading *A Dog's Journey,* the direct sequel. It's got an even higher reader rating than *A Dog's Purpose*!

Thanks to Steve Younger and Steve Fisher for representing me in Hollywood. Thank you, Scott Miller, for rescuing my career and deftly repackaging me as a novelist after I'd spent years as a humor writer, though I thought we agreed that everyone's name should be Steve.

Sheryl Johnston is not only the name of Ruddy's preferred psychiatrist, but she's also one of my dearest friends and a former NASCAR driver. Thank you, Sheryl, for getting me places quickly. Very, very quickly.

I am lucky enough to know some very talented writers on a first-name basis. Remember how Marlene Dietrich said, "It's the friends you can call at four A.M. that matter?" Well, it's talented and caring writers like Claire LaZebnik, Jenna (not Jenny!) McCarthy, Samantha Dunn, Jillian Lauren, and Andrew Gross that I can call on when I need help (sometimes desperately) who really matter. Busy with their own successful careers, they've all taken time, occasionally with little notice, to step in and assist me when I was considering dropping this whole author thing and going back to what I was always good at, which was stealing cars. I will be forever grateful.

The astoundingly talented Nelson DeMille and Lee Child were early supporters of this franchise—thank you so much; what an honor to have your names associated with mine.

You know who else has been supportive? My publisher, Forge. You'd think they would have turned up their collective noses that the "dog book guy" wanted to write a sort-of detective series based on a washed-up football star turned repo man who happens to have a voice in his head, but they've all gotten behind Ruddy McCann and supported my novels every step of the way. It's a huge team, but I want to specifically thank Tom, Karen, Kathleen, Patty, and Linda for everything they've done to promote my work and my career. And thanks, of course, to Kristin Sevick for being my editor and friend through the rewrite process.

Thank you, Carolina and Annie, my goddaughters, who still pretend I have relevance in their lives despite the fact that they're cool college kids now.

Lauren Potter has just joined the team of working dogs at the Cameron World Wide Headquarters. Hopefully by the time this novel comes out she'll still be there. Thank you, Lauren, for making my in-box look so gloriously empty.

There are very few people I can write and say, "Quick, I need a disease!" I may not be the only person with this particular problem. My sister Julie Cameron, my "doctor sister," has very patiently stepped into that role and guided me back to reality whenever I started to make up illnesses that don't actually exist. Meanwhile my "teacher sister," Amy Cameron, has written study guides for my novels and offers advice on what teenagers are like today. (No less horrifying than they were when I wrote *8 Simple Rules for Dating my Teenage Daughter.*)

My mother does more to promote my books than any other human on earth. I don't think she does anything *else.* Thank you, Monsie Cameron, for meeting your self-imposed sales quota every quarter.

There are other family members who pitch in and help, to the point where I am not sure I can list them all, but surely Georgia, Chelsea, Chase, James, Chris, Evie, Ted, Maria, Jakob, Maya, Ethan, Gracie, Amanda, Vicki, Kitty, Nancy, Dean, John, Charles, Jane, Ted, Bill, Michelle, Marta, John, Patsy, Jim, Cam, Sara, and Emily all deserve both mention and gratitude. Gordon and Eloise, you haven't even read my books! Come on, you're both only a few years away from kindergarten, get with the program!

Thank you, Jody and Andy Sherwood, for picking us up at the airport; hosting us in your home; driving us all over the place; buying us all of our meals; enabling, assisting with, and attending the Phoenix premiere of *Muffin Top,* pouring us delicious and necessary wines, driving us back to the airport, and then saying, "Thanks for coming to visit."

Thanks to Life Is Better Rescue (www.lifeisbetterrescue.org.) in Denver for saving so many death row animals.

And last but certainly not least (in fact, certainly *most*), thank you, my readers, for supporting this and all my other books. Without you I'm nothing. I mean that—with thousands of books being published every day, your decision to read my works means the world to me. And a special thank-you to the "secret group" on Facebook, who care about the world of dogs, of my novels, of the movies my wife directs—each and every one of you is wonderful.

If you like my stuff and would like to chat with others who hold the same views, come join us on Facebook and ask to be let into the secret group. There's a handshake and everything.

Now, here's a good question: Will Ruddy, Alan, and the rest of the gang be back? It's too soon to tell, but I'm inclined to say yes. There's just so much more to cover. Like, who killed Milt? (I know, but I'm not telling.) Will Rogan return? Is Ruddy crazy, or is Alan really some sort of ghost? (This last question is an interesting one. Would it amuse you to know that my wife and I hold opposing opinions on this issue? That's right, even though I write the books, I don't hold the answer to anything nebulous or subjective. You, the reader—your answer is as good as mine.)

Anyway, we'll see what happens. In the meantime, I promise you, I've got more stories on the way.

—W. Bruce Cameron

Frisco, Colorado, December 7, 2015